UNFIN

Frankie McGowa[n] ... after leaving coll... teenage magazin... Street. She freelanced while bringing up her chil- dren, contributing to national newspapers and magazines, including the *Sunday Times*, *Daily Mail*, *Cosmopolitan* and *Company*. Since then she has launched and edited a number of maga- zines, including *New Woman* and *Top Santé*. She has twice been nominated as Editor of the Year. Frankie McGowan lives in London with her husband and their children.

FRANKIE McGOWAN

# Unfinished Business

HarperCollins*Publishers*

HarperCollins*Publishers*
77–85 Fulham Palace Road,
Hammersmith, London W6 8JB

A Paperback Original 1996
1 3 5 7 9 8 6 4 2

Copyright © Frankie McGowan 1996

The author asserts the moral right to
be identified as the author of this work

A catalogue record for this book
is available from the British Library

ISBN 0 00 649627 X

Set in Linotron Sabon by
Rowland Phototypesetting Ltd,
Bury St Edmunds, Suffolk

Printed and bound in Great Britain by
Caledonian International Book Manufacturing Ltd, Glasgow

For Amy,
with love

# Acknowledgements

Most of my friends are working mothers so while researching this book I was able to draw on not just my own experiences but theirs too, and I'm grateful I have such funny, clever, and inspirational women in my life, too many to name, but they know who they are.

Many talented people in the world of interior design and antiques spent a great deal of time with me, but in particular I would like to thank very much indeed some leading players in that world without whom ... namely Sarah Meysey-Thompson, Vincent Dane and Rosemary Noden.

Thanks are also due to Lee Wilson, Julia Kirk, Nick Sayers and Susan Opie who, in their various ways, pointed a very appreciative me in the right direction when I was getting stuck. And, as ever, Peter, Tom and Amy for being there.

# Unfinished Business

# Prologue

Rosie looked at the man who had deserted her six years before and asked him to repeat what he had just said.

He was half leaning, half sitting on the edge of a small console table. He didn't look at her, just idly picked up a silver-framed picture of their small son and studied it carefully. Then he gave a quick nervous smile before turning towards Rosie where she stood against the fireplace.

'I said, I want you to have me back.' He watched her face carefully, amused at her expression. But it was an edgy amusement. More apprehensive, she decided, than confident.

'Please,' he added softly.

She glanced at the clock and then back at her ex-husband's face. Not yet four o'clock, nearly dark. Unlikely to be drink talking. But with Rory Monteith Gore, anything was possible. Turning, she picked up her bag, yawned and rose to her feet.

'Mmm. That's what I thought you said. Look, I didn't drag all the way over here to listen to your silly jokes, so why don't you call me when you're in a less frivolous mood? By the way,' she said, vaguely looking around, 'Tom left his football here, can you get it for me?'

Instantly Rory was on his feet. 'Rosie, listen to me. I'm not drunk. Yes, yes, I'll get Tom's football in a minute. But just listen. You haven't seen me, really talked to me, for such a long time, haven't noticed how I've changed. I'm very, *very* serious. Won't you listen? I was just having a problem finding myself . . .'

She wheeled round, her eyes wide in disbelief. 'That was

a *problem*? Why didn't you try the usual places? In front of any bar or in any bed but your own.' Shrugging off his arm, she tried to move past him but his grip simply tightened.

'Rosie, hold on. Surely your dazzling career can wait a few minutes . . . just for once.'

This time she did stop and stared back at him. A flush crept into her cheeks. Her eyes flickered briefly with a not-quite-forgotten pain.

'My *career*? *My career* . . . ?' Her voice was barely a whisper. Disbelief rather than anger controlled it.

'Don't start that again, Rory,' she warned. 'It wasn't true then. It isn't now. Do you honestly think that after six years of struggling to keep my job – *job*, mark you, not career – with precious little help from you, that I could take anything you say seriously?'

Rory's dark mouth moved into a familiar angry line. 'If you'd been prepared to stay at home, spend time with me, you wouldn't have had to struggle over this or any other job . . .'

They were on familiar turf. The same argument, the same weary stances, like actors in a rather bad play. They knew their familiar lines and she knew before they had even started that neither of them could change the ending.

The panic was rising to her mouth. She folded her arms tightly across her chest. When she spoke, her voice was dangerously calm.

'And what, Rory, was your solution to our financial problems? Living in a house on money loaned by your father because we couldn't afford one of our own, doing whatever he said otherwise he pulled the plug at the bank?

'Never buying myself any clothes, terrified this is where we'd be forever. No social life because we couldn't rely on you being there even if we could afford it. Always on my own . . .'

'. . . You were not, I rang home all the time . . .'

'When? *When* did you ever do that?'

'You only remember what suits you. You wouldn't *let* me support . . .'

'. . . *Support?* What support? When I finally got a job to get us away from him, out of the mess, where was the support? Or thanks?'

'Oh, c'mon,' Rory protested. 'I *always* took an interest in your job.'

'Interest?' Rosie's voice was scathing. 'What interest? Don't make me laugh. It was just terror that your wings might be clipped. You took more and more jobs that got you away from home so you wouldn't have to help. *Your* career, *your* job, that's all we ever heard.'

Well into her stride, her face flushed, gripping the back of an armchair, it came tumbling out. He tried to speak, but she didn't want to hear.

'The only weapon you needed to keep me quiet and you free was to make me feel I was a whining, unreasonable woman. And as for money, you were *obsessed* with it. God, if I heard you once more moan about not having any . . . And when I needed you most, what did you do?'

'Oh God, not that again. I've said I'm sorry . . .'

'You took off on some pitiful business trip dreamed up by James bloody Cooper, with a half-witted American in tow who obligingly allowed you to screw her . . .'

'. . . that's not true . . .'

'. . . in return for getting her a job as your *assistant* and who thought "The Hon" meant you were royal, oh my God, *royal* . . .'

'. . . that wasn't my fault . . .'

'. . . then you came home in a foul mood, pushing me and Tom around because you had to face life, *real life*, here. Real life, Rory. Me and Tom . . . And you know what you said?' Rosie could hardly breathe.

'I know what I said, I know . . .'

'You said . . . you said . . .' Rosie mimicked the lines that

3

had haunted her for six years: '"*I'm in love with her, I'm sorry I don't love you any more. I'm afraid I'm not sure I ever did.*" And when I asked you not to see her for a while, to protect my feelings, give us a chance to work it out, you just shrugged and said you couldn't see what good that would do. That you'd always care about her.'

'For Christ's sake, Rosie!'

'What did you expect me to do? Sit around waiting for you to get over her? And where is she now, Rory, this paragon who made you so happy? Gone. And the one who succeeded her, and the next one? And your family? We're gone too. And now you've decided for God knows what reason that you want it all back again. *Jesus*. You are not real.'

'I didn't know what else to say,' he muttered. 'She was forcing the issue. You know I wanted to end it. You threw *me* out, remember? Where else could I go but to her? I was terrified of your reaction. I'd never seen you like that.'

'More's the pity,' she flashed back.

'The pity is,' he said, pressing his fingers against his eyes, then letting them drag down his face, 'that I didn't make you pay attention to me.'

'Made me what?' She stopped.

Rory said nothing. Grinding out his cigarette into a curling, smouldering heap, he immediately lit another. She noticed his hand shook as he tried to steady the flame, his eyes puzzled as he gazed at her through the haze of exhaled smoke.

He didn't understand then. He didn't now. Reality appeared to continue to elude him.

'Rory.' Rosie's voice was resigned. 'We should never have got married. At the very least we should have waited until after Tom was born, the way I suggested. To see if it was what we wanted without everyone telling us what to do. The way your father did.'

'He advised me, that's all. I took his advice.' He looked weary. She sensed his defeat.

4

She wanted to push him to delve a bit deeper to find something new to say. Something to make the hurt go away. But even as she spoke she knew it was a wasted effort.

The rage that he had slept with someone else had long subsided. She had dealt with that. But living for so long with a deep hollow inside because she had been taken for a fool was what she resented. That he had shared jokes with, whispered in the night with, felt at ease with someone of whom she knew nothing and thereby rendering his time in her life a lie, was what had shocked her.

'You didn't have to have an affair, abandon me, to prove your point.' Her voice was gruff. 'I needed a husband, not another child.'

'But you know I never meant any of it,' Rory pleaded. 'It was all a mistake. I never loved her. It was just . . . just escapism if you like. I've changed, Rosie. You went back to work, you were successful so quickly, it unnerved me. I thought you would meet someone else. All I ever wanted was for you to stay home . . .'

Now she simply stared at him. '*Stay at home*?' she repeated slowly, incredulously. 'Stay at home and live on what? Thin air? Hope? The four thirty at Lincoln?'

Silence. She lifted her hands in a helpless gesture and turned away from him. His expression irritated her. Like the coldly austere furniture he had inherited in a house bought by a great-grandfather he never knew, Rory, like all the Monteith Gores before him, was unlikely to change. Rosie was conscious of disappointment rather than anger.

'Please.' She spoke impatiently. 'Just move out of the way, I'm late, I have a life to lead and it doesn't include you. Ever.'

# Chapter One

Out on the street, Rosie strode towards her car, parked a short way along the tree-lined square. Her head was down, her expression so forbidding that more than one passer-by hurrying in the opposite direction glanced back at her as she swept past, her coat flying open, digging furiously into her bag for her car keys.

She was still searching when she reached her car. Cursing silently, she moved into the light of a street lamp to try to locate them among the assortment of letters, pens, and notebooks that went everywhere with her. Nothing. And then she recalled putting them on the mantelpiece in Rory's drawing room. She slumped against her car door, letting her head drop back, closed her eyes and turned her face up to the cold sky.

Her first instinct was to get a cab home and then return when she was calmer. Pointless. Tom wanted his football and she needed her car tonight. Turning, she leaned her head on her arms and stared across the square.

She would go back, refuse to re-open the discussion, collect her keys, and go.

Rory looked startled when he opened the door. 'My keys,' she explained as his eyes widened. 'I left them behind.'

He stood back to let her walk past, giving a huge sigh that sounded like relief. 'Thought it might be because you'd forgotten to kiss me goodbye.'

He was grinning at her. She struggled to keep her features blank. 'You should have been a stand-up comic, Rory.

You're obviously used to being ignored. The football. Please?'

While he disappeared to retrieve it, Rosie collected her keys from the mantelpiece and waited.

She'd made her point. When he returned, she would simply remind him that Tom was expecting to see him the next weekend and then she would depart, safely back to where she had been before she had unwisely agreed to call round. Back to normal.

Rosie sighed inwardly, already regretting that Rory had goaded her into such anger, feeling better now that the fury had been released by a blast of fresh air.

There had been a time when such an exchange would have sent her stumbling in tears from the house, unable to concentrate for the rest of the day. As it was she took a couple of deep breaths. Calm now, she pushed a stray lock of hair out of her eyes. Glancing at her watch, she knew she wouldn't make it to Nancy's before seven.

Livvie, Rosie's invaluable assistant, would be frantic. The design boards for Sylvia Duxborough's country house needed completing this afternoon to deliver by this evening.

She couldn't bring herself even to think of the mountain of messages that spewed out from her fax machine overnight and awaiting her each day from Wu Chang, trying to organise renovation of his newly acquired townhouse in Wimbledon from his present home in Hong Kong.

There was no time now to pick up the new curtain samples that had just arrived at Preston and Lowe for her meeting at eight the next morning with Miriam de Lisle – who was becoming more impossible by the day. Worse, Rosie's accountant was starting to range himself on the side of the tax man, so desperate was he to finalise her accounts since she had cancelled two meetings in as many weeks.

Bloody man. How was it that all her friends had

8

accountants prepared to massage the figures yet hers behaved as if he had been force-fed a truth drug? How could she qualify to pay VAT on a struggling interior design company when she was living virtually hand-to-mouth? Had he never heard of company goodwill to rich and much-needed clients who were slow to pay their bills? He had not. He also wasn't interested.

And bloody Miriam. Changing her mind, first wanting her London townhouse to look like a Roman palazzo and then last week waving a picture of her favourite soap star's penthouse in *Hello!* – a triumph in both cases of money over taste.

One more try, and then she'd tactfully have to dump the dreadful but obscenely rich would-be socialite, cocktail bar and all. Some clients, no matter how much money they had, old or new (and so new in Miriam's case you could smell the ink), were not worth the hassle.

Seeing Nancy was now going to be difficult. Crossing London at this time of the day was a nightmare. And letting Nancy down did bother her.

Nancy was not a client but she had been influential in sending clients to Rosie. Unlike Sylvia or Miriam, Nancy had a feeling for design, a feeling nurtured in the bosom of the wealthy Alexander family and its acclaimed art collection to which she was heiress.

She was, like many of the paintings her family owned, an original. Spoilt but amusing, plunging impetuously to embrace new ideas often quite at odds with the exquisite homes she inhabited. Thankfully, owing to the league of experts she could call on, they rarely came to fruition.

Rosie admired Nancy, liked her up to a point, but found her absorption with her own needs too overwhelming to feel a real rapport with her. However, in recent months, Nancy had taken to ringing her up to come to dinner or drinks and since Rosie knew that Nancy surrounded herself only with people who were useful to her, she accepted cheerfully, rarely had a dull evening, made several useful contacts and regarded the heiress as good business.

On the whole, Rosie was inclined to feel a certain loyalty to the lanky American who was currently so enamoured of London, she was seeking a more permanent home there than the imposing building she currently occupied in a leafy avenue in Holland Park. Rosie hadn't minded – indeed felt faintly flattered – being taken along to inspect a possible purchase. She did not place any great store by it when she heard Nancy had dragged others on a similar errand; Nancy only ever used American designers anyway.

Tonight was another of Nancy's regular drinks parties and Rosie had promised to be there. It was looking increasingly doubtful. She glanced impatiently at her watch. Where *was* Rory?

The well-ordered drawing room, filled with the last fading light of a sharply cold day in November, registered for the first time. She had not seen the place for over a year. The last time she had been in here was just before Rory's sudden departure for America, when she'd picked up Tom from a rare weekend visit. She remembered that she had winced at the neglect.

The cream silk blinds had been grey and tinged with yellow, the clinging smell of nicotine impossible to disguise, the depressing evidence of Rory's nocturnal existence lying in piles around the room she had once so lovingly and naively, so optimistically, pulled together. Half empty tumblers of whisky, overflowing ashtrays, videos separated from their cases were littered everywhere.

Now it was surprisingly different. Filled with flowers, cushions plumped up, magazines and books neatly stacked. The silver gleamed and someone – impossible to believe it was Rory – had clearly had the heavy silk curtains cleaned.

The Kneller portrait of one of the first Monteiths before they became aligned to the Gores still hung above the mantelpiece, but for some reason Rory had now put back on display family treasures that Rosie had urged him to put away for fear they might be stolen.

A pair of delicate Bow figurines gazed at each other across either end of a fitted display of bookshelves. A china cabinet housed the exquisite Meissen Swan service. On the table where Tom's picture held centre stage, there was also a collection of Meissen double-ended snuff boxes. Their price was incalculable.

The decor lacked her touch but it was almost the house she had lived in as a young bride, briefly happy, the misery yet to come.

She gave a gently mocking laugh as Rory reappeared and tossed the football to her.

'Taking a few risks, aren't you?' She indicated the valuable ornaments as she caught the ball. 'I thought all this was too good to show?'

'Oh well, it's insured. And it makes the room come alive. You're the expert. What do you think?'

She shrugged. 'Not that much of an expert. I do interiors, not antiques. Who are you exploiting these days?'

Rory carefully studied the tall, willowy figure of his ex-wife as she began to gather up her bag. Clear blue eyes held his gaze from under lightly curling, chocolate brown, glossy hair, shoved casually back behind her ears framing a slender face. If only, he reflected, she was as biddable as her appearance suggested, he might not have thought he could get away with the final affair that broke her heart and wrecked their marriage.

He moved after her as she made her way to the door, reaching out to grab her arm to slow her progress.

Rosie pushed past him.

'Don't you even want to know why I want you back – although I would have thought it was obvious.' Rory propped himself in the doorway, preventing her from walking out.

Rosie hesitated. Even if he wore beaten-up jeans he

would still look expensive. For the first time she noticed he looked different. What was it? The same lean body, narrow hips. Of course, his hair was shorter, the pony tail had gone. It was a hesitation that was swiftly seized on by Rory.

His expression switched from resentment to rueful apology. 'Sorry, sweetheart. Did all that very badly, didn't I? What a mess I made of everything. You're quite right. Why should you listen? It was just that Tom was so happy here all weekend, we had a great time but we both knew what was missing.'

'What was what?' She was impatient, she had a business to run. 'Missing, I mean? Apart from you in your son's life for over a year?'

As she spoke she pulled a red leather appointments book from her bag and began flicking over the pages. At this rate, Nancy would have to be cancelled.

'I don't think you're listening.' Rory was edgy, watching her as she reached for the phone. 'I said, the thing that was missing was you.'

'Well, that isn't surprising, is it?' Rosie said, unable to keep the sarcasm from her voice, tucking the phone under her chin, punching out her own number. 'Honestly, Rory, I don't know why you asked to see me so suddenly after all this time. Livvie? Hold on, it's me.' She put her hand over the mouthpiece. 'Or want to have this pointless conversation, but I really *am* late . . . Livvie?

'Sorry, got held up . . . look, you just go, but make sure you take all the labels off this time . . . yes, I'm sure it was an accident, but I don't want one of Wu Chang's minions nipping down to the carpet warehouse and getting the whole lot cut price once he knows who makes it . . . I'm leaving now. I'll sort out the scheme board for Sylvia. I know about Wu Chang's faxes. Oh God, paper the master bedroom with them. That'll teach him. I'll call Nancy when I get there . . . yes, I'm out of the door now . . . What workshop? Oh, that one. No, of course you mustn't be late, see you tomorrow.'

She replaced the phone and started for the door. Rory shrugged as she pushed past him. 'Okay, fine. Go. It's just that Tom brought the subject up . . .'

Rosie wheeled round. 'Tom? *Tom* brought this up? I don't believe you.' But even as she said it, a more truthful voice in her head told her it was not impossible that her young son had expressed such a wish. He'd done so often enough to her.

'I swear he did,' Rory said earnestly. 'He said, why couldn't he be like his friends with me meeting him from school like their fathers did. I promised him that I'd talk to you. Think about it, Rosie, just for a second. I don't need an answer today, but for Tom's sake, and mine . . . ours. It could work.'

He got up and came over to where she was still standing against the door and took her by the shoulders. Rosie stiffened and tried to move away.

'Don't, Rosie, don't,' he said urgently. 'You know there's still something there. I know there is. You would have married Piers by now . . .'

'Piers is over.' Her voice was sharper than she had intended. He was standing too close. 'It had – has – nothing to do with you. And we are over too. Is that clear?'

'Actually, Rosie, no,' he said carefully, studying the carpet before glancing up at her. 'As a matter of fact it isn't clear at all. What about my feelings in all this? You've dictated events, you've called the tune . . . none of this is what I ever wanted and you know that. Rosie, wait. For God's sake, don't just walk out, listen to me.'

She ignored him. She had to. It was the only way. Just keep walking.

His voice followed her as she strode across the square hall to the door. Wrenching it open, she almost collided with James Cooper, older, plumper, enough oil in his hair to fry chips. The sweet smell of cologne clung to his pin-striped suit and tightly buttoned waistcoat. And he was still clearly dancing attendance on Rory. She glared at him as his eyebrows soared.

'Dear me, just like old times,' he drawled, taking in her flushed face and Rory's wreathed in anger.

'Get lost, James,' snapped Rosie.

'Goodness me, you should ask that charm school for a refund.'

Behind him Rory was cooling down. 'Rosie, please listen. Don't be unreasonable.'

'Unreasonable?' she breathed, instinctively pushing James aside to glare straight at her ex-husband. James flattened himself against the door, ignored by both of them.

'Rory, get this into your head. I have a business to run, I barely have time to see Tom these days as it is because I don't have the backup I need. But there is no way that I will allow Tom to live under the same roof as you again. Have you got that? Never.'

'Okay, okay. Anything you say. But you tell Tom that you wouldn't even listen. Wouldn't even give me a chance to explain. You tell him, Rosie. Your decision. You hear?'

# Chapter Two

The journey from Rory's large and imposing house in the very fashionable Marlborough Square in Mayfair to Rosie's compact terraced house in the less-sought-after Drake Street just off Kings Road, was a matter of fifteen minutes.

The door crashed shut behind her. She threw her bag onto a chair and made her way down the stairs to her basement kitchen. But bright yellow walls and cheerful blue gingham on the curtains and seat covers for once failed spectacularly to lift her spirits as they were designed to do.

A fork-lift truck would have fared no better, as she slammed cupboard doors and dragged a bottle of Chablis from the fridge. Splashing ice-cold wine into a glass that was in danger of cracking under her grip, she found it hard to recollect one second of the journey.

Carrying the bottle, she went back upstairs into the workroom that had once been her drawing room and tried to reason with herself. Impossible to try that with her ex-husband. He was beyond reason, in every way.

Livvie – short for Olivia – Blake had left a stack of messages which Rosie scooped up as she slumped on the green chaise longue in the corner by the window and gave herself five minutes to calm down. And promptly wished she had sat somewhere else. The view compounded her problems. But she was too tired to move.

Cream linen blinds maximised the light and in place of the rose taffeta curtains that had once graced the windows, looped into heavy silk tie-backs, a swathe of cream voile was now suspended from heavy wooden poles, falling in a cloud to the floor either side of the frame.

Floor-to-ceiling white bookcases separated by a sandstone fire surround were each stacked with neatly folded fabric samples on the top half, providing a breathtaking rush of colour against the putty-coloured walls, while the sample books, the tools of her trade, filled the lower half.

On cold days like today, a cheerful gas fire was lit, its flames licking companionably into the chimney, but Rosie simply scowled at it.

In the centre of the room stood a round lime-washed pedestal table where Rosie and Livvie both worked, cluttered with coloured pencils, pens, pins, scissors and sketch pads.

To the outside world this room was evidence of her skill as a designer, a constant reassurance to those who had invested in her talents, instilling confidence in new clients recommended by influential people like Nancy or Wu Chang to *Rosie Colville Interiors*. At first she had not understood just how tricky some of them could be.

But it wasn't Wu Chang who caused her the most grief.

Mrs Salina Bhandari, wife of a millionaire Indian film director who churned out productions at the rate of one a week, had an obscene amount of money and servants and made Wu Chang look in need of financial help.

Rosie couldn't think why the imperious and insensitive Salina continued to call her. Nothing she did was right. Everything was criticised. It was generally believed among Salina's friends that her own taste and expertise were responsible for the enviable decor of her homes. Certainly not Rosie's. She had heard on the grapevine that she had been relegated to a mere messenger for Salina's requirements.

Sitting waiting for sometimes an hour while Mrs Bhandari terrorised her staff, indignation would well up in Rosie's mouth, but the minute Salina swept in, all Versace jeans and high heels, laden with the contents of her jewel case, Rosie would find herself insisting the wait was nothing.

She could not afford the luxury of telling Mrs Bhandari what she thought of her. She remained silent and, with the prospect of money to pay her bills and more out of disbelief than gratitude, found herself saying 'yes' next time Mrs Bhandari's assistant telephoned.

To Rosie it was a trap of her own making. Behind the confident facade lay unpaid invoices that were pushing her to the edge of ruin.

Thus it was that now, balancing a wine glass on her chest, stretched out and glaring ahead of her, Rosie saw only the depressing lack of space making her job so difficult, in the certain knowledge that if she pulled out any of the files tidily stored on the other side of the room, she would have to confront some unpleasant financial facts.

Bloody Rory didn't help. This house had been bought in a rush. Neglected and dark until six years before when Rosie had come along, it had been rejected by a score of buyers who failed to see how it could be transformed into a comfortable, sunny home. But Rosie could. She preferred the house that way; she didn't have the expense of undoing other people's botched alterations, no false ceilings to remove or walls to restore. Most important of all it was also drastically reduced in price for a quick sale.

Carey Templeton, one of Rosie's oldest friends and anchorman on Television News Network, was fond of regaling their friends with the sight that met his eyes when he turned up to help move the newly single, desperate working mother into her new home.

His then four-year-old godson, Tom, ran excitedly from room to room, leaving a trail of toys behind him. Crouched on the floor hogging the only telephone was a horrified Norwegian au pair, furtively calling her agency, begging to be removed instantly. She actually crept out at two the next morning, leaving a note stuck to a cupboard in a kitchen that made a bombsite look alluring.

And Rosie in jeans, muffled to the ears in several scarves and hats because the house was freezing, yelling down the phone to the electricity company, when she finally wrested it from the sobbing Inga's indignant grasp, that she would sue if she was not connected by five o'clock.

In the space of six months, the house had gone from a desolate waste to a clever mix of timeless charm combined with a controlled casualness that made it all seem effortlessly comfortable. Rosie tried not to look smug when her friends heaped compliments and envious glances at her new home.

It was still charming and admired, but it was never intended to house a business as well. Rosie knew it. Livvie knew it. Soon the whole bloody world would know it, unless someone paid up on time. Or indeed at all.

Livvie had gone, very pointedly leaving Rosie a pile of labels stripped from the back of the carpet hand-trials which she had taken to show Wu Chang's London emissary. Rosie sighed and began to work her way through Livvie's scribbled notes.

'*I will be in by nine. My Environments In Crisis meeting has been cancelled because of the rail strike.*' Rosie gave a reluctant laugh but the list of messages, some starred and underlined, simply made her groan.

Joyce, who made up all Rosie's curtains for her clients, had phoned to say the measurements on a set of drawing-room curtains didn't make sense and would have to be rechecked. That was underlined twice with an exclamation mark. '*Joyce says, either they've altered the windows since last time or you've made a mistake.*'

Rosie ran her eyes down the rest of the list, muttering as she went:

18

'*Mr. Bhandari's assistant called. Says her majesty's husband wants to know what was the name of the fabric you said you thought her chaise longue should have*' ... I bet she bloody does ... no way ... '*Jim rang to say he's got a gap Thursday, could do electrics in Miriam de L's house then, but Miriam says it's not convenient and also she has changed her mind about the curtains, wants goblet pleats instead of pencil.*' Rosie sighed, automatically reaching for her calculator to reassess the quantity of fabric that would now be needed.

The phone rang as she was scribbling sums onto a workpad at her elbow.

'Yes,' she snapped, tucking the phone under her chin as she wrote.

'Hey, hey. Cool it. It's only me,' said a pleasant laughing male voice. 'Who's annoyed you?'

'Sorry, Kit. Just encountered bloody Rory ... you know how it is.'

'Er, yes. Unfortunately. Bad moment. Want me to come round? Stick pins in effigies, that kind of thing?'

'Well, it might save money. Why are you phoning, wouldn't it be cheaper to come round anyway?'

'I'm in the bath, that's why. And if you're going to be in a bad mood I wish I hadn't taken the trouble to deliver that very large parcel propped inside your door.'

Rosie got up, trailing the phone with her, and glanced into her small hallway to where the brown parcel from Preston and Lowe was leaning against the stairs. In her haste to get to the wine bottle she hadn't noticed that Kit had used his spare key to let himself in.

'Thanks, Kit. They said they might deliver. Livvie had to get off sharpish and in the morning I'm seeing the dreaded de Lisle, who's just changed her mind again.'

The sound of water swishing into the bath obliterated Kit's opinion of Mrs de Lisle.

'I know. I'm sorry,' Rosie sighed. 'But it wasn't my fault.

I had no idea she would be such a pain about being photo-graphed. Anyway, you didn't have to do it.'

'And you didn't have to redesign her ghastly house,' he retorted. 'But we both need the money, darling heart, or a rich lover, and that's a fact.'

There was no arguing with that, even if she'd wanted to. One of the unexpected bonuses of moving to this house had been finding that her neighbour was a kindred spirit.

Livvie, who openly disapproved of Kit's sleeping part-ners, had told Rosie that his problem was a series of cheap and meaningless encounters that made a mockery of inter-gender relationships.

'I knew it,' he'd chuckled when Rosie had passed this on. 'She fancies me. Anyway, women are not my problem, it's more understanding editors I need for commissions that don't include airhead models and neurotic fashion editors.'

'Ask Jaye, not me,' Rosie had retorted, not bothering to rise to the bait since she herself had been a fashion editor before turning to interior design. She moved his legs from the wooden table so she could get past to the dishwasher at the business end of the kitchen, refusing to look at the pile of invoices stacked perilously on a rack by the dresser.

'*Jaye?*' he'd repeated scornfully, replacing his legs. 'She's the worst. You'd think that budget the *Clarion* allots her is her own money, the way she doles it out ...'

'That's not true.' Rosie defended her friend, used to Kit's periodical attacks on Jaye Wingate. 'Everyone's had their budgets slashed on newspapers. Just because she's features editor doesn't give her a slush fund she can dip into when you come along. Besides, she pays you more than anyone else ...'

'Because I'm the best,' he'd replied simply.

Rosie had laughed at him. 'Look, if it were just Jaye's hold on the purse strings, I'd agree with you, there are other papers and magazines you could throw in your lot with, but she gives you the best photographic assignments and you know it. The problem is that you are thirty-five, have lashes most women would die for and if I didn't know better I'd agree with Livvie that you must use something on your hair to keep it that blonde and you're becoming fussy. Simple.'

Simple indeed, but a little simplicity in her own life would be more than welcome, Rosie decided now as she replaced the phone on Kit and ran a quick shower. She could just make it to Nancy's after all.

If asked, Rosie would have had no hesitation in saying that, tough though it was, her life was the one she had chosen, enjoyed and revelled in rather than resented. She loved her cheerfully cluttered kitchen, the cool sanctuary of her bedroom, the chaos that trailed behind Tom when he was home from his weekly boarding school.

Tom was her joy, her job absorbed her. Her friends were essential, her love life – well, nothing was perfect, she reminded herself when the forces of financial necessity appeared to be on collision course with her happiness, usually about the time that the demand for Tom's school fees plopped onto the mat.

All of this she understood, struggled with and largely overcame because she knew where it was all coming from. Rory was different. Unpredictable, mercurial, capricious. And back in their lives, a sharp reminder that he was capable of creating chaos in a convent.

No-one who later that evening saw her conversing effortlessly with Nancy's guests, laughing off her late arrival as just one of those things, would have hesitated to say that Rosie was on good form. Even the sight of David Belmont making no attempt to deflect the sly enquiries asking if it was true that Nancy had commissioned him to design her new house, could not dent her cheerful good humour.

And why not, Rosie thought enviously. David was

flamboyant and dramatic, adored heiresses, was openly gay and inclined to patronise Rosie when he felt she might be a threat to his position of leading player in interior design in London. Tonight he kissed her affectionately and insisted they lunched the following week.

Rosie slipped away before the party broke up, pleading an early start but knowing the truth was that the encounter with Rory had wrung her out. It was not easy acknowledging it. All that should surely be behind her?

Once home she climbed the two flights to her bedroom but, too tired to sleep, she eventually gave up the struggle and propped herself up against a soft mountain of pillows, closed her eyes and hoped the nagging pain behind them was simply the effects of close proximity to Rory which would disappear now that his presence was no longer confusing her.

And confuse her he did. After coming back into their lives, she had to say until today he had been behaving reasonably, and surprisingly reliably, even asking her about her commissions. Clever Rory, so clever that he had lulled her into believing she could handle him.

It was easier to be civil than curt. Friends rather than enemies. But nothing else. Surely he could see that? He couldn't have mistaken all that mild friendliness – a truce was all it was, for Tom's sake – for something else? Not Rory. Dear God, why did she even listen to him, let him upset her?

It was what Rory did to her, muddle her judgement, trigger uncertainty. Always had, right from that first time. She shivered but it had nothing to do with lack of heating in her bedroom on a sharp November evening.

*'You're young to be doing this.'*

*'Doing what?' Rosie asked, trying two shirts against the model's bare chest, holding her head this way, then that and discarding both garments.*

'Standing in small cubicles like this with half-naked men you only met a few hours before.'

She laughed, eyeing his chest, her hand poised to select another shirt from the rail. 'I'm twenty-one. It's my job. It's what fashion assistants do. Not all glamorous, you know.'

'Thanks.'

Her eyes flew to his, her hand clapped across her mouth. She giggled. 'Sorry. Didn't mean it like that. Stand still, you're distracting me from finding your size. James Cooper – is that your agent? Well, he just guessed.'

'Do you like your job?'

'Uh, huh. Here, try this.'

'Do you like me?'

'I've no idea . . .' She glanced up at him. His eyes were the darkest she had ever seen, almost black, his hair matched. He let his eyes travel across her face and down to where the open neck of her denim shirt showed a glimpse of tanned breasts, lingered and returned to her eyes. It took an effort not to wrap her arms protectively around her body.

'Look,' she said, her voice sounding odd. 'I hardly know you. Until this moment I haven't even noticed you.' She was lying and he knew she was lying. She hadn't noticed anyone else from the moment he had walked into the studio looking like a man who came to work from a different direction every day.

Hair rumpled, clothes creased, laughingly borrowing a razor from the photographer, a chum from the club scene, kissing the fashion editor on both cheeks, stopping her from scolding him about his time-keeping and appearance.

On the other side of the thin wall of the narrow dressing room she could hear the make-up girl gossiping to one of the models as they prepared for the next shot. The photographer was ordering his assistant to move the

23

lights, the fashion director was on the phone to LA.

The cubicle was small. Rosie had stacked a pile of discarded shirts on hangers behind the door which was now closed. The light from the bulbs framed around the mirror added to the heat.

Rory was leaning against the edge of the low worktop, his hands taking his weight, bare-footed, bare-chested, the top button of his jeans open. Smiling lazily at her.

'Please,' she said, making a fuss about replacing shirts onto their hangers. 'Get a move on, I've been in this studio since eight this morning. All day I have kept happy a photographer the magazine can barely afford, put up with a fashion director who couldn't direct traffic and I would quite like to get on with what I am paid to do.

'Now,' she continued, taking a deep breath, turning back to the rail and noticing he hadn't moved. 'What size are you?'

He ignored the question. Reaching out, he pulled her gently against him. She knew she had gasped. His hands were resting on her hips, her legs pinned between his. He leaned forward and kissed her, slowly, leisurely moving his mouth across hers, immobilising her brain.

'Now, answer my question and I'll answer yours,' he murmured in her ear. 'Do you like me?'

'Yes,' she lied weakly. 'I mean,' she said, trying and failing to sound unconcerned, 'why not?' But it wasn't true. It was what he was doing that she liked. Not him. How could it be him, when she didn't know him? But she didn't stop him. Even as he reached for the zip on her jeans and slipped his hand inside.

He laughed, watching her, her eyes half closed, clinging to him, biting her teeth into his bare shoulder so in the next cubicle they wouldn't hear her softly gasp as he slid one hand slowly down her bare thigh. Nor did she *resist as he reached for her hand and pulled it down with his.*

She turned her face into the pillow.

# Chapter Three

It should have been Piers with his brilliant photography, his world of high fashion, his inability to accept Tom, but now it was Rory with his wild ideas who haunted her days.

Like a heavy fog, memories of their time together would wrap themselves around Rosie when she was least expecting it, halting what she was doing, while she gazed unseeingly out of a window.

Sometimes when she was with a client, she would have to shake herself to focus on the task in hand. Whole chunks of time could be taken up listening to Tom describing goals he had missed, fights he had won, jokes he had played without any of it registering.

The leaden feeling had taken to disturbing her sleep so that she would find herself sitting in her silent kitchen at two, three, even four in the morning, shivering because the heat was off and lack of sleep was crushing her judgement.

Only when the fax began to whir and Wu Chang's instructions despatched from his office in Hong Kong about the pace at which his house was progressing began to slide silently onto the floor was she driven back to bed.

'Oh, maybe you're right,' she sighed to Jaye one evening, two months after Rory's shocking proposal, as they sat together in the little yellow-and-blue kitchen. 'Maybe I don't know what I want.'

She gave her friend a watery smile and began to feel better. 'Now if I could just find a man who will understand the way to Tom's heart is through loving Arsenal, who also cleans the house and is a great screw, life will be perfect.'

'Pass him around,' yawned Jaye.

'No chance,' Rosie grinned reluctantly. 'But you know what really gets me down is the way people treat me – when I get the car mended or at the bank – just because I'm a single mother.'

Jaye glanced uneasily at Rosie, elbows on her kitchen table, running her hand distractedly through her hair. It was a scene that was becoming a little too familiar. Rosie looked up.

'Don't look like that ... Anyone would think I'm a financial risk or a dickhead instead of being capable of running my own business. Do you know what I've done? I've taken to saying, "I'll just consult my husband", so they won't think they can con me. And it works,' she added. 'Well, sometimes. Most of the time I'm too tired to give a sod. Trouble with that is that it's beginning to affect my work.'

At the mention of work, Jaye took real notice. She might not understand the exhaustion of being a working mother, but she understood careers. 'God, that's dodgy. You want to slow up, my girl. You're doing too much.'

'That's the problem,' Rosie pointed out. 'I'm doing too much all right but not enough of any one thing to be a success. You know that wonderful moment when you show a client all the sketches and drawings and the colours, trying to inject a sense of excitement and confidence into them – just like a portrait being revealed for the first time?' Jaye nodded.

'Well, those moments are now in danger of being accompanied by me telling them to use their imagination. You know, "Ta-ra. Here's your portrait, I'll add details like the eyes, nose and mouth when I get a minute."'

'And Miriam de Lisle – *aaghh*. To think I've listened to her boring on about her bloody child being bullied at school –. which Tom says he isn't – and about the other one fixated by her ponies. She's now insisted on a

27

"snagging" clause for six months.' Rosie mimicked Miriam's affected twang:

'Rosee, miyah de-ah, it's not you I don't trust, but you just never know. In six weeks, sweetee, the curtains could still look great but in six months, my precious, *six months*? What then? They could have dropped or the parquet flooring could have lifted. These things happen, Rosee.'

'You haven't agreed?' Jaye asked, grinning at Rosie's unnerving impersonation of her tiresome client.

Rosie sighed and nodded. 'Well, it's a matter of honour to be around to correct faults, I don't mind that, but I just can't stand the way that woman thinks she is being rooked the whole time. Must come from being married to a bookmaker. Takes no chances.

'I mean, one of those kids of hers could swing on the curtains – *anything* – and she wants me to be responsible for that. The problem is her old man's trained her better than anybody. Del boy isn't in it with those two.'

Jaye patted her hand. 'Well, at least you know you can say goodbye to her at the end of each day . . .'

'You're kidding,' Rosie exploded. 'Two days ago I was called at seven in the morning, because she is so dependent now on what I tell her, she couldn't decide what colour to use to line her underwear drawer.'

In spite of herself she ended up with Jaye rolling about laughing. 'And now she wants me to go shopping with her – "*such an eye for colour, de-ah*".'

Twice Rosie had gone out to dinner with friends of Kit's, to see if it was just loneliness that was the problem. After all, Piers had been part of her life for nearly two years.

Alone in her bed after the second date, having successfully prised her escort's hand from investigating her thighs, she mournfully came to the conclusion that it wasn't. She simply felt she desperately needed a success of some kind. She was sick of failure. Sick of it.

'What is it you want?' Kit demanded after the second failed date.

Rosie shrugged. 'I want to stop feeling I'm trapped. I want to fill in the missing piece. I want . . .' She stopped. It wouldn't make sense to him, she wasn't sure it made sense to her, but she tried anyway.

'I want,' she said simply, 'to feel complete.'


One weekend she drove down to her mother's, collecting Tom from his weekly boarding school on the way, for a visit which perhaps wasn't – in her present mood – the wisest thing to do. Rory had protested when she changed their arrangements and she was too cowardly to tell Tom on the phone, knowing but not wanting to hear his disappointment. But Rory's sudden enthusiasm for family life had unnerved her.

Although, she noted, his enthusiasm had not extended to altering his plans to spend Christmas in St Lucia, where he had disappeared for two weeks, leaving lavish presents behind for Tom and a small sapphire brooch for her. Insurance, she told herself, putting the first present she had received from him in six years in the drawer of her dresser. Just to ward off any accusations of total neglect. Her mother was much the same.

It was not as though her mother encouraged her to visit but there was a sense of duty that spurred Caroline Mellbury to ring them every few weeks and suggest they come for lunch.

And each time the call came, Rosie would feign pleasure – because it was easier than pointing out that she would like to stop being an emotional crutch. Each call tallied with another of her mother's imagined crises.

As emotional vampires went, Caroline was in the Oscar class. Her own needs transcended those of everyone within her orbit – and sometimes even beyond it if her immediate circle of friends showed signs of flagging at her exhausting demands.

Any attempt to be blunt with her mother simply resulted in Caroline raising her outraged voice several decibels, talking Rosie into resigned silence. This outburst was inevitably followed up by a terse letter describing her own tortured (and in everyone else's view self-inflicted) suffering and how very little Rosie had to worry about in comparison and telling her to pull herself together.

No-one, least of all Rosie, had summoned the nerve in the face of Caroline's overbearing and often insensitive moods to tell her she was a crashing bore.

Rosie picked up Tom from his school and always felt a traitor when she tried to turn the visit into a treat, since even at his tender age he had Caroline well figured out and hated the way his grandmother could so easily upset his mother. But as Patrick, Rosie's older brother, had with great foresight opted several years before to emigrate to Chicago, Rosie felt it was up to her to maintain some semblance of family ties.

'Oh Mum, do we have to?' Tom protested, wriggling instantly out of his school jumper and into his Arsenal sweatshirt as Rosie turned out of the school gates and headed north towards Oxford instead of back to London. 'Dad said . . .'

'We haven't seen her for weeks,' Rosie interrupted him firmly.

'Not *weeks*. It's only January and it's not our fault we didn't see her at Christmas, she went on that cruise . . .'

'And it's only for the afternoon because she wants to give you your birthday present . . .'

'I bet it's a cringy sweater,' he muttered gloomily. 'Why can't she give me money like Grandpa – then I could buy something I really *wanted*?'

Rosie's voice was measured. 'Because she sees you and Grandpa doesn't.'

'Will I ever see him?' Tom turned his head to look at her profile. Rosie concentrated hard on the road.

'One day, I expect. Goodness, I wonder if there's going to be any more snow.'

Tom was hard to deflect. 'Why doesn't Daddy just ring him?' he persisted. 'I'd quite like to see Grandpa. I haven't got a proper grandfather, have I? Felix says . . .'

'Tom,' she interrupted, recognising the theme. 'It isn't that easy. Grandpa has his reasons for not speaking to Daddy and you wouldn't want to offend Dad by going behind his back and ringing Grandpa, would you?'

'No-o,' Tom said slowly, beginning to stuff his blazer between the front seats onto the back one. 'But I haven't got a dad to live with, Grandpa doesn't want to see me and Uncle Patrick lives in America.'

Rosie swallowed hard. What a family to inflict on the poor kid. Instead she switched subjects.

'Tom, stop chucking your blazer around. They're expensive.'

'It wasn't,' he objected, making a half-hearted attempt to straighten the sleeves. 'Dad says . . .'

Rosie ignored him. Even second-hand blazers cost, whatever Rory had said. She pressed the buttons on the radio, shushing any further protests from Tom, feigning interest in road reports when she knew the journey backwards.

Not for the first time Rosie reflected that it was bad enough that such a pleasant drive was always at such odds with the unpredictable greeting awaiting them at her mother's without being riddled with guilt at the lack of men in her son's life.

Once they were through Berkshire and off the short motorway drive, the Oxfordshire countryside opened up. They sped through wet roads, snow piled deep at the edges and perched inch-high on the grey branches of trees. A further snowfall had drifted silently down during the night, and was now rapidly melting as the sun struggled weakly to warm the day up, bathing the countryside in a sharp new light.

'Pity I can't melt away and reinvent myself,' Rosie thought, negotiating the winding road that would eventually curve its way through the small village of Hambleton to her mother's house, a mellow Georgian vicarage that was much admired locally and fiercely cared for by its house-proud occupant. Or as Rosie and Patrick used to say when they were children, house-slave proud, since their mother was famed locally for the number of cleaners she got through.

For once Tom cheered up after they had been going for less than ten minutes. Thrilled that Ryan Giggs was being interviewed by Frank Bough on the radio, he quite forgot that only the day before he had thumped his friend Garth de Lisle for saying that such a star player could knock spots off Tom's own hero, Ian Wright.

'And we both know,' Rosie teased him, glancing in the rear mirror before overtaking a swaying lorry, glad to be able to distract him from his dysfunctional family, 'that Gavin Peacock is more talented than either of them.'

'*Gavin Peacock?*' cried Tom scornfully, mystified by his mother's preference for the forward. 'Daddy says he couldn't kick the skin off a rice pudding. Daddy says . . .'

'Did he?' she interrupted discouragingly. 'Ssh. Tom, you'll miss what Ryan's saying and I'll hit something.'

'But it's int'resting, what Dad says . . . he says . . .'

'Tom,' Rosie exploded. 'If you mention what Daddy says one more time, I'm going to turn that radio off, do you understand . . . and stop sulking. Oh for God's sake, Tom, grow up,' she finished with a snap. 'Bad enough having to spend the next two hours listening to what Granny says.'

'But you said you didn't mind going . . .'

'I know what I said,' she replied, knowing it was totally unfair to confuse him but unable to help herself. 'It isn't what I meant.'

Tom's view of Rory was strictly the one Rosie had fostered, one that few who knew the man would recognise. But Rosie had pledged that her own unsuccessful relationship with Rory would not be inflicted on their innocent son.

It was a pledge she had often deeply regretted. Struggling to steer a delicate line between urging Rory to take an interest in his child while not maligning him to Tom, even encouraging him to have respect for his largely absent parent, had backfired on her.

If only she had listened to Carey, who had warned her that encouraging Tom to believe Rory was a hero had 'disaster' written all over it. Instead she had insisted that there was a world of difference between encouraging and simply not correcting him when he spoke of his neglectful and uninterested father as a perpetual font of wisdom.

She glanced sideways at her son and instantly felt contrite. The mop of black hair fell untidily around his eyes, thick black lashes framed deep blue eyes. He was going to be stunning. Like Rory.

She took one hand off the wheel and stroked his cheek. 'Hey, sorry. Grumpy old thing, aren't I? I'll make it up to you.'

Tom grinned back at her. 'You're okay,' he said easily. 'I expect the dreadful Miriam's been playing up.'

'*Tom*,' she gasped. 'You mustn't talk like that. She's Garth's mother.'

'That doesn't make her nice, though, does it?' he pointed out so reasonably that Rosie had to struggle not to laugh. But he was right. Merely being a mother was not always enough. Her own was undeniably devoid of maternal instincts.

'But Garth loves her,' she maintained.

'He likes his father best,' Tom confided. 'He goes to Spurs with him and next weekend they're going camping. Just the two of them.'

'Perhaps Miriam doesn't want to go,' she suggested hopefully.

'Don't know. Garth said it was boys' stuff. You know, just him and his dad.'

'But not all your friends go camping with their fathers,' she laughed impatiently. It was the guilt, of course. 'Felix doesn't.'

Tom put his feet on the dashboard and looked wistfully out of the window. 'No, he's going to cricket camp at Easter. His father's on the board of a sports company and he fixed it for him.'

'Well, I'll find something for you to do,' she told him cheerfully.

Tom stared resolutely ahead. 'That's okay, Mum,' he said. 'It's not the same.'

Rory's voice floated back. '*He wants to be like his friends.*' Oh God.

Rosie's mother's displeasure at her daughter turning Piers down after such a promising relationship was nothing compared to how she behaved when Rosie had finally split from Rory all those years ago.

Being denied a titled son-in-law and unlikely, in the greater scheme of things, to live to see her grandson inherit had hit Caroline's pride to such a degree that at the time Rosie began to wonder if her own suffering was, by comparison, as totally self-indulgent as her mother claimed.

Frankly Caroline had been as much mystified as appalled when Rosie had insisted on divorcing Rory after his affair and had demanded she sought counselling.

If Tom kept referring all afternoon to his father as the oracle of wisdom they were in for an even thinner time than usual. It simply encouraged Caroline silently to flash Rosie an I-told-you-so look of triumph mixed with despair.

Maternal support had never troubled Caroline. If she

34

couldn't solve her children's problems by a quick trawl along the shelves of Mothercare, hiring the right nanny or choosing the right school, she simply shrugged them away. Even Rosie's unplanned pregnancy had evoked not so much shock as irritation at the inconvenience of it all.

*'Are you sure?'*

*'Yes,' she whispered. 'Quite sure.'*

*Tears were dripping down her cheeks. Caroline walked across to where her distressed daughter was standing and grasped her shoulders.*

*'For God's sake don't sob like that. Here, take this.'*

*Over her shoulder as the weeping girl scrubbed the tissue over her face, Caroline gazed at a picture of Rosie taken on her twenty-first birthday just a few months before. She was at the centre of a laughing group of friends, all raising their glasses. Just after her graduation from art school. So much to look forward to. Really, this was too much.*

*'My dear girl, didn't you take precautions? You are going to marry him?'*

*In that moment Rosie knew her mother was not going to help beyond what was absolutely necessary. Caroline's children were her duty, not her life.*

*Now she shook her head at her mother's carefully posed question. 'I mean, probably not. He ... we don't want to get married.'*

*'What about his parents? Do they know?'*

*'His mother's dead – when he was twelve – his father is Sir Callum Monteith Gore. Rory's an only child. He's going to see him this weekend.'*

*'And you?' Her mother's voice was sharp. 'You as well, surely? What about the baby?'*

*Rosie shook her head. She was twenty-one years old, pregnant by a man she was obsessed with who, she knew, had never given a thought to marriage, confronted by a mother who didn't want an unmarried daughter with a child on her hands, and feeling so sick she would have agreed to shaving her head if this nightmare would end.*

*'I am thinking of the baby,' she said dully. 'But I can't marry someone who doesn't want to marry me. Can I?'*

'Tom darling, don't put your feet on that chair . . . that's better, dear, sit up straight.'

Rosie flashed a smile of sympathy at Tom, who had sprawled full length with his trainers still on along Caroline's Percheron-covered sofa.

He was thoroughly fed up with his grandmother's unstoppable monologue on the life and times of Hambleton, and wanted to go. It was one-sided, clearly prejudiced and littered with well-massaged facts about her disagreement with her current best friend or the whereabouts of his ex-step-grandfather on the political tree, a subject which held little interest for Tom since David Mellbury had divorced his grandmother.

The only time Tom looked hopefully at her, Rosie noticed, was when Caroline openly voiced her disapproval of his current school.

Old Farrells was distinguished by two things. One, it returned all its little inhabitants to their homes at the weekend and two, Rosie could just about afford it.

It was not the moment to remind her mother that the choice to send him there had been forced upon her while Rory was uncontactable and Caroline herself had been on an extended visit in the Bahamas.

The au pair had moved out overnight, leaving a message on Rosie's answer machine saying she would not be returning. Unfortunately she chose to defect on the morning Rosie was due to go to Rome for three days on a fashion shoot. The embarrassment of calling the editor to explain the situation, followed by a frantic call to Piers as he was en route to the airport, had decided her. Her reputation only narrowly escaped damage, thanks to Piers who persuaded a freelance fashion stylist in Rome to cover for her by doubling her fee.

Later on that nightmarish morning, alone in her kitchen after having delivered Tom to the local primary school, she faced the grim fact she had been avoiding for the last two years. Her nerves and her belief that Tom was the one who would suffer the most if this went on, could take no more.

It was a toss-up whether Caroline or Rory had created the biggest fuss when they heard what she'd done, but since neither had been there to help nor prepared to put themselves out to find a school for Tom worthy of their social aspirations, they both let the matter drop, confining themselves to pursed lips or a sulking shrug respectively when the subject cropped up.

Tactfully distracting her mother away from Tom, Rosie carried a tea tray into the conservatory. From there she could have an uninterrupted view along a perfectly manicured lawn banked on either side by rose walks, beech trees and, tucked into a small clearing, a summerhouse that Rosie and Patrick had as children pretended was their real home, it being more comfortable and comforting than the carefully plotted decor of her mother's house.

'That friend of yours, Nancy Alexander,' her mother was saying. There were some people of Rosie's acquaintance that she now approved of, and one such was Nancy; being a multi-millionairess had promptly elevated her to *friend* in Caroline's mind. 'I read she's involved with Joel Harley. What's he like?'

'No idea,' said Rosie. 'Never met him.'

Her mother looked disappointed. 'I thought you mixed with architects these days?'

'Not mega ones like him,' Rosie replied, pouring tea and feeling an instant nervousness at her mother's interest in a figure of such renown. God, her mother was such a snob. 'He doesn't do houses, more reshapes the skyline,' she added. 'Why?'

'No reason if you don't know him. But my friend Valerie Cottisham's son is at the same school as his son and she met him at Founder's Day. Asked me if you knew him, because I must have mentioned your friendship with Nancy.'

Must have? Rosie was in no doubt at all. Her mother only dropped names if she was sure they would bounce.

'Valerie said he was amazingly unsmart for an architect.'

Rosie looked surprised. 'Unsmart? You're kidding. Or Valerie Cottisham is. He's one of the few architects I've heard of who got a degree from Yale in Business after he qualified as an architect.'

'I thought they all did that?'

'No, they don't, which is why only a handful make a fortune out of it. It's only recently that architectural schools have started to attach business studies to their courses. There's no real money to be made in architecture unless you're rich to start with or get a great break. Bit like interior designers actually,' she added as a gloomy afterthought.

Caroline sniffed. 'You don't follow up the right contacts,' she admonished. 'Business studies indeed. Contacts, my girl, that's what does it, contacts.'

Rosie sighed. Caroline was probably right.

'I know,' she conceded. 'It isn't all pretty drawings and that's that. You've got to have a head for business as well to survive these days. Joel Harley quite obviously twigged that when he qualified. He doesn't sound exactly dim to me.'

'No, no.' Her mother waved an impatient hand. 'Not his brain. Valerie said he's quite frightening in that department. I meant his dress. The way he dresses. Valerie said on Founder's Day he was wearing a creased linen jacket, something perilously close to jeans and no tie.'

Her mother pronounced it with capital letters, since it was almost worthy of capital punishment in her book of etiquette. No wonder she had adored Rory, who whipped out a tux at the first sound of a stiff white card plopping onto the doormat.

'Perhaps it was Friday dressing,' Rosie giggled. 'Americans are into all that.'

'But he's not American,' objected Caroline.

'True,' agreed Rosie. 'But I haven't met him, so there you are.'

'Well, who do you meet? The only person I ever hear when I ring you is that lunatic you employ – what *is* her name – Olivia, that's it, telling me she's just dashing to or coming from a lecture on End of Era Crisis therapy or something.'

'Workshops,' Rosie corrected. 'Not lectures. Livvie's brilliant at her job, she's just very into women's issues.'

'Well, what about your old friend Judith? She's doing so well. When does she go to New York?'

'March,' Rosie replied. 'She'll be back and forward for the next year while the office is established.'

She let her mother drone on. 'My point is, all your friends are making successes of themselves. Ellie was interviewed by Melvyn Bragg the other night – some documentary she's got an award for. And there's Judith setting up a New York office and Jaye being quoted everywhere. You had exactly the same opportunities that they did, education, a good home, connections . . .'

Rosie just listened. Her friends' more focused lives disturbed her. It wasn't envy, but it was hard to make her mother understand that having to cope with Rory without any real family support had dealt her one crushing financial and emotional blow after the other.

At least her friends had backed her when she decided to switch from being a fashion editor to interior design. A chance opportunity had come her way, one she thought would solve her problems trying to care for Tom and earn a living simultaneously. Working for herself sounded like freedom. She wasn't sure now, with the benefit of hindsight, if she hadn't created her own designer prison.

Her mother's reaction at her decision to be her own boss had been to forecast complete disaster and a withdrawal of all support until Rosie had come to her senses, telling all her friends that Rosie was taking a year's break to research a book on design. All of which sounded more acceptable than her daughter setting up shop in her living room and being at the beck and call of Hong Kong businessmen buying into London and wanting their homes done up overnight.

It was infuriating the way her mother dismissed her talent and her job as though she was a bored housewife who fancied being an interior designer without any training, innovative skills or real talent to their name.

To her friends Caroline still referred to Rosie as Mrs Monteith Gore, ignoring completely that the day Rosie set up her own business she had with relief returned to her own name of Colville. *Rosie Colville Interiors*. It had sounded good. Successful. Independent. Her mother thought there should be a law against it.

'You simply can't go on forever living on your own,' her mother was saying.

'Well, I'll have to.' Rosie refused to be rattled. 'I haven't met someone that fitted in with me and Tom . . .'

'Nonsense,' her mother snapped. 'All this rubbish about step-parents. My divorces never affected you or Patrick, did they?'

Rosie wished Patrick could hear this. But like her, well versed in the hysteria that surrounded and ultimately drowned their protests, he too would have allowed the distorted facts to go unchallenged. Not worth it. Both out of it now.

Tom yawned. Not understanding his grandmother's pre-occupation with everyone getting married, he was getting restless.

'First Rory, now Piers. If you're not careful you'll end

up lonely and old. Life is not perfect, Rosie. That's your problem. You want perfection. Expect too much and you'll end up with nothing at all.'

Rosie could feel the familiar anger beginning to stir. It was time to draw this visit to a close.

'Perhaps.' She tried to smile. 'We'll see. Anyway, at the moment my most pressing concern is to find somewhere bigger to work from or maybe live.'

A happy and helpful thought struck Tom. 'Daddy says we can live with him,' he piped up, hastily swinging his feet to the ground as his grandmother swivelled her head to look at him.

Caroline stopped in mid-sentence, in the act of sipping her tea and gaped at her grandson.

'*Really?*' She slewed round towards Rosie, making no attempt to conceal her delight. 'Darling, why didn't you mention it before?'

Rosie clattered her cup back into the saucer. 'Tom,' she ordered sharply. 'Collect your things, we really should be getting back.'

Obediently and totally relieved at the magic words, he raced off to round up his blazer and books.

'And there's no need to tell you, is there,' Rosie said firmly to her agog mother once he was out of earshot, 'that such an idea is of course completely ridiculous. So don't even begin to entertain it.'

# Chapter Four

January remained freezing, February was unseasonably warm, while March arrived on a cyclone of bitter winds labouring under an impression that it was meant to be rivalling the Arctic.

Rosie, dashing from clients to showrooms and workrooms, was only too aware that antique fairs she should have gone to had to be ditched, galleries missed out and auctions conducted without any input from her.

Instead she became incapable of passing a travel agent's window without staring at posters showing acres of deserted sand, desolate mountain ranges and isolated farmhouses, in the same way she had once lingered over a design by David Hicks or Jane Churchill.

The final straw, however, had been her sharp ten-minute exchange with the accountant employed by Sylvia Duxborough, wealthy, demanding, patronising and spiteful. Rosie could reel off, as she frequently did after a meeting with Sylvia, the litany of character defects the woman possessed. Her flawed grip on how women like Rosie earned a living was pitiful.

'Your invoice doesn't add up,' Sylvia's accountant declared loftily as Rosie clenched the phone.

'In what way?' she asked politely, drawing her copy of the offending document in front of her.

'The total cost of materials and labour doesn't match your final figure. It's much higher,' he pointed out.

'The rest is my fee.' Rosie was polite. The pencil she was holding snapped in half. 'But now that you've drawn my attention to it, I can see that I haven't added cancellation fees for when Mrs Duxborough failed to show up for meetings and the day she went to the country having arranged for me to measure her new curtains. So that will have to be added on.'

But Sylvia wasn't the only one to drive Rosie to near despair and to wonder at the venality of some of her clients.

Each month she paid her suppliers out of her dwindling funds and learned to turn down commissions when the client asked too many detailed questions on their first encounter, revealing they simply wanted information to do the whole thing themselves. She now resolutely walked the other way when they flourished torn pages from glossy magazines demanding *that* look when their budget clearly couldn't stretch to the price of a paintbrush.

Earnest, dedicated and addicted to women's workshops, Livvie was the reason Rosie had not gone under. She earned every bit of her admittedly small salary and Rosie felt very responsible for her assistant, who had joined her when she first started up.

Livvie was a rare design talent and also a sounding board for many of the feminist tracts that Jaye featured on her pages in the *Clarion*.

Currently Livvie was reading *Dealing Safely with High Expectations*. Her conversation was always loaded with her favourite words; at any given time, Livvie could be found 'dealing with her feelings' or 'coping with unrealistic aims'. Sometimes she would be 'exploring his guilt', or 'dumping her denial syndrome'.

Quite a lot of the time she would feel motivated to try to get Rosie to join her in these sessions, and never lost hope that one day her boss would see the light.

'I think I'm beyond saving,' Rosie would tell her with a rueful grin.

'Not "save", Rosie,' Livvie would gently correct her. 'Just "staying with who you are". Just tell yourself each day, "I'm okay, my job's okay", okay?'

'Okay,' Rosie would dutifully repeat. She could only imagine the pleasure Livvie would get if she knew that increasingly Rosie was beginning to think Livvie's views on shared parenthood had something to them.

'Parenting,' Livvie pronounced, 'is a business like any other. Shared responsibilities, a partnership. Just because you no longer want to screw each other doesn't mean one half should be loaded with all the day-to-day stuff.'

Rosie tried to defend herself. 'But I read here,' she rustled up that morning's paper in which a leading feminist columnist had spoken on the subject, 'where is it . . . yes, here it is: "Having a father helps kids stop being poor, educationally retarded and delinquent. Apart from that, it remains unclear what fathers do that is so damn important."'

'Exactly,' Livvie beamed. 'It's the poverty aspect, the lack of education, that's important. You should create a self-dynamic that challenges white middle-class values about bourgeois child-care arrangements,' she advised.

Rosie couldn't quite figure out how you made someone like Rory do something he didn't want to without costly legal advice or action. Neither appealed to her. However, because Livvie was sincerely concerned, she meekly agreed that she would be tougher.

'I saw a great studio up the road this morning,' Livvie told her shortly after this, wedging her shoulder against a precarious pile of sample books which were stacked on the shelf behind her worktable as she wriggled one out from the bottom of the heap. 'It would be brill to work from. Why don't you think about it?'

'Because I have a straight choice,' Rosie said, stapling a sample of stiff paper onto a board that showed a watercolour of how the wallpaper in a client's mews house would look when finished. 'A bigger workroom would be wonderful but it costs money, so something would have to be sacrificed. And I need an assistant more than I need to find a king's ransom for rent.'

'Oh,' said Livvie and didn't mention it again.

Even the recruitment of Livvie when she first started the business had not solved as many problems as Rosie had envisaged. Clients wanted Rosie's personal input; Livvie simply did not have the image that inspired confidence in the Sylvia Duxboroughs of Rosie's world.

Sylvia understood Bond Street, not Red or Dead. Livvie's spiky cropped blonde hair, sharp red plastic earrings the size of small satellites she habitually wore, black lycra skirts stretched tightly across her thighs were tolerated by Sylvia because she knew the likes of Jaye and Nancy took her seriously, as did quite a few of Rosie's other clients.

There was, in Sylvia's book, no accounting for it, so she continued to ignore as best she could Livvie's presence, never troubling herself to wonder how the young woman graduated from the Slade with such excellent references.

Especially when Livvie had offered to lend Sylvia her book *New Goals and Directions Without Him* when Sylvia had kept them waiting a whole week for a decision about her master bedroom carpet until her husband, Oscar, returned from a business trip.

'But she defers to him all the time,' Livvie protested after the angry call from Sylvia threatening to return to their great rival, Jessica Milford.

'I don't care if she defers to the entire regiment of the Queen's Own Highlanders,' snapped an exasperated Rosie. 'We're here to make Sylvia feel terrific about herself, not turn her into a seething mass of doubts.'

Although on reflection she had to admit such a thing was not even a remote possibility with Sylvia.

'You're going to a football match?' the dreadful woman exclaimed on hearing Rosie was tied up on Saturday after- noon instead of being free to discuss plans for her country house. 'Oh, poor you. Oscar does all that with Felix.' Sylvia waved a perfectly manicured hand in the air. 'At this age, they do rather feel they want to get away from Mama ...

oh dear. I'm so sorry . . . but you know what I mean?'

Sylvia had raised her hand to her mouth to disguise a small gasp. Rosie smiled back, annoyed that Sylvia had rubbed it in that Tom was stuck with just his mother, annoyed that she had a point, annoyed that such a silly woman could make her feel so guilty, annoyed that Tom should have chosen this silly woman's son as a friend . . .

It was not, however, the foolish Sylvia who had triggered her gloom on this cold March day, long after Rory's astonishing proposal that they should live together again and weeks since her mother had given up nagging her about it.

The farewell party for Judith, as she took off for New York to set up a branch of her highly successful PR company, was certainly a factor.

Rory's sudden insistence on driving with her to collect Tom from school each weekend was another. Taken by surprise, Rosie hadn't the heart to refuse, even though on the first occasion he had twice taken wrong turnings, so unused was he to the route to Old Farrells.

Her ex-husband's continued belief that he held some power over her feelings nagged at her. Judith's parting words lingered.

'Stop humouring him. He's a shit. Ask him what's really in it for him.'

'All very well for Judith,' Rosie had grumbled to Jaye the day after the party as they strolled along Christopher Place to collect a jacket that Jaye was keen to buy but on which she needed, as ever, Rosie's opinion. 'She's used to direct dealing. I'm trained to make people feel terrific about themselves, not defensive.'

'Then stop being such a doormat – so submissive all the time where he's concerned.'

'Submissive? *Me*? Just a minute . . .'

'No, you listen. You're just as capable of saying what you want when you want it. It's just you're so bloody busy

46

you don't have time to think what that is these days. Unless pride's getting in the way . . .'

'Pride? I can't afford *pride*. I have a business to run, a child to bring up. There isn't *time* to argue with him. It's quicker to do it all myself. Tom stays undamaged, if disappointed.'

'Well, remember Rory's wrecking your business, he's contributing to that by not being supportive. He's a total liability.'

Tall, outspoken, with a sweep of silver blonde hair, tucked carelessly into a coil or fixed with whatever came to hand, Jaye's clothes were as dramatically glamorous as Rosie's proclaimed her unerring eye for style.

Really, Rosie thought, walking silently beside Jaye, she's as bad as Livvie. Theory is great and that's all this is. It's just words.

Jaye was in full stride: 'Stop letting him call all the shots. He's Tom's father, still responsible. Why should he be able to tell you when he will or won't turn up? I'll tell you something, my girl, your future would be a lot brighter if you tell him to start shaping up. Unless . . .'

'Unless what?'

Jaye hesitated and then with a swift shake of her head grabbed Rosie's arm. 'Nothing . . . c'mon, the jacket I want is in Whistles.'

'I said, unless what?' Rosie persisted, following her into the shop.

Jaye marched straight ahead. 'Unless . . . okay, unless you're enjoying having him chase after you . . . here, it's the red Lolita Lempicka. Waddya think?'

'Chase after me? Are you crazy? I have enough problems without recreating old ones. I couldn't wait to unload him. You know that.'

'Do I?' Jaye replied bluntly. 'As a matter of fact I recall you said you felt so betrayed you had no option.'

Rosie paused. 'You don't understand,' she finally

muttered. 'I don't want to encourage bad feeling between me and Rory. I have Tom to think of.'

Jaye plucked the jacket from the rail and headed for the changing rooms. 'Tom to think of?' She hesitated and then with a tiny shrug, 'Yes, Tom, of course. Now I wonder why I'm not convinced?' she said, and disappeared into the cubicle, ignoring Rosie's outraged glare.

# Chapter Five

Even worse than the worry over Rory was the prospect of confronting her dismal financial affairs. The interview with her accountant later that day was so dispiriting Rosie walked all the way from Battersea to Kings Road in a biting wind rather than take a bus, determined to make every economy count while mystifyingly trying to work out how much it would cost to disappear to a remote desert island.

Matthew Ormond's advice was as blunt as Judith's, as uncompromising as Jaye's. Threaten late payers with a significant interest percentage slapped on their bills after thirty days without payment or, better still, threaten legal action to the ones who were still outstanding after three months. And let Livvie go. Rosie didn't even have a choice.

'No company in the world would tolerate this,' said her long-suffering accountant. 'I know you say it's not done to chivvy them all and that they'll pay eventually but this is ridiculous. Look at this invoice . . .' He peered at the figures, 'You finished the work in December. The balance for your invoice went in in January, it is now March.'

'They've been abroad.' Rosie knew she sounded defensive, but she didn't know whether it was her own dismal accounting or the clients' lifestyle she was defending.

'And this. A second invoice. Nothing. Really, I'm not at all sure you're tough enough to be running a company.' Rosie suspected he might be right. Her face remained impassive.

Matthew Ormond led an orderly life. He understood the finer nuances of interior design, and he understood late.

He simply couldn't fathom ignoring late. Especially when a business like Rosie's was going under faster than the *Titanic*. He tried again.

She stubbornly shook her head. 'There must be another way. Can't you get any tax relief on anything? I don't have any help with Tom or the house. Livvie's all I've got.'

'You're much too easy on people like this,' Matthew countered, tapping a sheaf of unpaid invoices. The top one, the largest, was for Sylvia Duxborough. So embarrassing. Wife of a millionaire, mother of one of Tom's best friends at school. Impossible to threaten her. Of course the *idea* of threatening Sylvia was certainly attractive, one couldn't deny that it would afford Rosie a great deal of pleasure to unsettle the stick insect.

'You can't afford to go on as you are,' Matthew warned her, ushering her out of the door. 'You've got to be tough somewhere. Livvie's on three months' notice. Either she goes or the business does.'

'It isn't like your business,' Rosie protested. 'One *word* that I might be in trouble and I'll be ruined overnight. It's like a village. Word spreads.'

'You make it sound like a jungle,' he retorted. 'Here's a piece of advice for you. Think about it. Failure isn't losing everything – it's an opportunity to start again more wisely.'

'What with?' she asked bitterly. He made her sound like an impulsive airhead. But she hadn't gone into such a business sacrificing a substantial salary as a fashion editor on a successful magazine – albeit one blind to the needs of a working mother – without being shrewd enough to understand that skill, taste, flair would be rendered useless if she stopped being charming.

Bluntness was not at her disposal. Tact had become her companion. If she did what her accountant said, she'd have no clients at all, then no job, no home, no . . . Livvie. The very thought made her feel sick with nerves.

And Rory was still plaguing the life out of her. Just

because he now fancied the idea of a beautiful and engaging son around, he thought he could wipe out the years when the restrictions the same little boy had once generated had been a source of aggravation to him.

Thankfully she was used to him. The novelty would soon wear off. Mind you, she mused gloomily as she strode purposefully across Chelsea Bridge, the wind from the river searing her face, it was nearly three months and he still hadn't let up about getting back together. Dream on, Rory, she muttered under her breath.

Pathetic, she told herself in disgust as she finally reached home. What parents Tom had been given. One on the point of insolvency and the other lost in fantasy.

By now it was nearly four. Livvie had gone early to see Joyce, the curtain maker, in Kennington. Slinging her bag and coat into the kitchen and shoving the buff folders containing her depressing accounts into the bottom drawer of her desk, Rosie picked up the list of messages Livvie had left, checked the machine was still on 'answer' and mounted the stairs to her bedroom. The prospect of a hot warm bath had been sustaining her on her cold walk home.

Rosie's bedroom was her favourite place in the house. Piers had said it was like sleeping in a page from *House and Garden*. Jaye loved it so much, she eventually told the style editor from *Special Interiors* who featured it in the magazine.

White linen curtains and blinds hung at the window. Crisp blue-and-white cotton bedhangings matched the bedspread and were complemented by the palest grey fitted carpet. All were reflected in mirrored glass doors concealing a small dressing area, out of which she had coaxed enough room to house a bathroom.

The phone rang as she wrapped herself in a bath robe, her wet hair shrouded in a towel. Jaye sounded ragged, cancelling supper which Rosie had in any event forgotten.

'Bed and lights out by ten. Alone,' Jaye recommended.

'Nothing new in that of course and Alex is in a fury because I won't sign off the pages.'

'Why not?' Rosie yawned, used to Jaye's high-octane performance at any given moment and her daily screaming match with the editor. It was part of her charm, what Rosie had liked about her when they had first met all those years ago when she was fashion editor of *Focus* magazine and Jaye was in charge of features.

'Because he wants me to drop the American from my single mother series ... and don't panic, I know better than to ask you to fill the gap.'

'Sounds reasonable,' Rosie pointed out, pulling the pillows into a comfortable shape behind her. 'This is England, after all. Oh, don't do a Livvie on me, all that affirmation stuff.'

She could hear Jaye's exasperated sigh. 'More's the pity. You could really learn a thing or two from Alicia. She's cut through all that guilt trip. American women have stopped taking it on the chin, they make demands, breach the rules, the sacred cow of parenting ...'

'What sacred cow?' Rosie demanded. 'What *is* Alicia, whatever her name is, talking about?'

'Oh, c'mon. All this stuff that unless you sacrifice yourself they'll grow up to mug old ladies and never speak to you again.'

Rosie was irritated. 'Rubbish,' she snapped. 'I don't spend all my time with Tom, but I do have certain responsibilities ...'

'Of course and you do a great job, but you won't let a man into your life unless he passes the Tom test ... don't deny it. Whereas Alicia says, she dumped all that guilt, married twice more and had four children by three different fathers. She simply said "I have a life too", farmed them all out to their individual fathers whenever she needed to get her own life in shape, and one of her children is now running for Congress,' Jaye finished triumphantly.

'Well, no-one's perfect,' Rosie said lightly, privately horrified at the antics of Alicia but too tired to voice her opinion because Jaye would regard it as her duty to convince her. 'Now, supper tomorrow instead? Oh, I can't. Friday? Got to get Tom.'

Jaye's yawn down the line matched Rosie's. 'Could be worse, you could be twins. Just joking. I'll catch you later. Must go, I've been buzzed.'

Rosie gave a wry grin. Where she herself had a cool charm about her, a laid-back humour that was quietly but accurately delivered, Jaye was pure Manhattan – the result of two years at Columbia in New York studying English.

After the conversation, Rosie lay back and studied the ceiling for a while. Hard to admit without feeling such awful disloyalty to Tom that there were some things about Alicia's philosophy that were very appealing.


'Darling?' Rory enquired. Rosie sighed, knowing the bed was too comfortable for comfort.

'No, not "darling", Rory, "Rosie",' she told him patiently, knowing the point was wasted on him. 'What is it?'

'I wondered if I could pop round . . .'

'Pop round . . .' she echoed. 'Why?'

'Apart from seeing you – which would be nice – I've just been reading Tom's school report. Thought we should discuss it.'

'What's to discuss? He's in the top third of the class, he's in the first team for football and in the reserves for swimming . . . what's the problem?'

'No problem, just this comment from the head: "He needs to assert himself in class discussion" . . .'

'Rory,' she began carefully. 'Tom is eleven years old. He's doing well, I really don't think we need to worry too much about his contribution to a class discussion.'

'Well, I do,' Rory insisted. 'It's at this age that the foundations . . .'

'Rory,' she interrupted. 'Can we talk about this another time? I have just come in. Lunch? No, Rory, I mean it . . . I'll . . . Yes, okay, okay. I'll think about it.'

Just as well Jaye was the one having to make the professional decisions, she sighed. These days she couldn't decide which side of the bed to sleep, let alone what to do with her life.

Sleep. Just ten minutes. No. It was only five. She turned her back resolutely on the inviting mountain of pillows. Today had been a bitch. Tom had left two messages on the answer machine and her heart sank, knowing they were to say he was unhappy. And his Easter break was due at any moment. Rosie hated herself for dreading it.

Striking a balance between a need to put Tom first and flying into a panic when he demanded her attention was exhausting her almost as much as her work.

Miriam de Lisle, not content with having tried Rosie's patience since Christmas, was now making Rosie seriously consider refusing to take any more of her calls. She began to daydream about unloading her onto Jessica Milford.

If anyone was designed to cater for Miriam's mercurial moods and changes of mind, it was Jessica, who found no difficulty in slavishly copying any Hollywood mansion irrespective of whether the house was 1930s mock-Tudor or based on Balmoral itself. With a shrug she would pocket her fee which she baldly doubled when her own taste had to be compromised.

There had been many moments when Rosie wished she cared less for her reputation and more for her bank account as she had struggled to meet Miriam's demands. Discreet low-voltage lighting, clever paint effects, the very latest fabric trends and strategically placed mirrors had all been rolled out in an attempt to turn Miriam's already generous-sized bedroom into the size of a hockey field.

Whatever Miriam had she wanted it bigger and bolder.

'Everything needs doing. It is simply a shell for me to bring to life,' Miriam had announced grandly down the phone earlier in the week when she called to say she was moving. 'With your help of course,' she'd added quickly.

'If you moved her into Buckingham Palace and gave her the ballroom for a bedroom, she'd still want the walls knocked through,' Rosie had complained bitterly to Kit.

The blinds were flapping against the window, sending gusts of cold air into the room. Rosie sighed. No wonder she was chilly. Getting up, she slammed the window shut, and the muffled roar of traffic in Kings Road deadened. Rosie eyed her bed longingly and then, slipping off her robe, slid under the cover just until the room warmed up.

She yawned. Waiting for her in the small room across the landing that she had been forced to turn into an office was a workload that was dangerously close to engulfing her. She did her best, but there was never enough time.

Time? She stifled a mirthless laugh and slid further down under the cover. She felt safe here. Warm. She would close her eyes for a few minutes and then she would feel ready to compose a few uncompromising letters, starting with Sylvia, and work out how to keep Livvie. Let Livvie go? Unthinkable.

Just for a minute. No harm in that.

The phone shattered her sleep. Disorientated by waking in a darkened room, the blinds still open, light from a street lamp throwing shadows across the walls, Rosie tried to grab the receiver and succeeded in sending it plunging to the floor.

'Yes, hello?' She gasped blearily into the mouthpiece, her head hanging over the side of the bed, while with her free hand she flailed around searching for the switch on the lamp. God, it was six o'clock.

'Rosie? Rosie? Is that you? It's Nancy. Are you okay?'

*Nancy*. Oh God. Nancy. She'd forgotten, she was meant to phone her. 'Yes, Nancy. It's me. I'm here.' Christ, she breathed, trying to make sense of everything. Are you trying to lose the only decent contact you've got?

'Sorry, got held up.' Rosie tried to keep her voice calm as she struggled to push the cover off her legs. 'Client meeting,' she lied, wriggling into her robe. 'Yes, hellish traffic. I've just walked through the door. Let me just put my briefcase down and I'll be with you.'

# Chapter Six

Nancy Alexander was being massaged by her personal aromatherapist as she spoke to Rosie.

'Can you make it by seven?' came the clipped if muffled New York accent of the American socialite. 'I'm tied up tomorrow and Wednesday I leave for Vermont. I'll delay dinner. Better still – join us.'

Rosie pulled her robe more warmly around her. 'That's sweet of you, Nancy, but I have a huge workload,' she said, eyeing the pile of letters she had vowed she would tackle. 'What's the problem? Has someone let you down with something?'

Nancy's track record of alienating the internationally acclaimed designers who worked for her was legendary. She snorted down the phone. 'Let me down? Me? No way, and I don't need any help with designers either. Ouch . . . my neck, I thought this was supposed to relax, not paralyse . . . sorry, honey. My problem is getting them off the phone, not on it. But yes, I do need your help.'

Nancy was tricky but immensely influential. There was a directness about her that left her network of contacts, like Rosie, in no doubt what their use was to her.

Last time it had been to ask Rosie to persuade a client to sell her a couple of Regency chairs that Nancy had noticed when she'd gone there to dinner. On another occasion she had collared Rosie to come and re-arrange the furniture in her library, having slung out the household name who had arranged it in the first place.

At forty, she looked ten years younger thanks to the skill of an expensive surgeon in New York. She had been twice married and divorced, neither of her husbands ever speaking to her again. This did not trouble her in any way. Her own exceptional wealth eclipsed the need for anyone's good opinion. When she wasn't collecting paintings, she was fully occupied as president of the Alexander Foundation, named after her family, which donated or loaned works of art to worthy charitable causes.

At least, that was the simple explanation used in the financial pages and the social columns to justify the frequent inclusion of the name.

'Art for art's sake and money for Christ's sake,' Rosie whispered to Jaye, who'd raised her eyebrows when once on the same night she and Rosie had been invited to Nancy's for drinks, two cabinet ministers and an American senator were also among the guests. 'They couldn't tell a Vuillard from a Van Gogh. Alexanders are great bankrollers for political office.'

'I thought it all came from the art collection,' Jaye whispered back, pretending interest in a small Picasso drawing.

'Lord, no,' Rosie told her. 'That's just the beard for the real business. Nancy loves it. Takes after her great-great-grandmother who started it while grandpapa was out buying up railroads and trying to be governor of some state or other. Then he got a taste for politics which he mistook for power, only he discovered fairly quickly that real power lay in holding the purse strings and not in the White House, so he founded the First Finance Bank instead. And then the Alexander Foundation came along because his wife had more scruples than he did and found it easier to entertain her friends surrounded by all that wealth and corrupt politicians if it looked like they were doing it all for charity.'

'Didn't rub off on Nancy,' Jaye pointed out, watching their hostess who had inherited her great-great-grandmother's mantle, quite shamelessly ordering the visiting senator to make a sizeable donation to the Foundation while looping her arm companionably through his.

'Thank God for that,' Rosie said. 'Grandmama would have been annihilated today. Nancy takes after the male Alexanders – well, mostly.'

In an unguarded moment Nancy had revealed to Rosie that marriage must mean public as well as private compatibility.

'Gotta have a guy who can cut it on the same scale. And the ones that I wouldn't mind waking up with each day are not thick on the ground. Meanwhile,' she said with a shrug, 'a girl's gotta have fun.'

And it was rumoured that she did. She was discreet but Rosie knew that Nancy's very public sponsoring of new, cash-strapped young artists was providing her with a more basic diversion.

Unaware or perhaps uneasy about libel, gossip columns ignored these facts and confined themselves to describing Nancy's outstanding collection of eighteenth- and nine-teenth-century American furniture in her Vermont home, which rivalled anything to be found in major museums, and her London house in Holland Park, which contained a seriously important collection of art.

'I could manage a quick drink at seven thirty,' Rosie told Nancy, not wanting to use up a whole evening that could be better spent clearing up her accounts. 'If that isn't going to hold you up?'

'You have to eat,' objected Nancy, determined to get her own way. 'Besides, it may well serve a double purpose.'

In spite of herself, Rosie was suddenly intrigued. Wary of Nancy at the best of times, she relented. 'Goodness, you do sound mysterious. It's just that I would have to leave early,' she began but Nancy cut across her.

'No problem. So let's say eight, so that I can talk to you before everyone else arrives at eight thirty. Okay? Must go, I have to turn over.'

Rosie was still holding the phone as Nancy rang off. Oh well. It was just six thirty. Black coffee, that's what she needed, and she'd make it through the evening comforted by the fact that the dreaded conversation with Livvie could be delayed for another few hours.

The phone rang as she was plugging the coffee jug into the socket.

'Mum? It's me.'

'Darling.' Rosie pulled off one earring and sat down on the kitchen stool, spooning a handful of ground beans into the percolator while she listened to her son.

'Are you all right? Okay,' she teased, hoping to divert him from a problem she couldn't solve by giving him one she could. 'What have you forgotten?'

'Nothing. I just wanted to tell you I really do hate it here. I don't want to stay. Why can't I come home?'

'Tom, darling,' she began carefully. The opening line was as familiar to her now as the accompanying deep breath she took to deal with it. 'What's happened? You always do this and you know why you can't just come home. If you still hate it at the end of the term I'll talk to Mr Farrell . . .'

'He won't care, you know he won't. Garth said his father told him Mr Farrell thinks we're all just punters . . .'

'Tom,' she admonished, silently agreeing with Conrad de Lisle. 'Now stop that. You mustn't talk about your headmaster that way.'

'Why not? Everyone else does. Mum? Did you speak to Daddy about my cricket bat? Did you?'

Rosie hadn't. So pushed for time. 'Oh Tom, I'm so sorry. I forgot, but look, don't worry, you won't need it just yet, will you? I'll call Daddy and get him to drop it off before Friday afternoon and bring it with me when I come to collect you. Howzatt?'

There was a brief pause. The usual giggle from her son didn't follow her mild joke.

'Mum? Did Dad talk to you about anything . . . next weekend, I mean? He thought . . . I mean, he said . . . we,

60

I mean, me and him, might go to Grandpa's or something like that . . . Grandpa asked him. He *really* did, Mum. He wants to see us.'

*Callum's?* With Tom? Since when had Rory been back on speaking terms with his father?

'Mum? Mum, are you there?'

'Yes, sorry, darling.'

'I won't go if you don't want me to.' Rosie's heart was wrenched. She could hear the apprehension mingled with hope in her son's voice.

'Yes, he did mention something of the sort,' she lied, not wanting Tom to feel torn between them, her voice as matter-of-fact as rising panic would allow. 'Tell you what, love, Scotland's a bit far just for a weekend, even if you do fly up there. Maybe you should do that during the summer break. It's a bit late to start organising for Easter.'

'But that's ages away,' he protested. 'Well, could we . . . I mean, we could have lunch with Dad. He said lunch as well. He said both of us, Mum?'

Rosie could deny her son very little, certainly not over the phone when he was away at school. 'Leave it to me,' she said soothingly. 'I'll talk to Daddy about it. You can be sure of that.'

She replaced the phone and sat very still. Callum? My God. After all Rory had said about him. After all Callum had accused his only son of.

And for what? Shortly after the marriage that Callum had found so distasteful had ended, he had quarrelled with Rory over his dissolute lifestyle and relations between them ceased. Not a word since. Nothing.

She began to dial Rory's number and then stopped. Picking up a large black pen, she scrawled 'Cricket Bat' on a memo pad.

Staring up at her from the basket where she threw her post were the unpaid invoices that had suddenly lost their importance. Absently she tucked them out of sight, instead of taking them up to her cramped office. For a minute or two, she drummed her fingers against the phone, staring into space. Then she pushed the phone firmly away.

There was just time. Ten minutes later, changed into narrow black trousers and a mulberry crushed velvet English Eccentrics tunic with a plain silver necklace resting at the collar, she was ready for Nancy's dinner party.

She slipped on her coat and let herself out of the house. At the end of the road she flagged down a cab and directed the driver to Rory's house.

The door was opened not by Rory but by a fair-haired woman dressed in black leggings and a loose black T-shirt.

There was a small flicker of surprise on her face as she stepped aside for Rosie to come in. 'I'm sorry, I should have recognised you,' she said with a strong New Zealand accent. 'I'm Abeline, Rory's housekeeper.'

Housekeeper? That explained the gleaming silver and the plumped up cushions. Rosie tried not to laugh. Who did Rory think he was fooling? She wondered if Callum was paying the woman's salary. God knows how Rory could, since he appeared to be just as allergic to work as ever.

She was shown directly into the drawing room where Rory, sitting with James, exchanged a startled look with his housekeeper, leapt to his feet, stubbing out a cigarette as he did so.

'Darling,' he said. 'What a surprise.' Rosie ignored the endearment, annoyed to see the dreaded James was once again in the house.

James rose as she entered, smiled serenely and asked her if she felt better. Rosie gave him the briefest of nods, her attention riveted by the third occupant of the room.

Sitting splayed out in an armchair was a girl so slender she had no hips to speak of. Yet her breasts strained so voluptuously and unmovingly against a white tank-top, it was clear to any woman who read about these things that nature had no part in their shape. In the gap between the top and her jeans, a smooth brown midriff was visible.

Her hair was chestnut, oiled back from fiercely pitched eyebrows; her olive skin was free of make-up except for a vivid red lipstick and two slashes of blusher reaching up to her hairline. A studded leather choker was wrapped around her long neck, a matching armlet gripped the area above her elbow.

She looked expensive and predatory. Goodness me, thought Rosie, now there's a girl who likes men for dinner and dessert. I'll have to sling both Rory and James at her to keep her from launching an attack.

The girl didn't move, allowing her eyes to travel over Rosie and taking in the enviable necklace that matched the chunky silver loops which moved gently from Rosie's ears in the same manner as her expertly cut glossy hair when she swung her head around to glance enquiringly at Rory.

Seeing Rosie was making no effort to speak to her, ignoring her in fact, the girl finally extended a long, slender hand as Rory hastily introduced them.

Rosie slid her hands into her pockets and returned a brief, indifferent nod. Then turned and began to examine a nearby picture of Tom.

First the girl glanced uncertainly at James and then to Rory as she scrambled less than elegantly to her feet. James' description of Rory's ex-wife – what was it he'd said? An insecure mess? Well, that most certainly didn't tally with this exercise in cool confidence standing before her.

Rory was speaking with deliberate emphasis: 'James and er . . . Syra are just leaving. Aren't you, James?'

James' eyes widened in surprise. From under her lashes Rosie caught the look that Rory shot him. She almost laughed. Just like old times.

James got to his feet and, taking the girl with him, left

them alone only too aware that Rosie's quietly understated appearance and manner contrasted sharply with Syra's exotic choice of wardrobe.

As they emerged onto the street, James experienced the familiar sense of outrage that Rosie's presence invariably induced. Before she turned up he would have challenged anyone who'd said Syra didn't look like sex on legs; now he was dimly aware that it was Rosie's class that held the real sex appeal.

Meanwhile, Rory turned to Rosie. 'Ghastly girl,' he grinned. 'James always had lousy taste. Have you got time for a drink? Please? Five minutes?'

She nodded.

Handing her a glass of wine, he wrinkled his nose appreciatively. 'Nice perfume. Who's the man?'

'No man,' she said briefly. 'Business.'

'Sorry, I wasn't prying. Just interested. You look wonderful.'

Leaning against the opposite side of the doorway, she studied her nails.

'What's all this about, Rory?' she asked, frowning as she sipped her drink. 'Why now? Six years after we're divorced? What am I solving? What's the problem? And since when did you start talking to Callum again?'

Rory did not miss a beat. He answered her as though a conversation with his father was routine instead of unthinkable.

'The old man isn't so well. It's about time I organised my inheritance – well, there's Tom to consider, isn't there? I don't want to hand over something that isn't in great shape.'

Rosie was relieved she was leaning against the door. 'Well, well,' she mocked, slowly applauding him. For a brief while she had been unsure of his motives, half believing he'd changed for the better, even *wanting* to believe him. What had Jaye said? *'Are you sure you're not enjoying having him chase you?'* Inwardly she winced. 'This *is* a surprise. The mists lift. You get Callum's money when your own house is in order. No . . . don't deny it.

'What a performance. No wonder you want us back. Daddy still holds the purse strings, eh? Daddy still wants to fool the neighbours. But Rory, *such* a sacrifice and all for a tinpot title.'

He opened his mouth as if to argue, then shook his head impatiently. 'I'm not lying to you and I couldn't give a fuck about the title. I've been thinking about it for a long time. I swear it was the other way around. I told him my plans first. Okay, I did go and visit him – he's sick. What do you expect? I'm not inhuman. But I came back from New York to see you two. I told him what I had in mind. Yes, I admit I wanted his approval. What's wrong with that? He *is* my father. You've never stopped trying to get your mother to say something decent about you, have you? All right, all right. But it's the same thing.

'I'd like you to believe me. But frankly, Rosie, I'm getting to the point where I think my past is always going to cloud my future. You were the one who wanted to marry me, remember? Your mother was *very* keen, I recall. I could have walked away, don't forget that.'

Rosie gave a wry grimace. 'Daddy wouldn't let you get away with it, would he? An illegitimate heir? *Tsk.* Shock, you said, you weren't thinking straight. Of course you loved me, wanted to marry me. I was the one who said wait, remember? Odd how one visit to Glencairn changed your mind. And I believed you. Trusted you.'

Rory ran a hand distractedly through his hair and began to pace up and down.

'Oh c'mon, Rosie. I didn't rape you. I didn't get pregnant. You did.'

'An immaculate conception I suppose?' she flashed back at him.

*       *       *

65

'Christ, are you sure?'

She nodded, not daring to take her eyes off his face. Searching for comfort. Reassurance. She felt so sick.

'And you're sure it's . . . ? Oh God, of course it's mine.'

Her face was white. 'I had that tummy bug. I couldn't take my pill. I'm sure that must be it. And sometimes I miss the curse – the doctor said it often happens with girls who are underweight, which is why I didn't realise it could be that. Well, at least I kept hoping it wasn't. But I swear it wasn't deliberate. Darling, please. We'll manage. I've got some money, it won't be so terrible . . .'

His face cleared. 'Oh sweetheart, of course. Oh poor bunny. Yes, of course it will be all right.'

He wrapped his arms around her. With a sob and a sigh of relief she clung to him. 'I'll take care of everything,' she said into his shoulder. 'And I'll work for as long as possible . . .'

She stopped. He was holding her away from him.

'What do you mean, work? I thought you said you had enough cash to get rid of it? You're not going through with it, are you?'

She was shaking, the roaring in her ears making it impossible for her to speak clearly. 'I have to, Rory. I'm sorry you don't understand. I'm nearly four months gone. No-one would do it. And besides, I wouldn't let them. I want this baby.'

Rory was watching her. Exasperated. 'Rosie, this is silly. Why can't I just want my family back? What's wrong with that? Why don't you just listen to me for a change?'

They stared uneasily at each other from either side of the doorway. Rosie searched the familiar face in vain. No clues. Smooth skin, a dark shadow around the chin, faint white lines fanned out around his eyes, the kind that are evidence of a life in the sun. But no lines that, by right, hard living should have induced.

She felt annoyed. No grey hair either. Unfair. He was thirty-four. That's what selfishness did for you, she thought. Still in good shape.

'All right.' She sounded curt. 'Give me one good reason why I should stay and listen? Personally, I don't think we really do have anything to say, do we?' The words faded.

'But then we never did need words, did we?' he said deliberately. The room felt suddenly very still. Rosie looked down at her hands and shot a quick nervous look at Rory's face.

*'Rory, Rory, it's eight o'clock.'*

*'So?' he said sleepily, resisting her attempts to wake him.*

*'I have to go to work. I'll get fired if this goes on.'*

*'Tell them you're sick or something.'*

*'I can't, I did that yesterday. Rory please, wake up, listen.'*

*'I am, but I can hear better if you come back to bed.'*

*Without opening his eyes, he reached out and gripped her hand, pulling her on top of him, ignoring her protests, laughing at her attempts to get away. Her dress now half off, his body rolled over onto hers and over again until she was on top of him, he drowsily watched her the whole time, as she closed her eyes and pressed her knees into his sides and told him to do whatever he wanted even if it took the whole day. And all she could think was that she fervently hoped it would.*

Rosie and Rory had nothing in common except their mutual attraction, not even their jobs. She'd been an eager graduate from art school, longing only to be involved in fashion.

But Rory? Nightclub greeter, professional party guest. Selling vintage cars to Houston oil barons or playing host at hired-out stately homes to Japanese tourists, who left convinced that they had been entertained by a Duke of the Realm, were regular features of Rory's life.

As James used to giggle: 'You can tell them anything you like – who's going to check?'

And amazingly no-one ever had. Last time she had heard of Rory working during daylight hours was when James had the idea of launching a society magazine which survived several weekend think tanks in smart country hotels and a week's stay in New York on a fact-finding mission, before the advertisers agreed with their backers that the one thing the venture lacked was a future and closed it down.

After which Rory had disappeared to America for a year. And now, his need for a reconciliation was no longer a mystery, just an immediate solution to getting back into his father's will.

That's all it had been, she thought morosely. Typical Rory. Oh, the title would be passed on along with Glencairn, the rambling granite built house on the West Coast, but the rest wasn't entailed. Callum could leave his personal fortune to anyone he fancied. Without it the title was useless.

'So,' she said, trying to keep her voice under control. 'How do you propose to earn Daddy's approval? James going to help, is he? What is it this time? Custom-built Morgans? No, no, let me guess. A model agency . . .'

'What do you mean?' he asked sharply.

'Exactly what I said. Which branch of the twilight industries are you planning to raid now?'

Surprisingly he flushed. Then he blurted it out. 'I'm going to learn estate management.'

'I'm sorry?' she said blankly. 'You're going to do *what*?'

'Learn how to manage the estate – a degree course. I've

checked it all out. I was an estate agent for a while, so I qualify.'

Rosie glanced swiftly at the whisky decanter. No great inroads there. Estate agent? He must mean the month he spent helping James unload a couple of villas outside Malaga as time shares.

'I've had enough, Rosie,' he sighed, with a weariness that surprised her. 'I've done some pretty daft things. I just wasn't ready for marriage – and honestly, baby, you weren't either. I've had to face some terrible truths and you should too. Everyone makes mistakes. God, I know it's been tough for you, but you know, you're a hard person to help. But there's only ever been one woman I've ever wanted to share my life with . . .'

His voice trailed off. He gave a helpless gesture, turned and gazed down into the fire. He took a deep breath: 'Rosie, can't you let go of the past? What else can I do? Do you want me to beg? Because I won't. If that's what you want, I'm out of here now.'

He was serious. Perfectly serious. Rosie gazed uncertainly back at him. She was on new ground.

'Why on earth would I want you to beg?' she asked, more gently than she'd imagined she could. 'I just want the truth from you until Tom's old enough to make his own decisions.'

'And if I had told you straight away about seeing the old man, what would it have looked like? Exactly.'

Suddenly she felt an unexpected rush of sympathy for the man in front of her. At least that's what she told herself it was.

'Rory, don't do this,' she pleaded. 'Look at my life now. I have a business of my own, a house, friends. You might have changed, Rory. But I haven't. I like my freedom, my independence. No-one in their right mind would go to hell twice. And that's what it would be. Let's be friends. Just friends. I'd like that . . . but nothing else.'

He stood back, disappointed, with hurt in his eyes. 'I don't blame you. I've never fooled myself about how I feel about you. Always afraid of losing you and in the end I did.'

'Yes,' she agreed, surprised he was caving in so easily. He must have changed. 'You did.'

'And the chance to make amends along with it.'

'No chance.' Rosie paused. He hadn't taken his eyes from her face. 'Don't, Rory,' she warned him. 'Don't. I've turned my back on the past. You must as well.'

She left him sitting on the leather fender, massaging a tumbler of whisky between his hands and pretended not to hear his parting words.

'We'll see,' he smiled. 'We'll see.'

# Chapter Seven

Nancy asked Rosie to design the decor for her new London house in Knightsbridge as she poured her a glass of champagne.

Straight to the point. 'I liked what you did to Jane Grantham's new house. You know about light and you're not afraid of colour.'

Jane was a client who had become a good friend, particularly as she had a son of Tom's age and was as wise as she was supportive. Rosie detected her hand in this commission.

Outwardly she acknowledged that she was both delighted and flattered, and asked to hear more. Inside she was screaming with relief and experiencing something bordering on delirium. Livvie saved. Her company saved. If Nancy had asked her to redesign her shoe cupboard, Rosie would have been thrilled. Such a name on her client list with a commission of whatever size, and she would have been on her way. But *this*.

So what if Nancy had fallen foul of everyone else? Who cared how she got the commission? All that mattered was that she had. If she could handle Miriam de Lisle, she could manage Nancy.

Asked to hear more? How much more did she need to know? She was made. *Made, made, made.*

Nancy had leaned over to tell her personal assistant on the house intercom to hold all her calls. Rosie was hard put not to wrench the phone from her hand and call her accountant. Call Rory. God, of course not. What was she thinking of?

'I'm not,' Nancy said, refilling her own glass and keeping a straight face, 'going to hold it against you that you have the bad taste to take on the Duxborough woman as a client. But,' she passed her hand theatrically across her eyes, 'Miriam de Lisle? What are we talking about here? Silicon or helium? She must have forty pounds of the stuff pumped into her mouth alone. She *cannot* be surprised that Conrad is screwing that weather girl?'

'No idea.' Rosie shook her head. It was not sensible to discuss one client with another, tempting though it was to reveal that Miriam had spent one of their meetings instructing her solicitor to sue a Sunday tabloid for libel.

After which the poor man was somehow to pay off the little whore who had told them in the first place about her 'nights of passion' with Miriam's husband, in the hope she would remain silent about the fact that they had done it several times a night, on the M23 and on Eurostar as the train went through the tunnel.

'Liar,' Nancy said affably. 'Anyway. This is the plot.'

It was not so much a house but a mansion that Nancy had bought. Rosie swallowed hard. It occupied a corner site a stone's throw from Hyde Park, hidden behind a high brick wall and screened from the road by trees. There was a surprisingly sizeable, if sadly neglected, garden at the back, leading from a spectacular terrace.

There were at least eight bedrooms, a staff flat, a set of offices and, while the main rooms were large enough to hold any number of people at the receptions so vital to Nancy's fund raising, Rosie knew that Nancy planned to use it as her home. It needed a lot of thought.

'And,' finished Nancy, studying the ceiling as she spoke, 'you wouldn't gossip to the papers.' She lowered her gaze to look straight at Rosie. 'Would you?'

'I doubt I'd have time to read them, let alone talk to them if I were doing your house,' replied Rosie calmly, recognising Nancy's hidden agenda: the need to keep her name out of the limelight, whether coupled with Joel Harley's or, more likely, that of her latest protégé; and the even greater need to have someone working on her house who wouldn't argue with her.

Nancy threw her a shrewd glance. 'Once went through it yourself, I hear.'

'Mmm,' Rosie murmured, sipping her champagne. 'Long time ago.' Rosie had never had any illusions that the American had any interest in her life beyond how it affected her own. And she had no interest at all in the problems of parenthood. Tom was acknowledged but not discussed. Nancy's interest in a child was restricted to having once been one. So now Rosie didn't react, but waited for Nancy to move on.

Nancy was lanky, witty, shrewd, faintly eccentric, with close-cropped streaked russet hair, a minimum of jewellery, and was famous for the severity of her clothes, which were invariably black, bewilderingly expensive and relieved only by one of her impressive collection of brightly coloured silk scarves, usually trailing down around the hem of her garment.

As she shifted her long limbs into an armchair opposite Rosie, she tossed the ends of her emerald green choice for the evening over each shoulder and stretched out. The faint, lingering scent of her earlier massage settled around her.

'So,' she said abruptly. 'Let's talk money, and get the tough stuff out of the way before we fix up some meetings.'

If Nancy only knew it, the fee she suggested was so large, Rosie felt like the famed Elsie de Wolfe who demanded and got ten per cent of the million dollars she spent doing up Henry Clay Frick's house on New York's Fifth Avenue.

Honesty compelled her to say so. 'And he got a bargain,' Nancy growled, finding Miss de Wolfe's reputation as the founder of modern interior design more impressive than the amount she charged to a tycoon in the 1920s.

It was an illuminating insight into Nancy's thinking. She

admired women who went and got what they wanted but until now she had not trusted any woman designer, let alone an English one, to come near any of her homes dotted around the world.

'Wouldn't have minded letting Sybil Colefax loose on this though,' Nancy amended, a reference to the English society hostess who lost all her money on the Wall Street crash and rose to become one half of the formidable Colefax and Fowler team. 'Game girl, that one,' Nancy said approvingly. 'Got herself up and made a fortune.'

Rosie agreed that once she had toured the house more closely, she would give Nancy the specification as soon as possible. Nancy waved her aside.

'Whatever it takes, deal with my accountants. I pay them enough, for Chrissake.'

Rosie's only concern was that the local firm of architects that her builder always used had never tackled such a mammoth task either. Nancy was demanding and professional. Being loyal to trusted colleagues would not impress her.

'No problem.' Nancy made a note in her diary. 'I was planning to ask Joel – Joel Harley, he's a . . .' Rosie didn't miss the hesitation but she politely ignored it '. . . a good friend of mine, he'll be here later. I'll ask him to advise you. He's on the board of trustees of the Foundation, and he's giving our lecture in Prague at the beginning of summer. So waddya say? All settled?'

Rosie grinned with delight. It was spelt 'ecstatic' in her head. 'Of course. Yes, I mean . . . Nancy, are you sure?'

'Sure? What's there to be sure about? Fuck it up and I'll destroy you. What could be more simple than that? Now let's look at some dates.'

Leafing through the pages, Nancy screwed up her eyes and was lost in some brief mental calculations.

Rosie was doing some calculations of her own. Her fee for the commission was Tom's school fees for the next year, the mortgage for the next few months and enough kudos attached to feel pretty sure that more prestigious clients would feel confident to employ her.

To think she had tried to get out of dinner with Nancy.

She couldn't wait to start. It was every designer's dream commission. The whole job, she figured, would occupy her for about a year. Tomorrow she would call her solicitor, get him started on a good, tight contract to cover anything going wrong, such as bad weather holding up outside work (this was England after all), but she knew Nancy.

It could be done. Just. Money was not a problem. And Tom would benefit from this. At least with such a long-term commission she could organise it so that she could get away for a week at either end of the holiday time. Livvie would be able to handle a lot of the details from other clients, freeing her to concentrate on this project, and this year she could afford to send Tom to one of those daytime activity camps.

Nancy had disappeared to consult her assistant. Rosie stretched happily in her chair. Personally the light at the end of the tunnel was in sight. Professionally she was already absorbed in what lay ahead.

Structural alterations, removing that false ceiling in the hall and restoring what she knew would be exquisite cornices underneath. And the public rooms, as Nancy called them, might present a problem where light was concerned but Rosie already had ideas to overcome that.

The magnificent staircase, hugging the far wall. It would have to be resited. Centre of the marble hallway. Centre stage where it belonged.

Rosie was already converting the house into a home of unparalleled elegance. Opulent, serene, confident back-drops to Nancy's international lifestyle.

'How about early November?' Nancy was saying as she came back into the room.

'You mean for the main building work to be completed?'

'No, the whole lot.' Nancy looked surprised.

Lighting, plumbing, the building alterations alone ...
Good God, what was Nancy thinking of? But even as she
stared in consternation at the American, Rosie knew it was
not the timescale that troubled her, but Tom. How on earth
would she see Tom if she was working around the clock?

She swallowed hard. 'That's quite tight, Nancy. I
thought ... I think I might need a little longer.'

'Oh pooh, why?' Nancy asked in astonishment. 'You
mean you might not get the labour you want during the
summer months? Leave that to me. I'll get my own guys
in. You just supervise, okay?'

Rosie was silent. Nancy looked puzzled. 'Is that a prob-
lem? You know me well enough to know how I live, what
I want the house to be used for. We're not into all that
twenty questions trying to find out what I'm like, are we?
We can skip all that. Anyway, when we go over to New
York ...'

*New York?*

'... you can take a look at the Fifth Avenue apartment
and we'll take a look in up at Hartford to see the farm.'

Nancy clearly thought this a more efficient way to let
her newly acquired designer get a firm grip on her taste
than endless discussions about lifestyles.

Rosie tried again. 'It's not that, Nancy,' she began carefully. 'I need to do colour boards for each room showing
fabrics, furniture, layouts. I mean, surely you will want to
see all this before we start ...' She rambled on in a desperate fashion.

Trying to find the right words to tell Nancy she needed
time with her son was out of the question. She would
simply have to say she had other commissions that crossed
with it, must consult her diary.

Nancy waved her aside. 'Sub-contract. Take a cut and
keep an eye on the work. And how long will it take to
knock up a few boards for Chrissakes? You went to art
school, didn't you?'

Inspiration faded. She heard herself saying, 'But the alterations, you'll need a great architect, they're hard to get.'

'Rosie,' Nancy said sharply. 'What *is* this? I've told you Joel is a friend. I don't even have to wait until I see him, he'll do anything for me. He'll advise you. He's going to be at dinner. An ogre, but divine. Frankly he was against me hiring you, he thinks I should be with a much bigger firm. I don't want him to be proved right. He'll get his own team in.'

Rosie would not have cared if the entire team from *Architectural Digest* had been drafted in. She simply did not have the domestic backup she needed to help with Tom. So convincing had she been to the world that she was on top of the case, she was now poised professionally to slit her own throat.

Rosie thought she was going to scream.

'Oh, and just one other thing,' Nancy called back as she headed off to greet the first of her guests. 'I want that new design from Colefax and Fowler – you know the one I said I liked? – something like that for the morning rooms.'

Dear God, what now, Rosie thought miserably as she trailed after Nancy. Joel bloody Harley might dismiss her as inexperienced without even knowing her, but she knew that was exactly how the world would see it if she turned this down, and all for want of time.

# Chapter Eight

There were twelve people altogether at dinner. None with a care in the world, Rosie thought bitterly as she followed Nancy down to the flower-laden, elegant ground-floor drawing room which was slowly filling up.

White-coated menservants were unobtrusively serving drinks. A low buzz of conversation was given an extra spin when it went around that Joel Harley, who had been persuaded to give the prestigious Alexander lecture in Prague, would be joining them.

Only too aware that she was passing up a chance that would be about as likely to come her way again as hearing Rory had entered a monastery, Rosie's interest in the evening was now minimal.

David Belmont, wearing a toupee, carrying a paunch, and with a heavily striped shirt and white collar looking more like a banker than a designer, spotted her as she came in. Counting a clutch of royals and several ambassadors as his clients, David adored publicity. He had been contracted to redesign in a blaze of publicity, the new house bought by the stunning new TVN presenter Heather Woodman.

He swooped down on Rosie, kissing her warmly on both cheeks, and whispered his congratulations. 'Well done, my darling,' he cooed.

Rosie, who knew he must have been ruled out by the fussy heiress because of his penchant for dining with gossip columnists, was touched but surprised he knew about her involvement barely half an hour after she did.

David was on good form but even the confidence about where some of the much-publicised Spencer family treasures had now turned up after they were flogged earned no more than a faintly smiling, 'Oh, how amazing.'

Rosie had stationed herself by a deep window embrasure where she could sip her drink and gaze out over Nancy's brilliantly lit garden beyond the terrace and let her mind race over possible courses to salvage such a life-saving opportunity without affecting Tom too much. Deep in thought, she consequently failed to see Nancy approaching.

'Rosie, this is a dear friend of mine.' Nancy was standing in front of her, her arm linked with that of a tall, lean man with a light tan, who looked vaguely familiar. His carelessly swept-back hair was blonde with streaks that looked like the result of too many days in the sun.

'How do you do,' she smiled politely. A quick glance at Nancy's face made her realise something more was expected of her. 'I'm so sorry, I didn't quite catch your name.' Her mind was on more important things. What else could she do? Tom needed her.

Nancy looked faintly embarrassed. '*Ro-see*. I said, this is Joel Harley. He's so kindly agreed to advise you on the alterations to my house.'

'Americans always exaggerate.' He grinned at Rosie but spoke to Nancy. 'Nancy, I said I would get someone to do it and keep an eye on it.'

'Oh pooh,' Nancy pouted. 'Well, get someone who's on the case, this lady is a tiger when it comes to getting things done properly. She'll keep you on your toes.'

'Really?' he said but his tone and glance suggested he had merely confirmed his view that this lady, who had difficulty in recalling his name, would have trouble keeping an egg on the boil let alone a team of crack designers working at full tilt.

Rosie looked up into a pair of quizzical grey eyes. Every other man in the room was wearing a tie, but this one had on a carelessly opened dark blue denim shirt under a fine black cotton jacket.

'Oh, of course,' she said, vainly trying to recover some credibility and for once blessing her mother's store of trivial information. 'You didn't wear a tie to Founder's Day either.'

Nancy blinked.

'Possibly not,' Joel replied carefully, without missing a beat. 'But then I rarely do. In fact I'm not even sure I got married in a tie. You seem remarkably well informed.'

'Oh, I'm not really,' Rosie began, realising too late that ahead of her lay an admission that she listened to gossip. 'I don't remember how I know,' she ended lamely. She was spared any further embarrassment when Joel's attention was claimed by a couple he clearly knew well.

Rosie let out a sigh of relief. How could you defend such an inane comment to a man who had designed a clutch of prestigious buildings around the world, including the futuristic Alexander Museum in Detroit which had won three major awards and much press coverage?

How could she have given him all the evidence he needed that she was an inexperienced designer with more ambition than skill?

Since the architect had divorced his wife a couple of years before, the tabloids quite freely coupled his name with that of any number of beautiful women, as he was rich, successful and that rare commodity – currently available. Thankfully such a potent combination was having its inevitable effect. He was surrounded.

At that moment Rosie would not have noticed if the combined charms of Tom Hanks and Keanu Reeves stood before her. She tried to ease her way out of the group. But even in that she failed miserably; having claimed a place by the window, there was no discreet escape route.

Joel Harley had obviously asked her a question. 'I'm so sorry,' she stumbled. 'I'm afraid I was miles away.'

'Designing Nancy's house? She says you're so busy she wasn't sure she'd get you.'

'Did she? Goodness. That *is* a compliment. I mean, it isn't absolutely decided. Well, it *is* if you see what I mean, only,' she looked hopefully at him, 'you might be too busy to advise me. Are you?'

Rosie was tall, but even though Joel had perched himself on the window ledge she was looking almost straight into his face. Probably about forty, she decided. Leaner than his photographs suggested. Grief, wouldn't her mother be thrilled with this first-hand account.

'I'm busy but not too busy for a friend. I'll see what I can do. Perhaps we could fix a meeting? I hate talking shop at this kind of thing, don't you?'

Oh God, he could do it. The last avenue of hope was jettisoned. Now what was she to do?

'Okay,' he said, this time with a resigned sigh. 'Your turn.'

'Turn? My turn for what?'

'To keep the conversation going. It's almost compulsory at dinner parties. Especially between strangers. I know, awful drag, but there it is.'

'Sorry.' Rosie shook her head. 'You must think I'm awfully rude. You said something about fixing a meeting. Great. I'll call you. Yes, that's right. I'll call you . . . no, your secretary, of course you wouldn't make your own appointments, would you?' She laughed, desperately trying to get back on track.

'Oh, I have been known to,' he said solemnly and in such a way that she knew he was humouring her. 'Stops the fingers from seizing up. All that dialling and pressing buttons, see?' He wriggled his fingers at her.

Rosie looked mortified. 'I'm so sorry, it's been a long day.'

'Don't give it another thought,' he said politely, standing up. 'It wasn't important. Don't let me intrude. It was pleasant meeting you. I'm sure Nancy will know where to find you,' and with that he smiled briefly and moved away as

David Belmont seized his opportunity to remind Joel where they had previously met.

Throwing her a puzzled look, Nancy took off after him, leaving Rosie wondering if she really had had such a bizarre conversation.

Starting by telling Joel Harley she hadn't caught his name and finishing by ignoring him, was just about bearable. But being dismissed with such undisguised boredom by a man whose agreement to give a lecture anywhere in the world guaranteed a sell-out audience, put the seal on an evening of total and unalleviated misery. Knowing he had no faith in her didn't help either.

She watched as Nancy piloted her prized possession around the room. The smiling recognition, the burst of laughter at something he was saying. The polite deference to his views.

At dinner she found herself sitting between one of Nancy's financial advisors to the Alexander Foundation, who was interested only in the wine, and a photographer she vaguely knew through Jaye, who had just finished a commission for *Special Interiors* to photograph the new London home of a recently married young royal of whom he was a distant relation.

Across the table a young male model resembling a moody Sicilian bandit but who, as Rosie knew from her days as a fashion editor, came from Clapham, sat in silence throughout the meal.

It didn't matter. Nancy had not asked him along to hear what he had to say about the Bundesbank interest rate. His particular skills would be tested later, when they had all gone and the sophisticated, rich American needed a mindless screw, no strings, an expensive gift bestowed and above all no questions asked.

Odd he was here though, thought Rosie, as well as Joel Harley. Nancy was playing a deep game if she had two lovers at the same table.

Rosie glanced up to where the architect was seated next to Nancy and had the oddest feeling she had just missed him looking at her. Not surprising, she thought gloomily. Can't be every day he meets someone incapable of sensibly following two perfectly unchallenging consecutive sentences. He must think Nancy had gone mad.

She left first as the party began to break up on the terrace, starting to walk to the end of the street where she hoped to pick up a cab. A black Range Rover pulled up just ahead and reversed slowly.

'Can I give you a lift?' Joel Harley asked.

A lift would have been welcome if it hadn't meant small talk even for the mere ten minutes or so it would take to reach her house.

'Well, thank you,' she smiled as appreciatively as she could. 'But I really think the walk will be better for me. You know, inside all day, that kind of thing.' She knew she was rambling. It was written all over his face.

'But thank you,' she repeated, backing away. 'Nice meeting you. Great night. See you again.' She stepped back onto the pavement with a theatrical smile and a wave of her hand, willing him to go away.

'Are you sure you're all right?' Joel asked.

Rosie gave a forced laugh. It sounded more hysterical than she had planned. 'Couldn't be better. Really. Lovely night,' she said indicating a night sky so cold the wind was already cutting through her skin. Rain couldn't be far away. 'I think I'll just go this way. Shorter,' she added, seeing Joel's puzzled look as he glanced first up at the sky and then over his shoulder to where she was pointing as the first drops of rain began to hit the pavement.

She started to walk backwards down the road in the direction from which she'd come, waving as she went. God, if he wouldn't go, she had no option but to get away from him.

Joel looked curiously at her. 'Is it? Shorter, I mean? I

had no idea. I thought you only came to the park gates that way and they might be locked at this time of night. Of course, I haven't been in London for a couple of months and things might have changed. But I'm sure you know best. Nice meeting you,' and with that he drove off as the heavens opened.

Rosie stared after him, furious with herself. Of course it was a dead end. It was a square with only one way in, the road leading straight around and out again. Would this dreadful day never end?

She waited until she saw the tail lights of the vehicle disappear and then she sprinted in torrential rain to the main road where, after a frustrating delay, her hair and clothes drenched, she flagged down a cab and less than fifteen minutes later was sinking against her own closed front door.

Clutching a cup of coffee, she flopped into the rocking chair in the corner of the kitchen, slipping off one shoe with the toes of the other, reaching out to check the answer machine before easing off the other. There were six messages.

Her mother, saying she would be staying at the Pelham when she came to town next week, and could manage lunch but not dinner. Carey Templeton, reminding her about dinner to celebrate Jaye's birthday. He and his partner Josh would go straight from work and would she remind Kit to try not to be late?

Tom – her eyes flew open and then relaxed as his familiar little voice simply said he needed his cricket stumps as well. Miriam de Lisle, cancelling her morning meeting. Sod her, Rosie groaned.

This was followed by the voice of Conrad de Lisle's secretary on behalf of Miriam, reinstating the morning meeting. No apology. Sod her as well. Yawning, Rosie sipped her coffee and waited for the click to signal the final message. This time she held her breath.

'Rosie. It's me. Rory. Look, I'm sorry about tonight. I didn't want you to go away thinking I don't understand. I do. Really. Just wanted you to know I meant what I said. Okay? I'll call you.'

Then she took the phone off the hook. Never again would she be there waiting for him to call. Never. Anyway, ten to one he wouldn't call back.

# Chapter Nine

Livvie spoke to her twice before Rosie looked up. 'I said, Joel Harley's office called. They're calling back. Hey.' She passed a vacant-looking Rosie a steaming mug of tea. 'Are you okay? You look fagged to death.'

Rosie took the cup. 'Sorry, late night. Have I got to call them back?'

'Well, generally speaking when people telephone they quite like it if you call back. It's called doing business. Actually it was an odd message.' Livvie wrinkled her nose, trying to decipher her notes. 'She said . . . oh yes, here it is. *"Mr Harley said to tell you he would have called himself only he didn't want to overdo the exercise and he knew you would understand."*'

Rosie gave a thin smile. 'Just a private joke.'

Livvie's eyebrows soared. 'With Joel Harley? Goodness, you *are* in there,' she exclaimed as Rosie reached for the phone.

'Heavens, no.' Rosie didn't want Livvie to know about Nancy's offer, especially as it was going to come to nothing. 'I expect he wanted a phone number or something like that.'

'Oh, right.' Livvie clearly didn't believe her but left it at that. 'Oh, and while you're at it, can you ring your ex? He called while you were over at Miriam's. He said he would drop Tom's cricket bat off. He's found it. Sexy voice,' she added.

'Sexy man.' Rosie stopped. Appalled that the thought had even occurred to her let alone that she'd blurted it out. She must be more tired than she thought.

Livvie shot her a curious glance, but said nothing. Rosie never discussed her husband. But plenty of other people did. Joyce devoured gossip in between making curtains, which she did not only for Rosie but for David Belmont and Jessica Milford too. While they wouldn't lower themselves to gossip to each other, Joyce was different. A great deal more than curtains would be discussed and details of the troubled Monteith Gore marriage were confided over many a cup of tea in her neat terraced house in Kennington.

Rory said he would drop by at seven with the cricket bat. Maybe they could have a drink. No time, Rosie lied. Dinner with a client. She would call for the cricket bat en route. There was no way she wanted Rory to see the over-filled house, the chaos that engulfed it. Nor did she want to talk to him any more than was necessary.

As she drew up outside the elegant house, backing into the space she had always used when she'd lived there, she saw herself as she had been when they first married and when Tom was just a baby.

Pulling the buggy over the two sloping front steps, Tom nearly asleep, shopping stacked in the white rack underneath. Nothing more troublesome ahead of her than giving him his tea, bath and bed. And waiting up for Rory.

In those days her name invited a snobbish deference which, tedious though it was, was useful. Particularly in shops when the credit they relied on to keep them going was tolerated longer than anyone else's.

'Rosie Colville' did not carry the same weight as 'Mrs Monteith Gore'. She stopped, giving herself a shake. Slamming the car door, she ran lightly up the front steps and knocked, steeling herself to see Rory.

Only Abeline was in. Friendly, polite, but uninterested. Rory had had to go out. She was going out herself, and was only waiting for Rosie to arrive. Rory sent his apologies. The bat was here. She could see, she laughed, that the little chap was as keen on the game as his father.

Rosie agreed he was. As she walked away, she gave herself another shake. He wasn't that desperate to see her either. Just as well. Giving up this house had saved her sanity. Remember?

How could she forget? 'Had to stay *so* late,' he would yawn, emerging hungover at tea time, not looking at her as he prepared to leave her for another night on her own. 'James wanted me to meet someone who's going to put money up. We're crunching numbers tonight.'

At first, before reality shattered her illusions and she took to sleeping in the spare room, Rosie would doze fitfully until she heard him come in and endure the confusion of anger and relief fighting each other, waiting for him to slip into bed beside her, waiting for him to touch her, cajole her into a good mood.

But in the end it was she who, torn with misery and loneliness, would turn and wrap herself around his back, relieved he was home. Lonely for him. For them. All the questions, the accusations, the ultimatums she had planned would evaporate with his body beside her. Hopeless.

Sliding her hands up his bare back and down between his thighs, whispering that she was sorry for being so grumpy, she knew he was now deliberately making her wait. It was all part of his performance. He was good at waiting. Controlling.

He would remain still until her increasingly frantic body pressing into his unresponsive back began to thrust to a lonely climax, and then, only then, he would abruptly roll his body onto hers with a brutal intensity that left her senseless, shuddering and moaning with grateful pleasure. And of course prepared to forgive. Anything.

If only she had not been so obsessed with him. But it was why she had married him. Put up with him, willing his lies to be the truth. If only she had simply had an affair, walked away from him. In time, she might have done. But

Tom put an end to that plan and to the temporary happiness she had known.

'Does he have to sleep in here?' Rory groaned, twisting up, bleary-eyed in the bed as she tried to soothe the screaming baby.

'Haven't you ever heard of cot deaths?' she hissed back fiercely, shushing her baby son.

'No, but I've heard of murder,' he retorted angrily. The baby's cries were getting louder. 'Oh Christ, I've had it,' he muttered, shoving back the bedclothes.

'Where are you going?' Her breasts were sore, her body ached. Sleep was becoming an obsession. The baby's knees were drawn rigidly up to his chest; frantically she stroked his back, rocked him as she paced the dimly lit room.

'Where do you think? Somewhere where I can get some sleep.'

'He's got wind, that's all. For God's sake, Rory, can't you stay and . . .' Her voice tailed off, she was talking to an empty room. 'And just be here?' she finished. Reaching behind her she picked up the book that had become her bible, pushing the pages open with her chin.

'Colds, colic, croup, crying.' Right, now which one hadn't she tried? '"From wind",' she read. '"Is it indigestion? Or maybe baby is wet,"' she scanned the page, '"or maybe baby is overstimulated and suffering fatigue?"'

In the mirror, she gazed at the infant's red and furious face against her own exhausted one. She took the sanest option for both of them. Wearily dismissing the strong need to punch the writer of this patronising rubbish, she pushed her long hair back from her face, out of reach of the clawing little fists.

Holding him with one arm, she undid the top of her nightgown and for the third time in an hour, guided the screaming, screwed-up little face to her breast.

Everyone had said such moments were a peaceful,

*ecstatic union between mother and child. A time to cement the bond between you and your baby. So why was this child so ungrateful, so demanding? Where was the peace? Why had serenity eluded her? Why was her new husband now in the spare room? And why was she crying?*

Staggering blearily downstairs, Rosie switched on the coffee and tried to focus on starting the day.

In the cold light of dawn, the enormity of fooling Nancy, no matter how unintentionally, into believing she was in the league of those who routinely accepted commissions from Manhattan to Mustique made her cringe. She had even fooled herself.

Glancing at the clock she threw the familiar pile of bills onto the dresser. Later when she was feeling stronger she would call Nancy in New York and hope to catch her before she left for Vermont and say ... say ... well, anything. She'd think of something.

'Bad night?' Livvie enquired when she rang to suggest she instead of Rosie went to see what crinkle had occurred in Miriam's demands.

'Sort of,' Rosie replied truthfully. Livvie's offer was tempting. 'Don't worry, I'll try and get an early night instead.'

'Have you phoned Joel Harley? They rang yesterday after you'd left.'

'No. But I will. I just haven't had time.'

The morning paper was propped up against the milk jug. Yawning, she sipped the strong black coffee, idly flicking over the pages. She noticed the item about Nancy straight away. It was on the diary page. A picture of the American and Joel taken a few months before accompanied the item.

*'At an exclusive dinner party earlier this week in her Holland Park mansion, multi-millionairess Nancy Alexander entertained international architect Joel Harley, who*

*is set to deliver the prestigious Alexander Lecture in Prague shortly. Divorced from his American-born wife Marianne by whom he has two children, his presence continues to fuel speculation that he and Nancy are an item.'*

Rosie raised her coffee to her lips, reflecting that Joel Harley looked much nicer when he smiled than when he was looking bored, and read on.

*'Also there was Rosie Colville, ex-wife of baronet's heir, Rory Monteith Gore. Friends had expected Rosie to marry society photographer Piers Imber – now soon to marry Scottish heiress Catriona Forsyth – but while the relationship cooled last year, they remain on cordial terms.*

*A rising star in the world of interior design, Rosie has been chosen from a highly competitive line-up to design Nancy's new London home.'*

The rising star choked over her coffee and in her haste to grab the paper, knocked the percolator flying.

Dark brown liquid snaked into a perfect lake across the table, ignored as Rosie, eyes streaming from coughing, stared in horror at the item. *Fait accompli.* No way out.

The story must have come from that dreadful photographer, who clearly had wasted no time in earning himself a small fee for sitting next to her at dinner. The grander they were, the less they were to be trusted.

Shaking with fright, she mopped up the table and only just made it to Miriam de Lisle's by nine. Maybe no-one will have seen it, she consoled herself as she negotiated Hyde Park Corner en route to Hampstead.

But her hopes were shortlived. Miriam's customary greeting was to keep Rosie waiting for thirty minutes while she trawled through her husband's post and diary, after which she would call whoever she suspected he might be sleeping with and pretend she was selling double glazing to find out if his latest sexual interest was at home. Rosie, with mask-like patience, usually flipped through the *Racing Post*, the only paper around, while this sad little pantomime was played out. However, this morning Miriam had seen the *Telegraph*.

An hour later Rosie left. One mention in the *Telegraph* had succeeded as she had failed to do in weeks in persuading Miriam to lose the Austrian blinds and replace the cocktail bar, then fill the space with something more tasteful like a Biedermeier sofa.

At midday she went to the Wimbledon home she had raced to finish for Wu Chang, intending to inspect it before he arrived. The fax that morning had said early afternoon. He was already there with the estate agent who had let him in.

Her eyes flew rapidly around. Nothing was amiss. Everything from the curtains to the bed linen was in place, the cupboards filled with the crockery she had chosen for him, the living rooms filled with the furniture she had bought to blend with his own.

The entire decor of the house in a leafy expensive avenue was bright, airy and blissfully elegant. The sight of it had brought a delighted thumbs-up from the estate agent.

Wu Chang walked carefully through each room, silently noting the smoky blue and yellow of the master bedroom in accordance with his wish for something restful, the ebony chairs with barley-twist legs that Rosie had discovered at an auction. The blonde efficient woman from the estate agents followed equally silently and respectfully behind.

The Venetian windows earned a grunt as he gave a cursory glance at the wine-and-green swagged and tailed curtains with their ornate valance. Rosie briefly closed her eyes. The hours that had gone into that pelmet, each element fitted separately even though it looked like one continuous piece of fabric.

'Everything done?' he asked, swinging round to inspect her. 'Package complete?' Rosie nodded. They were standing in the kitchen. Wu Chang pulled open a drawer in the kitchen dresser and peered in.

'No teaspoons,' he pronounced. 'Not part of deal?'

Rosie could not bring herself to meet the estate agent's eye. 'Yes,' she replied gamely. 'Part of the deal, but I'm afraid they've been overlooked. They'll be here within the hour.'

'Okay.' He walked past her. 'I call my wife. I give your fax number to her. Her sister buying house here.'

Outside Rosie fell into a heap and laughed all the way back to Chelsea.

Her mother, whose phone calls had become thankfully rare since Rosie had not rushed back to Rory, rang to say one or two of her friends *might* have the odd little commission and how about bringing Tom to see her. Mmm?

Rosie, inured to her mother's transparent and unlovely addiction to social mountaineering, said she could not take on commissions from her mother's friends but yes, Tom would be intrigued to see the real thing instead of a series of recent photographs of his granny which she had been thinking of requesting.

'Awful word, darling,' Caroline complained. 'You know he never calls me that.'

Rosie didn't know anything of the sort but she couldn't be bothered to argue. She might need her mother if she couldn't get out of this fix with Nancy. She gave a hollow laugh. *Her mother?* Oh good grief. Now she really was going loopy.

Strange that a simple item in a national newspaper could have such an effect. It had transformed her – on paper at least – from struggling working mother facing insolvency to a sought-after interior designer. The problem was that the rising star had one problem. How to live up to it all?

There were moments when she was brought back to reality. When Joel Harley's office called again – obviously reminded by the item in the paper – to see if she could be pinned down for a meeting about Nancy's house, her first instinct was to fix one. Then panic surged back and she hedged for time.

'Let me see,' she said, rustling the pages of her diary so they could be heard down the phone, implying that she too was having trouble locating a mere half hour in her busy schedule. 'Next week? Wednesday? Hmm. I don't think so. Perhaps I could call him when I have a clearer idea of my schedule?'

Twenty minutes later the girl rang back.

'Mr Harley said Thursday would be better. He has thirty minutes at four o'clock.'

Defeated, Rosie replied helplessly: 'Fine.'

'And Mr Harley also said,' the girl paused, clearly reading from notes, 'he hoped the park gates weren't locked.'

'Please thank him for his concern,' was all Rosie answered.

By six next evening when Kit called round for a drink, two more enquiries had been made from potential customers, both of whose names Rosie recognised, and neither of whom raised a quiver of a question when their appointments were fixed for weeks ahead, which would take her over the Easter break.

On the contrary, both new clients were pleasantly surprised they weren't being asked to wait longer.

'I was meant to be in New York,' Rosie had lied, not wanting to appear to be too available. 'But my client there has been called urgently to LA, which means I have an unexpected gap.' She was catching on fast but nevertheless, she avoided her gaze in the mirror above the phone.

'You see,' Kit grinned when she described her day. 'You only have to apply the bullshit factor – or in your case have it applied for you – and you have them beating a path to your door. Know anyone on the *Telegraph* who can do the same for me?'

It was all very well for Kit to tell her she was being pathetic but the immoveable fact remained that she had to own up and give Nancy time to get someone else.

She wasn't sure which she would most loathe if she turned Nancy down: losing her reputation or being the centre of a buzz of excited whispered speculation.

Eyebrows would be raised, commissions would dry up, and she'd be relying once again on the patronising goodwill of the Miriam de Lisles and Sylvia Duxboroughs of the world.

Later the next day, when she returned from sorting out Wu Chang's disagreement entirely by fax with the builder who would be renovating his newly purchased office block in Knightsbridge, her machine had just two messages. One from Joel Harley's office, cancelling the appointment because he had to leave for New York. She breathed a sigh of relief.

The second call was from Rory. She sighed and listened to her ex-husband while she made a strong cup of coffee.

'Rosie, it's me. I called round earlier but you were out. Tom called me from school – everything's fine. Listen, *please*. Couldn't we just have dinner? I'm going to New York tonight for a couple of weeks. I'll call when I get back. Oh, and congratulations on the Alexander commission. You always were the best.'

This had to stop. When he got back from the States she would make him see reason, make him see that it wouldn't work. She called Kit and told him she was going to go with him and Carey to the movies after all.

Cheered from two hours of watching an endearingly romantic performance from Hugh Grant and laughing at Kit and Carey all the way back down Fulham Road as they tried to re-arrange their hair to fall with the same boyish charm into their eyes, she left Carey to have a nightcap with Kit and resolved to go straight to bed.

Just for tonight, she would not think any more about dreaming up a reason that would at once retain her credibility with Nancy, save her company and allow her to pull out of the deal.

'Like Scarlett,' she told herself in the mirror, 'I will deal with it tomorrow.'

In the event she dealt with it within the hour, standing in the street wearing only her pyjamas, as the fire services rescued what remained of her workroom, not to mention her home.

# Chapter Ten

How it had started and the miracle that she had woken to prevent the fire destroying the entire house, was all she could think of. And that she was alive and Tom away at school and not trapped in his room above hers.

The sounds of glass shattering followed by the alarm and the distant roar of a motor bike ripped through the night, just as Rosie was drifting into sleep.

For a brief second, heart thudding, she sat staring into the dark. Not bothering with a robe, barefoot in just pyjamas, she clambered out of bed and made her way down the two short flights of stairs. A noise like paper being systematically crushed reached her. As she rounded the tiny landing she heard something crashing to the floor.

My God, *no*, she breathed.

Jumping the last steps, she reached the door of the workroom and pushed it open. A blanket of flame had gripped the wall surrounding the window. The heat sent her staggering back against the far side of the passage, she flung one arm up across her eyes, lunging forward with the other to slam the door shut. In that brief glimpse she saw that the flames were licking up the white voile curtains, the blind had already crashed to the floor and tongues of fire were stabbing at the rolls of fabric in the bookcase. Her hands trembling, her legs shaking uncontrollably, she fumbled with the locks on the front door.

The noise of breaking glass and the urgent ringing of the burglar alarm had now alerted most of the neighbours. Jumping the shallow steps, she collided with Kit and Carey who had been talking late into the night, who pushed her aside and raced into the house, yelling at her to get out and get help.

Livid yellow flames were clearly visible in the street, as Rosie raced into Kit's house and frantically dialled the emergency services.

Then she ran back to her house where Kit had had the presence of mind to grab a fire extinguisher and was standing in the doorway of the workroom, unleashing a torrent of white foam. Rosie could see the fire was winning.

Carey was in the basement kitchen, pulling basins, buckets and saucepans randomly from cupboards, filling them with water from the taps turned full on. Rosie raced to help him.

'They're coming. They're coming,' she yelled as he pushed past her with a bucket, water sloshing over the sides as he mounted the stairs.

Not thinking, just reacting, their hearts were in their mouths as crashing masonry hit the workroom floor, coughing and choking as the acrid smell of smoke swept through the house. Water and foam fused together, but the fire roared on. Black clouds began to engulf the staircase as they raced up and down.

'Get out, Rosie,' Kit screamed, his face blackened by ash, as he stumbled into the hallway. 'It's no good. Carey? Carey? Out, out!'

Rosie wasn't listening. Her home, her livelihood was being melted into a black charred mess in front of her. As Carey, slinging one last bucket of water into the flames, tried to grab her arm she ducked under it and raced back down to the kitchen.

Grabbing a towel, she plunged it into the basin in the sink, and then wrapping the cold, soaked material around her head and mouth she crawled back upstairs, trying to keep under the smoke as it filled the lower half of the house. She could hear Kit and Carey shouting as she began to sling what belongings she could into the narrow road outside, half sobbing, half choking, diving in and out of the burning room.

Black clouds of smoke filled her lungs, her eyes streamed, she was fighting to breathe, to stay conscious.

As she swayed through the doorway clutching an armful of files, she felt rather than heard Kit and Carey pull her struggling into the street as the first fire engine, siren screaming, blue light frantically flashing, rounded the corner.

Torrents of filthy water were gushing out of the house, gurgling into drains. Sodden carpets were now piled dankly onto pavements. A young girl who lived opposite handed Rosie a steaming mug of tea and squeezed her arm; other neighbours, hastily evacuated by the firemen, began to drift back to their beds now that the blaze was under control and Rosie seemed to be supported by her friends.

The house on the other side of Rosie's was empty, the occupants, an aspiring young politician and his wife, being away. Once the fire officers had decided that it was safe for Kit to return to his house, he and Carey tried to push Rosie inside, but a doctor summoned by the fire officers insisted that all three were checked at the local hospital. Smoke searing into their lungs had left them all hoarse. Rosie appeared to be in shock.

Two hours later they were allowed to return, with minor burns and bruises now treated.

Rosie stared almost blindly ahead of her as the taxi bringing them back turned the corner. A fire engine was still in place. All she had was what she stood up in.

Kit asked if some clothes could be rescued for her. But since her bedroom was directly above the blaze and the floor was blisteringly hot from the flames below, it was too dangerous for Rosie to attempt it.

Instead a cheerful young fireman following her directions, balancing on the beams supporting the floor from below, managed to locate enough clothes for her to go to Kit's for the rest of the night.

Shortly before eight, Livvie, who had been woken by a phone call from Kit half an hour before, fell out of a taxi to find Kit and Rosie standing on the pavement, listlessly trying to organise the mess in front of Rosie's house which was nothing compared to the devastation within.

The fire had destroyed most of the workroom, and the water pumped into the room to contain it had virtually wiped out the ground floor. Rugs had been rolled up and dragged into the street, windows were opened, furniture cleared, but the stench from the smouldering remains mingled with the smell of the damp and sodden hallway, would, Rosie knew, take weeks, months even, to obliterate.

'My God,' Livvie breathed, gazing horrified at the charred mess. 'How did it start?'

Wearing cotton track suit bottoms, canvas boots and a T-shirt under a hooded jacket, Rosie looked numbly at the room, her eyes red-rimmed as much from no sleep as the effects of the smoke. Wearily she shook her head.

'Don't know,' she said hoarsely. The smoke had left her throat raw. 'They'll let me know later. The wiring is okay. Neither of us smokes, no-one was in there. I just don't know.'

Livvie put a comforting arm round her. 'It's awful, Rosie love. Awful, I'm just so thankful you're okay. You might have slept through it . . .'

'Don't,' Rosie whispered. 'Sorry, Liv, I'd rather not think about it. Not yet. Matter of fact, I can't think straight at all.'

In spite of Kit's insistence that she, and Tom, could easily stay with him, Rosie knew his kind offer was not, in the long term, practical.

Jaye immediately demanded she stayed with her. Carey

did the same. Kit indignantly asked if they thought he was not capable of organising her.

A row ensued involving several phone calls from each of them laying claim to her, but Rosie, more frightened than she had ever been, her throat still raw and aching and under instructions from the doctor to talk as little as possible until it healed, sat huddled in her car which was the only place she could now be alone, and tried to think.

She knew they were being kind, but she wanted silence. Their concern for her was comforting, but she just wanted to emerge from this nightmare.

Everything she owned was in that house. Six years of recovering, struggling, juggling. It was all too cruel. Too much. She stared forlornly out of the window to the blackened exterior of her home as two workmen fixed a huge brown plyboard sheet into place and she was glad the windows of the car had misted up so that no-one would see the tears rolling down her face, or hear the racking sobs as she buried her head in her arms and wondered if there was a God after all.

# Chapter Eleven

'Look, Rosie,' Livvie said firmly. 'I know how everything must stand. I'm not daft. But there's no way I'm leaving you in the lurch.'

Rosie hugged her. 'Oh Liv, think about yourself. You're right. It's pretty bad. But I can't expect you to stay in this mess. Maybe when I'm back on my feet, we'll get together again. I'll pay you until you get another job.'

Livvie sighed. 'I don't think you heard me,' she said patiently. 'I said, I'm going nowhere. At least not yet. Give me all that stuff and I'll take it to my flat. We're not finished yet.'

Touched as she was and because she was too tired to argue, she agreed to let Livvie store their files.

In the end she asked Kit if he could put her up, just for a fortnight until she could get herself straightened out. She didn't want Tom to see the mess. Her first plan had been for Rory to have Tom with him while she stayed with Kit but even as the phone rang, she realised he was already in New York.

Typical, she sighed heavily, and fell back on her next plan.

For once her mother came to the rescue and said she would collect Tom and keep him with her for the weekend, Rosie making a lightning visit to him on Sunday in time to take him back to school.

Tom was indignant that he hadn't been allowed to see the legacy of the fire but more out of fear of his grandmother's idea of amusing him than any real attempt at good behaviour, he assured everyone that he liked nothing better than to sit in front of the television all day.

Rosie, feeling drugged through lack of sleep, her body aching as the aftereffects of shock set in, and by now keeping a very tenuous grip on her nerves, felt there was enough going on without a curious and over-excited schoolboy to cope with as well.

Finding somewhere to work from was of course much harder. All thoughts of Nancy's project had been eclipsed in the face of her more urgent needs.

At the end of two weeks, still insisting on paying Livvie's salary and for the work already being carried out by her suppliers, Rosie had fought back tears when she had to agree to some of her commissions being taken over by other designers as she had no hope of completing them herself. The bank chose that moment to send her a letter asking for her plans to settle her overdraft, and Mr Farrell telephoned from school saying they were disturbed to hear that Tom was homeless.

Having assured him that Tom had exaggerated the case, she replaced the phone, still clutching the letter from the bank. The awful part as she knew, but was trying not to acknowledge, was that Tom had not exaggerated in the slightest.

''Bout six months, I should say.' The earnest young insurance assessor stuck his hands in his pockets and squinted around at the damage.

'You mean before I can start to clear up, or before I can move back in?' Rosie asked.

'Well, depends on how you like living,' he replied cautiously. 'Some people have no option but to move back in once the house has dried out and the structure is safe again. That's up to you.'

She knew already that her house was not habitable upstairs. The beams between the floors had suffered and extensive structural work would be needed before anyone would give it the all clear to house Rosie, Tom and *Rosie Colville Interiors* again.

Once she had been taken up to see the first floor and the sight of her once light and airy bedroom, its blue-and-white hangings, the pale grey carpet blacked and sodden from the water and the smoke, depressed her so much that once she had removed her clothes and as many of her possessions as she could, she never asked to see it again.

Tom's room was easier. Helped by Kit and two workmen sent to secure the house, she packed up his belongings and gratefully accepted Carey's offer to store them in his spare room.

Rosie listened dully before suggesting the assessor followed her inside to Kit's to finish the discussion.

Initial investigations indicated that whatever had started the fire had possibly been thrown through the window because Rosie was certain it was the sound of breaking glass that had woken her and the swiftness with which it had spread suggested it had been helped with petrol or spirit of some sort.

'But why?' Rosie asked, appalled. The insurance company were at first openly suspicious, and when Rosie's accountants had submitted her financial statement they were even more so.

'Listen,' she said angrily to the smooth-faced young man sitting opposite her in Kit's kitchen. 'I gain nothing by burning my own house. How dare you. I've nearly lost my livelihood. I could have lost my life.'

Eventually the police decided that it must be a case of mistaken identity. Having satisfied themselves that she had no enemies and it wasn't, as Kit mischievously suggested, a disgruntled client or that the insurance on the house would enable her to retire for life, it was their only option.

'We think it was more likely your neighbour they were

targeting. He's a bit right-wing for some, specially on immigrant issues.'

Rosie was horrified but not surprised. He was a pompous prat, and had made some provocative, highly racist public remarks. 'Trust me to be the one to have him for a neighbour,' she groaned.

Jaye showed her an article in a magazine that said people who were feeling low attracted bad luck. Rosie tore it up. Bad luck? Good God. Disaster is how she would describe it.

It was, in the end, Nancy's phone call that pushed her into agreeing to sign the contract to do her house. Fighting down panic, she asked herself what other chance did she have to pull in some money? The call coincided with a note from her accountant with a horrendous choice. Get some work or face bankruptcy. Something had to give.

On the surface, Nancy's call was one of concern, but the underlying message was unmistakeable. Was this going to delay her own plans? Curiously Rosie wasn't offended, but almost relieved. It meant she owed Nancy nothing more than producing a brilliant job on her house. This was business. It was also her last chance to stay afloat. Keep Tom safe. Gritting her teeth, she set off on another round of househunting.

From Rory there had been sympathy and an immediate visit on his return from New York, during which in her distraught state Rosie had forgotten that for years she had avoided all physical contact with him and did not resist when he hugged her and kissed her hair.

'You know you can live with me. You know I want you to,' he offered almost at once.

'Please, Rory.' She stopped him. 'Not now. It wouldn't work.'

Rory walked swiftly over to the door of Kit's kitchen and closed it so that Kit would not overhear.

'It could,' he said urgently, coming back to her. 'Do it

just for a year. See if it works. If it doesn't, your own house will be ready and you can move back in. Just a year, Rosie, surely that's better than this.' His eyes swept over the over-crowded little room, Rosie's white face.

'And then in a year, I uproot Tom and say he has to live back here? How could I? I'll find somewhere. Thanks, Rory, but I couldn't. And besides, it would only complicate everything.'

But by the end of the next week, having failed to find anything that could function as a house and a workroom, she was in despair.

Her feet ached, her head was permanently engulfed in a tight band that threatened to snap if one more person told her that what she wanted for the money she'd got was only available outside London. The sight of her blackened front door, the window boarded up to prevent squatters or loot-ers, was almost the final straw.

Taking her key from her bag she let herself into the cold, still damp house and leaned disconsolately in the doorway of what had been her workroom, the once-warm hub of the house, now shrouded in a ghostly silence. Electricity and gas supplies had been suspended for safety's sake. She shivered.

Life was so simple for Rory; when he had a problem he just turned to the first available person to solve it. Kit was being wonderful, but it couldn't last. Suddenly she stood very still.

What was it he had said: 'Rosie, this is silly, Kit must be going mad. It's not just my problem you would solve, but I could help you with yours. We could help each other. What's wrong with that? Call me?'

She walked across to the door. Outside the sun was shining, a tradesman was delivering something across the road, a car backed into a space and disgorged a girl in wellies and a parka accompanied by a huge sheep dog. Life went on.

She took a last look back. '*Not just my problem you would solve.*' She closed the door behind her. Just what, she thought, as she tucked the key into her bag and turned towards Kit's, what if Rory could be the solution to hers?

# Chapter Twelve

Shortly after three o'clock two days later Rosie left Livvie battling with a temperamental client's moveable moods and instructions, saying she had to see her accountant over in Battersea.

The indecisive Mrs Compton had phoned with fresh instructions to replace the diamond smocking pleats with the goblet pleats she had rejected in the first place. She had also insisted on an overpowering shade of red in a tiny dining room, having listened to her friend Miriam de Lisle who said it would create *ambience*, disregarding Rosie who said it would look like Fingal's cave, and now wanted that reversed too. Livvie was about to remind her, but was stopped with a warning shake of the head from her boss.

Determined that no more clients would turn to other designers, Rosie had told Livvie that Mrs Compton had to be accommodated, even if she decided to restructure her entire home on the lines of the White House.

'What she needs,' suggested Livvie, flicking through her list of forthcoming workshops, 'is this: "Is Your Indecision Final?"'

What I need is her bloody money, Rosie thought savagely, closing the door on her temporary office in Kit's spare bedroom and setting off for the main road.

But instead of heading across the bridge to Battersea, Rosie took a taxi to an address in Lincoln's Inn, where she ran lightly up the wide, shallow steps past two stone lions gazing haughtily across to the tree-lined square opposite, and disappeared into the dim interior of the building.

Minutes later she was being ushered into a thickly carpeted and panelled office where a middle-aged, slightly balding man rose to his feet and greeted her with a kiss on both cheeks.

'Nick.' She returned his embrace, bestowing on him a smile that was more strained than she realised. 'Lovely to see you.'

'This is a pleasant surprise for me, my dear girl,' the man said, pulling out a chair for her at one end of a long, highly polished mahogany table that dominated the centre of the room, seating himself next to her.

'I do hope we can talk this through fully, before you make a decision. The fire was such a shock ... oh dear, you have that look on your face. I can see you've already made up your mind.

'Ah, Margaret,' he said as a young woman came in with a tea tray, 'Mrs Monteith Gore's file, if you please, and don't put any calls through, this might take some time.'

The business of the meeting took a bare half hour. The remainder was taken up with Nick Newall earnestly asking Rosie to reconsider what she had asked of him.

'Is Rory really so changed?' he had asked bluntly. 'I must urge caution, Rosie.'

'Caution?' She gave a hollow laugh. 'This, I have to tell you, will be regarded as a long-overdue display of support for Jaye Wingate's readers and, mark my words, the right-wing press would see it as coming to my senses.'

Nick peered over his half-moon glasses at her, bewildered.

'Surely you know about women like me?' Rosie's voice had a hint of hysteria. 'Single-handedly responsible for creating the poverty trap, a drain on society's resources? The fact that I have never taken a penny in assistance is neither here nor there – we're clogging up the housing list in every borough in the country and producing the next generation of muggers and yobs . . .'

Nick broke in protesting: 'They're not referring to women like you.'

But virtually homeless, her business disappearing before her eyes, the support Rosie was getting from the world had sunk to zero.

It seemed to her that banks, building societies, accountants and tradesmen had never encountered a single mother except in the pages of Dickens, and had formed their attitude accordingly. The fury, the rage she had been unable to direct at the source of her frustration was dumped in a tirade on Nick Newall.

'Really?' she snapped. 'What am I then, if not a single working mother? I'm treated like a blight on society, spoken to as though I'm at best a half-wit and at worst as someone who won't make a fuss if I don't get paid for months on end if at all and get threatening letters from the bank if I exceed my overdraft facility by a quid.

'Look at this.' She dug into her handbag, produced the letter from the bank that had arrived that morning, and brandished it at him. 'That bloody man knows he will get his money. I told him about the fire. What does he say? "*I am of course sorry to hear about the fire in your home.*" That's it. That's all. After that comes a list of suggestions about reducing my overdraft and protecting the sodding bank. Care? He couldn't define the word if his life depended on it.

'Does it matter to him whether I'm living in a high-rise with five children by as many fathers or a hard-working woman who doesn't want to burden anyone with her problems? He does not. He sees One Parent Family. He sees A Statistic. Not me.'

She stopped. Nick remained silent. Rosie let out her breath with a shake of her head. 'Sorry, Nick,' she mumbled. 'Not your fault.'

'You should have been a politician, Rosie,' he remarked mildly. 'Now just sign this and I'll do the rest.'

At five Rosie left, hailing a cab to take her back to Chelsea. From the window of his office Nicholas Newall, who was the senior partner in Newall, Knight, Newall, Solicitors, silently shook his head as he watched the slight figure give brief instructions to the driver and followed the cab's progress as it circled the square before disappearing into the thick of the rush-hour traffic in Kingsway.

Behind him the door opened to admit one of his colleagues, a man of similar age, but round where Nick was angular. He crossed the room and splashed whisky into two cut-glass tumblers, added a dash of soda and then joined Nick Newall at the window, handing him one of the glasses.

'Any luck?'

'Luck?' Nick's eyes remained on the empty square. 'Luck?' he repeated thoughtfully, mulling over the word. He sighed and turned back into the room. 'Only in the legal sense. You know, John, you and I have been in this business for too long. We both know merely signing a contract does not ensure a satisfactory outcome. You can't legislate for what is going on in someone's head. Can you? I only wish I knew the game plan.'

'Rosie's?'

'Rosie's? God, no. That flaky ex of hers.'

Livvie took a call cancelling Rosie's next appointment. News of the fire had brought much sympathy but also a frightening loss of business that no insurance claim in the world could recompense.

'I quite understand,' she told the latest caller politely. 'No, I'm sure Rosie would not expect you to wait, and nor was she planning that you would. I see . . . of course. Shit,' she muttered, replacing the phone. It was the third such conversation in two days.

Reaching over for the address book, Livvie ran her finger down the A's and called Rosie at her accountant to head her off from the now-cancelled appointment, only to hear she hadn't been there nor was she expected.

Only a flicker of unease on her face when Rosie returned indicated that she was not being truthful when Livvie mentioned it. Nor did she volunteer why she had disappeared for two hours.

'Wrong date,' Rosie lied. 'Took a bit longer to get back than I thought. Any other calls?'

Livvie threw her a suspicious look, but refrained from pursuing it any further. She was, however, uneasy. Livvie was sure Rosie was about to do something drastic.

'And er . . . did Rory ring?' Rosie asked after Livvie had delivered half a dozen messages that had come in while she was out.

'No, 'fraid not,' Livvie said with a stab of surprise, seeing the frown that crossed Rosie's face although she had just shrugged on hearing yet another client had jumped ship. Joyce had always said the Monteith Gore relationship was a real case of unfinished business.

That was probably it, she thought as Rosie nodded absently. On top of the fire, more trouble. Must be her sexy ex.

'No temperature,' pronounced Kit, removing his hand from her brow. 'Any insanity in the family? Your mother sounded a fork or two short of a dinner party when she was last here. No? Then I'll arrange for Tom to be taken into care and you have just won two years of heavy sedation in the psychiatric wing of any hospital of your choice. Pass me the phone book, Jaye. This is an emergency.'

'Not unless you want to hit her with it.'

'Oh, be quiet, Kit,' snapped Rosie, pushing his hand

away and accidentally splashing wine onto Jaye's Donna Karan shirt. 'This is serious.'

'You're *serious*?'

Jaye, who had joined them for supper at Kit's, looked dazed as she dabbed at the wet stain on her shirt sleeve. Rosie gazed defiantly back, unrepentant at the alarm she was causing her friends. This was, she said, just about the smartest move a single mother could make. Particularly a homeless and bankrupt one.

'Told you,' smirked Kit, who had had trouble convincing Jaye on the phone that Rosie had finally cracked and was now leaning back in his chair enjoying watching Jaye's horror as well as the spreading burgundy stain.

'This is a *career* move,' Rosie insisted. 'Not a reconciliation. I am pushed to the edge of my limits. No, I know you think I should either stay with Kit until I work something out, or move in with you, but it won't work.

'Honestly, I *am* grateful. Truly. But I need stability. Tom is ricocheting from my mother's to any friend who will have him, and I'm losing so much business. My house will take months to put back together again. So I am left with no choice. Don't you see, I'm not asking for an emotional commitment but a business one. And it will be done properly. I've taken advice . . .'

'From a psychiatrist, I hope,' moaned Kit.

Rosie ignored him. 'Jaye, you've always said parenting should be shared. Remember Alicia, that American? She stopped shouldering all the responsibility and is now running her own multi-million dollar company and her son is running for Congress . . . yes, I know what I said. It was a joke . . . Well, it worked for her and Rory sounds seriously changed.'

'But, Rosie, that was different,' Jaye wailed. 'Alicia didn't *live* with her ex . . .'

'How could she? There were so many. At least I've only got the one.'

Jaye looked helplessly at her. 'She just redefined co-parenting in a way that made sense. *Please*. Let me lend you the money. *Please*. Carey is begging you to let him *give* you whatever it takes. And you still think Rory is your best option? Rory is a shit. I know that, you know that. *Everyone* knows it. And you think Rory has changed? Will the Pope become a Buddhist? Will Livvie become a house-wife? You'll end up like this shirt, I just know you will. Ruined. Bloody Rory.'

'Don't say a word,' Jaye hissed savagely to Kit as Rosie went to take a phone call. 'That bloody fire. That fucking ex of hers.'

Rosie saw no reason to mention that a dozen times in the days following her decision she had wavered and pulled back. Jaye's and Kit's open horror at such a move weighed heavily on her, but Tom's needs transcended it.

And the quality of his life depended on her ability to finance it. Stuff all that stuff about love being enough for any child. The fire had put paid to that.

So a few days later, Rory at Rosie's request made reservations at an expensive but not particularly fashionable French brasserie off Brompton Road, where the tables were spaced far enough apart to disappoint eavesdroppers, but which had a pleasant hum and bustle in the background to maintain a decent level of intimacy.

'You look terrific,' he said once they were seated, but his attempts at anything more personal were thwarted by the twin obstacles of the waiter arriving with two large menus and Rosie's determination to keep the meeting on a businesslike footing.

After the waiter departed Rory tried again, reaching for her hand. Rosie did not miss the swift glance around to see if the way she had pulled her hand back had been noticed before he focused on her face, demanding to know what was her problem.

'I don't have a problem with you, Rory. That's over. But I thought about what you said, and Tom can't have his needs overlooked because we don't get along . . .'

'. . . *You* don't get along with me,' he interrupted. 'I don't have any problems with you. You're the one who . . .'

Rosie began to twist her napkin. 'Rory, if you're going to rewrite the past in your favour, we might as well stop now.'

'Sorry, sorr-eee.' He held up both hands. 'Sorry. Okay? Just anxious. You know how it is. Actually, if you want to know, I feel like I'm on a first date with you. You always did know how to produce a knot in my stomach.'

He was good. She had to hand it to him. Instead she laughed. He couldn't touch her feelings this time. This time she wasn't a mesmerised, pregnant bride. This time all she wanted was a business partner.

He relaxed. 'You were saying. About overlooking Tom's needs.'

Rosie nodded at him. 'Tell me what you think.'

'I think that's something we should discuss together.' He exhaled, signalling for the waiter to bring him a brandy. Rory used his body a lot. An imperceptible nod brought a waiter to his side. A raised eyebrow in Rosie's direction simply brought a shake of her head.

No need to ask her. It was just courtesy. He knew her well. He knew that she never had breakfast, read papers from the middle to the front, cried over sad movies and felt sick if she rowed with anyone.

He knew she kept her clothes well-cut and understated and he had always adored the way she could transform the plainest outfit into glamorous chic by the simple addition of a scarf, chunky bracelets, unusual earrings or securing her hair up with tortoiseshell combs, which he loved to unpin, seeing it fall in a tangle onto her bare shoulders.

No matter how strong she appeared, he knew she was shy and funny, and the reason her hair was now bobbed was because after he had told her about his affair she had hacked it off in front of the bathroom mirror and never worn it long since.

'Look,' he said, tracing a pattern on the tablecloth with his lighter. Dunhill, she noticed. 'A certain amount of trust between us has gone. But not entirely. You wouldn't be here if you weren't prepared to consider my proposal, would you.'

His voice trailed off as he absently lit his cigarette. Smoking had always been his prop. The device to play for time. But this time he frowned, flicking ash into the ashtray beside him. She wanted to believe he had changed.

The warning voice of Nick sounded in Rosie's head. And Kit's solemn lecture on never going back anywhere. Jaye urging caution. It was, they had warned, for once united in their views, a road strewn with broken promises and the debris of shattered illusions.

She took a deep breath. Being truthful was the only way. She did not want Rory to believe her reasons for sitting opposite him were anything other than completely practical.

'I need help,' she said levelly. 'No, stop trying to grab my hand. I've said I'll level with you, not sleep with you.'

'Shame,' he said lightly. 'Could be fun.'

This was getting nowhere. The contract Nick Newall had drawn up was in her handbag. She took a deep breath. 'Look, Rory. A year, you said? Just a year?'

He nodded. His eyes narrowed as he inhaled on the cigarette.

'Okay, Rory.' Rosie extracted the long slim brown envelope from her bag and placed it in front of him. 'I'll do a deal with you.'

# Chapter Thirteen

'Tom? Tom, darling. What are you doing? Daddy's been waiting for ten minutes. You'll miss the start.'

His anxious young voice floated down the wide staircase. 'I'm just coming. I can't find my Nintendo.'

'Nintendo? Tom, leave it, you can't take that to a football match.'

Rory's impatient voice bellowed up the stairs and over hers. 'Tom? One more minute and then I'm going. Understand?'

There was a clatter and the bang of a door. In seconds Tom appeared at the top of the stairs, the laces of his trainers still undone, still pushing his arms into a T-shirt that was an enduring, if well-worn, favourite.

Rosie ruffled his hair affectionately. 'You'll just make it. Go on with you . . .'

'Not in that T-shirt, he won't,' Rory interrupted as she bent to kiss a breathless Tom who had jumped the last four stairs. 'Go and change it for something decent. And no arguing.'

Tom shot a quick, appealing look at Rosie, took in his father pointedly studying his watch, opened his mouth to argue, thought better of it and raced back to his bedroom.

Rosie dug her hands into her pockets.

'Bit severe, weren't you?'

'If you mean firm, then yes. I was never allowed to go out with my father looking like a yob . . .'

'*Yob*? Don't be ridiculous, he's only eleven. How could he possibly look like a yob?'

'He doesn't but he might if I don't tell him now. Anyway, he knows who's boss around here . . .'

'I *beg* your pardon?' Her voice held a deliberate note of surprise, one eyebrow raised.

'Just joking,' he soothed.

'By the way, have you signed those papers? Nick phoned yesterday. Said he hasn't got your copies back.'

Rory sighed. 'Why couldn't this just have been between us? Why did you have to drag solicitors into it?'

'You know why,' Rosie said firmly. 'This is a business arrangement.'

Tom's noisy return in a clean but plain T-shirt stopped them. Just as well, Rosie reflected as they left for the Chelsea stadium in Rory's Porsche. She'd forgotten Rory's strangely pompous view of dress and his abhorrence of football grounds. However, in spite of this, Rory had agreed to take Tom to the match, which was evidence that he was trying. Rosie had to admit she had been preparing herself for a blunt refusal when Tom had suggested it and had kept herself in readiness to step in.

The Porsche was ridiculous. But Tom, to his mother's surprise, had made it clear that he was deeply impressed and wouldn't consider Rosie dropping them both off in her more serviceable old estate car.

Abeline, who preferred to be called Abbie, had disappeared for the weekend which was one less thing to get used to while they all tried to adapt to a family life to which all three were strangers.

And now a whole Saturday afternoon entirely to herself lay ahead which was both a novelty and a luxury and she couldn't help but look forward to it. In fact at breakfast Rory had insisted that she just relaxed.

'This is boy's stuff, isn't it, Tom?' he smiled conspiratorially at his son. 'Last person we want along is a bored woman.'

'No way,' Tom shouted gleefully, banging a spoon on

the table but stopping abruptly when he saw Rosie's face. She had opened her mouth to rebuke him for his manners, but bit her tongue. She could see he didn't want to offend her. She knew it was because he was excited at being like his friends.

'I mean,' he mumbled, 'Mum likes football. She sometimes takes me.'

'Yes, but *I'm* here now,' Rory pointed out. 'So what are you going to do with your freedom?' He turned to Rosie.

Smiling reassuringly at Tom, who was looking rather anxiously at her, she told Rory she would be shopping and maybe meeting Jaye for a coffee at Harvey Nicks.

But in fact she had arranged to meet Colin, the dependable builder she used for her clients' work, at her own house to get some idea of how long it would take to make it structurally sound.

Even in the short space of time she had been living under Rory's roof she had decided that also living with his irrational dislike of her getting her house repaired was tricky. While she saw it as a necessity whatever the future held, he merely saw it as her lack of commitment to their arrangement.

'You're not giving me a chance,' he complained. 'I said I wanted to prove I could give you all the support I never gave you the first time round. How can I if you're planning to move out before you've hardly moved in?'

No matter how much she argued, he remained adamant. Rory was on a mission to please. She didn't have the heart to stop him.

Deceiving him wasn't therefore something she liked, but it was her life. This time Rory was not going to dictate its terms. Those were thankfully already well documented in the agreement drawn up by their respective solicitors.

After Colin had inspected the house and said he would give her and the insurance company an estimate, they parted, Colin to take his wife to IKEA and Rosie to have her hair cut. As she set off the young girl across the street, recognising her neighbour, came over to talk.

'What a terrible night,' she exclaimed. 'I gave a description of the bike rider to the police but I doubt they'll find him. He was gone in a flash. Anyway, you're safe. You will be coming back, won't you? I liked having you living nearby.'

Rosie was touched. 'Yes,' she promised, glancing up at her shell of a house. 'Yes. I'll be back.'

She emerged a relaxing hour later from the hairdresser, but almost immediately guiltily consulted her watch. And then she stopped. Guilty about what? Crowds of shoppers pushed past her as she stood on the pavement, glancing curiously at her as she let the reality of her situation descend on her.

She looked thoughtfully in both directions, with only a moment's indecision. Her bag was slung confidently over her shoulder, and she set off along Sloane Street.

London in springtime was magical, she decided. She saw only trees breaking into pale green leaf, not the fumes from traffic, the hanging baskets of sharp red geraniums over shop awnings and not the pushing and shoving crowds entering and leaving shops.

She even managed to laugh when the gleaming Bentley carrying Salina Bhandari scattered pedestrians as it deposited its occupant at the side door of Harrods, Salina making no attempt to acknowledge Rosie, who was a mere three feet away as she swept past.

She continued with a leisurely stroll along Knightsbridge, only turning off the route home to take in Nancy's house, standing empty and imposing behind its high walled garden, as much to satisfy a couple of questions in her head as to justify her freedom.

Directly opposite was a small memorial square with a

bench placed underneath the statue of a long-dead warrior gazing sightlessly into the middle distance. Rosie sat down and, resting her chin on her raised knee, surveyed the project that was going to make or break her as a designer.

Nancy had been alerted to this shell of a house by an exhausted estate agent who had failed to find the perfect house for her. It was considered cheap at a figure that could have rebuilt an entire housing estate, but she would spend that again restoring it. It was hard to equate the stillness of the house with the scenes of near-hysteria Rosie knew had ensued before the purchase was completed. She smiled to herself as she recalled Nancy's description of the estate agent who, almost weeping with relief, raced the deal through in a fraction of the time usually allocated to such arrangements, and had himself transferred to another branch before Nancy could change her mind.

It was a grand house. Majestically small, is how Kit had described it. Obscenely large, countered Jaye, who disapproved of Nancy's unreasonable wealth.

It was built at the time of Regency London, had escaped the ravages of bombs during the war, but in the end had had more damage inflicted on it by a rock star in the 60s who made most of his decisions heavily influenced by copious use of a mind-altering substance.

Miriam de Lisle's taste was a model of restraint by comparison. False ceilings to give more ambience to his well-documented love-ins had been hurled up while the delicate artistry of Regency windows had been torn down at random to be replaced by iron-framed picture windows.

The most beautiful feature of the house, a staircase sweeping up and round to a gallery on the first floor, had been resited to hug the wall, the oak handrail removed and a poor art deco structure put in its place. It was where Rosie was going to start. Or rather, Joel Harley would.

The rock star's interest in the house had faded simultaneously with his career and the next owner, unable to find time or tenants to maintain it, had let it fall into disgraceful disrepair.

Nancy thought it perfect. A stone's throw from Harrods, a stroll to Harvey Nicholls and easy access to the M4 straight out to Heathrow and New York in a few hours on Concorde. The urgent priorities satisfied. And the money to do it.

The wind stirred Rosie's hair. Absently she moved it away from her face, catching sight of a familiar black Range Rover as she did so. She jerked herself upright as it pulled up outside the house. The tall figure of Joel Harley got out, followed by a young girl – about thirteen, Rosie guessed.

For a moment she was convinced she'd been spotted and she started to rise to her feet, but he turned almost immediately to face the house. He couldn't have seen her, for which she was relieved. Uncertain what to do and conscious of the fact that the night at Nancy's had hardly endeared her to him, she moved quietly towards the end of the road.

Rosie looked back to see Joel, hands dug into the pockets of his navy wool bomber jacket, being joined by the girl in a short plaid miniskirt, black tights and Caterpillar boots, who ran round the side of the vehicle and stood next to him, hanging lazily onto his arm as he stared up at the house.

After a few seconds she could see that he was being badgered by the girl to continue their journey. Dark glasses hid his eyes, the collar of his black shirt was open. He was wearing very faded jeans.

She watched him bending over slightly to hear something the girl said, throwing back his head and laughing, ruffling her hair. She began to pull on his arm, trying to get him to go. Rosie smiled. So like Tom. Bored with grown-up stuff.

He put both his arms around her, holding her firmly in

front of him to stop her wriggling as he checked out the house. It was affectionate, familiar. A father with a much-loved daughter.

Rosie found it hard to equate this figure with the urbane, indifferent man who had made her feel so gauche. She was tempted to cross the street, say hello, but she wasn't sure of her welcome. She gave them a last backward glance before threading her way through quieter residential streets to Rory's house.

If, however, she had turned before she got to the corner she would have seen Joel Harley lower his glasses and stare after her, before allowing the girl to drag him back to the Range Rover and drive slowly away in the opposite direction.

But Rosie, blissfully unaware, walked contentedly on. For the first time in months – no, years – she felt that she was leading something approaching a normal life.

Just wandering aimlessly through London on a Saturday afternoon had been denied to her for so long, she found it difficult not to smile with relief and the prospect of a dinner with Rory and Tom was a welcome one. Who, she thought as she let herself into the silent house to await their return, would have thought it?

# Chapter Fourteen

Rory continued to be so disconcertingly easy-going in the first few weeks that Rosie checked the terms of their agreement twice to make sure there had been no misunderstanding.

*'Joint care and control ... all bills to be split equally, except mortgage because the family house is entailed to the Monteith Gore estate and owned outright. Joint decisions about Tom's schooling, weekends spent as a family to ensure Tom's stability.*

*'When the agreement is terminated – on completion of the renovation of Miss Colville's house – a scaling-down period to allow changeover to take place to be implemented. After which both parties will agree to live within reasonable distance of each other to ensure ease of access to Tom.'*

Rosie read on, searching for anything that Rory might have misinterpreted.

*'While at all times endeavouring to maintain a harmonious co-existence, both parties may exercise the right to privacy in business, social and domestic arrangements provided this does not inconvenience the other party unreasonably.'*

Nothing. Each day Rory left a list of instructions for Abbie, which made it unnecessary for Rosie to do anything more than concentrate on her work. Abbie followed these with an enthusiasm that left Rosie overwhelmed.

'It's almost as though she thinks I'm an invalid,' she confided to Jaye with a giggle. 'I've only got to plug the kettle in and she's there, whipping it away from me and saying that's her job.'

'Don't knock it,' Jaye recommended. 'Enjoy it.'

And each day, Rory disappeared to work, usually at James' office where he was a consultant – although Rosie suspected he was still just a name to James – and from where, he explained, it was easier to get in as much ground-work as possible before his course in estate management commenced in the autumn.

In spite of herself, Rosie could not help but be impressed. Although his penchant for nightlife had not significantly diminished, since this was no concern of hers she refrained from asking why he was still so addicted to it.

Occasionally she would be inveigled into having a drink with him at which he surprised her by asking her advice on the future of Glencairn. Mostly she demurred, seeing it as his future not hers, but just occasionally alarmed that Tom might one day be confronted with a financially drain-ing old house to maintain, she was prepared to offer her views. Rory did not hide his delight in her interest.

'I think it would be more cost effective to turn it into a Museum of Scottish Arts,' he declared, tapping his pen thoughtfully on a document lying before him.

'A museum?' She was startled, knowing Callum's fierce pride in the Monteith Gore heritage. 'What would your father say?'

Rory looked up eagerly. 'Oh, he'd be delighted, provided one wing of the house was left to live in. And of course I agree with that. Don't want to let it go out of the family.'

He began to call to say if he was going to be late. On Fridays, if Rosie was collecting Tom he would suggest they met him for hamburgers and a movie. He took Tom to football and was pleasant to Rosie's friends.

Only Piers' name could arouse an acid remark, but Rosie was convinced it was to flatter her that he was jealous rather than anything else. After all, Piers was history.

Nothing Rory did contravened the terms of their agreement. He was charming, courteous, sometimes gently teasing her, but while Rosie knew he was smudging some of the demarcation lines, he made no attempt to move their relationship onto more intimate ground, rarely sought her out if Tom wasn't around and would often pass her in the kitchen with little more than a 'Hi, everything okay? Just let Abbie know,' before disappearing for maybe two or three days at a time.

Good God, she thought. He has changed. The trick now was for her to stop looking for flaws and get on with the business of co-parenting which was, after all, what this was about.

James Cooper was not so convinced. More than once it had occurred to Rosie that James' dislike of her was not so much about her personally – it was what she stood for. Or rather, between. In this case, it was the use of Rory's house.

The re-emergence of her and Tom after six years had clearly put a stop to James using it as a venue for entertaining his clients and finding alternative locations was proving a drain on his pocket. It was, however, impossible not to notice the sudden silence if she happened to walk in when James was there.

'Darling, he's just being discreet,' Rory once told her, racing after her as she apologised for accidentally interrupting them in the drawing room. 'He's like that with everyone.'

Rosie said nothing. Discreet indeed. She knew it was James who had told the gossip columns all those years ago that Callum believed she had married Rory for the title. Because he envied Rory's title in a way that Rosie found preposterous, no-one could persuade James that Rosie's motives for moving back were for any other reason than to advance her career.

Rosie ran into him by chance in Rory's kitchen when she arrived home early from an exhibition of new fabrics and designs. She halted on the threshold. 'Sorry, I had no idea you were here. Don't let me disturb you.'

'No fear of that,' he smirked. 'I'm not one of your fans.'

'Such a relief,' she replied, calmly pouring a cup of coffee. James' eyes were bloodshot, he was clutching what appeared to be a triple shot of whisky. 'If you were I might have to be nice to you.'

'Oh, please.' James looked pained. 'Don't let me overtax you. Being nice to Rory must exhaust you enough – pity you don't work for him full time. You could make him a fortune.'

'I thought you were doing that,' she said lightly, knowing the drink was loosening his tongue. 'Besides, turning ancestral homes into cultural museums is not in my line – nor, I would have thought, yours either.' He really was a toad. He was also looking at her in a way she found disquieting. It crossed her mind that he was no longer angry, just amused.

'Really?' he drawled. 'So tell me, Rosie . . . what do you actually *do* for him? When it suits you, you're Rory's wife. When you've made use of him, you're Miss Tight-arse Colville. What happened to "*I will never let Tom live under your roof again, ever*"?'

Rosie's face was white with anger. It had been a long day. The last thing she wanted was to be so pointlessly insulted by a man she had come to loathe over something that wasn't his business.

'Whatever happens between me and Rory is totally private,' she said in a shaky voice. 'Nothing to do with you. Just be grateful he bothers with you at all.'

The chair he was holding was pushed aside. James' face was livid. He leaned both hands heavily on the table. His eyes were bulging. 'Bothers with me? *Me? Jesus* . . . are you thick? It's him who needs me. I know enough about him to put him . . .'

'Behind bars? *Tsk tsk*, James . . .'

They both wheeled round at the sound of Rory's voice. Rosie flicked her gaze over James' pinstriped suit, the slicked back and greased hair, the old school tie, the fleshy face, soft before its time and now flushed as he glanced uneasily at Rory strolling casually into the middle of the room.

'I honestly don't think anyone's going to be interested in a little youthful high spirits, do you, James? I mean, we both got off with a caution. James still has nightmares every time we sign a contract. I don't know,' he sighed. 'Who didn't do drugs all those years ago? Hi darling, you're home early. Good trip?'

'Not terrific,' she said briefly, looking uncertainly from James to Rory. James really was vicious. Thank God, she was totally aware of Rory's past. Only James would still think he could control someone with that sort of information.

'Actually, Rory,' she said, 'I don't think James is feeling very well. Perhaps you could take him home?'

'Of course,' he agreed smoothly, not taking his eyes off James. 'In a minute. See you later.'

The scale of Nancy's job was awesome. Only time had prevented Rosie from looking for another assistant and of course somewhere to accommodate her business.

Matthew Ormond, who only weeks before had said she could have no assistant at all, had dramatically revised his ideas and now urged her to think about it, even congratulating himself that Rosie must have remembered his advice that from failure comes a chance to begin more wisely.

It was odd how many people saw living with an ex who had made her life a misery as a source of reassurance when they now dealt with her.

Those who had hitherto seen her as a social misfit and responsible for the national debt because she was a single working mother had been transformed on hearing of her new status.

Tom's headmaster, who had made no secret of the fact that he blamed a boy's poor performance on a working mother and particularly a single working mother, cheered up enormously when she wrote to him to say that her business and home address would now be in Mayfair until the fire damage at her former home could be repaired.

The garage that a few weeks previously had said her car needed repairs running into almost four figures suddenly found it was possible to make it roadworthy on a fraction of the cost and in half the time, when they were told very bossily by Abbie that she would get *Mr* Monteith Gore to call them.

And he did. Rosie tried to stop him. But he had swept her aside, saying he would enjoy making them feel uncomfortable.

Sharing the load with Rory had not quite eased the horror of opening her post in the morning and once when it produced a letter from the bank manager her initial apprehension made her laugh and squirm in turns.

Uriah Heep lives, she reflected. When only a few weeks before she had watched her house nearly razed to the ground and had had to beg him for time to pay her overdraft, the man had addressed her in tones reserved for those planning to flee the country to take up permanent residence on the Costa del Sol. Now when she didn't need his unctuousness, he had turned it on in full.

Anyway, she no longer cared. This agreement with Rory had opened the way to accepting Nancy's lucrative contract and with an eight-bedroom house with five reception rooms, one of which was nearly the size of a ballroom, not to mention a conservatory and a garden room, all of which had to be ready by November, she simply didn't have time to care too much.

Besides, there was no immediate need. Rosie Colville had been a liability to everyone she dealt with. But Rosie Monteith Gore was an asset. And all she'd done was change her address and turned her parental duties into a business arrangement.

'You see,' she said to Kit, falling about laughing. 'It's true. If you owe the bank and live on your own in a small house in Chelsea, you're a risk. Move the same business to an address in Mayfair, acquire a name that sounds loaded, employ a housekeeper, and you can have credit up to your armpits. Don't you think that's hysterical? Kit, what's the matter?'

Kit was looking at her with an odd expression. 'Matter? Oh, nothing. Yes, very funny. By the way, are you going to Carey's for supper on Saturday?'

'Yes, of course,' she said at once, wondering why she imagined he was withdrawing from her. 'But that isn't what you were thinking, is it?'

'Listen, kid, it's your life. I was just thinking this is starting to sound like a case of knowing which buttons to press,' he replied sourly and not a touch sulkily. 'The only thing an ex has got going for them. Well, don't come running to me when it all goes wrong.'

Rosie was aghast, and deeply hurt that he was not prepared to be more optimistic. 'I agree I wasn't out of love with Rory when I threw him out. Remember, you can't hurt someone the way he hurt me, if there's no love there. But that's over. We're just striving to be friends. And he *is* trying.

'Honestly, Kit, don't give me that rubbish about "you've got to love someone to make something work". That would only be true if we wanted to get back together again. And we're not doing that. I just know I've got to give it my best shot. For Tom's sake.'

Kit was genuinely bewildered. Platonic relationships didn't exist for him. Rosie had escaped his attentions only because for the first two years they lived alongside one another she was involved with Piers.

By the time Piers disappeared, Kit's friendship with Rosie had settled into that comfortable area where shifting things onto another level might not be any less interesting, but would be plain inconvenient if it ended in tears. Easier to get a new girlfriend than move.

'Surely you can't believe that he won't start coming on to you?' he asked. 'Rory couldn't resist sex with his ex.'

'You've forgotten something,' she pointed out.

'What's that?'

'I could.'

Tom was transformed. His new bedroom was his paradise, and he shared the top floor of the house with Abbie who occupied a pretty and spacious room with its own bathroom.

It wasn't long before Rosie realised the New Zealand girl took her job very seriously and that while Rory left endless instructions about how things were to be managed, Abbie simply did things as they pleased her. Since the end result was that Rosie did nothing, she said nothing. Particularly as Rory only seemed to notice when something went wrong.

Abbie admitted to being in her late twenties, although she looked older. Rory had found her through an agency when, as he openly confessed to Rosie, he had set out to court her back.

Abbie's hair was a thick tumble of teased curls which she pulled back into the nape of her neck. She never wore jeans. 'Hate the things, just *hate* them,' she told Rosie who mentioned that it was a shame to risk such nice clothes when she was doing the housework. 'Just because I've taken this job for a year, doesn't mean I have to look or behave like one of those backpackers.'

Her voice betrayed a good education at some point in her life, but Abbie had apparently wanted to see the world. A couple of failed relationships had been the trigger that had made her put Auckland a long way behind her, she explained in a rather strained voice.

'I had my own company supplying domestic help so I know what I'm doing. Rory said he would need someone for at least a year, and then anything could happen, couldn't it? Just let me know how you like things done, Mrs Monteith Gore.'

'Rosie will do fine,' she interrupted, feeling a pang of sympathy for the girl. It must be difficult for her to take orders when she had been used to being the one doling them out. 'And please don't think you have to do anything special for me, whatever you've arranged with Rory is okay by me.'

Abbie's face remained impassive. 'Whatever you say. I have weekends off unless we have a prior arrangement and every evening. But if you want a baby sitter . . .'

Rosie shook her head. 'Thank you, when Tom's home I spend my time with him but when he transfers to a day school in London, it might be different.'

'Day school? I thought the little chap boarded?'

'He does but he doesn't like it and I would prefer to have him home. Anyway for the moment he's only home at weekends.'

Abbie was an odd choice for Rory, but Rosie soon discovered a tenous but sufficient link to explain to her satisfaction why they understood one another. Rosie had never been able to temper Rory's delusions of grandeur; he adored being a baronet's son even if he didn't always adore his father.

But Abbie was surprisingly intrigued by Rory's lineage, and bewildered by Rosie's preference for the informal rooms, which led onto the paved courtyard at the back of the house, over the severity of the drawing room.

Once or twice when Rosie had come back earlier than planned she had found Abbie with a cup of coffee, feet up, absorbed in a book about the stately homes of England, in the sumptuous surroundings that Rory used exclusively for entertaining.

Rosie just laughed as Abbie scrambled guiltily to her feet.

'Be my guest,' Rosie invited. 'Or rather, Rory's. Don't rush off.'

Rory had arranged with Abbie that Rosie should occupy a bedroom at the back of the house on the same floor as his which had its own bathroom and double doors leading out onto a flat roof surrounded by a stone balustrade. But it had not been touched since Rosie had lived there. The wallpaper was fading, she noted, but otherwise it only lacked thought.

It also had the advantage of having a dressing room the size of a broom cupboard, which meant that she could dispense with wardrobes in her bedroom and turn it into a comfortable sitting room should she feel the need for space.

When she discovered a size eight black velvet minidress languishing in one of the two wardrobes, along with a black lace wired bra and suspender belt, she suspected she would.

Plucking them from the wardrobe she held them at arm's length and dropped them into the dustbin on her way out.

Rory's rooms were at the front of the house. He slept late while Rosie was generally on the move by seven each day. She went to bed early. Rory's idea of an early night was reaching his room by two in the morning.

'Maybe we could have dinner or see a film together?' suggested Rory as they met in the kitchen, having not crossed each other's paths for a while.

'Not a good idea,' she replied firmly. And then seeing his disappointment, she relented. 'At least, not yet. By the way, are you still okay about collecting Tom on Friday?'

For a brief moment Rory looked blank. 'Friday? Oh yes, *Friday*. Of course. Ringed in red. Absolutely.'

Passing his study a few minutes later she wasn't at all surprised to hear him on the phone as she went into the dining room to resume work.

'Sorry, James. Can't do Friday lunch. Forgot. I've promised to collect Tom. Yes. I know. Well, that's the arrangement I'm afraid. Make it dinner. What? Oh, fuck that. Look let Betsey know will you? Say I'll call her. Oh Christ James, say anything you like. You're the brain behind all this. I'm just the bait.'

Rosie closed the door, shutting off the rest of the conversation. Some things never changed.

Thus it was that they settled down to a living arrangement that prompted speculation privately, publicly and unavoidably.

'*Friends have wondered at the apparently sudden reconciliation between Rory Monteith Gore and his ex-wife, fashionable interior designer Rosie Colville,*' reported the *Express*.

'*Neither is prepared to comment, but clients of Ms Colville say she is looking more relaxed these days, having recovered from the fire that destroyed her Chelsea home, and is looking forward to completing the interior design of the new London residence of New York heiress, Nancy Alexander,*' countered the *Mail*.

The result of that was an interview in *The Times* with an expert from Relate, warning of the dangers of expecting too much too soon or indeed at all from marital reconciliations.

Ignoring the gossip seemed the wisest course of action. But the gossip was her only flicker of misgiving. For

Tom's sake she did not want to spell out publicly the finer points of her deal with Rory – it would sound bizarre – but privately to friends she was perfectly open with the arrangement.

'It just made more sense, since we both work and both love Tom,' she told Judith who had rung from New York with the name of a good shrink she knew in London.

'Honestly, love, I know what I'm doing,' Rosie said crossly. 'Now, don't forget. I'll be over soon. Nancy wants me to look at some of the furniture she's having shipped over for the house, and in between I'm just longing to raid Saks.'

'I didn't know they were big on brain transplants,' Judith remarked gloomily.

# Chapter Fifteen

It was, however, harder than she had thought to live with Tom's devotion to Rory. After a couple of weeks she felt it incumbent on her to remind him that this arrangement was temporary. A year at most.

'And then what?' he asked, squeezing a river of ketchup across his plate and obliterating all trace of the food on it. Rosie cringed.

'And then our house will be repaired and you'll be at a school nearby.'

'And then what?' He sounded just as he had at four when every sentence was a question.

'Then you'll be able to spend lots of time with Dad when . . . when he's here.'

Tom digested this along with the chicken he was spearing up like a child denied food for a month. 'I s'pose,' is what she thought he said. It was hard to decide since his mouth was inelegantly stuffed full.

'Mum?' he began and stopped. Rosie waited. 'S'pose I stay at Old Farrells. S'pose it starts to be all right. What then?'

Rosie almost took his temperature. 'But you don't like it there.' She sounded amazed. 'Do you?'

He looked uncomfortable, swallowing mouthfuls of Coca-Cola to deflect her.

'Why the doubt, Tom?' She wasn't fooled for a moment. 'What's changed?'

'Nothing. Just . . . oh, nothing. I'll talk to Dad. Can he come to get me next weekend, instead of you?'

'Maybe . . .'

'Not *maybe*. Please can he? Can I go and ask? And Mum? Has Daddy decided where we're going on holiday – I mean and you?'

*Holiday?* And her too? Well, *pardon me*. Thanks a lot. Oh God. 'Tom, shouldn't you be doing prep or something? I don't want Mr Farrell nagging again this term.'

Now when he was at home, he shadowed his father like a devoted puppy. Once when Rosie had discovered Tom ensconced with Rory and James, in Rory's study, she casually suggested that perhaps Daddy would like a little space, especially when he had visitors.

'Dad doesn't mind,' Tom retorted with such defiance that Rosie looked at him in surprise.

'No, but if you get in the way of his business friends he might,' she pointed out, ashamed of herself because she knew the real reason was that she didn't want him involved with James.

'No he won't. He likes me. So does James.'

'I see,' Rosie replied.

Privately Rosie thought it was his father's hand that encouraged this new aggression in Tom. Shrieks of *pow* or *splat*, even wrestling, became standard greeting between the two. But Caroline would have none of it.

'Perfectly normal,' she pronounced. 'Stand back. Tom is fast approaching the age when he needs to let off all that masculine energy with another male, and who better than his own father?'

And this from a woman who recoiled in horror when she heard that Kit regularly took Tom to Laser Quest or Alien Wars. 'Next thing he'll have him running around the countryside in camouflage gear, wielding a bayonet and shooting at everything,' she had shuddered.

Not for the world would Caroline spell it out, but Rosie knew her mother had been completely thrilled by her return to live with Rory, refusing to see it as anything other than a reconciliation.

'No chance, Mama dear,' Rosie had insisted when she broke the news to her. 'This is a business arrangement.'

'Nonsense,' Caroline exclaimed. 'Just don't make a mess of it this time.'

Infidelity was a hazard of married life that Caroline Mellbury had long endured from both her husbands. Having loved neither sufficiently to understand the anguish of betrayal felt by her daughter – whom she had told sharply not to over-react – she was swiftly aware of how Rosie's social standing had soared since she was now once again in pole position to become a lady. That, in Caroline's book, was ample compensation for being saddled with a straying husband.

But one thing Caroline did get right. Tom was a different person since he had resumed life under his father's roof.

When Rosie collected Tom for half term, he scrambled into the car already making sure Rory hadn't forgotten they were going to see the new Star Trek movie. Rosie looked blank.

'What movie? I thought we were going to Jane's for supper. Johnny's at the school I think will be great for you. He can tell you all about it.'

Tom shot her a sulking look. 'Johnny Grantham's a prat,' he complained. 'And I don't want to go to that school. Dad said Star Trek was great, he saw the whole lot in one day.'

Rosie gripped the wheel. 'Daddy did what? When?'

'Last week,' Tom told her. 'He said there was a special all-day showing and he knew you wouldn't let me go all day . . .'

'Certainly not.' Rosie was appalled that even Rory had done it. It took another half hour's driving to remind herself that in the first place what Rory did was none of her business and furthermore she really must stop feeling so rejected.

After all, she was the one who, inspired by Jaye's American single mother who had it all, all the time and at the same time, wanted Tom to have a special relationship with Rory.

Half term passed easily and rapidly in a round of outings and treats mostly organised by Rory and Abbie. The latter troubled Rosie.

'She isn't employed to look after Tom,' she protested when she discovered that it was Abbie who had taken Tom and Felix Duxborough to Planet Hollywood for lunch and not Rory. 'I thought you were taking them.'

'I was, but something cropped up. I would have told you, but you were so busy. Livvie said you had gone to an Art Deco fair in Kensington Town Hall . . . well, some exhibition or other. You're always at them. Okay, okay, it's work, but whatever it was you wouldn't have been back until late. Look, Tom had a great time and Abbie does what I tell her to do.'

In fact Rosie had reformed her view of Abbie. She still found her superior manner irritating, but since if anything her ex-husband had become even more demanding, it was just as well Abbie was a live-in housekeeper.

But his insistence on tagging onto the end of these demands to Abbie a rather embarrassing and usually very public rider that Rosie was extremely busy with her job and mustn't be bothered with any domestic matters, caused her a problem.

Sometimes his fury was vented in front of visitors like James, who usually carefully studied the ceiling. On another occasion Sylvia Duxborough, returning Tom and Felix after an afternoon spent at one of Oscar's leisure centres, got the full impact of Rory's concern.

He did, however, flash a mischievous smile at Sylvia saying he was in training for house husband of the year, which left Sylvia laughing, in Rosie's view, a little too excessively at his mild joke.

It was one of the few areas where she knew she had an ally in Abbie. The housekeeper would deliberately absent herself so that she would not be obliged to wait on the very snooty Mrs Duxborough, whom she described to Rory as a 'nouveau'.

Abbie bore the brunt of Rory's orders. Rosie could hear him working himself up into a fury from where she sat in frustrated despair at the top of the stairs having failed to convince him that she actually *wanted* to tidy Tom's room and her own.

These days it was one of the few avenues she had to keep tabs on Tom's life, since he spent increasingly more time with his father.

Rory made no secret of the fact that he thought Tom would benefit from boarding school while Rosie tried to point out that his parents living in the same house had opened the doors to Tom having his dearest wish granted.

'What does it matter if you went to boarding school?' she asked, exasperated, when Rory produced it for the fifth time as the strongest case for Tom remaining at boarding school, although not necessarily at Old Farrells.

'Because I know I gained from it,' he said, a remark which gave Rosie difficulty in remaining straight-faced since Rory had been expelled from both establishments his parents had selected for him.

Curiously this was now the only stumbling block she met with Tom. Tom, who had once complained bitterly each Sunday evening being driven back to school that it was a form of child abuse.

Tom, who aggrievedly pointed out all the advantages of home life, suddenly did not now think it such a wizard scheme. Totally perplexed, Rosie finally put this down to the fact that he had realised he would be leaving Felix and Garth behind.

'The only case against that school is the company he keeps,' said Rory who had taken an instant and immoveable dislike to both the Duxboroughs and the de Lisles. '*Arrivistes.* You can smell the shop.'

'I must be going mad,' Rosie replied. 'But didn't you mention something about Tom benefiting from staying there?'

'I didn't say a social sacrifice, did I?' he retorted. 'I said boarding school as a *principle.*'

The chances of them ever agreeing about the benefits of Tom enjoying a home life were slim.

And Rory, for all his disdain at the families of Tom's friends, threw himself with unaccustomed enthusiasm into Tom's school life.

On Sports Day, when Rory had come second in the father's race, the veins in his temples straining as he was beaten by Oscar Duxborough, Tom was beside himself with delight at his father having acquitted himself so well, although Rory – as only Rosie who knew him better, recognised – could barely contain his fury.

Then came Founder's Day when Rory had utterly captivated the head's wife, reducing her to an almost unrecognisable simpering flirt over tea in the cricket pavilion.

'Daddy's just being nice,' Tom said, catching Rosie's dismayed expression.

'Absolutely,' she replied stoically. He's so afraid I'll criticise Rory, she thought to herself, as she noticed the increasingly anxious look on Tom's face whenever Rory was with her.

In turn, she made sure that she learned to smile indulgently or even give Tom a conspiratorial wink. He seemed relieved. She was glad he wasn't around when on Parents' Day Rory had to her astonishment deferred to every single suggestion Tom's tutor had made about their son's education when she had believed it settled at least between them, that Tom was going to be removed in the autumn and sent to a local school.

Discussions about schools were, however, kept to a minimum since each time she raised the subject with Tom, it brought on a wailing protest which she couldn't understand at all.

'Daddy doesn't keep trying to make me,' Tom stormed, his head slumped on his chest.

'But you hate Old Farrells,' Rosie pointed out to him, sitting on the edge of his bed, trying to get his attention from the television. 'All you've done since you went there is to phone home twice a week to say you want to leave.'

Tom's face never left the screen, mouthing 'pow' and 'crunch' as the action hotted up. The television had been installed with Rory's permission and without Rosie's. It had taken a good deal of teeth-gritting not to berate Rory when she had been presented with this *fait accompli*.

Anxious not to undermine Rory in front of Tom she had given in with a 'no watching after lights out', a condition that was totally ignored almost every night.

'Everyone hates Old Farrell,' claimed Tom, kneeling on the bed, firing off a laser gun, glued to the arrival of the invading alien onto the spacecraft on the screen.

Impatiently Rosie reached across and snapped the set off ignoring Tom's protests.

'When you've given me your attention you can have it back on again,' she told him severely.

Sulking on a spectacular level, Tom returned monosyllabic answers until, sighing, Rosie got up and left him to it, refusing to turn the set back on.

Half an hour later as she came back to see if he was asleep she was annoyed to hear the unmistakeable sound of the television again.

'Tom,' she exclaimed wrathfully as she walked in. And stopped. Sitting propped up with Tom was Rory.

'Daddy said it was okay,' Tom explained defensively.

142

Rory didn't take his eyes from the screen. 'Just a treat. He's back at school tomorrow and you'll be working so hard soon, he won't see you.'

'No,' she replied carefully. 'I did try to reschedule the whole thing but it was impossible . . .'

'No trouble,' Rory interrupted. 'If you have to, you have to, eh, Tom? Mummy shouldn't feel so guilty about being busy, should she?'

'What do you mean? This is work.'

Tom giggled as Rory gave him a broad wink. 'Ok, work. Don't make such a fuss. Anyway, now that you're here why don't you come and join us?' Rory invited, patting the bed beside him.

'Oh yes, come on, Mum,' Tom said eagerly, beginning to make a space for her.

She took a deep breath. 'No. No thanks, darling. Not my cup of tea, I'm afraid. I er . . . I have a couple of things to do in the workroom, I'll be back later.'

Until that moment she had no intention of working. But the cosy domestic scene was moving her onto more intimate and dangerous ground. She wasn't ready for that. If ever. No, not if. Never again, she reminded herself sharply.

'Work, work, work,' Rory complained to Tom. 'Mum doesn't do anything else, does she? Neglects us both,' he sighed in a theatrical way.

'Poor us,' Tom agreed mournfully, joining in the teasing.

Rory looked lazily over to where she was standing. 'Just joking,' he told her.

She pushed her hands into the pockets of her trousers. 'I see,' she said and quietly closed the door.

Nancy's contract was signed and preliminary work had begun. Two meetings on site to pin down the look Nancy wanted had gone successfully, but the all-important one with Joel Harley could not be organised until Rosie had completed her ideas and got Nancy's approval. Nancy said he was in New York, and not to expect him back in London for a couple of weeks.

'He's frantically busy,' she explained. 'When he's not in New York, he's in Frankfurt. I'm joining him in New York so I'll make sure he fits you in at some point. To be honest,' Nancy added giving her a penetrating look, 'he thought you'd be out of the picture after that fire, but I explained that you had moved back with your ex. That's right, isn't it?'

Rosie started to point out the difference, but changed her mind. Why would either of them be interested in where she lived or worked, beyond knowing she could come across with the goods? Instead she just nodded: 'Something like that. Don't worry. I'll make sure Joel is reassured about . . . the job finishing on time and to your brief.'

So it was that two days later she was surprised to see Joel at the preview of an art exhibition at a small gallery in Cork Street.

The gallery was crowded. A pleasant hum of conversation, mingled with glasses tinkling and bursts of laughter from groups around the room, greeted her as she arrived shortly after six.

Rosie pushed her way through to find Simon Ballantyne, the gallery owner and an old friend since art school, recognising several famous names as she did so. She stopped for a word with Jane Grantham, exchanged a hug with Nick Newall who was there with his wife. Regretfully she declined dinner with Simon and after an hour, having felt she had done her duty by the unknown artist and more importantly Simon, she was edging her way slowly to the door to make her escape.

Next day it was her turn to collect Tom, which meant she would be leaving town early. She was anxious to run through the notes she had made with Nancy so that Livvie could chase things up in her absence. She had just mimed across the room to Nick that she would phone and turned to make her way to the door, when she recognised Joel Harley's back barring her way.

Taking a deep breath, she tapped him on the shoulder. He turned and for a moment stared at her waiting as if for recognition to dawn.

'Rosie Colville,' she reminded him. 'We met at Nancy's.'

He smiled. 'Of course. I was just surprised to see you.'

He was so much nicer when he smiled. No tie. Rumpled hair. Crumpled cotton trousers, black jacket. But then she was no judge of men. She had no way of judging Joel either. Except he had rushed to judge her.

'Are you okay?' he asked, guiding her out of the line of the door. 'I heard about the fire. I mean, you *look* fine.'

Caught off guard by his genuine concern, Rosie grimaced. 'A fire certainly knows how to . . . well, *tries*,' she amended smoothly, 'to wreck a girl's life. It's okay. In fact it's worked out much better. I thought you were in New York.' She switched subjects, not wanting to dwell on something that could still wake her, sweating, at two in the morning. And annoyed with herself for betraying the smallest sign of stress.

'Got back last night. Just bringing my children over to school. How are you managing? I hear you're still doing Nancy's house. Even storming ahead with ideas. Any problems?'

A warning note sounded in her head.

'No problems.' Her voice was easy, confident. 'Not now that I'm living in my old house for the next . . . the foreseeable future. Well, strictly speaking my husband's. That is, my ex-husband's.'

She plunged recklessly on. 'In fact everything there is just great. Better, in fact. Bigger.' She demonstrated with her hands, forgetting her bag was tucked under her arm. It slipped from her grasp. 'More space,' she added, retrieving her bag, attempting to slide it onto her shoulder. She missed. 'I'll probably take my time finding a workroom.'

'Good job your ex didn't need it,' he said, nodding a greeting over her shoulder to someone. 'The house,' he explained as she looked blank.

Rosie swallowed hard. This was going to be tricky. It sounded odd even to her friends.

'Well, he's there too. We live together ... I mean, we share.'

He looked at her carefully. Rosie dug her hands into the pockets of her linen trousers. It was May and very warm. Under her blue linen jacket she was wearing a black silk sleeveless vest. She felt very hot.

'With your ex? How civilised.'

'Yes, isn't it?' she returned defiantly. So stupid. What was it to him? 'He's been ... very ... supportive.'

'And it works?' Joel asked curiously.

It was so easy. Fighting for survival had taught her some hard lessons. Bullshit was one. 'Of course,' she said lightly. 'As you said, it's very civilised. Look, I was just leaving. Client to see. Nancy's fixing a meeting ... look forward to it. Must dash. *Lovely* seeing you.'

Walking up Cork Street in the warm spring evening, hugging her shoulder bag to her chest, she wondered if she really had ducked under his arm like that. And it was rotten luck that James Cooper had chosen that moment to arrive and she had stumbled straight into him and all three had had to retrieve her bag where it had fallen. Damn. Damn. Oh fucking damn.

# *Chapter Sixteen*

Getting the key players to address themselves to the task was always the tough part of any job. David Belmont and Rosie had once decided that all commissions would be completed on time, within budget and with a happy outcome if they could only dispense with the client. The perfect client, they decreed, was one who listened to their advice instead of insisting on making costly mistakes, made themselves available for consultation, and paid up promptly.

Nancy failed the test on every level. Rosie was finding out the hard way why so many designers went into therapy after working for her. If there was a design trap to fall into, Nancy would plunge in headlong.

'I think festoon blinds for the reception room,' she would airily announce. Rosie struggled to disguise her alarm.

'Good idea, Nancy,' she croaked. 'Let me see what I can come up with. Of course, Salina Bhandari has just had hers removed, so there's no worry there about competition.'

She could hear Nancy pause. Knew the expression that would be on her face. She and Salina collided head on courting the rich and powerful to grace their charities. If Salina was removing them, there was no way Nancy was installing them.

Rosie spent time-consuming and unproductive days tactfully redirecting her client's thoughts, knowing that Nancy's input was to demonstrate that she was ahead of the game rather than from any real belief that she knew best.

It was so one-sided. Nancy could reach her any time. But trying to get Nancy to respond to her was a full-time job in itself. Phone calls were ignored. Urgent messages flashed to her round the world occasionally brought a vague answer that she would be onto it soon.

There was nothing Rosie could do but wait. Few people outside the business understood the frustrations of gritted teeth and brave smiles in the face of a client's lack of co-operation. Surprisingly Rory showed real sympathy if no great understanding as she grumbled to him about it one evening.

'Nancy's difficult to tie down. But it doesn't help my image if Joel Harley thinks I can't control the client. And I can't move an inch until she gets his approval on everything.'

'Then make them wait to see you,' he advised. 'Play hard to get.'

Rosie winced, already regretting having been drawn into that small confidence. But Rory had noticed the harassed look when she arrived back and insisted on breaking the rules and pouring her a drink.

'Oh stuff that,' he said easily when she pointed it out to him. 'Even business partners have to be kept happy.'

So she took the drink and found it disturbingly easy to outline the dilemma she found herself in.

'Not a good idea in my world,' she told him, sipping the drink he brought to her. 'Particularly with someone like Joel Harley.'

'No, but a good one for my wife – sorry, ex-wife,' he amended as her eyes widened pointedly at the slip.

Rosie shook her head, beginning to recapture some of the ground she had conceded. 'Difficult to explain. He's so bloody good at what he does I don't blame Nancy wanting his input. He influences everything Nancy sets up . . .'

'But he doesn't influence you?' He was watching her closely. Inexplicably she felt herself blushing.

'God, no.' She hastily took a gulp of her drink. 'No-one

does that. Least of all Nancy's . . .' she stopped. What was he? 'Nancy's confidante,' she finished. 'But I'll just have to wait for him to ring. Such a bloody waste, but there you go. Hey, is that the time?' She got to her feet, draining her glass. 'I've got some work to do. Thanks for the drink.'

At that moment Abbie appeared with a list of messages for Rory, hesitating as she saw them in close conversation. Rosie assured her she was on her way out and left him studying the list, chiding herself that it wasn't just Rory who had broken the rules and she mustn't let it happen again. Or, at any rate, too often.

Rory told her that he was taking Tom to see his father during the Whitsun break.

Rosie felt a pang of misgiving, partly because it was the first time her side of the bargain would really be tested but mostly because she could not recall, as Rory insisted, that he had already mentioned the subject to her.

'Monday,' he reminded her. 'We were in the kitchen. You were on your way out. The day you said Nancy was having a tantrum and you were irritated with that Harley fellow. You said. "Fine. Let me know when." Didn't she, Abbie? So now I'm saying when.'

Abbie shuffled uneasily, clearly not wanting to be dragged into this. Rosie came to her rescue, rattled that Rory had discussed Nancy so openly – and inaccurately – in front of Abbie.

'Don't worry, Abbie, I must be busier than I thought. By the way, do you think you could collect my dry cleaning for me?'

Once she had got Abbie out of the way, she turned firmly to Rory. 'I don't think you could have told me properly. I need to know about your plans for Tom where your father is concerned, that's all.'

There was a momentary flash of the old Rory having his

wishes challenged but, seeing she was serious and unmoved, he instantly relented.

'Sorry, sorry.' He held both hands up in a defensive gesture. 'It's just that we did agree our relationship is with Tom. Not my father. I'm not going to inflict you on each other until you're both ready to meet.'

He moved across the room and gave her shoulder a hug. She didn't move. 'Darling, of *course* he wants to see his grandson. He hasn't seen him in six years. Okay, okay, not your fault. You too, of course. In time. But he's not at all well, and I think it's only fair to do it gradually, don't you?'

Rosie thought it would only be fair if she never had to see Callum at all, as she moved as unobtrusively as she could from Rory's arm. A perverseness had gripped her, a feeling that instead of going forward she was being pushed back into familiar territory.

There was nothing she could do, although she thought Tom's shrieks of joy a bit much. Rory had kept his side of the bargain. Practicalities were easier to observe, she decided. Emotionally it was a wrench. It was, however, part of their agreement.

If it were not for Tom, she was dimly aware that work would easily become her obsession. Between them, Rory and Abbie were effectively removing all the markers that had until now halted her progress. Shopping, cooking, cleaning. All catered for. It was what she had dreamed about. Hadn't she?

During the five days Tom spent in Scotland renewing his relationship with his grandfather, there was nothing to stop Rosie working round the clock and she did. With so little to do in the house she suggested that Abbie took some time off but she chose to remain in London.

'I'm kind of seeing someone,' the housekeeper confessed with an awkwardness that Rosie guessed came from not wanting her privacy invaded by her employers. 'I'll just hang around if that's okay.'

Rosie was relieved to hear it. For a while she had thought that Rory was working his usual charm on Abbie, but thankfully his contact with her clearly stopped at paying her wages. In fact Rosie had begun to suspect that Abbie thought she was above the pair of them, particularly with her meticulous observance of the order of things.

Tradesmen were rerouted to the basement kitchen if they chose the front door and callers were made to wait while Abbie discovered if Rory or Rosie were available. Even if they were in she made it plain to callers that this did not automatically guarantee an audience.

Rosie thought it was over the top. Rory was puzzled that she found it weird.

'Anyway, Rory said you're having some problems at work,' Abbie was saying.

'I think you'll find Rory meant a lot of work rather than problems,' Rosie corrected. 'Finding a workroom is a real bugger.'

'Whatever,' Abbie said in an uninterested voice. 'But at least I can keep the time wasters away.' It was said with a firmness Rosie hadn't noticed before. 'I can never understand how those silly women think you ever get anything done, the way they hang around.'

'It's part of the business,' Rosie told her. 'Sometimes it's useful, mostly I find it a dead bore, but there you go.'

Tom's return the night before he was due back at school was not a success. The only flight Rory said they could get had been well into the evening, which meant he was yawning and in no mood to talk.

'Never mind, darling,' she consoled him – or was it herself? – as she went in to say goodnight. 'We'll talk on the way to school tomorrow. It was a shame you couldn't have got an earlier flight.'

Tom yawned. 'Not Dad's fault. His flight was late.'

Rosie paused as she folded his scattered clothes. 'You mean your flight, don't you?'

'No. Dad's flight with Gordon.' And with that he shut his eyes and was asleep in minutes.

But they didn't talk on the way to school. At least Tom didn't. Her questions started to sound like an inquisition. His answers grew more irritable. Everything was fine. Grandpa was fine. Yes, yes, his room, the food, the scenery were all terrific. No, Grandpa hadn't mentioned her. He didn't know where Dad had gone with Gordon.

Rory laughed at her anxieties.

'I went for a spin in his new plane – you remember the Johnsons? – that's all. Tom misunderstood.'

Apart from Tom needing more discipline than he had clearly been used to, Rory informed her, the visit had gone well. Rory was teaching Tom how to fish and shoot.

Rosie's nerves were getting the better of her.

Gordon Johnson – of course. An old crony of Rory's. Part of the hunting, shooting and fishing crowd – and now apparently flying as well. She backed off and refrained from enquiring if it was perhaps Rory who had misunderstood that he had Tom in his charge and not a fledgling prince of the realm.

Meanwhile, Nancy had phoned, which was something. 'FedEx all the schemes to me,' she instructed. 'I'll talk to Joel myself. No, don't you. He's tricky and if there's anything wrong, I don't want him saying "I told you so".'

What a pair, Rosie thought, irritated that she should be seen as such a weak link in the chain. But at least she was beginning to make progress. If Nancy wanted to deal with the tricky architect, then good luck to her. She would rather not deal with him at all.

To Rosie's amazement and to Livvie's ecstatic delight, within a few days of Rory returning from Scotland they found themselves the occupants of a wonderfully unexpected new workroom.

It coincided with a call from Nancy approving all her ideas, so now it was just a question of what Joel would say. With Nancy's go-ahead, Rosie was determined to recapture the time she'd lost. She had decided that the house was crying out for drama and had suggested that the vast reception hall should have the starring role.

Resiting the staircase was a bold move, but Rosie could see it, rising magnificently from the centre of the lobby to meet the gallery on the first floor.

'Shades of Rhett Butler,' Livvie gasped when she saw the rough sketches. 'It's a stunning idea.' Rosie grinned. She thought so too. She knew it would appeal to Nancy's sense of grandeur. It also meant she could scale down her client's predilection for overdecorating. Keeping the house simple was becoming a battle. Ultimately Nancy would have the final say, but Rosie dreaded having her name associated with a house that made Versailles look restrained.

Her relief was obvious when Rory came up with his idea. Part of his Marlborough Square property included a very small mews house at the back, currently occupied by a young advertising executive in need of the right address rather than space.

Rosie was stunned when Rory made his suggestion. The Mews House had always been rented out. She had only once seen inside it and that was when she was asked years before to deliver the keys to the next occupant when the tenancy switched. Rosie was thrilled at the fortuitous way it had come back into Rory's hands.

He simply shrugged. 'Didn't think that man would last. Said he wants somewhere cheaper, no real money behind him. Why are you looking like that? It's true. And besides, much as I want you to succeed, some of your clients are a pain.'

Bathed in goodwill, Rosie grinned sympathetically, suspecting the real root of his generosity lay in that last remark.

Sylvia Duxborough had decided to call round to inspect personally the paint chart that Rosie was preparing for her. Rosie wasn't fooled. Faced with a title, Sylvia's manner made a nonsense of even Caroline's ruthless social ambitions.

It was sheer bad luck that Rory happened to choose the moment to arrive home. He got the full blast of Sylvia's idea of social intercourse.

'We've never met,' she gushed, sticking out a hand. 'But our sons are at the same school, *such* great friends. I haven't had the pleasure of meeting your father but I *did* once stay at the same hotel although of course we didn't actually *meet* but next time Oscar and I are going through Peebles we plan to stop off now that I've met you, I'll feel *quite* one of the family.'

Rosie gazed at her in awe. Sylvia had been at pains to pile on the glam factor. Expertly made-up, wearing a cream Chanel suit, a quantity of gold bracelets, with Cartier gold plaited earrings, she looked like a kept woman while Rory looked thoroughly overwhelmed. And disdainful.

For once the estranged couple were in full agreement. Abbie, hovering in the hall, also heard it all and muttered that Sylvia sounded orgasmic. That vision, along with Miriam de Lisle looking equally inappropriate for an afternoon visit, several tradesmen at Rory's front door and the tedious noise of Wu Chang's sister-in-law's faxes whirring through the night, clinched it.

Rosie chuckled to herself. She would not, however, accept the Mews House rent free. While she was prepared to live in Rory's house and not have to concern herself about the mortgage since neither did he, renting work space was something else.

She insisted on paying him. A brief argument ensued

which was resolved by a letter from Nick Newall instantly pointing to a contravention of the terms of the agreement.

'This is a *business* arrangement,' she reminded Rory.

'For you, it is,' he said. 'I've never disguised what I think – want – it to be.'

'*Ro-ree*,' she warned.

Within a few days the place was transformed. It had to be. Rosie's new schedule would not allow her to stop work and move, the two had to be done simultaneously. It meant working late into the night, but with Rory around Tom didn't seem to mind not having Rosie's exclusive attention when he got back at the weekend.

'That's okay,' he said, spraying pretend bullets at Rory who was feigning being shot. 'Dad's taking me to The Imaginator – *pow* – Dad, that's not fair. You *can't* get up, I've zapped you twice.' He took off after Rory, who was now absorbed in trying out the latest addition to Tom's computer game on the television.

Rosie gave an exasperated groan, partly irritated at the moronic level at which they conducted their relationship but mostly relieved that Tom was distracted.

'I'll drive you back to school on Sunday,' she called after his retreating back. Tom skidded to a halt in the doorway.

'I'm driving back with Dad. We're giving Felix a lift back. I offered,' he added. For a moment she looked at his flushed face. For Tom, she knew, a small ambition had been achieved.

'Great,' she grinned at him and tried to be sensible about not being needed.

Jaye often said that if Rosie had been around at the time, the roof of the Sistine Chapel could have been knocked off over a weekend. Certainly the former tenant, who arrived back to collect some stray mail a week after he had vacated the Mews House, had difficulty in recognising it.

Livvie was just handing a cup of coffee up to Rosie who

was standing on a ladder, paint pot in hand, wearing an old shirt of Rory's which was now spattered with paint, when the former tenant came in accompanied by a redhead.

'No wonder you fought so hard to get it,' was the girl's opening remark as she gazed around at the freshly painted entrance. Rosie thought she had misheard as the young man tried to hush her. The girl switched her glare from Rosie to him.

'I didn't fight hard for anything,' Rosie began, but the girl cut in, ignoring her boyfriend's sigh.

'No of course you didn't,' she sneered. 'Women like you let the men do it for you. Mustn't get your hands dirty, oh no.'

Rosie gaped at her. She must be mad. Livvie, cup in hand, glanced in amazement from one to the other.

'Look,' Rosie began, coming slowly down the steps, wiping her hands on a rag. 'I haven't got a clue what you're talking about and nor am I interested. If you want your mail, it's on the shelf behind you.'

'C'mon, Trish,' the man urged her. But it was clear his companion wanted to unload the speech she had been nurturing for days.

'We could have gone to court, could have taken you to the cleaners, but Bob is too nice for that. And if it wasn't for your husband's generosity . . .'

'His *what*?' This girl clearly had confused her with someone else.

'You heard. Don't play the innocent . . . in a minute, Bob . . . He said you weren't to be bothered. *Not bothered*. My God, someone who's been a model tenant kicked out and all because the owner's wife insists she wants her toys back.'

'Now *just* a minute,' Livvie intervened firmly, having heard enough, but her voice was drowned by the embarrassed Bob. 'Trish. Stop it. Mr Monteith Gore was very generous.'

'*Generous*? Only when I threatened him with court action. Oh, what's the point,' she finished, having got no response from Rosie. And nor could she. Rosie was paralysed with a mixture of bewilderment and dawning rage at what had gone on.

'Pity the women's movement was lost on you,' was Trish's parting shot. 'Rich man's plaything lives. Your poor husband having to do your dirty work,' and, yanked out of the door by Bob, she left.

# Chapter Seventeen

'Rory, that's not the point. I don't want ... it isn't our agreement. You kicked that poor man out. His girlfriend was livid.'

'His girlfriend is a nonentity,' he replied indifferently, studying his nails.

Rosie gazed helplessly back at him.

'But you said it was all my doing. That simply isn't true. Livvie was listening, it was hideously embarrassing.'

'What difference does it make?' Rory sounded bewildered. 'You needed somewhere. He was prepared to go. I'm only trying to help.'

'But you had to pay him ...'

'So what?'

Rosie paced up and down running her hands distractedly through her hair, an incongruous sight in her paint-spattered shirt and jeans against the calm ordered opulence of Rory's drawing room.

'So ... so ... you can't go round doing things like that,' she exploded. It was like talking to Tom. 'I'll have to pay you back whatever it is you paid him ... or your father ...'

'Who we will leave out of this,' Rory snapped as he pushed himself off the fire surround, closing his eyes in exasperation. 'God, you are a difficult person to help. I've always said that. Look, we have an agreement. We both want the best for Tom. How can that be achieved if you're not able to work? You're the one that's always going on about it.'

'Rory, *I am not*,' she protested, a terrible sense of *déjà vu* descending on her. 'Wanting to be independent isn't the same thing at all. We have a business arrangement.'

'And now it's taken one step forward. For goodness' sake, Rosie, what's the matter with you? My former tenant is happy. I thought it would make you happy. You *were* happy until his ridiculous girlfriend piped up. It's just you bloody women. I have to go. Stay in the Mews House if you want. If not, I'll have no trouble letting it out.'

For a moment she stared at him, baffled. And then he smiled and started to laugh.

'Hopeless, aren't I?' he said. 'I thought you would be pleased with me. Oh c'mon, Rosie, I did it for you. I was just trying to help.'

She relented. 'I know. I'm sure you were. Perhaps I'm just not used to someone . . . well, you know, putting me first. I didn't mean to blow up like that, sorry.'

'That's okay,' he said easily. 'You're easy to put first. I just can't help it. Friends?'

'Mistake, Liv,' she told her briefly when she returned. 'Rory meant well. Anyway, we're staying.'

Livvie nodded. Rosie could see she was relieved. The last few months had stretched Livvie's loyalty. Hearing she was party to an eviction, no matter how innocently, might have snapped it.

Thus it was that Rosie played down the odd values Rory worked by, emphasised his generosity and made a mental note never to let him loose on her behalf again.

'Wish someone would have presented me with a lump sum to move,' she joked. 'Now, c'mon, we have work to do.'

Two wicker chairs with green-and-blue striped cushions, a matching sofa and a glass coffee table with a wide shallow bowl crammed with a myriad of coloured satin ribbons, rosettes and fringes of lace sitting in the middle, now occupied the reception area.

Instead of displaying flowers, spare corners of the room

were draped in fabrics falling carelessly from Victorian jardinieres or out of Victorian trunks. The latest glossy interior magazines from London, New York, Rome and Paris were piled casually across the remaining space.

A narrow winding iron staircase, now painted a gleaming white, led up to a large studio room with three sets of sloping windows along one wall. A skylight stretching across half the ceiling gave the room a wonderfully airy atmosphere.

A smaller room led off it, once the bedroom but now Rosie's office. Livvie's first task was to climb on a chair and unhook the dusty curtains, replacing them with white linen roller blinds, so that light could flood the room and, in her seventh heaven, arranged her worktable where she could see into the cobbled street below.

For the first time Rosie stopped feeling guilty about Bob being asked to go. It really was disgraceful the way he had let the place fall into neglect.

The rather worn sisal carpet was taken up, and the stripped wood of the floor underneath sanded, limed and polished. All of this, plus the assembly of some shelves, was completed over a couple of weekends by a friend of Livvie's who also repainted all the woodwork a pristine white and fixed cork workboards along two walls.

'Brilliant,' enthused Rosie as she and Livvie surveyed Becky's handiwork. 'Does she want any freelance? We could certainly use her.'

Later in the week she found a real treasure in Mrs Milton, who cleaned a couple of other houses in the Mews. Rosie waylaid her and asked if she could fit them as well.

Walking around the corner to work was a pleasure, and having somewhere to be away from the house all day had provided an unexpected relief. It also meant Rosie avoided most of Rory's business contacts. Particularly James. And Abbie clearly felt more relaxed about getting on with things when Rosie wasn't around.

James Cooper had never liked Rosie, based solely on the grounds that she occupied too much of Rory's attention which he needed to boost his multifaceted business interests.

That remained a vague area. While Rory showed every sign of being a man who worked, Rosie was never quite sure what exactly it was that involved lengthy hours out of the house and the occasional weekend away. As far as she knew, the estate management course didn't start until October. James' almost constant presence, the odd snatch of conversation, the messages she heard Abbie relay, seemed to indicate that acting as James' consultant still dominated Rory's life.

The exotic Syra hovered in the background; occasionally Rosie spotted her dropping Rory off or collecting him en route to one of his business appointments. But since Abbie refused even to acknowledge Syra's presence with a disdain that made Rosie laugh, the sightings were few and far between.

Of course she heard gossip about Rory and the way he seemed to surround himself with women who in her view were either bored or brainless but nearly always beautiful. None of this troubled her since, true to his word, Rory kept his social life away from the house.

Sometimes hearing him come in late at night, going to his room along the corridor, she thought wistfully of a life with someone to share her hopes and dreams and much else besides.

Good job you have a massive workload, my girl, she told herself severely. Otherwise the celibate life would not do for you at all.

House parties were big in James' obscure line of work and inevitably Rory would be involved. Rosie's eyebrows soared when she saw a letter confirming reservations for Riannan Castle in Galway for a few weeks hence. Rory playing the Duke again.

Once she would have made a note of the date, questioned it, even attempted to persuade him to let her come too. Now all she wondered was who it was this time. Houston oil barons or Japanese businessman?

Rosie did not go into Rory's study unless she needed to consult him, even though there was no sign of working life in there. In the same way that her bedroom door was kept firmly shut, so was the study's. If all other areas of the house were open access, they respected each other's privacy because that was the deal.

Strangely it was Rosie who broke the deal first. Nancy turned up unexpectedly in London from Paris, saying she wanted Rosie on site to consult while she had the lighting people in and to check a couple of points Joel had raised about the proposal to resite the staircase.

Rosie bit her lip. Not entirely because she felt slighted that Joel Harley could have had the courtesy to call her instead of Nancy, if he had a problem. They were, after all, her plans, even if it was Nancy's house.

Nancy had adored the idea – as Rosie guessed she would – particularly as she had let Nancy believe she herself had inspired the whole concept. But her real dilemma was that it was her turn to collect Tom.

Nancy's erratic timetable had caught Rosie by surprise. As usual the American had just jetted in and demanded that everyone simply dropped what they were doing.

Perhaps Rory could swap with her. He knew how important it was to her to get things moving, and he was sympathetic. Failing to locate him at James' office and the Sloaney receptionist having no idea where he had gone, she went home and hastily scribbled a note asking him to call her at Nancy's when he got in to see if they could swap tasks.

She left it propped up on the kitchen table. And then stopped. Abbie was out all day on some personal business, and Rory might go straight into his study and not see it.

The most sensible thing to do was to leave another note in there.

Rosie crossed to his desk, searching for a blank piece of paper to write a message. Moving a file of papers just fractionally to one side, it fell open. She found herself looking at what appeared to be half a dozen airline tickets.

Fanning them out, she frowned at them. Why would Rory want so many? Sorely tempted to check inside, she was struggling with her need to satisfy her curiosity when the front door slammed. Hastily she grabbed the note and was busily sticking the message on the desk lamp, when he walked in.

He stiffened when he saw Rosie. She knew she was looking guilty. He knew her too well to miss the signs. And yet what was there to feel guilty about?

'Sorry, Rory, I just wanted to leave a note where you could find it,' she explained, noticing that his eyes were flicking around his desk and to the picture on the wall where she knew the safe was located.

'Yes?' He came further into the room, moving towards the desk so that Rosie had to back away from it.

'I wondered if you would get Tom tonight, instead of me? I have a meeting at Nancy's that's suddenly come up.' She could hear herself gabbling.

She noticed he deliberately sat on the edge of the desk blocking her view of its haphazardly spilled contents. Casually he had moved a file across the tickets.

'Yes, of course,' he smiled. 'Anything at all to help. That's what I'm here for.'

'Thanks, I appreciate it. I . . . er . . . must get back. Well, thanks again. And of course if there's anything I can do for you in return?'

He looked thoughtfully at her. 'As a matter of fact,' he said, reaching out to touch her cheek, 'there is.'

Rosie held his gaze, her hands began to feel clammy. She folded her arms protectively across her body.

'What's that?' she asked in a voice that was far from steady.

'Would you drop these off for me at James' office. It's on your way to Nancy's. They've been sent here by mistake.' Rory turned and pulled an envelope from the desk, scribbling James' name and address across it and carelessly slid the airline tickets inside before sealing it. 'You don't mind, do you?'

Rosie felt weak with relief. 'No, of course not,' she managed to get out. 'No trouble.' She really must stop being so suspicious.

Rory didn't appear to be involved in drugs any more. He had insisted that period was over. She tended to believe him. The perennial sniff, followed by clearing his throat, had ceased. But drink he did.

'Went to say goodnight to Tom,' he told her, encountering her outside her room the following Friday night. Tom had stayed over at school for cricket practice. 'Forgot he's not here.'

'What a fright you must have got,' she remarked, the bloodshot eyes and carefully enunciated words not lost on her, 'seeing an empty room. Go to bed, Rory. You've promised to collect Tom in the morning. Will you be okay? You're not making much sense at the moment.'

'You could change all that,' he said softly, moving in front of her, blocking her way.

Rosie took a deep breath. Not afraid. Not surprised. 'I'm so tired I couldn't change a lightbulb,' she told him firmly. 'Let alone sober you up. Now, move, I need my bed.'

She went to move past him, but he moved as well. 'Rory, please.'

'You guys okay?' came Abbie's voice. Rosie turned to see her coming downstairs from the next floor, wearing a dressing gown. 'Heard a noise, sorry I didn't mean to interrupt.'

Rory retreated and leaned against the wall. 'Just exchanging world news,' he told a clearly disbelieving Abbie.

It was no surprise that the following morning there was no sign of him. Rosie went up to his room, ready to drive to the school herself, although knowing how disappointed Tom would be that his father had failed to show.

His room was in semi-darkness, the curtains closely drawn. Clothes everywhere. Some things never changed.

'Rory? Wake up. You'll never get to the school on time,' she warned him from the door. 'You should have left by nine.'

'That's what *you* do,' he yawned. She stood just inside the door, watching him stretch in the bed, making no move to get up.

'I'll get there some time after eleven,' he promised.

'But Tom always . . .'

'Seems to get his own way,' he interrupted, now clearly fully awake. 'It won't harm him to wait.'

Rosie stiffened. 'I'm sorry Rory,' she began carefully. 'But I know Tom. He'll be anxious.'

Rory rolled over in the bed and looked at her through half-closed eyes. Barefoot, in faded jeans and white cotton shirt, her hair still wet from the shower, she waited impatiently for him to say something.

He said nothing. Without warning he pushed the covers back, swung his legs to the floor and stood up, stretching, his tanned, bare limbs still as lean, still as good.

Rosie took a step back. A curious panic gripped her. This was a scene she had lived with for four years. It was a body she knew well, had dreamed about, yearned for, but as she gazed at him, mesmerised, she had the strangest feeling that while she knew the body, she didn't know the man. Not at all.

With a familiar uninhibited ease, knowing she was

watching him – performing for her – he strolled to the window and opened it. Sunlight flooded the room. He yawned and looked back at her over his shoulder, the muscles in his legs cleaving dark shadows along their length.

'Okay, sweetheart,' he drawled lightly. 'You're the boss. I'm on my way. Incidentally,' he mocked gently, his hands resting lightly on hips, watching her through narrowed eyes as she remained where she was. 'Thanks for getting me up. You were always good at it.'

'Dear me, Rory,' she smiled sweetly, letting her gaze travel with an unexpected amusement over his body. Rory suddenly looked less certain of himself. 'And there was me,' she finished, sounding bored, 'thinking all you ever needed was a full-length mirror. Buck up, will you? Tom's waiting.'

# Chapter Eighteen

Nancy's new house now eclipsed everything in Rosie's working life and the necessity for another assistant became urgent.

With only Livvie to help, the newly created aura of success that surrounded her was likely to evaporate if clients had to be kept waiting. Crossing London, keeping and making appointments, pulling together a team now that Nancy had given the go-ahead on the colour schemes at least. Twice she had mentioned her delayed meeting with Joel Harley, only to be told that until both he and Nancy had had time to consider her ideas, it was on hold.

There was no limit to what she could earmark in London showrooms for Nancy's approval, but some things could be picked up in New York. She called a couple of contacts and located some pieces she thought might work and made a note of where to go when she went over.

Rosie's small trusted team of workers had been dramatically expanded, making Livvie ask with awe if Rosie was planning to rebuild Nancy's house rather than simply revitalise it.

Knowing her workmanship would now be on display in one of the most prestigious drawing rooms in London, Joyce was lording it over a small team of outworkers that she had recruited the minute Rosie had told her of the commission.

'Rosie, that's t'riffic, dear,' she'd warbled. But Rosie well knew that while Joyce had of course put up a creditable display of surprise at the news, the power of the grapevine had got there ahead of her. Before even mention of Rosie's commission had been recorded in the *Telegraph*, Joyce had been waiting in daily anticipation of the call.

Colin, Rosie's usual builder, immediately recognised his small workforce would not be able to handle such a massive job, and promptly undertook to find the right craftsmen, taking a cut and keeping some of the smaller building tasks for himself.

Teams of electricians, plumbers, lighting experts and kitchen designers were rounded up while Rosie all but lived at the derelict house, measuring or sketching when polaroids could not grasp the corner or angle she was investigating.

Nancy had undoubtedly been the catalyst for Rosie's sudden elevation to the big time, but now, lying awake at night in her bedroom at the back of Rory's house, or staring out over the darkened garden from the stone balustrade, Rosie dwelt pleasurably on laying the foundations for a business that was on course for continuing success once Nancy's house was finished and had become an established part of her reputation.

Once when Abbie had gone to stay with a friend overnight, Rosie had encountered Syra at an hour when social calls could not really explain her presence in any way that made sense except a night in Rory's bed, but she had simply allowed her gaze to travel over her for a brief second before moving wordlessly past.

It was only when Abbie had included in Rosie's fresh laundry some very brief knickers, little more than a thong, that she took action.

'Not mine,' she said to the housekeeper, who saw her replace them in Rory's laundry.

'Not yours?'

Rosie grinned. ''Fraid Rory must have had one of his aunts to stay,' she said solemnly.

'Aunts?' Abbie looked bewildered. 'What aunt?'

'I'm just going to find out,' she replied.

'But Tom isn't around, he's at school,' Rory defended himself. 'And how do you know Syra was with me? She could have been in the guest room.'

Rosie raised her eyes in exasperation. '*Oh puh-leese.*'

'Okay, okay, don't panic.' He pushed himself upright from where he had been lounging against the doorway. 'Have you told Abbie?' He groaned as she nodded. 'God, she's such a bore about Syra. Okay, no more naughty nights. At least not here. But . . . you know, sweetheart,' he said, strolling over to her and running a finger gently along her jawline. 'There wouldn't be any need for anyone to stay if things were different. I mean, you must get awfully lonely sometimes . . .'

'Not that lonely,' she replied smoothly, pushing his hand away. She heard him laugh as she closed the door firmly behind her, unable to resist a small smile herself, almost colliding with Abbie coming in.

In spite of the odd flirtatious lapse, Rory was keeping his word. Nor did he show any interest in where she went in the evenings. He was pleasant and friendly if Jaye or Kit dropped round for a drink, although Carey was treated with a little more reserve.

Carey went back too far to be fooled easily. He was also glamorous, well known and his long-term relationship with the scholarly Josh unsettled Rory. Yet even Carey had to admit Rory was trying.

But instead of all that reassuring her, Rosie was frankly puzzled. She knew Rory liked the excesses of life in every way. When he drank, he didn't stop until the bottle or the bar was empty. If he smoked it would be a chain reaction. Sex was high on his list and the answer to everything in his view.

Even now, Rosie noticed he could not pass her without absently touching her arm, slipping a hand around her waist, holding her shoulders to move past her, or carefully studying her progress across a room.

Even stranger than the fact that he hadn't made a move was the inexplicable pleasure she got from knowing that her presence in the house clearly unnerved Syra – still being floated as James' property. It was illogical. She never wanted to be that involved with him again. But the feeling that everyone else thought she could if she so chose, did not displease her. And she knew from the way she sometimes caught Rory's eye, that it certainly did not displease him either.

# Chapter Nineteen

Nancy had infuriated Rosie by relaying a message to her
via her PA, Tanya, that Joel Harley had asked to see some
of her previous work before they held their long-overdue
meeting.

'Because?' she queried, knowing her temper was only
just under control.

'Probably wants to see what your style is like,' Tanya
told her. Rosie said she would call her back. She got Joel
Harley on the line just as he was about to start a meeting,
which she later reflected was perhaps not the most favour-
able moment to flex her muscles and too late to recall that
Nancy had expressly forbidden her to deal directly with
him. In a few minutes she knew why.

'I'm extremely busy,' she said firmly. 'And this matter
has taken much too long to resolve. So now if you could
be a little more specific about what you want to see and
indeed why . . .'

'Could we discuss this later?' His tone was pleasant. 'I
have a roomful of people with me.'

But already indignant at being shoved to the end of
everyone's list, being ignored by both Nancy and until now
him, Rosie was no longer in a mood to be reasonable.

' 'Fraid not,' she returned crisply. 'I'm not used to having
my work picked over by anyone other than my client. After
all, I haven't asked to see yours.'

Even as she said it, she realised on a scale of absurdity
this was right up there with asking if Buckingham Palace
was quite large. Possibly someone with no interest in art
or architecture on any level would have no idea who had

designed many of the prominent buildings that dominated the City skyline, but she could not claim that as an excuse.

'Have you ever been responsible for getting such a large staircase shifted?' he asked abruptly.

Honesty compelled her to hesitate, but an evil genius prompted her to say, with a smugness that appalled even her: 'No, but you must remember what Frank Lloyd Wright said. If it goes wrong you can always plant trees. And I know a great gardener.'

Two days later a note arrived from him saying he was prepared to be surprised and looked forward to a meeting with her. He would get his secretary to call her. He added a PS: 'I think you'll find FLW said "vines" not "trees".'

Rosie tore the note up. Finding the right assistant was top of her list of priorities, not scoring points with Nancy's boyfriend. But it was frustrating waiting for him to ring. If it killed her she wasn't going to lift the phone to him ever again.

Jordan Buckhurst sounded like a cowboy but was built and moved like a dancer. If it hadn't been so funny, Rosie told Jaye, she would never have hired him had she known how excited he was to become at the very sight of Rory, even if he was undeniably the most talented designer out of the scores who had applied.

The cleaner, Mrs Milton, simply sniffed and said it wasn't natural but even she unbent when he showed a real interest in her entire family and agreed with her that her daughter-in-law clearly hadn't a clue about how to bring up her grandson.

'Nature's bloody unfair,' grumbled Livvie, observing Jordan's lithe and very watchable body in its skintight black T-shirt, leather trousers moulded to his long, lean legs, pony tail flying, jeté across the workroom floor every time he heard Rory's car in the street below. 'But he needs to learn to overcome his fear of staying with his feelings. There's a lot of free-floating anxiety in him that needs to be dealt with.'

'Yes, okay, Livvie,' Rosie agreed meekly, knowing her assistant too well not to recognise when she had a perfect recruit to her workshop philosophy in her sights.

If Jordan responded with enthusiasm to Livvie's addiction to exploring her reactions to everything from food to fear, it was nothing to the way she absorbed his total, unequivocal belief in astrology.

Snatches of conversation greeted Rosie each day, jostling in an incomprehensible jumble. 'Fear of intimacy ... Uranus rising ... try dumping your aggression ... sensational aspect between Jupiter and Pluto ...'

'We're having a Life Evaluation quickie,' Jordan whispered to Rosie on his third morning, handing her a mug of coffee when she arrived just after nine to find her assistants already huddled in conference.

'I'm really beginning at last to feel comfortable with some of my life decisions,' he said excitedly.

'Really?' Rosie said dryly, not in the least amazed that he was already talking Livvie's language. 'Well, try and feel comfortable with Jane Grantham's blinds instead. I've got to be there in an hour with some ideas.'

'No wonder my Travelling with Crisis meeting was cancelled,' Livvie exclaimed to an amused Rosie. 'I should have guessed.'

'How?' asked Rosie, more concerned with wondering if Nancy would appreciate the charm of a butler's sink in her kitchen than something more hi-tech. After all, she wanted more English than American.

Livvie looked amazed. 'Because Mercury was in retrograde, of course.'

\*    \*    \*

While anything that went out in the name of Rosie Colville carried her distinctive input, Rosie was prepared to encourage Livvie to take on small commissions under her own steam.

A nurturer by nature, she found delegating a reasonably easy task, even if sometimes she had to be tough about her assistants' ideas, sending them back again and again until they got it right. It was, however, what inspired Livvie's loyalty and what Jordan found so attractive.

And it had its compensations. *Rosie Colville Interiors* took on a new lease of life. Jordan lived a peripatetic existence, moving easily and without a backward glance around the capital to be certain he was living in the area that mattered.

Currently he shared a wonderful studio loft in Notting Hill with his friend Bunty, but they lived in daily dread that it might cease to be socially acceptable.

Both were high on the list of social surfers, seen everywhere on double-kissing terms with half of Debrett's. Hostesses across town obligingly turned a blind eye to the fact they were neither personally known to them nor indeed had they been invited at all, and at weekends they adored trawling through the countryside searching out antique markets.

Since Rosie had little time herself, it was a bonus that Jordan was happy to do it and keep her up to date. Both Jordan and Bunty were so delightfully camp they were better than a cabaret, a source of usually intriguing, almost always illicit, alternative amusements.

In turn Jordan adored the houses of the rich and famous and worked the social internet with an energy that made even Livvie blink. He was able to reel off an apparently artless, but faultless, description of the interiors of most of the homes of the good and the great, which was often useful. Rosie decided on the quiet that the newest addition to the business wasn't as scatterbrained as he tried to make out.

He also knew that a new commission by David Belmont was already being lined up to appear in *Special Interiors* and that the designer, he shrieked gleefully upon returning from a lunch with his friend who worked in an exclusive antique shop near Portobello Road, had become so star-struck he had now hired his own PR.

'Can you imagine,' he giggled as Livvie corpsed in the corner. 'Today *Special Interiors*, tomorrow Ten Ways with a Bedhead on "Richard and Judy".'

He had, for reasons that were unclear to Rosie – and she refrained from enquiring – been a guest at Nancy's present house, and knew who Oscar Duxborough was sleeping with, not to mention Conrad de Lisle's latest exploits.

He was deeply impressed when Jaye dropped by to see Rosie and nearly fainted with pleasure at the sight of Carey lounging with his feet on Rosie's desk, being earnestly counselled by Livvie to come to terms with his spiritual ineptness.

Since Jordan also declared James Cooper would be more at home in a trailer park than Belgravia, Rosie congratulated herself on such an excellent choice.

While Jordan didn't have Livvie's eye for detail, the grand plan was where he excelled, the drama of swags and tails, the daring mix of colours. He was constantly in love with highly unsuitable people and worshipped anything and everything Rosie did. When he wasn't, of course, hovering in the hope of catching a glimpse of Rory.

When Rory discovered this he laughed out loud and sometimes quite deliberately waved up at the window when parking his car across the garage of the Mews House. Sometimes Rosie thought Rory made a noise roaring into the cobbled street outside for that very purpose, and hoped the novelty would soon pall.

What didn't amuse her but left her enraged to the point

of murder was when she discovered Rory had told Joel Harley not once but three times that she was too busy to take his calls.

# Chapter Twenty

An impromptu lunch with Carey brought it to light. They met at their favourite French restaurant in Soho. It was cheerful and packed and they only got in because Carey's name pulled a table.

Feeling unsettled at the lack of co-operation she was getting from Nancy and in turn from Joel Harley, disoriented by Rory's protectiveness and frankly irritated by the grandness of Abbie's manners, Rosie needed a friend.

'So how's it all going?' Carey asked, running his eye down the menu. 'Okay, is it?'

'Fine. Too fine sometimes. Rory *is* trying to make it work. He's making mistakes – oh, you know, like the way he got the workroom for me – he meant well. It's . . . it's he just sometimes overdoes it, ordering Abbie not to let me do a thing – and God, Carey, she is *so* grand. No wonder Rory hired her, she practically bows backwards out of the room when he's there.

'There are some good things, of course. Tom adores being with Rory and I get on with my work. So why I'm feeling – dependent – that's the word, I don't know. Maybe it's a reaction from the fire and everything. Just uneasy generally, don't you think that's it?'

Carey nodded soothingly. 'You need a bit of familiarity. Everything's strange. Bit like leaving home – which I suppose is what you've done. Can't you come to supper, catch up on the goss? I've had the most hysterical fax from Jude. Listen to this.'

She was laughing delightedly at Judith's wicked

assessment of New York business life when Carey stopped, raising his eyebrows slightly.

'Excuse me a moment, Rosie,' he murmured, at the same time getting to his feet and extending his hand to someone approaching behind her.

'Good to see you,' he was saying, sounding genuinely pleased. She glanced round straight into the gaze of Joel Harley. The look he gave her was as surprised as hers but it was Carey he addressed, as though she didn't exist.

'I believe you two have met,' Carey began.

Joel Harley was not even smiling. Just nodding.

'Indeed we have,' Rosie replied politely. There was a silence. 'Maybe we can fix that meeting soon?'

'Certainly.' He sounded bored. 'If of course you have time. Your husband said you were very busy.'

'My husband?' she repeated stupidly. But the words died on her lips. He *wouldn't*? Would he?

'Yes, we've called a few times,' Joel was saying with such marked indifference, Rosie briefly closed her eyes in horror. 'So I now think it better if we wait for you to call us.'

'I'm so sorry,' she stumbled. 'I'm afraid there's been a breakdown in communication.'

'Really?' He pointedly turned to Carey. 'Good to see you. I gather we're seeing each other in Prague?'

'Indeed,' Carey replied. 'For a moment there I thought you would turn us down. But we can't do a documentary on Prague without an architect's input.'

Joel smiled at him in the most attractive and friendly way while Rosie sat scarlet-faced, utterly humiliated, trying to pretend the menu was the most riveting document she had ever read.

'You have Nancy to thank for that,' Joel was saying to Carey. 'Like most women she has a habit of getting what she wants. Lucky I happen to be free at the same time. Hope it helps.'

A minute later he moved away to join a smiling redhead waiting at a nearby table, who greeted him with a kiss.

'Don't tell me,' Carey whispered, slipping back into his seat.

Rosie nodded, barely able to speak.

'Rory,' they said together.


'But you were busy,' Rory protested. 'I told him to call back. In fact you're so fucking busy these days, you haven't got time for anyone. And what's dishonest about what I did? Nothing. You told me you were being treated like an employee so I simply upgraded you.'

'But Rory.' She tried again. 'He's business for me. Important business. I spoke to his PA just now and she said they phoned *three times*. *Three times*, Rory. And she said the housekeeper had repeated the message. What *is* Abbie thinking of?'

He had been pacing up and down, furiously dragging on a cigarette. At that he stopped, nearly bent double with laughter.

'I do not believe you.' He spelt it out. 'Give me strength, will you? You said he couldn't blink without permission from Nancy.'

Rosie thought she was in a scene out of *Alice in Wonderland*.

'Yes.' She took a deep breath, speaking carefully. 'That's true, I did. But I didn't mean it like that. Oh, don't you see, of all the people who phoned me last week, he was the most, above all else, without a shadow of doubt, the most important. You may well have lost me Nancy's commission. He is *livid*.'

'Oh, don't exaggerate. What are we talking about here? A fucking architect. Not God. And you said he doesn't mean a thing to you, didn't you?'

It was impossible. Her head slumped into her hand. Rory was around the table in a second, stubbing out his cigarette.

He put an arm around her and squatted down in front of her.

Rosie looked up, startled. He seemed genuinely dismayed.

'Oh God, Rosie. I'm sorry. I honestly didn't mean it. I really thought I was helping you. You looked so fed up and I was livid that you were being treated that way.' He shook his head with a groan. 'Let me call him.'

Rosie leapt to her feet, throwing a warning hand out in front of her. 'No. Definitely not. I'll call Nancy. I'll try and explain. Just promise me. You won't ever do it again.'

His face looked just like Tom's, anxious and sorry. Was he acting?

'Promise?'

Later a huge bouquet of roses was delivered to the Mews House. The card just said: 'Promise. R.'

Rosie groaned and dropped her head onto her desk in despair. Livvie and Jordan glanced uneasily at each other.

'Liv.' Rosie looked up. 'Get me Nancy Alexander on the phone, will you? And don't be surprised if she hangs up.'

Nancy's secretary, Tanya, phoned next day. She asked Rosie if she could keep three days free the following week. Nancy had pencilled her in and would see her at some point during that time. She had also arranged for her to see Joel Harley the next morning.

'He's leaving for Prague tomorrow night,' said Tanya. 'This is the last chance you'll get.'

'Leave it to me,' Rosie assured her. 'I'll be there. Now, which days and what time?'

'Well, the whole week is tight. It might mean snatching an hour or two here and there, but Nancy will make sure you leave with all decisions made. You don't mind including the weekend, do you?'

'No problem,' Rosie said. Rory, so eager to make amends, could be around. Abbie never seemed to mind her schedule being renegotiated at short notice. Rosie was simply rather awed at the energy Nancy possessed to be in Prague attending the Alexander lecture in the same week that she had to be in London overseeing alterations.

'So shall I go to Holland Park or would Nancy prefer to meet at the new house?' She flicked the pages of her diary to the following week.

'Holland Park?' Tanya sounded surprised. 'I'm sorry, didn't Nancy explain? No? She'll be in Prague for the Alexander lecture. I've booked you on the early morning flight on Friday. Is that okay?'

It was far from okay. Hanging around for three days for a meeting that shouldn't take more than a couple of hours, and she was already behind schedule.

Tanya rang back. Nancy had insisted. Rosie bit her lip and looked down at her diary. It looked horrendous. Nancy might be her most important client, but she was not her only one. She tried again. This time Nancy's message was that she would see her immediately after lunch on Friday. There was nothing for it. She would have to leave on the early morning flight on Friday and come back on Saturday.

Later that evening, she had dinner alone with Kit.

'It's more I'm *nervous*,' she told him when he came to pick her up.

He watched while she pulled together a colour chart for the library at Nancy's house. Greens, blues, maybe yellow . . . no, not yellow. Too insipid for someone as strong as Nancy and just about the hardest colour to get right. Memories of exhaustive repaints trying to stop a delicate primrose turning into egg yolk or a deep ochre ending up brown banished yellow to the bottom of the list.

'It was such a big thing to do – not wrong,' she amended hastily as Kit's expression started to display 'I told you so'. 'But it's all happened so fast, don't you think?'

'Maybe,' was his cautious reply. 'All ready for Joel Harley and Prague?'

She gave him a weak grin. Kit had heard the saga.

'Ask him if he wants his photograph taken.'

'I'm not soliciting for you,' she retorted, searching around her cluttered desk for the swatches of fabric she had picked up from Mary Fox Linton. She held them out for his inspection.

'What do you think?'

'I think I could do a great job on him. Surely the board of his company would fork out for something suitably fitting for the man whose name is stamped on the skyline of a dozen capital cities around the world.'

'I meant, what do you think of these swatches? And get real, will you,' she added as Kit kissed his fingers in appreciation of the fabric she was holding up. 'Anyway he doesn't have a board, there's just him. Nancy told me. Well, him and a friend who goes back to their days at the Architectural Association, more a financial partner than anything. Daniel something or other . . .'

'What I could do with that nose, definitely neo-classical, and those eyes above the high cliffs of those cheekbones, intense – what you might call post-modernist. Yes,' he rhapsodised, ignoring her. 'Almost certainly post. Those clean angles, faultless sweeping curves . . .'

'Listen, my fine friend,' Rosie cut in, bringing him down to earth. 'I'll probably only get an hour of his time and that's quite something, I can tell you. If you think I'm going to waste any of that getting work for you . . . anyway, what's so special about him? And get off that fabric, will you?'

'He offers them monuments to their power and wealth,' Kit was saying, shifting his weight to a pile of catalogues Rosie had stacked on a chair.

'Does he?' She looked startled.

Kit sighed impatiently. 'Of course. That's what's special

about him. He's got a stream of clients because he gives them a chance to write their names in the sky for everyone to see and wonder at. He plays games with light and space and structure that mock the rules of gravity.'

'You seem to know an awful lot about him,' Rosie remarked, well used to Kit's flights of poetic fantasy.

'I read as well as paint,' he replied loftily. 'I subscribe to *Architectural Digest*. But I like what he does. The Chan Centre in Hong Kong, the Alexander Museum in Detroit. There's a recklessness about him that is attractive . . .'

Rosie closed her eyes in horror. 'Oh God, how *do* I find them? Surely not another reckless man in my life. He isn't like that.'

'What, not neo-classical?'

'Nope.'

'Not even post-modernist?'

'Nope.' She wrinkled her nose, starting to put her work aside. She tried to summon up Joel's face. The bored expression at Nancy's party, the laughing affection with his daughter, the smiling concern at the gallery, cold indifference when she met him with Carey. But a sense of humour too. The note about Frank Lloyd Wright proved that. And Nancy hung onto his every word.

'More complex than that.'

Kit looked astounded. 'How can you get more complex than that?'

'Don't know,' she said absently. 'He seems tough to me. Changeable. Difficult. At least,' she paused and looked thoughtfully out of the window, 'at least I think he is.'

'Ms Colville. You have no soul,' declared Kit, rising with hurt dignity from his chair, wanting to eat. 'Just don't go into overdrive. You're not being asked to live with him. Only work with him. Where are you seeing him?'

'At his office,' she grimaced.

Kit laughed. 'Well, don't look so pained. It's only a discussion, you're not on trial. You haven't got to prove a thing to him. Now what have I said?'

# Chapter Twenty-One

The building in which Joel Harley worked when he was in London was near Chelsea Harbour. It was also where he lived.

As Nancy had once pointed out in surprise when Rosie remarked she thought he had addresses in several cities around the world:

'He has an apartment in New York. But then why should Joel travel when his reputation does that for him?'

Why indeed?

Rosie parked her car and walked in the early morning sunshine through a wide cobbled passage that led down to the embankment. Harley Associates was at the end facing out over the river.

She was early, but she had resolved to reverse the impression Joel Harley had of her: that she was not only incapable of producing two consecutive sentences but she had allowed her ex-husband to decide whether she was too busy to see someone.

Rory's interference still made her cringe. Abbie had taken the mild ticking-off rather better but had apologised with a curtness that rendered it rather pointless.

Abbie, she decided, was definitely a Rory employee. She could tell that Abbie believed it was Rory alone who paid her wages and therefore only Rory had the right to complain. Rosie didn't bother to tell her that she religiously contributed half her wages in the cheque she sent each month to Rory's bank covering her part of the deal.

Rory, coming in as she was hurriedly leaving the house, raised an appreciative eyebrow as she whizzed past in cream linen trousers and a dark blue short-sleeved silk shirt.

'Someone special?' he enquired.

'Is that a question or a statement?'

He threw up his hands. 'Just showing a friendly interest. I promise not to act on it.'

Rosie paused on the steps. 'Sorry,' she said more gently. 'Water under the bridge now. It's a . . .' she stopped. Joel wasn't a client, but he could hardly be called a colleague either. 'It's Joel Harley.'

His eyes narrowed. 'I was going to say good luck, but you won't need luck looking like that.'

On the roof of the narrow mellow brick building that was the London headquarters to Joel Harley Associates was the penthouse he called home when he was in town.

Flanked by a deep wide terrace the length of the entire building, it looked out over an expanse of the Thames. Beneath it in the basement was a swimming pool and in between a set of studios and offices, his own kitchens and dining rooms that were used exclusively by the surprisingly small nucleus of staff that he kept around him and of course for entertaining clients.

The steel-and-glass front doors were operated by a security system that was activated from within as Rosie announced her arrival. A pleasant voice asked her to take the lift up to the second floor where she was met by a tall young woman with bronzed, cropped hair, and bare tanned legs, wearing a straight black skirt and a plain white T-shirt, with both arms jangling with silver bangles. Joel certainly had glamorous staff. Her eyes were ringed in kohl and a lipliner had reinvented her mouth into a generous smile.

'Hi. I'm Virginia Willoughby – Ginny. I'm a junior architect. I've been looking forward to meeting you.' As she spoke she ushered Rosie into a small studio the size of

186

which didn't matter since it had views to take her breath away. Sliding doors led to a small terrace on which she could see a couple of director's chairs and a small table.

'Is this Mr Harley's office?'

'No. His is upstairs. This is mine.'

They shook hands, Ginny indicated a seat for Rosie. 'Joel has asked me to work on his plans for Nancy Alexander's house with you.'

'*You?* But I thought . . . Nancy thinks Joel himself is handling this.'

Ginny, pulling a large folder tied with black ribbon towards her, hesitated, looked apprehensive. 'Well, he's done the design, I've just got to see it through.'

This meeting was important to Rosie. Designed to reverse the very odd impression he'd got of her so far. He'd never wanted her to do this job. Too inexperienced is what Nancy had said. Now he hadn't planned to be there at all, handing her over to a junior member of his staff.

Clearly the moment had come to demonstrate just how big she was even if her company wasn't. Her voice was firm but calm: 'I think there has been a misunderstanding. My instructions are that Nancy has asked Joel to be instrumental in the design of her house.

'If that has altered, perhaps someone should have told me. Otherwise I'm afraid I must insist, in my client's interests, that the architect she appointed attends this meeting.'

In truth she had never heard such claptrap. But it sounded good. It made her feel good. And by the time she had turned the sentence over in her mind, it had begun to sound like a legal requirement.

Years of being brushed aside, or treated as though she was working on half a brain, being a single working mother, came flooding back. Rosie was angry. Very angry.

Pointedly she looked at her watch. 'Perhaps you could find out why I wasn't told,' she said coldly.

Two minutes passed. She was now positive she'd blown

it. He'd refused to see her. Rosie discarded the magazine which had not interested her in the first place and which turned out to be *Engineering News*. What a performance. Now see what you've done?

Wandering over to the window, the vagaries of the Thames skyline were lost on her. Ginny returned, breathless. Clearly she had been running.

'I'm sorry, I must have made a mistake. He'll be here when he's finished his phone call. Let me get you a drink while we're waiting. The terrace . . . that's it. The terrace is very pleasant.'

Hiding her relief was not easy. But as she briskly gathered up her bag and notepad, Rosie wasn't at all sure the feeling wasn't also one of amazement.

Following Ginny outside, she was glad she had dark glasses with her. Her mouth felt dry. Her hand was shaking.

The bullshit factor worked. It actually worked. A more honest voice told her that was nonsense. Fear as usual had worked wonders. Fear that she might slip back, be pushed down the ladder.

Someone from the dining room on the next floor appeared with a tray of iced drinks. Rosie asked for mineral water. She took a sip, admired the view, felt calmer and grateful for the respite before the meeting started.

Out of sheer politeness she asked Ginny if she was particularly busy. She began to wish she hadn't. At every turn Ginny referred to Joel in a voice that suggested he was a deity on earth. Or at least with regard to buildings.

'He has this kind of artistic impudence,' she said eagerly as Rosie tried hard to keep a straight face.

*Impudence?* Oh, for heaven's sake.

'Amazing,' Rosie agreed solemnly. 'I gather stars in the architectural world are as rare as great tenors.' Really, Ginny was very intense.

It worked. Ginny blushed and grinned. 'Sorry, it's just

that most of us only scrape by. I mean, if Joel hadn't taken me and a couple of others on, I doubt I'd ever have got past designing extensions for semi-detacheds. Joel's one of the few who have really made it big. That's why it's so great working for him, he's got such vision.'

'Useful when you're an architect,' Rosie pointed out.

'Oh, of course, but so many of them haven't. You see,' Ginny glanced back through the open doors to make sure Joel was not in the vicinity. Then dropping her voice to almost a whisper, she earnestly explained her theory.

'I think he's got a natural feeling for the hardware of modern buildings, an almost,' Ginny paused, clearly finding the existing English language not nearly extensive enough to do justice to her boss' genius, 'an almost *feline* sensitivity for the texture and strength of brick, steel, stone, even concrete.'

Rosie's shoulders shook. This was too much. She threw back her head and laughed delightedly. 'That's the last word I'd use to describe him.'

'So what would you use?' came a voice from behind her.

'Late?' she suggested, as Joel emerged onto the terrace. She knew it was churlish but he simply apologised, handing some files to Ginny, who hurriedly disappeared.

Joel took the opposite chair to Rosie, sliding on dark glasses as he sank down. He was wearing a grey cotton crew-neck sweater and his hair looked as though he had dragged his fingers through it and back off his face.

More a case of a strong presence, Rosie decided, than drop dead good looks. But there was something. Her memory of him at Nancy's party was blurred since she had been so preoccupied. At the gallery she had had an impression of glamour, but she could see now that this wasn't correct.

His face had an unexpected strength which robbed him of glamour, but gave him a sense of power which Rosie thought much more potent.

Rory was glamorous. Breathed it, exuded it, lived it. Joel Harley was careless about his appearance. Rory was fastidious to the point where Rosie had once asked if he would like his socks ironed and had laughed when Rory had considered his answer.

'I hope Ginny has been looking after you,' Joel began politely.

She nodded. 'Beautifully. Ginny is very committed to . . .' she nearly said, to you, but changed it to: 'Her job. Ginny sees architecture very much as an art form.'

There was a silence. Joel Harley did not seem to think he had to exert himself with small talk. She cleared her throat.

'I thought architecture was the meeting of art and science – the science bit being ever so slightly necessary as well,' Rosie struggled on into the silence. If he was going to answer she never knew, Ginny reappeared and did it for him.

'Oh, it is. It's just that you know how architecture arouses such fierce hatreds in people. Everyone's got a "view" which can throw less experienced designers.

'Architecture these days is condemned before it gets off the ground. Either the design is damned as being too modern, or passé, and if it's acclaimed someone's bound to pop their head over the parapet and say, "but it's useless". Oh sorry, forgotten a file. Just a second.'

She disappeared in a rush. Without looking at her, Joel murmured: 'Good God, why didn't anyone tell me I had a choice? I didn't realise I could spend all that time on making something both ugly *and* useless? I thought it had to be one or the other.'

It was a good moment. He seemed more relaxed.

'Look, I just want to say I'm so sorry about the confusion over the telephone calls.'

'Nancy explained,' he said curtly, the humour vanishing.

'What did she explain?'

'That your husband was merely being protective ...'

'No, you're wrong. He made a mistake, that's all. He misunderstood what I had said. What I wanted.'

'Really does it matter, now?' He had started to sound bored again.

Rosie gave up. This was deeply unfair.

'Clearly you're *much* better with buildings than people,' she remarked. 'Most architects are. You can see it in the way they design them, usually impossible for people to use.'

Ginny, returning with her lost file, looked horrified. 'Oh no, not Joel. He believes in people-friendly buildings, don't you? Not just monuments to some corporation's ego.'

'Well, that is good news,' Rosie beamed. 'Now,' her voice moved from amusement to briskness, as Joel Harley continued to stare out over the river. 'Shall we get on? It would never do for you to miss your plane and upset Nancy.'

'Upset Nancy?' He turned his head sharply to look at her.

'Mmm,' she smiled brightly, pulling the sheets of designs towards her. She blinked. They were excellent. Brilliant in fact.

The disputed staircase instead of rising in one stage as she had wanted, now divided halfway up into two arcs sweeping up each side to join the gallery above. The proportions were perfect, because now the staircase started deeper into the entrance hall, making the whole area more spacious and impressive.

Rosie swallowed hard. 'Yes.' She reached for her pen, slowly unscrewing the top without taking her eyes off the designs in front of her. 'Yes, I'm sure we can do something with these.'

'Thank you,' she heard him say through what she sincerely hoped was clenched teeth. Ginny audibly gasped.

# Chapter Twenty-Two

Only Tom could get her attention in the frantic days before she left for Prague. And the odd thing was that Tom was the one person who now didn't seem to need it.

Thank God she had had the sense to come to that deal with Rory. She would never have managed this commission and kept Tom happy. And her satisfaction showed. Everyone from lighting specialists to gardeners responded to her laidback charm. The completion of Nancy's house now became her waking obsession.

The plans she had agreed with Joel, the final drawings, were all carefully packaged to take to Prague for Nancy's approval.

'Certainly extravagant, that woman,' Jaye remarked, helping herself to a glass of wine, her feet propped comfortably on Rosie's worktable. 'What's so desperate that she can't wait a few days to get back here?'

Rosie paused. 'She's going to New York straight from Prague. But also because getting on and off planes is like taking taxi rides to her.'

'Does it suit you, that's what I'm interested in?' Jaye persisted, not at all liking the way Nancy snapped her fingers and everyone came running, particularly as she was having a dinner party on Saturday night and had lined up a man she was convinced Rosie would adore.

'No it doesn't, as it happens,' Rosie confessed. 'I could use the time here, and I'm sorry about the dinner – can't risk it though, might not get a flight until Saturday night. But I'll only be gone for two nights at the most. It isn't all bad. Carey will be there and he's included me in the TVN group going to the gala opera. And besides, I mustn't lose sight of the fact that this commission has really turned my career around.'

'Thought you had allocated that honour to Rory ... sorry, sorry. Just a joke. Oh well, Dominic will get snapped up by someone else, you'll die an old maid and I hope you'll be very happy.'

She left Jordan and Livvie to cope with routine commissions and immersed herself in getting as much under-way as she could at Nancy's house since so much time had already been lost. A fact that hadn't escaped Nancy's attention. While it mattered nothing to the millionairess who she kept waiting, her objections to those who held her up were ill-disguised. Her tone became more abrupt.

Rosie tried to comfort herself that she was just inheriting the mantle worn by so many of her predecessors.

But Jordan was different. In Rosie he saw the embodiment of what a designer and a boss should be: breaching traditional ideas at a pace to satisfy her growing clientele who wanted to be ahead of the game and confident enough as a boss to give both Livvie and him their head. Jordan was perfectly satisfied that his future lay with Rosie.

Each day, after the ritual exchange of identifying life-enrichment opportunities with Livvie, he had taken to studying Rosie's horoscope, on the alert for any unwelcome planetary collisions that might alter this happy state of affairs.

'You must be careful. It says here,' he told her, reading from the newspaper as she left clutching folders with Joel's plans inside to give to the foreman of the builders, 'the solar eclipse this weekend heralds the end of an era in your life. Neptune changes direction on Monday and Mercury – oh my God, listen to this – is at odds with Mars.' He lowered the paper, a look of horror on his face.

'What's wrong with that?' Rosie asked. Livvie was

already reaching for the book of logarithms Jordan had given her now that she was into astrology, to check the planetary aspect that was causing him such grief. Jordan's hand was clapped across his mouth.

'I bet Nancy will change her mind about all our ideas.'

'Oh, don't say that,' Rosie pleaded, amused by him. 'Anyway, Nancy's in Prague and has approved the building plans.'

Jordan stared at her, wide-eyed. 'But she isn't,' he said, surprised. 'Didn't Rory mention it? She's here. I saw her last night. By accident. Rory was there too . . . I expect he forgot,' he trailed off, catching a warning look from Livvie which was not lost on Rosie, who now gave him her full attention.

'No, he didn't mention it. But then I haven't had a chance to talk to him.'

This wasn't true. She had seen Rory at breakfast and they had chatted for at least ten minutes but no, he hadn't said a thing about it. Jordan looked relieved.

'Oh good, I thought I had dropped a teensy bit of a brickette,' he laughed. 'We all collided at the opening of that new French restaurant. Nancy was there and I just couldn't resist saying hi . . .'

Rosie waited, not wanting to appear too interested. An irrational feeling of unease was creeping into her mouth. Jordan took a gulp of coffee.

'Anyway, Rory – he is so protective of you, isn't he? – he said how pleased he was that Joel had finally seen sense and acknowledged you were the right person for the job. Frankly I didn't know he'd even said it, but Nancy . . .'

'Thanks, Jordan,' she interrupted, faint with horror. 'I get the picture. Joel hasn't got misgivings over me doing the house, just a difference of opinion of how it should be done. Must dash. I'll check in later. You know where to find me.'

*　　*　　*

'All I said was that you had changed your opinion of him and he really *liked* what you were doing and that he was never off the phone. Now what on earth can be wrong with that?'

'Nothing. I just wish you hadn't said anything at all. I have no idea if he thinks that.'

Rory drained his glass and poured himself another shot of whisky indicating the decanter to see if Rosie wanted to join him. She shook her head.

'I thought it was what you'd like to be said. Everyone knows Nancy won't have anything to do with anyone he dislikes, not to mention that she's trying to hook him . . .'

'Is she?' Rosie asked politely.

Rory swung round in astonishment. 'Good God, sweetheart. I hardly know the woman but even I know that. Where do you hide yourself?'

'So how does that affect me?'

Rory answered her with painstaking patience. 'Because if she thinks he doesn't approve of you, she'd rather ditch you than him.' He looked at her over his glass and then smiled broadly at her, his head on one side. 'Hell's teeth, ducky. Take it from me, I know women. Oh c'mon – at least admit that.'

Rosie gave up. It sounded petty to find any more fault with what he had done. He meant so well. 'Okay. But tell me first next time. And I'll pass on the last question.'

For a moment she saw a flicker of anger in his eyes. She raised her brows. He switched to a smile.

'Oh, bugger off, my treasure.' He made it sound like a caress. 'Enjoy the trip.'

She gave him an airy wave as she left. She felt ridiculously lightheaded and put it down to seeing Prague again.

# Chapter Twenty-Three

Rosie gazed out from her room on the sixteenth floor of the hotel in Vysehrad. Ahead of her a host of Baroque and Gothic roofs spread across the skyline in a tangle of shapes and colours.

Green and silver domes, important-looking towers all jostled haughtily into an azure sky. A glimpse of the Vltava through a gap in the buildings, sparkling in the evening sunlight, a faint shimmering haze of heat hanging over the city, added to the mesmerising charm of Prague.

Tomorrow night at the castle on the hill, next to the Cathedral, Joel Harley would be delivering the Alexander Lecture before an international and specially invited audience.

Rosie turned away, her face registering her annoyance. All day she had waited for Nancy to find time for a meeting, chivvying the harassed Tanya to pin Nancy down to something. Since ten when she had arrived on the first flight out from London, she had been reluctant to stray too far from her room in case Nancy should call.

But it was now nearly five. Impossible to think after a day organising the details surrounding the big event in the Alexander Foundation calendar, Nancy would be in the mood for a meeting with her interior designer. Rosie bit her lip and resolutely made one last attempt.

'It's not your fault,' she agreed with Tanya. 'But this is such a waste of time. I could have flown over tomorrow morning.'

Tanya sounded anguished. 'I know, I know. But Nancy and Joel have had to do a lot of entertaining today ...

drinks, lunch, honestly, Rosie, it's been impossible. No, they won't be around now. God, I'm really sorry, but they've gone off somewhere – it's the opera tonight and they . . . I mean, they had some personal stuff to attend to.'

Rosie was furious. So much time wasted. So much to do. Other clients postponed. Jordan's contact, who'd wanted to meet her on Friday night to talk about a small block of flats his company had purchased, had flown back to Madrid, disappointed and possibly with the intention of commissioning someone else.

Who the hell did Nancy think she was? Back in London Colin the builder would be liaising with Jordan, pushing through planning permission on the alterations needed which, except for the staircase, seemed to be well within the guidelines and unlikely to prove a problem. Even so, she was fretting at not being around.

A drink, that's what she needed. She tried ringing home just once more before she went in search of a pavement café. A few minutes later she replaced the phone, puzzled that Rory was not around with Tom. No Abbie either. Maybe they'd gone out to eat, she decided, leaving her third slightly less jokey message on the machine that she would ring when she got back.

Outside, she crossed over to the metro, the blast of heat after the air-conditioning of the hotel taking her by surprise, and took the first train to Muzeum, emerging into Wenceslas Square ten minutes later.

The square was thronging with backpackers, sidewalk cafés were filling up with footweary tourists eagerly seeking relief from the sun under striped awnings and inside cool bars.

Neatly dressed Czech students pressed endless flyers into her hands as she strode along, publicising everything from Chopin to piano recitals at the Castle to five versions of the Ave Maria being performed in the Klementinum.

'Don Giovanni' at the Marionette Theatre on Zatecka vied with 'The Bartered Bride' at the State Opera House. Even sex clubs openly touted for business in the bustling square which after dark would be crawling with hookers, resisting all attempts by Prague City Hall to remove them to a more discreet location.

Rosie made her way through a maze of backstreets towards the Charles Bridge passing quartets, solo violinists, blues singers, guitarists on every corner. The air was filled with Vivaldi, Bach and Bob Dylan. Rosie's spirits began to lift. The memory of her last two trips here to shoot fashion with Piers was pleasant rather than painful. She grinned to herself. She was winning.

So what if Joel Harley and Nancy Alexander rated her needs as somewhere due south of their own, she thought as she abandoned the idea of a drink in favour of a stroll across the bridge. The sun was shining, she was in a beautiful city and in a couple of hours she was going to be Carey's guest at the opera.

Artists and craftsmen selling their wares packed either side of the medieval bridge, jugglers, musicians competed for space, while a small army of Hare Krishna singers, banging tambourines, chanting their mantras, jogged across the bridge in perfect unison to their rhythmic beat and were swallowed up in the crowd.

She was smiling at the sight, pausing to peer over the parapet, when she froze. Ahead of her, hands dug into his pockets, sunglasses pushed back into his hair, Joel Harley was standing with Nancy, their heads close together studying a display of wooden framed prints.

The sight of them irritated Rosie so much she had to turn her face away in case she exploded. Sightseeing, casually strolling around the city when she had work that must be done, left cooling her heels in a boring bloody hotel all day.

Hurriedly she stepped behind one of the stalls and waited

until they had moved on. Rosie felt dangerous. After a few minutes she peered round to see where they were, but they were no longer in sight.

In no further mood for sightseeing, she strode quickly through the crowds to make her way back to the hotel to book herself on the first flight home in the morning.

Too late, she saw him sitting alone at a sidewalk café, reading a paper, a waiter about to deposit a cup of coffee in front of him. No sign of Nancy. He saw her almost immediately and lowered his paper.

'Nice to see you,' he began as she drew level with every intention of giving him a curt nod before walking straight on. 'Won't you join me?'

Rosie shook her head. 'I have a lot to do back at the hotel.'

'Of course,' he said. 'Where have you been hiding yourself?'

'Hiding myself?' she snapped. 'I'm hardly hiding in the middle of Prague in a public square. I think the word you're looking for is waiting. Waiting for a meeting with Nancy which doesn't seem to be important to anyone but me.'

He was surprised: 'I would have thought you'd be pleased having so much time off . . .'

Rosie's eyes flashed. 'Time off? *Time off?* Nancy has bought my ticket, not my time. It might be news to you but I haven't dragged all the way over to Prague for fun. I never wanted to come here. Nancy insisted. I could have used the time more profitably at home, not to mention seeing my son, instead of waiting on a couple of spoilt brats . . .'

She stopped, appalled at herself. It was hot. She was tired.

'I'm sorry,' she added lamely. 'I shouldn't have said that. What you and Nancy do is none of my business.'

'No, it isn't, is it?' he said. He looked up at her where

she was standing, face flushed, her hair shoved behind her ears, uneasily trying to find a reasonable exit line.

'But spoilt brat, eh? Now I wonder why?' he mused.

'Because people like you and Nancy have no regard for other people's schedules. You both have people running around you to do whatever you want and you lose sight of anything that doesn't directly affect you. Look, I'm sorry, it's hot. If I hadn't had such a wasted day, I would never have said all that. Good luck with the lecture.'

She left him staring after her. Annoyed with herself for losing her temper, but glad she had. Uneasily aware that he would probably tell Nancy she was unstable, but in no mood to care if he did.

Turning back into her room, she decided to give Rory one more try before calling Livvie and asking her if she would check the house. And where was Abbie?

Still no answer. Livvie called her back within half an hour, saying there was no-one around.

'I checked everything, but it was all locked up. I banged like mad in case Abbie was asleep, but I think they must all be out for the evening, or away. There's some milk on the doorstep so I've taken that back here.'

Was she going mad? Had she forgotten something Rory had told her? Had there been an accident? She rang the school. It was ages before they managed to track down the matron who came on and said Mrs Duxborough had collected Tom as arranged.

'*Mrs Duxborough?* Arranged with who?'

'Well, Mr Monteith Gore, of course. He explained you were away for the weekend and Tom would prefer to stay in London rather than go with him on his business trip.'

Business trip? What business trip?

Sylvia's housekeeper said the boys were out with Nanny and wouldn't be back until nine. Mrs Duxborough was with her aromatherapist and couldn't be disturbed.

Rosie drew a deep breath. 'Would you say I called. I have to go to the opera this evening so I'll call again in the morning. And . . . and give my love to Tom, please.'

Bloody Rory. He'd never mentioned a business trip to her. She stopped. Riannon castle. Of course, it was this weekend. Why didn't he just say?

Bloody Sylvia, Joel, Nancy. All cosying up to each other and not a single thought about her. With a grim satisfaction that she had the power to dump them all, Rosie called the airline and was put on standby for an early morning flight. She called Tanya and told her to let Nancy know her plans. Then she caught sight of herself in the mirror on the far wall and groaned.

The sun had caught her cheeks and the tip of her nose was certainly pink, her hair was standing on end and her clothes were suffering from heat fatigue.

Fortunately the mini bar wasn't. Armed with an ice-cold glass of wine, she stepped out onto the small terrace that led off her room, eased her white canvas sneakers off, dropped with relief into an easy chair, swung bare legs onto the low table in front of her and gave the day up as a lost cause. She might have lost the job but she had struck a blow for her self esteem. She was asleep in minutes.

The opera house was a blaze of lights. Ornately gilded boxes climbed in dazzling tiers above the auditorium, each packed to capacity for the gala performance of 'The Magic Flute'.

An audience to rival a film premiere, more concerned with inspecting each other than what was about to unfold on stage, milled around, a sparkling mix of politicians, actors, directors and local dignitaries.

TVN's group were relaxed, friendly and enormous fun, even after a day filming evidence of the political and social changes that had transformed Prague since the velvet revolution. Before then, events like the Alexander Lecture would never have been mounted. An interview with an internationally renowned architect already in Prague was welcomed by the TVN crew, who couldn't believe their luck at getting someone so eminently qualified to add authority to their programme without having to pay for him to fly in. In sweltering temperatures in the city they were ready to enjoy themselves, helped by copious draughts of champagne. They made a cheery group, dressed in exaggerated glamour, each outfit being loudly awarded points by the others.

Rosie's loosely flowing black silk trousers, with a long white chiffon scarf wound loosely around her neck, were much admired, but it was the white-and-black satin basque which did wonders for her slender shoulders and cleavage that produced the appreciative cheers and whistles when she arrived to meet Carey, whirling theatrically around to another delighted cheer.

Not to mention long, dangling silver earrings which on close inspection spelt Mozart, bought that afternoon in a local craft shop.

A polite ripple of applause alerted them to the arrival in the State box of the Minister for Arts along with the English Duke and Duchess who had flown over to listen to the lecture.

Rosie noticed that Joel was next to the Duchess on one side with the ambassador's wife on the other. Nancy was departing very slightly from her habitual black by wearing a crepe dress with stitched jet beading, the lights reflecting in flashes as she moved. She was reacting in a very animated way to the Duke.

From her box on the opposite side of the theatre, sandwiched comfortably between Carey and David Mesinski, his producer, she watched events in the main box with interest.

Overdressed, formal, strangers brought together for an evening for the sake of diplomacy and whatever their invested interests were in the Alexander lecture. Joel was stuck with people who wouldn't recognise neo-classicism from a pre-fab. Rosie could easily understand so casual a man detesting the rigidity of it all.

He was not, she noticed, wearing a tie, having compromised with a black shirt, a double-buttoned round collar negating the necessity for one.

He chose that moment to take stock of the theatre, his gaze sweeping the baroque ceiling, the packed auditorium, before alighting on Rosie. For a moment he just looked at her. To her embarrassment she was suddenly aware that she had been staring steadily at him for at least five minutes. And then quite deliberately he stood up, gave her a small elegant bow and sat down.

There was, she decided, something interesting about spoilt brats. They always had to have the last word. Such a shame to deny him the pleasure, she thought, but what else could she do, as in turn she rose and, whipping an ornate fan from the continuity girl's clasp, she gave an exaggeratedly deep curtsey, spreading the fan across her shoulders as she did so.

'What's all that about?' Carey chuckled as the others crowded forward demanding an explanation.

'Oh, just wasting time,' she said lightly, noticing that Nancy was leaning across to ask Joel the same question as the TVN crowd, giggling helplessly, practised bows and curtseys to each other, wildly waving cheap fans they had bought from a gift shop in the old town.

Whatever Joel whispered made Nancy glance across at Rosie and simply nod her acknowledgement. David then claimed her attention and by the time the brilliant, surreal performance had come to a close and the standing ovations had subsided, she had decided that her earlier encounter with Joel was something she would rather keep private.

She had begun to hope he would prefer that too. An

uneasy feeling that she might have been a bit too hasty was flickering in her head. But it was hot. And Rory hadn't answered the phone. Understandable.

# Chapter Twenty-Four

Tanya had left Rosie a message that Nancy would see her at midday.

Rosie was sorely tempted to ignore Nancy and just get the flight she had arranged at mid-morning. Now she would be stuck here for another night. However, a wonderful and funny evening spent with Carey and the very attentive David Mesinski had adjusted her mood and she called Tanya to say that would be fine. After which she called Sylvia.

'I suppose Rory never thought to phone me? He has got the number.'

'But he did, Rosie,' Sylvia replied curtly. 'You were at the Opera. He found someone called Tanya who said she would give you the message. I believe he also tried earlier but you were sightseeing with someone.'

'Sorry, Sylvia,' Rosie interrupted as politely as she could to one she would rather have been rude to. 'That isn't the way it was. But thank you for having Tom.'

When Tom came on the line, Rosie took a deep breath and sounded cheerful. 'Hi, darling, sorry to drag you to the phone. Everything all right?'

'Sure,' he said easily. 'Have you got me anything?'

'*Tom*.' She began to rebuke him. But she was in Prague, his father was in Ireland, and he was staying with the dreadful Sylvia.

'Well, maybe.' It sounded lame and she knew it. 'Wait and see.'

She heard Tom talking to Sylvia. 'No, it's all right. Mum forgot Dad was in Ireland, that's all.'

\*     \*     \*

There was certainly no apology, not even a sheepish look. Merely a curt, brusque good morning and a: 'Let's get down to work, shall we?' when she kept her appointment.

An hour later, drained from Nancy's incessant nit-picking, it was only her experienced patience with difficult clients that stopped Rosie from tipping every scheme over Nancy's head and suggesting she did it all herself.

'Blue?' Nancy asked doubtfully. 'You think that'll work? I mean, it's kind of cold, isn't it?' The American frowned, tossing the swatches of fabric over. 'What's wrong with that idea I had for lining the walls with mottled tissue paper? A guy I know in New York is a dream on this kind of thing. Looks like a stone block effect.'

'I know the man you mean,' Rosie answered, unruffled and trying to appear interested. 'He's extremely good. I just wonder if such an idea would work in London? The twenty-fifth floor of a New York duplex has more light to make it effective. London has a colder, more northern light. It might end up looking a little bleak. But I agree it's an interesting idea.'

She didn't agree at all. It was a mission to madness, but Rosie had dealt with more difficult clients than Nancy.

She could see Nancy was struggling to make her criticisms sound credible. For the life of her, Rosie couldn't think why she was getting this treatment. Surely she wasn't still annoyed over the misunderstanding with Joel?

The white with just a hint of rose to warm it, which Rosie had suggested for the main rooms, Nancy thought should be cream. The saffron in the gallery would fight with the lighting for her art collection.

After twenty minutes she decided that rose was okay, provided Rosie changed the curtains from the sharp crimson silk she had chosen, swagged and cascading to catch the ripples of light on the dramatic drops of the window, to a powerful print which she grudgingly discarded when Rosie patiently pointed out that it was hardly the way to enhance the drama of a reception room the size of a ball-room. Particularly when the curtains would never be drawn.

With one ear listening to Nancy's views on everything from Colefax and Fowler to the Designers' Guild, Rosie was also anxiously looking at the time. As if on cue Tanya appeared to remind Nancy she was due elsewhere.

'Okay. I'll let you know when we can continue,' Nancy said dismissively, starting to leave. There was a limit to Rosie's patience. She asked Tanya to wait outside.

'Unlike you, Nancy, I wouldn't dream of embarrassing you in front of anyone. I'm afraid we finish this meeting now, otherwise I'm catching the afternoon flight.'

Nancy looked outraged, her cheeks were crimson. Rosie simply ignored her. 'In spite of your belief that you own my time, I should mention you are not paying me any more for this job than we agreed. You're actually costing me money. Now either you want my services or you don't. If you don't, I'm out of here. Think about it.'

Nancy went to the door. 'Give me five,' she instructed Tanya. Rosie started folding away the schemes.

When Nancy spoke there was a wary note in her voice: 'Look, Rosie, I'm under terrific pressure at the moment, what I don't need is someone coming on to Joel . . .'

'Coming on to Joel? Are you quite mad?'

Nancy shook her head, talking over her. 'He's easily distracted.'

Rosie looked at her in blank amazement. 'Easily distracted . . . Joel. By who?'

'Well, I know you met up with him in town.'

'Who on earth said that?' Rosie was amazed. 'I bumped into him, that's all.'

'Rosie, listen to me. I would not want to see your relationship with Rory hijacked before it's even begun. He sounded so concerned when he rang yesterday.'

'*Rory? Rang you?* I thought he'd just phoned Tanya. Last night when I was at the opera?'

'Well, he rang twice. You'd already left to go to the opera and I said you were okay because you'd just been with Joel.'

'You told him *that*?'

For the first time Nancy looked flustered. Dear God. This had to stop. 'Nancy, I am here to do a job. All I want is to make sure you are happy with the plans I've drawn up for your house and then to go home and get on with them. Really, that's all.

'I hardly know Joel and, believe me, he is not distracting me. I don't think he's even tried. And if he has I didn't notice. It would take someone very special indeed to do that to me nowadays.'

Nancy hesitated, giving her a searching look. 'I'm glad to hear it for your sake and Rory's ... well, just yours then. Joel's a great guy, but tricky. Take it from me, honey, I know him. You don't.'

Mollified that Rosie's interest in Joel was professional and not overwhelming in that direction either, some of Nancy's former cordial manner resurfaced. They would meet again at three, she said. When Rosie returned to her room she found an invitation waiting for her to attend the lecture.

She grinned in the mirror. Just showed what a little assertion could achieve.

# Chapter Twenty-Five

Wave after wave of applause filled the medieval hall in the heart of the castle. The American ambassador was on stage shaking Joel's hand together with the Czech government minister in charge of the arts.

Rosie gazed around the sea of people roaring their approval. Nancy, both hands clasped to her mouth, eyes shining, was gazing rapturously at Joel.

A very young boy and a serious young girl who were going to benefit from the Alexander Foundation paying their college fees, stepped nervously up to present Joel with a bouquet of flowers, and still the applause went on. Joel hugged them both and spent a full minute talking to them, his head bent to hear their answers.

Of course, Rosie shouted to Carey who was on his feet clapping, straining to hear her above the noise, the venue helped.

The romantic and powerful atmosphere of Prague Castle, on an evening bathed in warm sunlight, certainly could not be ruled out. But Joel had been good. Impressive. One minute urbane, witty and wicked, the next passionate, stern. He delivered an hour's lecture without notes, one hand in his pocket, no props, just a beam of light picking him out standing behind a lectern on a specially erected stage swathed in midnight blue curtains.

He drew parallels with inner-city decay to the crumbling facade of the beautiful city they were guests in, condemning both.

The absurdity of competitions to design buildings that would never be built felt the lash of his tongue. The new opera house in England was singled out for special attention. Plus the Friedland Platz in Munich, and a Welsh Centre for Literature, which had lost vast sums of money because they had no hope of becoming a reality, and everyone concerned knew it.

'If the money's there, then fine.' His voice carried with quiet authority to a hushed audience. 'But in all those cases it isn't and they will never be built.

'The National Lottery in my own country has sent everyone rushing to set up even more competitions that will produce buildings of rare talent and vision, but they will never leave the paper they're drawn on.

'If of course you are content with a handshake, a letter to pin on your wall saying you've won, then fine. And of course if you can afford it, it's an exercise in addressing building problems which is good for experience and gives the opportunity to try to overcome them.

'Big companies like the prestige of winning. But for smaller companies there is no way they can afford the thousands of pounds it costs just to enter. The idea of tying up valuable manpower while the project is completed is not viable. Are we then really seeing the best architects, the best designers? Of course not. We are seeing the results of those who can afford to be seen.

'The Alexander Foundation is attempting to reverse that. Personally I would like to see fewer competitions to design art galleries, which are great for tourists, I admit, but how many hospitals are we ever asked to design? How many schools?

'Architecture like anything else is big business. I want to see an environment where young, talented designers get the chance to shine, I would like a generation to emerge who are interested in improving the way we live, not just building monuments to some corporation's ego.'

Rosie squirmed where she sat.

'Someone recently said to me that architects preferred

buildings to people, which is why so many of them were unlivable in – and I believe she also added the architects themselves must be unlivable with.'

There was a burst of laughter. Rosie eyed the exit.

'I look around my own city, or New York, or Hamburg, even here in Prague, and I can understand what she meant. I hope the future work of the students who have been awarded scholarships through the Alexander Foundation will be people-friendly, not a waste of space.'

Rosie knew she must be the only person in the entire auditorium who was sinking lower and lower into her seat, resisting a strong temptation to wrap her arms around her head and hide her face forever.

Oh God, she hadn't . . . *spoilt brat*? She had. *Wasting her time*? Dear heaven. And she thought *she* might make something of his work? She pressed her hands to her face. Where was the black hole, the bin liner, the humble pie?

Joel was surrounded and the day's work was complete. There was nothing to stay for, they were all booked on the first flight out in the morning.

Eyeing Joel across the room, Rosie and Carey decided he was the most relaxed person there. He was holding an untouched glass of champagne, listening good-naturedly to other architects who were teasing him about his own success.

He had his arm around a much older woman with grey hair, with a quiet elegance that spelt taste as well as money who occasionally glanced up at Joel with undisguised affection. The man next to her was clearly struggling not to let his pride show.

Without having to be told, Rosie knew they were his parents. It was an interesting scene. Rosie was always curious about family loyalty, having never experienced that closeness herself.

They were relaxed, rather than excited, full of quiet pride

rather than shrieks of excitement. Joel obviously knew his role. A kiss on the cheek for wives of colleagues from around the world. A hug and a shared joke from his business partner Daniel, who had flown over just for the evening, and a bear hug for a dark-haired woman Rosie assumed was Daniel's wife.

And Nancy hovering around, touching Joel's arm to bring his attention to another guest. She could have been his wife. Indeed it was an odd relationship.

Nancy had surprised Rosie by arriving back punctually at three and had finished their meeting in record time, even congratulating her on the inspirational themes Rosie had planned.

In the space of a few short hours, the saffron was now the only possible choice. The blue? Quite brilliant. Yes, yes, New York for the chandeliers in the drawing room and maybe even the dining room.

Amazing what clearing up a few misunderstandings could do, Rosie thought dryly, watching Nancy speed off to rejoin Joel for their TV interview.

With her task sewn up, Rosie relaxed and even looked forward to attending the reception at the castle which she would have willingly forgone if Tom had been waiting for her at home.

The night air was heavy with the smell of jasmine, the firework display was over. Rosie thought she would remember that night forever. In her black crepe slip dress, huge silver globes hanging from her ears, with a three-inch thick plaited silver collar lying flat against her slender neck, Rosie glowed and it showed.

Carey smiled at David's efforts to get Rosie to himself but mindful of Rosie's warning, he was steadily ignoring pointed looks from his boss and remained firmly by her side.

Nancy, sensational in a black-and-scarlet dress, radiant and ecstatic at the success of the evening which had produced enough money to fund four new scholarships and two fellowships to universities in Paris and Prague, wafted over with the American ambassador, suggesting Carey interviewed him the next morning before he left.

Joel joined them, talking easily with Carey. Perhaps he might not notice her in the crowd and if he did he might be too overwhelmed by the evening to remember their conversation. Rosie tried to look as though cowering behind David's back was normal behaviour at a glittering reception.

She felt Joel's hand on her arm gently pulling her into view, asking disarmingly if she was hiding from someone, introducing her and Carey to his parents, his partner and Stevie, Daniel's wife.

'Congratulations,' she said as the others moved on. 'Not bad for a spoilt brat.'

'Thank you,' he said meekly. 'I'm glad you were able to stay on. Here, sit next to me and pretend to be interested, the bloody Duchess insists I meet every boring official she wants to unload.'

Rosie flashed a look at the comic dismay on the Duchess' face as Joel mouthed, 'No', back at her.

'Have you spoken to your son?' he asked.

Rosie nodded. 'He's staying with a friend. Rory's away on . . . a business trip. Bit of a muddle. I forgot.' She changed the subject. 'What about your children? Do you see much of them?'

Joel laughed. 'I fight for their attention. Ben, my son, called earlier. Big dilemma. He wants to spend the summer in Cap Ferrat with my parents, but his stepfather has already arranged a trip to Martha's Vineyard, he has a house up there.'

'Poor boy,' Rosie sympathised.

'Hardly poor. His problem is too many people wanting his company, not unloading it.'

'Do they get on with their stepfather?'

Joel shrugged. 'They're only kids. It's hard on them. Sometimes even I feel sorry for my replacement. He does try with my two, but it isn't the same. Well, my daughter has a problem with him more than Ben. Lexie sees him as the man who threw me out of her mother's life.'

'And did he?' Rosie asked, surprised at her own curiosity.

'Not entirely. I asked for it. I was sort of temporarily distracted by someone else.' He stopped and squeezed her hand as she began to apologise for the question. 'Don't ... you're not intruding. We're having, I think, one of those conversations that being thrown together in a place like this produces.'

She nodded, smiling at him. 'Ships that pass in the night, you mean?' Wondering if Nancy had been the temporary distraction.

He smiled back. 'Something like that. Anyway, Marianne had met Dale and the inevitable happened. We both wanted custody of the kids. But even I could see it was better for them to stay with Marianne.'

'Do you mind them living with a stepfather?'

Joel shrugged and his face lost some of its humour. 'Quite a lot of the time, actually. He doesn't understand them as I do. But at least now they're being educated in England so I have them during termtime and Marianne flies over once a term to see them. Like you once said to me, it works. But then we could never have done what you're doing. Maybe you'll get back together for real.'

Rosie shook her head vehemently. 'Oh no. That's over. It's just a civilised way of bringing up our son, that's all.'

'Must take a lot of basic understanding, though. Even if no other people were involved I don't honestly think Marianne and I could have lived that closely together after we were divorced. I think you have to have something still going for you to be prepared to make that move. What happens if one of you meets someone you want to be with? Who gets Tom?'

Rosie was shocked. 'Why, I do, of course,' she said. 'But neither of us is involved with anyone else. With an eleven-year-old it isn't easy to include someone else in your life. You said it yourself. For the moment Tom has to come first.' She paused. 'Actually it will always be Tom first, until he wants to leave home.'

'Is that why it works with you and Rory?' Joel asked, clearly puzzled.

'Maybe. The circumstances are very unusual,' Rosie replied wearily. Compared to his more recognisable scenario, hers sounded like a leftover from the sixties when eccentricity reigned and society had been redefined.

'I'm not left wing, a separatist feminist or trying to revolutionise family life. I had certain problems to overcome, so did Rory. Sometimes, you know, the answer to your problems is there all the time, you just have to learn to approach it from a different direction.'

Suddenly she didn't want the conversation to go any further. She didn't want Rory to be part of this. She wanted the moment for herself, not shared. Like it used to be. So easy, she thought, the way real life could be suspended, and yet it was waiting just a day away.

'I'm glad you came,' he said, smiling at her in a way that made her catch her breath. 'What are you doing about dinner?'

'Dinner? Oh yes. I'm joining Carey and David.'

'Pity,' he shrugged. 'All sorted out with Nancy?'

She nodded. Not interested in Nancy, wishing she could dump Carey, knowing she couldn't. 'Fine. No problem. Look, I'm sorry about all that. She couldn't have been nicer in the end. Just me. Feeling a bit harassed.'

'Nonsense. You were quite right. I should thank you,' and then with an ease that lent nothing of any significance to it, since he seemed to be doing it to every other woman

215

in the room, he leaned over and lightly kissed her on the mouth. Not distract her. Who was she kidding?

Certainly, judging by the icy look on her face, not Nancy.

# Chapter Twenty-Six

The house was deserted when Rosie finally arrived back late on Sunday afternoon. The phone was ringing as she let herself in. Dumping her case, she reached for it, scooping up a pile of letters that were clustered on the mat.

'Miss Hart? Oh, you mean Abbie?' Rosie reached for a pen. 'She left what? Where?'

'In the car – one of ours, Miss – a scarf and some glasses. They were only found after we dropped her at the airport on Friday. Can you tell her we've got them?'

'Of course. Excuse me, but did you say airport? Where was she going?'

'No idea, Miss. The driver who took her isn't on this weekend. He might know. He'll be here tomorrow. Only the glasses are expensive . . . Gucci? Is that right? She'll be upset to lose those.'

Gucci, eh? On her salary it was unlikely she could afford them. Must have hidden resources. In the kitchen, Rosie sifted through the post, an unwelcome idea thrusting itself into her mind. Tossing the envelopes aside, she picked up the coffee and wandered upstairs.

Why not? She wouldn't be the first. History repeating itself. Stupid, stupid girl. Rory would now find her irritating and want her out.

Not that she cared that much. Rosie had grown tired of the New Zealand girl's polite 'Of course' and 'Whatever you say', in a tone that robbed the acknowledgment of anything other than recognition that Rosie had to be obeyed.

Just like the girlfriend from hell who had turned up at

the mews, it was obvious that Abbie had begun to regard her as a kept woman and clearly believed Rory was where the power as well as the money was to be found. Inevitably, compared with Rory's glamour and his crusade to make sure his ex-wife was waited on hand and foot, she must present a very unattractive proposition.

All that, she decided as she mounted the stairs, could wait. She needed a shower, distraction. Maybe Kit or Jaye would be free for supper. But then, not too much distraction. That's what the last couple of days had done to her. She needed normality. She gave herself a shake. You're not a teenager, she chided herself.

Rosie yawned and wandered upstairs to Tom's room, for no other reason than it was the next best thing to having him there.

It looked so tidy, untouched. Absently she picked up his Star Trek videos, and refolded his Arsenal pyjamas. On the wall behind his bed, the pinboard was crammed with Tom's essential paraphernalia.

His heroes, fixture lists, a birthday card he had loved that Carey had given him when he was six, and a rosette proclaiming his first place in the relay team on sport's day.

A signed photograph of Ian Wright had central position with a cluster of red arrows all directed to it; a silly note from Felix and an old photograph of him and Rosie pulling faces on the beach.

Tom in the football team at school, grinning broadly, arms folded, holding the ball between his knees. A picture of him standing on his head in his bedroom at the house in Drake Street, Kit swinging him around by the waist at a fair they had all gone to one bank holiday and there was another of Ellie, Jaye and Judith in the kitchen at Drake Street that was slightly out of focus. Rosie smiled. He'd insisted on taking it.

There was so much of his short history on that board. A whole life that Rory had taken no part in or interested himself in. Her eyes roamed the board again. How odd. Rory must be there somewhere. Tom adored him. But there was nothing. Maybe he hadn't had time to include his father.

When this job is over, Rosie decided, I am going to make Rory get to know Tom. Not the one who was performing for him. She stopped, gazing fixedly at the foot of the stairs, slowly making her way down. Performing? Yes, that was exactly it. The description that had eluded her. Performing was the right word. Of that she was certain.

Rory denied it with such genuine shock, Rosie hesitated. 'I have no idea where she went,' he said when she suggested Abbie might have gone to Ireland with him.

Rosie gazed uncertainly at him. Thus far in a five-minute exchange he had dismissed her annoyance about involving Sylvia Duxborough in Tom's weekend, saying with perfect sense that having to make a decision about where Tom should spend the weekend, he had chosen Tom's best friend.

'What you and I feel about simpering Sylvia is neither here nor there, I just wanted what was best for Tom. As for Abbie, I gave her the weekend off. Er ... no chance you might be jealous?' he ended, giving Rosie a hopeful look.

'Jealous?' she snapped. 'Don't be ridiculous. I just think you knocking off the help is sleazy. Like some ludicrous *droit du seigneur*.'

His eyes narrowed. 'I am not knocking off the help. Japanese businessmen poking your eye out with their fucking cameras every time you turn round is not my idea of a jolly weekend. You're an odd person, Rosie dear.' He stretched out in the armchair, giving her a thoughtful look. 'You spend an afternoon sightseeing with Joel Harley, who less than a month ago was irritating the hell out of you, well, that's what that Tanya person said you had been doing, and then a night at the opera with God knows who, and Prague is a *very* romantic city. And then you begrudge me a bit of fun. Not that I've had any. And don't slam the door, I've had a helluva weekend.'

Abbie returned to the house after Rosie had gone to work, so it was Monday night before she encountered her. If she had been expecting a blushing defence she was disappointed. Abbie seemed to be very quiet. Almost nervous. But not embarrassed.

She had spent the weekend with a friend in Paris. Rory had said it was okay. She had just assumed Rosie wouldn't mind.

Rosie began to feel foolish. Old habits. So used to Rory behaving badly, she had simply assumed the coincidence was too much.

'No, I didn't mind,' she said in a kinder voice. 'I would just like to have been told. Do what you like about the house, the shopping, even Rory. But where Tom is concerned, no matter how much Rory thinks I should be protected, I have to be told everything. Okay, let's forget it.'

Several times over the next few days she had to stop herself from glancing around restaurants, doing double takes in the street every time she saw a tousled blonde head.

Once, to his bewilderment, she dragged Kit off to the National Film Theatre when she heard they were showing an obscure subtitled Czech movie. She saw 'Immortal Beloved' with Jaye, as Kit flatly refused to indulge her any further, just because it had been shot in Prague.

'And this is all down to what?' Jaye demanded, giving her a shrewd look as they left the cinema. 'You'll be practising writing his name next.'

'Who?' Rosie asked innocently, humming Beethoven's

Ninth as they made their way across Leicester Square.

'The man in the moon.' Jaye was sarcastic. 'Who indeed?'

It was Ginny who brought her down to earth for which Rosie didn't know whether to be grateful or embarrassed.

'This looks great, Ginny,' Rosie enthused, making her way across the rubble that was now littering the spacious hallway in Nancy's new house, both girls wearing hard hats.

Rosie loved it all. Out of this chaos a beautiful, gracious house would emerge. The gallery of scaffolding to support the new structure for the staircase was already in place. The demolished walls, widened doorways, the dingy cracked plaster of ceilings revealed after thirty hidden years, she could already see what it would be like.

Ginny had been on site for part of each day since the work had begun to organise the removal of the ceilings and the extension of the double-height music room, which was to incorporate a conservatory and a galleried library, and to prepare the groundwork for resiting the staircase. It was going well. They left Gerard, Nancy's temperamental chef, relaying his orders to a suitably awed kitchen designer and the couple who were employed as housekeeper and butler poring over a choice of colours for their staff flat.

'Isn't that just adding to your problems?' Ginny asked, referring to the tail end of a conversation Rosie had had with them.

Rosie grinned, accepting the orange Ginny handed her as they settled themselves on the front step of the house for a breather.

She was feeling good. Mrs Bhandari had set her accountant onto Rosie the minute she got back from Prague to insist he went through her latest invoice item by item. Rosie had abandoned adding her fee as a separate percentage on her invoices, since it created such stunning misunderstandings with some clients, and had built it into materials and labour instead.

'The invoice I've submitted to Mrs Bhandari is for the figure we agreed, there is no other invoice. I'm afraid you must talk to my accountant, no, better still, my solicitor.'

The invoice had been paid in full that morning. Salina Bhandari as a client merited courtesy. As a tyrannical bully she no longer left Rosie feeling cowed by her despotic behaviour.

'No point in creating a stunning home for Nancy, if her little treasures aren't happy,' Rosie said to Ginny, settling herself in the sunshine. 'They'd just up sticks and go and then she'd blame me. Anyway, I've just asked them to make a choice out of the three schemes Nancy's already approved.'

'Same as Joel really,' Ginny remarked idly, biting into an apple.

'In what way?' Rosie asked, carefully peeling the orange, squinting in the strong sunlight.

'Well, he does that too. You know, keeps clients happy. Nice to everyone, listens to what they have to say. Trouble is,' Ginny giggled, 'it can be taken the wrong way. Some of the wives of those corporate heads have been so neglected, they mistake his professional concern for personal concern. Doesn't cost him anything and they're putty in his hands.'

'Wouldn't have thought Nancy came into that category.' Rosie pushed the orange aside.

'Oh, not Nancy,' Ginny said dismissively. 'She thinks she knows him better than anyone. Tanya said Nancy told her she thought you were going to walk out in Prague so she set Joel onto you. Ludicrous. As if you, of all people, would fall for something like that.'

'Ludicrous,' Rosie agreed, tipping the uneaten orange into a paper bag. 'And such a waste of energy. Must rush,

Ginny. The Lovetts will be asking for gold leaf round the Ajax if I leave them alone for much longer.'

When Joel phoned she was polite, charming even, but found she was already busy when he suggested lunch.

'Shame,' he said mildly. 'I'm going to the States and then onto Cap Ferrat with the kids, so I'll only be here on flying visits. Maybe another time. Everything all right with Nancy?'

Rosie clenched her teeth. 'Fine. Tomorrow I'm . . . I've promised Rory to drive down with him to Oxford to get Tom.'

It wasn't a lie. Since her misjudgment of Rory's weekend in Ireland she had decided her behaviour had been churlish. When he said he would have to be away again, he suggested they both collect Tom from school, have tea with him and then Rosie could drop him at Heathrow on the way back to London. That way Tom would see him.

She left it to Joel Harley to interpret that any way he chose. She thought there was a sardonic note to his voice. 'Glad it's working,' he told her. 'Enjoy yourself.' Rosie was left holding the phone.

Good, she told herself. History was not going to repeat itself. She knew about charm. The first time she was a naive girl. This time she was an experienced woman.

She would also quite like to have told Joel that Rory was laying siege to her, but she thought that might be going a bit too far. But at least, she comforted herself, if comfort was the right word, at least she was in control where that was concerned.

# Chapter Twenty-Seven

If Rory had to be away overnight, she didn't miss him in that hungry way she had all those years ago, but she was now very aware if he was not around.

Once or twice Rosie had not arrived home until after he had rung to say he wouldn't be home and was surprised when she got a call before she left the house the following morning.

Just to make sure she was okay, he said. Rosie felt unnerved rather than reassured. It was so easy to feel comforted by someone's concern. Far too easy to let it slide into something else.

Abbie looked bewildered when she began to politely but firmly reverse Rory's instructions that she was to be untroubled by domestic tasks.

'But why?' she blurted out. 'Have I got something wrong? You only have to say.'

Rosie reassured her it was not that. 'I am an independent woman,' she tried to explain. 'I want to look after my son myself. In fact I can't understand why anyone should think that was a chore.'

'But your work, surely . . . ?'

Work. Rosie gave a tight little smile. Abbie appeared to be more obsessed with it than she was. 'Tom comes first,' she insisted as gently as she could and then with a smile: 'Concentrate on Rory. Now *he's* a full-time job in himself. Tell you what you can do though.' She handed Abbie the roses she was carrying. 'Perhaps you could do something with these? Rory sent them this morning – for good luck. I'm off to my first meeting for a new commission.'

Abbie took the white roses without a word. Merely nodded.

Rory took it better, just saying, whatever she wanted was fine with him. He baffled her. He was a master at creating intrigue, one minute making his need for her plain by crowding her day with his presence. Then disappearing for two or three days at a time without a word.

Her desperate need for his approval had gone, along with the passion, but he could still hold her interest.

Maybe what I need is one of Livvie's workshops, she thought wryly. 'Dealing With An Identity Crisis Safely' might be a start.

The ease with which she had been drawn to Joel Harley frightened her. Her judgement was so bad. How could she have been attracted to a man who had all the potential to be as damaging as Rory had once been? When she looked back on their meetings she had to admit they had been stormy. Hardly the harmony she craved, the feeling of being accepted without question.

Jaye dismissed the damage theory. Getting serious about someone on a business trip, she maintained, was about as sensible as eating the local fish delicacy and not expecting to throw up later on. Barriers down, the rules relaxed. Entertainment thrown in, the chance to dress up, reinvent yourself.

'Frankly I think business trips should come with a government health warning. This trip could seriously damage your brain. All common sense extracted at the border. And all that nonsense about LDC relationships should be made illegal.'

'What's that?'

'Location Doesn't Count. Unfortunately in the real world it does. Cheer up, my duck.' Jaye paused to screw the piece of paper she was holding into a ball and lobbed it into the waste bin. Not looking at Rosie, she said: 'David is a great guy, but a lousy lay. You're missing nothing.'

Rosie looked blank. '*David*? What's he got to do with it?'

'Grief.' Jaye's eyes narrowed. 'Who are *you* talking about? Carey said he had to fight him off for you.'

'Not David,' Rosie spluttered, recalling the pains she went to, to keep him at arm's length. 'And just a minute. *You* screwed David? When did this happen? Does Carey know? Here, move those lampshades. Tell me *everything*.'

After a few weeks of his new particular brand of concern and denied the opportunity to remove all practical problems from her path, she knew for certain that Rory was laying siege to her. Knew him too well not to recognise the signs.

'*The one that got away*.' She heard Jaye's voice.

Rosie found herself reading articles with titles like 'The Lure of an Old Flame', or 'Is Sex with your Ex ever okay?'. When Jaye asked her if an article they had run from a single mother rang bells with her, she looked blank. No, she hadn't read it. Didn't want to. That was another life. She'd moved on.

Later, reflecting on her reaction, she was both scared and relieved that the world of scrimping and scraping was no longer hers and headlines about the plight of single mothers no longer drew her like a magnet.

'I didn't notice the time,' she told Rory when two days later he rushed in to the mews to see her, with profuse apologies for his absence. 'Look at this, what do you think?' she asked without thinking, holding up a drawing of a new scheme for a block of flats in Little Venice. 'Like it?'

He looked at her. Not hurt, just puzzled. 'Terrific,' he replied flatly. Rosie didn't notice. Jordan and she had held a hugely successful meeting with his friend Pedro. The fact that she hadn't been instantly available seemed to have had the opposite effect to the one she feared. The job was hers.

Jordan was thrilled and even more so when Rosie told him she wanted him to have a real input.

Rory took himself off, saying he would see her later.

Jordan was the only one who openly welcomed Rory's visits, squirming with pleasure when Rory would start by deliberately ignoring him and then blow him a kiss on the way out, leaving Livvie to deal with the consequences.

'I have a lot to be possessive about,' Rory would say when Rosie gently tried to deflect him from his new role as her protector. 'I'm Tom's father. You're his mother. There's a big investment in both of you for me. That's all.'

Touched by Rory's concern, she would make a huge effort not to let him see that this behaviour – once a sign to her, the only sign, that she was secure – was no longer necessary. It was easier to say thank you than argue.

Her discreet visits to Drake Street continued without his knowledge. Each time she saw another beam in place, rubble moved from the hall, plaster start to be laid on walls, she went home reassured that she still controlled her life.

Immersed in Nancy's house, but with other very prestigious commissions beginning to come her way, her reputation in the design world continued to grow. The woman's editor from *The Herald* telephoned to ask if she would be interviewed for a series on women who were successful in their field.

For once she consulted Rory, knowing that the publicity would be good for her but equally uncertain whether he and Tom wanted her to be so publicised. It was, after all, part of the deal that they respected each other's privacy.

'Maggie says they won't ask any personal questions, but inevitably some details will have to be included. What do you think?'

For a moment he looked at her without saying anything. Then he smiled. A quick, charming smile.

'Sure, why not?'

'And they want a picture of me with Tom,' she continued, studying Maggie's follow-up letter.

'And you've declined, of course?'

'Well, I hadn't. But I will if you would prefer he was kept out of it.'

Rory rose to his feet, lighting a cigarette as he walked past her.

'Mmm. Personally I don't mind at all, but you know it would be better for you if he wasn't. You told me once, remember, that women like Nancy Alexander – just for an example – felt it gave the wrong impression. Somehow not professional. I wouldn't want that to happen to you.'

'No, of course not,' she conceded reluctantly, rather touched by his concern although she disagreed, and informed Maggie that she preferred to keep Tom out of such things.

Jordan thought a picture of Rosie and Tom would be charming, even better with Rory in the background.

'So *intimate*,' he explained. 'I love Madonna and child, all of that.'

'But Rosie's hardly a Madonna,' Livvie objected. 'She looks too . . .'

'Sexy?'

'No. More sensuous. And Tom *is* very beautiful but a right little bugger these days.'

'But at least his parents love him,' Jordan replied mournfully.

Livvie, who knew that Jordan's parents had not come to terms with his lifestyle, thought Jordan would benefit from a one-day workshop on Dealing with the Hurting Inner Child.

'What's that?'

'It's part of an amazing personal growth course. It deals with unresolved conflicts – controlling parental hostility through visualisation techniques.'

'You mean I just have to feel good about them?' Jordan

wrinkled his nose. 'I don't think so,' he said doubtfully.

'No, no, no,' Livvie scolded. 'Just close your eyes and visualise who you would like your father to be most like.'

Jordan obediently closed his eyes. 'So who are you thinking about?' Livvie asked encouragingly.

'Keanu Reeves,' Jordan said, a dreamy look on his face.

Livvie glared at him. 'Well, if nothing else it would help you lose your childish admiration for superficial glamour. I mean, you never leave off about Rory but do you ever speak kindly of work Kit does, for example? Now *that's* artistic. No you do not. How can you not have not recognised that Rory's a control freak?'

If Rosie could have heard her she might have agreed. It would have shocked Jordan, who was utterly mystified at her ability to resist her beautiful ex.

Nothing stayed the same, Rosie knew that. It was persuading Rory that you could never turn back the clock that was more difficult. He wanted her to be the same pliant, biddable girl she once was.

But that time was over. She'd tried to explain that to him. But he had simply looked bored. She waited for the familiar feeling of hurt to sweep over her. But it didn't. Catching her looking at him, he was instantly contrite.

'Sorry, sweetheart, helluva day, and I've still got to go out. Business contact, you know how it is.'

Rosie gazed after him. Is this *déjà vu* or what, she asked herself?

A week later the feature appeared in *The Herald*. Ginny rang to say she had seen it, congratulated her and ended by saying she had included a copy in the air bag that was sent over to Joel every few days because it had mentioned she was working with him.

Kit called, having also been alerted to the feature by Jaye who felt *The Herald* had not handled the feature at all well, and admitted grudgingly that the pictures were stunning.

Only Rosie was dismayed. Of the four case histories which included a barrister, a well-known columnist and a glamorous TVN newscaster, only Rosie was photographed alone.

The others were with their partners and, in the barrister's case, with her three children.

'Oh never mind, sweetheart,' Rory said comfortingly. 'I only thought it would look better for you. More organised, less domesticated. Stupid me. Next time Tom can sit on your knee and I'll even stand behind with a washing-up mop if it helps.'

She had laughed and not shrugged him off when he gave her shoulder a squeeze and dropped a light kiss on her head. What was a picture, after all?

A life where the unexpected was no longer a disaster was more valuable to her. For example, the phone call from Tom's school just as she was planning to go to New York, alerting all parents to the fact that the school was closing for a week because of burst pipes which had flooded the kitchens.

Rory immediately suggested taking Tom to Scotland to see Callum while Rosie made her planned trip.

She gulped when she thought what might have happened if she had still been in Drake Street on her own.

Abbie was to go to Scotland with them, having not seen that part of the country, and because – and this Rosie was sure was the real reason – because Rory would not want the responsibility of caring for Tom on his own, especially as he had invited Felix Duxborough along.

The idea of staying at Rory's 'seat', as she kept referring to it, was blinding Abbie to exactly what these few days would entail.

Abbie would have her work cut out, Rosie thought with satisfaction, seeing the snobbish housekeeper carefully sliding into the back seat of the car waiting to take them all to Heathrow.

Abbie had shopped quite extensively in some expensive but as far as Rosie was concerned middle-aged boutiques before she left judging by the number of bags that had been put out with the rubbish.

'Careful,' Rosie murmured mischievously to Rory as the boys piled into the car. 'You're beginning to look like you should be waiting on her.'

Rory glanced quickly to where Abbie was patting her hair into place, noticing for the first time her carefully selected travelling outfit of white trousers, scarlet silk shirt with shoulder pads and a pair of wedged sandals.

She was totally oblivious to Tom and Felix Duxborough shoving and pushing each other, ignoring Sylvia's last-minute instructions.

Undercover of the general melee, Rory turned back to her: 'I've only ever wanted to look after one person,' he whispered with an urgency and intensity that surprised her. 'No-one can change that. Take care.'

Rosie was startled, but since Sylvia was dominating the scene, she had no need to answer.

'And Abbie.' Sylvia turned to the housekeeper, now busily investigating her handbag. 'Please make sure Felix changes into long trousers for dinner with Sir Callum. Felix, *please*. I'm giving orders to Tom's nanny.'

Rosie had to look away as she heard Abbie say through clenched teeth: 'I am the *housekeeper*. I am not a *nanny*.'

'Well, whatever you are.' Sylvia dismissed her. 'You'll find them in his brown suitcase. Please hang them up as soon as possible. They may need pressing.'

'But I told you . . .'

It was surprising that Abbie loathed Sylvia, they had at heart so much in common. Abbie had eventually been prevented from getting out of the car the better to deal with Sylvia by Rory bellowing at all of them to get ready to go.

He kissed Rosie on the cheek, and then he did the same

to Sylvia, who went crimson and became quite silly.

Rosie looked curiously at Sylvia dealing with Rory's social kiss. It was a nothing kiss. Polite, because she was the mother of his son's friend. Polite, because she was one of his ex-wife's clients. That was all. God, she felt so stupid. So very stupid.

# Chapter Twenty-Eight

After she cleared customs Rosie headed in a yellow cab for the West Village and the apartment of Ellie Carter, one of her oldest and closest friends and who was now an award-winning documentary film-maker based in New York.

With only a few working days to play with, Ellie demanded maximum time to catch up while Jed Bayley, the English gossip columnist, Rosie's friend from the days when all three had worked on *Focus* magazine in London, had arranged a dinner in her honour.

New York was already sweltering in temperatures that had soared well above the milder weather of London. Each day was packed as Rosie worked through an itinerary from Nancy's brownstone on Riverside Drive, to the sale rooms, shops and stores on the Upper East Side that she had already checked out from London.

As the midtown rush got under way Ellie dropped Rosie on East 84th, where she was to start her trawl of antiques shops, starting with Dean Levy's.

There she spotted a perfect Philadelphia highboy and a signed Newport chest and called Nancy's office to arrange to have them shipped to England.

Florian Papps came next, since Nancy was a believer in what was eternal and not temporarily fashionable, where Rosie discovered a pair of rococo chairs and phoned Nancy to insist she came down to inspect them before the Met bought them to sit alongside the others they had recently acquired.

While Nancy was driving to Madison Avenue to inspect

Rosie's find, Rosie herself took off for George N on East 11th, where she knew she would find just the right chandeliers for the grand reception room. In an exhausting but exhilarating trail across town, having forgone lunch, downing a quick cup of coffee in The Stardust diner on Sixth, she spent most of the afternoon scouring shops in the Village.

A whole day taken up with checking out Nancy's country home in Connecticut followed. Rosie reached New York after ten that evening, not wanting anything other than a gossip with Ellie then bed.

On the last full day in New York, she spent a paralysingly frustrating but necessary morning, sorting out shipping arrangements in Nancy's office, after which an exhausted but elated Rosie was looking forward to a relaxing evening before getting the early morning flight back to London.

She had no problem with Nancy now but since Prague she preferred treating her as strictly business. But that was fine by Nancy, who no longer made any effort to include her socially as she had once done when they were in London. More to the point, Joel's name was glossed over.

It was some time before she noticed Nancy's party in the same restaurant that Jed had chosen for dinner. But then the choice of fashionable La Grenouille was not all that surprising. Nor was seeing Joel.

She hadn't seen him since that night in Prague weeks before, nor had she been expecting to now. Or perhaps, her more honest self said, she hadn't ruled it out, knowing that he was in New York. She had just understood if she saw him it would be by chance rather than design.

'Uh oh,' Jed murmured in Rosie's ear. 'The Alexander league out in force. I may have to be vulgar and work for a few moments, my petal.'

'Jed,' Ellie hissed across the table as he rose. 'Marianne will bust a gut if you mention her again.' But it was too late; he was already on course for Nancy's table.

'What is it? Who are they?' Rosie demanded as Ellie gave an exasperated sigh.

'Oh, spare me,' Ellie muttered. 'Now we may get stuck with bloody Nancy.'

'Who's with her?' Rosie asked.

'Apart from Joel? His ex, Marianne.' Ellie slid her eye around the half a dozen or so people at Nancy's table, stopping at a woman with ash-blonde hair swept loosely upwards from a classically oval face. Rosie thought she was beautiful.

'With Joel?' Rosie asked, amazed.

'Why not? They're on good terms now. The surprise is she even speaks to Nancy,' Ellie was saying. 'Let alone has dinner with her. Joel's best friend, my ass. The guy next to her is Dale Klonack, her husband. Nice guy. Plastic surgeon. Did Nancy's eyes. I bet Marianne prayed the scalpel would slip.

'Nonsense,' Ellie went on crisply as Rosie looked shocked. 'So would you if she broke up your marriage. Well, perhaps not broke it up. More she encouraged Joel not to try and mend it. I *know* he *was* playing around with some deb from Houston or Dallas or somewhere, and Marianne *had* met Dale, but most people thought Joel really did want to patch things up and they might have done, if only Nancy had just butted out. They have two nice kids. He's crazy about them.'

Rosie didn't have to be told that. Instead she said: 'Is Nancy involved with Joel?'

Ellie glanced over to where the millionairess was exchanging wisecracks with Jed. 'Hard to say. She certainly encourages Jed to think they're an item. But you know what Nancy likes.' Ellie waggled her eyebrows. Rosie giggled.

'Problem with Nancy is she only tolerates people with intellectual clout or more money than she's got. Marianne fails on both counts. Always has. All first nights and charming the top half of the social register is what the Klonacks do best. Not discussing obscure European painters the way Joel can.'

Rosie turned back to Ellie. 'What if Joel actually prefers Nancy?'

Ellie looked doubtful. 'As far as Nancy is concerned, Joel is her territory because her father commissioned him all those years ago to design the Alexander Museum in Detroit and it made him. Jed says Marianne and Dale are much better suited to each other.'

'Better for Jed too,' Rosie remarked, observing him glean at least three stories for his column from the ex Mrs Harley. 'What about Joel?'

'What about him? Happy? No idea. We'll soon find out. He's coming over.'

'Joel, lovely to see you.' Ellie turned to be kissed by him. 'I was just saying to Rosie, this dinner party will never get under way.' Rosie had a mental picture of Rory kissing Sylvia on the cheek. She moved back out of his reach, earning a surprised look from Ellie.

'You're lucky to have got her,' he said lightly. 'I missed out on dinner in Prague and failed to get lunch in London. Nice to see you. How's your family?'

'Fine. Just fine. Rory and Tom are in Scotland.'

'Maybe next time I'm in London we can have that lunch. I'd better get back. You're right, Ellie, I think someone's got to get things moving on these occasions, don't you?'

'Rosie,' Ellie said as Joel returned to his table, regarding one of her oldest friends with an expression that clearly showed a most intriguing thought had crossed her mind. 'Is there something you haven't told me?'

It was unfortunate that Rory, via an American friend, saw Jed's column.

Jed had named all of Nancy's guests and quoted her

gushing about the success of the lecture in Prague, which was no surprise to Rosie. But Jed had also mentioned that he had met all these charming people while hosting a dinner in honour of his friend, and Nancy's English designer, Rosie Colville.

'The company you keep.' Rory's voice was teasing but Rosie knew he wasn't.

'More the company Ellie and Jed keep,' she yawned. She was still jetlagged and she had been home for a week. She simply couldn't get her act together at all. The wrong time to think straight.

'Anyway Scotland was a success, I gather?' She changed the subject. Tom and Felix appeared to have run circles around Abbie, who had never been more glad to see Tom return to school for the rest of term.

Rosie privately thought it might herald Abbie's resignation. Looking in need of a well-earned break, Abbie came as near as Rosie had ever heard to being rude to Rory and Rosie was relieved that the housekeeper's undoubted passion for her ex-husband's lifestyle must be waning. But she refused to get drawn in. Rory hired her. Rory could fire her.

'Ask Tom. But before you do, yes, I did leave them on their own with Helen for a couple of days. Thought I might do some business and I had to stay in Edinburgh overnight. But he was fine.'

'That's okay,' she said, not minding because Abbie had been there as well as Helen who she gathered was Callum's housekeeper. 'I would have been amazed if you'd stayed the course.'

'You'd be amazed at what I can do these days,' he said, smiling at her with an intensity she found disturbing.

Tom was, if anything, more edgy when he came home at the weekend. For some time now Rosie had noticed that if the three of them were strolling back from having supper together, Rory would gently ease his son to one side of him, Rosie to the other, only to find minutes later that Tom had pushed between them.

Watching television curled up on the sofa, Rory might arrive and slump companionably down next to Rosie. Tom would announce he was starving, knowing Rosie would instantly get on her feet and rustle up a snack.

'Shouldn't he wait for supper?' Rory grumbled when this had happened too often for his liking.

But there was an area from which she was excluded which involved Tom and that was still not being allowed to see Callum.

'If this year is a success,' Rory would say, smiling into her eyes. He wanted Tom and his father for the moment to be exclusive, really get to know each other at a gentle pace. It sounded like sense, but it didn't seem right.

The private line in Rory's study rang almost constantly from mid-afternoon onwards. Rosie was glad she had the Mews House, it would have driven her mad, and clearly Rory found her presence unsettling when he was talking business.

If she went into the drawing room while he was on the phone, he would cease his conversation until she had left, or politely pause and ask her if she wanted anything in particular.

'Sorry, sweetheart,' he would say coming to find her after these calls. 'Just boring business.'

Moreover, Rosie found it difficult to remain silent on the subject of James Cooper, who Rory paraded as a businessman of acumen and integrity.

'James? A powerful executive? Oh c'mon, Rory, who are you kidding? He couldn't negotiate his way round a bend in the road.'

'James might be a pain to you,' Rory said carefully. 'But he gets things done. He's not riding around in that Aston Martin or has an office in New York because he's stupid.'

'No, but owning a Harley Davidson he keeps falling off, is. What does he do all day?'

Rory shrugged. 'You don't really want to hear all this boring stuff, do you? Come over here and entertain me instead.'

No longer could he control her with youthful passion. But Rosie knew what it was like to be able to control someone by resisting them. It was a powerful place to be with someone like Rory. Very powerful. Safe.

Now she raised her eyes. 'Oh God, Rory, don't you ever think of anything else? Silly me. Of course you don't. Seriously, I'm curious. I thought you might have moved on. I never believed in James. I think he's shady.'

Rory tapped the ash off the tip of his cigarette. He wasn't angry with her assessment, just wary. And it showed.

'Sorry,' she said lightly. 'None of my business.'

'No, no. You've got it all wrong. But then you never did have any confidence in me where work is concerned, did you, Rosie?'

She started to protest but he stopped her. 'It's all right, sweetheart, I understand. You always felt it was coming between us. I expect it's something you will always feel. I *do* understand. Honestly.'

Knowing it would be quicker to let him unload what he wanted to say, Rosie listened patiently, sorry she had been trapped into having dinner with him when all she had wanted after driving Tom back to school was to kick her shoes off and prepare for the next day.

'All I do, these days, is help James to secure the odd deal. Those clients of his react to a title and you know, sweetheart, even my father has got to bring himself up to date.'

'What's Callum got to do with James?'

'Oh, nothing directly, but James has given me some ideas about how to finance the estate if it comes to it. Some of these people, particularly the Americans, love being entertained in a house where there's a bit of history. I have to think of the future and James will be useful to me then. Actually, whenever he tells his clients I'm coming along you can see they half expect me to turn up with Fergie.'

'And what about estate management? The museum?' Rosie asked, refusing to be deflected.

Rory hesitated. Annoyance flashed across his face. She raised an eyebrow. Their gaze held. Then he chuckled, and she laughed.

'Well, that too. But honestly, sweetheart, I have to be honest, that might be my – our, all right, Tom's future, but it can be fucking boring. Oh c'mon, you know me. I much prefer to have fun and talking of fun . . .' He reached out an arm to grab her wrist as she rose to go, but she simply laughed and walked ahead of him out of the restaurant.

Later that week, sitting alone after Livvie had gone, gazing around her stylish workroom, Rosie heaved a satisfied sigh. It was Friday night. Tomorrow she would have a lie-in because Rory had offered to take her turn to get Tom since he had noticed she was not leaving her workroom much before ten each night.

Even though Rosie thought Livvie and Jordan were the dream team, she had refused to relinquish her personal input on her old clients. Miriam de Lisle might be a pain but she had been loyal when Rosie was in need of work. Jane Grantham was one of the exceptions as she was a good friend as well as a client.

She took overall charge of new clients but increasingly she was testing some of them to see if they would be willing to let Livvie take over. When it was apparent they were, she presented Livvie with a set of business cards that she had secretly had printed proclaiming: *Olivia Blake for Rosie Colville Interiors*.

The charm of Jordan was his genuine delight for Livvie,

who immediately booked herself into a workshop on 'Why be afraid of Success'. All three went out to celebrate, joined later by Kit who had just unloaded another unsatisfactory girlfriend and for once listened carefully to what Livvie had to say on the interface of personal relationships.

Jordan announced the sun was passing through Gemini so Kit's volatile love life was to be expected.

For once Livvie disagreed. 'He's trouble,' she said tersely.

'But Livvie,' Jordan wailed as they escorted each other to the tube. 'I thought you said he was dysfunctional, unable to commit and the sun *is* in Libra adversely aspected by Uranus and Neptune which means that this relationship was bound to come to an end, Gemini . . .'

'Fuck Gemini,' she ordered. 'I know what I said,' she threw back over her shoulder as she preceded him through the ticket barrier. 'That doesn't make him any less trouble to women.'

Jordan thought about it. 'Oh,' he said. 'Sorry, Liv.'

Rory was being so genuinely concerned with her business that she had finally agreed to have dinner with some of his clients. The arrangement cropped up quite suddenly and because it had distracted Rory from noticing her sudden flash of interest when he told her he had seen Joel in London eating out with his kids, she let him persuade her.

A favour. Some of James' associates were unexpectedly bringing their wives, and they both needed a partner.

'It would be a terrific help for me just this once,' Rory pleaded. 'I do need to impress them and you would, you know you would.'

Her first instinct had been to refuse, but then she thought of his generosity over the Mews House. And the way he had taken Tom off to Scotland so she could go to New York. So she changed her mind.

Just this once, she told herself. After all, it was simply helping him with his business as he had with hers.

She lifted her head as she heard the unmistakeable sound of his Porsche turning into the mews. The detailed measurements of the interior of the eight flats she had to finish in ten weeks, were being turned into drawings which had absorbed her so much she had forgotten the time.

Idly she looked down from the workroom window as Rory parked his car hard up against the garage door, switched off the engine and doused the lights. She watched as he swung his long frame out of the car, glancing up as he locked the door. Seeing her, he waved and pointed to his watch. She smiled and acknowledged that she understood, and he strode off towards the front of the house.

Turning back into the room, Rosie began stacking stray catalogues into the right files, piling pens and pencils into a big china jug shaped like a pig and started to switch off the lights.

She flicked the last light out, ran down the stairs and it was only when she reached the end of the mews that it occurred to her what she was doing. She slowed her steps and halted, looking up at the silent house where Rory was waiting to take her to dinner. Business, she told herself firmly. Simply business. What else?

Ellie had suggested she was not getting enough attention. She didn't think that was the case. Not getting enough attention from the right person, was the problem.

# Chapter Twenty-Nine

No-one seeing the estranged couple arriving together at the exclusive Mayfair club chosen by James to entertain his clients would have described the picture they created as anything other than glamorous. Some might even have whispered 'reconciled'.

The same black dress she had worn in Prague but with the benefit of a light tan, earrings of gold-and-jet intertwined loops and a matching necklace, were all Rosie needed to look effortlessly at ease in her surroundings.

Rory always had been completely at home in designer clothes and Rosie could see he was not immune to the impression he was creating in a black Yves Saint Laurent double-breasted jacket and a dark blue Armani tie as they were guided to where James was waiting with his guests: two oil executives from Houston with their wives and a blonde with a practised charm that was tottering on the embarrassing. At least until Rosie got the full blast of what passed for social intercourse from the rest of the group.

Beyond nodding at Rosie, Betsey, the blonde, then ignored her, her time, attention and energy focused unrelentingly on the Americans.

To Betsey, nothing they said was dull. She admired the novelty of their thinking that wouldn't have strained an episode of 'Melrose Place' and marvelled at their grasp of English life, which was drawn almost entirely from bad historical novels.

It was clear that the Americans, who Rory said were keen to plough money into the museum and tourist centre at Glencairn, had not originally planned to have their wives present. And it was even clearer that James was not thrilled when the smiling Texan who clearly held the strings to the whole deal was taken with, not Betsey's unadulterated admiration, but Rosie's understated English sense of humour. Even he could see that the combination of that plus the fact that she looked untouchably classy, was a potent partnership.

By the time they finished dinner and someone suggested dancing, Grant E. Morgernstern had spurned the charms of Betsey and tried to give Rosie the number of his hotel room, while he described in graphic detail, growling into her ear, how he thought she might entertain him while his wife was checking out Harrods.

The dance floor was crowded, the music loud, it was several minutes before it registered with Rosie just what he was suggesting as he rammed explicitly against her to the music. Furiously she pushed him away.

'I admire your ambition,' she told him with an iciness that took him by surprise. 'But you're aiming far too high.'

'Hey, honey,' he crooned, his eyes narrowed, breathing heavily. 'I'm more than willing to learn.'

'Really?' She started to leave the floor. 'Since you've clearly left your brains in Texas, I wonder what would you use? Excuse me.'

'Listen, bitch.' He grabbed her arm, pulling her inches from his face. 'I am in this for a lot of bucks with your James . . .'

'He is not *my* James,' she snapped.

'Well, that's no way to get my business,' he hissed, red in the face. 'It was just a bit of fun . . .'

'James might want your business, but I am not part of it. Nor am I a bit of fun, I am . . . I am Rory's wife.'

'His *what*?'

'I mean, ex-wife, and you've obviously got entirely the wrong impression. Now excuse me.'

Marching back to the table, Rory took one look at her face and hurriedly muttered something to James.

'I knew it was a mistake,' James whispered back furiously as Rosie reached the table, ignoring the other women, snatched up her bag and told Rory she wanted to go. *Now.*

Grabbing her hand, he halted her just long enough to whisper urgently to James that he'd be back. But he never made it.

Outside ignoring her protests that all she wanted to do was go home, he pulled her into a nearby bar and ordered a couple of brandies. It wasn't until they were sitting down that she realised it was one of their old haunts. Well, an old one of hers. Rory seemed to have remained a loyal customer.

'The problem is,' he said into the silence as she angrily gripped her glass, 'you shouldn't be so fucking attractive. I'm sorry, sweetheart, and James is really too . . .'

'I bet he is,' she snarled.

'Well, perhaps sorry I got you involved. My fault. Those Americans don't know how to behave.'

She glared at him. He hung his head. She could see he was trying not to laugh.

After a while she relented. 'Nice to know I can still pull,' she said dryly.

'You wouldn't even have to try with me.' He held her gaze. The bar was crowded. They were sitting too closely together. Rory let one finger run gently down her arm. She didn't move.

'You know watching him come onto you like that was weird. Exciting. I just wanted to whip you straight back home.'

Rosie sat very still. Stunned. 'You *saw* what he was doing? *Knew?* And you didn't *do* anything? And you enjoyed it? How could you?'

'Calm down,' he urged, pulling her back down beside

him. 'I didn't say I wasn't going to do something. And no, I didn't enjoy the idea of him mauling you, just you looked so angry, it was very sexy. But then you always do. Piers was so stupid.'

She looked doubtfully at him as she sat back. It was hard to believe he meant either of those things. But it didn't seem to matter very much, not at this precise moment.

Rory ordered two more drinks. 'Let's forget what happened. I really want to talk to you, Rosie, just like we used to. Oh c'mon,' he pleaded. 'It's too early to go home, eh? And where's the harm?'

The house was in darkness when they finally arrived back. No Abbie. She was late too. Rosie knew she should have said no to the drinks. They made her sleepy and she was tired enough.

She made coffee, Rory watched her in silence. She yawned and said it was late, she would go to bed.

She thought Rory would be rejoining James. It was still early for him, but to her surprise he followed her upstairs saying he thought he would have an early night, watch the late movie.

'I was bored with that lot even before we left,' he grinned. 'What's that?' He indicated some folders she had taken with her from the kitchen table.

'I've got to check these,' she said. 'Jordan needs an answer in the morning.'

'Good, is he? Can I see?'

They were standing outside her door just to the left of the stairs. 'Sure.' She handed them to him. God, she was tired.

'Don't you ever think of anything else?' he asked, giving the rough sketches a cursory glance.

'Of course,' she said, reaching out to take them back, expecting him to hand them to her. In one movement he dropped the folders between them, and pulled her to him, twisting round so that his back was already pushing open her bedroom door.

'This for example?' he breathed, his hands digging into her bare back, pulling her after him into her room.

She gasped at his once so familiar touch and squirmed, trying to get away from him.

'Rory, stop it. I've got work to do . . .'

'It can wait,' he muttered, pushing down the straps of her dress. 'This can't. Not any longer and you know it.'

She didn't scream. She knew she couldn't. His mouth was grinding into hers, she felt herself falling backwards onto her bed, instinctively she clung to him, bringing him crashing down on top of her. Black lights flashed in her head. She knew she wasn't resisting. Couldn't, he was too strong for her. She felt her skirt being pushed up, his mouth was on her neck.

If there had been a moment, a second to think, it would have been different. But then she wasn't thinking and the unthinkable happened and she knew she hadn't resisted enough.

'This is how it was meant to be, Rosie,' he breathed into her hair, stroking her back as they lay sprawled across her bed. 'Me and you, just a temporary break, but we've always belonged together.'

She lay with her eyes shut, trying not to think. Best not to. Impossible not to. Long after she heard his even breathing, she had slipped from the room and sat hugging her knees in the kitchen, frightened, confused, wondering how had she been so stupid? How had she let it happen?

Why hadn't she seen it coming? But as dawn broke and she climbed exhausted into bed in the spare room, she knew she had seen it coming, undeniably, absolutely. And she had done nothing to stop it. Thought she could handle it. Thought that this time she held the power.

The question she asked herself as she shut her eyes and

tried to blot out the raging throbbing in her head, was not whether there was a difference between rape and consent but where did one stop and the other begin?

# Chapter Thirty

Slowly she eased herself up in the bed. She waited for the wave of remorse, the embarrassment to wash over her. Nothing happened.

Her head felt like cotton wool had been wrung out inside it, lead weights were on her eyes. The house was silent. Sunlight streamed onto the landing outside the door as she made her way back to her own room. It looked chaotic. Rory's clothes lay in a heap by the bed, her own tangled up with them. For the first time she thought she was going to be sick.

A gentle tap at the door was followed by Abbie, whose frozen expression conveyed exactly what she thought of the jumble on the floor.

'Rory asked me to bring this up,' she said, placing a tray of black coffee on the table. 'He said you might have a . . . a bit of a headache.'

'Thank you, Abbie.' Rosie tried hard to sound normal.

When she had gone, Rosie looked at herself in the mirror. Dishevelled hair, pale skin but nothing else. She thought at the very least her eyes would look haunted.

The same moves, the same pattern, familiar bodies, familiar demands, only this time it was Rory who had been uncertain when it was over.

But for Rosie? For Rosie it was different. Something was finally resolved, finished. Something had been lifted from her.

Her head throbbed. Her eyes ached. A shower, that's what she needed. Gingerly she bent down and picked up her scattered clothes, knowing she would never wear that crumpled black dress again.

Water gushed down her back, through her hair. Wrapping a warm towel around her she pushed open the windows of her room and winced in the sunlight. She knew Rory was in the house somewhere. At some point sooner rather than later she would have to confront him.

'Let's just call it a mistake,' she said quietly. 'Unfinished business if you like. Pretend it never happened. We were both not thinking straight.'

Rory was in the kitchen when she finally caught up with him. Tom had to be collected by lunchtime, and they'd promised to pick up Felix as well. She had no idea if what she was doing was the best thing.

Just looking at him pouring coffee as she spoke, she could see he knew last night was never going to be repeated. He knew when he woke and found her gone. Knew she was in the guest room.

'You mean, a casual, meaningless encounter?' His voice was matter-of-fact, almost chatty. He could have been Livvie.

'Call it what you like,' she said wearily. 'Just don't call it anything other than a huge mistake on your part and an even worse one on mine. Don't make me struggle to explain. I shouldn't have to.'

'My darling girl,' he exclaimed, pausing to replace the percolator on its stand. 'Why struggle? What is the matter with you? Why does everything have to be such a drama?'

'It's not a drama,' she protested. 'It was the one thing I didn't want to happen, didn't think would happen.'

'Really?' he asked politely, making no effort to hide the frankly sceptical tone.

'No. Of course not. How can you say that?'

He pulled a chair out and straddled it, taking a gulp of coffee, watching her over the brim. 'How can I say what?

That you weren't looking for it?' He ignored her gasp. 'What else can I think? You spend weeks deliberately making me notice you, you arrive for dinner in a fuck-me dress, so much so that one of James' guests also apparently gets the wrong idea and then I did too? *Tsk tsk*, Rosie baby, who are we kidding here?'

She felt sick watching his sneering disbelief. It took all her willpower not to smack him hard across his face. That and the fact that there was just a grain of truth in what he was saying.

'Fuck-me dress?' she said lightly in a voice that didn't sound anything like the way she was feeling. 'What charming expressions you use. I was going to say I don't know what gave you the idea I was looking for a fuck, because that was the last thing I intended.'

'Oh?' His tone was openly insulting now, his manner contemptuous. 'Then what did you intend? I don't think we're talking about me forcing myself on you, are we?'

'I think we are. I wasn't "looking for it" as you put it,' she replied as calmly as the searing injustice of what he was saying would allow. 'I simply didn't make enough effort to stop it.'

He laughed in her face.

All she could recall were the moments in the last few weeks when Rory had made it obvious he was making the running.

'Excuse me,' he interrupted. 'I don't make mistakes where sex is concerned. Unlike you I'm not stuck for a partner or two – as you so clearly recognised last night at a most passionate moment.'

Rosie flushed, knowing one of her few sane moments in the frantic physical activity that had robbed her of nearly all her common sense was to insist he used a condom.

This was pointless. Accusation and counter claim. Bitter exchanges about who was to blame. Somewhere it flickered that Rory was angry not because she had been honest, but there was something else.

Like a man who had gambled away something valuable. He had tested his power and it had failed. The control he wanted and had always exerted over her was gone.

'I'll get Tom,' she said quietly, not trusting him to drive. 'I'm sorry you feel like that. I couldn't allow you to . . .' she stopped. 'To think there will be a repeat performance.'

'My dear girl,' he drawled, getting up. His chair was pushed back with a sharp scrape. 'Let's pretend it never happened. In fact until you mentioned it, I'd completely forgotten about it anyway.'

Sylvia Duxborough turned up to collect Felix, maintaining an irritating air of composure as Rosie had to ask Tom not once but three times to turn the television volume down.

'Daddy says visitors should use the drawing room in his house,' Tom retorted, which earned him the penalty of being instantly ordered to his room.

'Sorry,' Rosie said briefly as she closed the door firmly after her son, who could be heard thumping up the stairs. Sylvia, who was smiling maternally and gently at her own son, stroking his hair which surprised Felix as much as Rosie, said nothing.

'I think Tom's going down with something,' Rosie told her firmly, knowing Sylvia had devoured every word Tom had said which had relegated Rosie very firmly to the status of a mere guest in this house.

'Of course,' Sylvia smoothly agreed. 'However, I can see you'll be able to cope more easily if we absent ourselves. Felix darling, Mummy's ready,' she cooed, ignoring his bewildered look at her unusually tender tone. 'Daddy's waiting.'

Having seen Sylvia and Felix out, Rosie strode off to find Rory. Eventually she tracked him down to his bedroom.

'Do you mind if I come in?' she called through the door.

'As long as you don't stay,' Rory replied. He was lying full length on his bed, the television on and a glass of whisky in his hand. A light blue fug of smoke hung over the room.

She waved her hand in front of her face, coughing.

'I can see where Tom gets it from.' She leaned against the door eyeing the chaos, and not quite believing that someone could actually want to watch Oprah Winfrey at five in the afternoon, knocking back whisky when the day outside was so sunny and warm.

Watching him lying in the midst of such chaos, she checked what she was about to say and began instead:

'We've got to start agreeing about certain things.'

'Like?' he asked lazily, not taking his eyes off the screen. 'Oh God, just look at that woman. No wonder he left her for her sister. Jee-zus, look at the mother. Oh, please . . . I don't be-leeve it. He's screwing *the father*.'

Rory howled with laughter, rolling hysterically around on the bed. She tried again. It was like dealing with Tom.

'I said we have to agree,' she raised her voice to compete with the screaming laughter of the studio audience, 'on certain rules where Tom is concerned.'

She knew he wasn't listening. He ignored her trying to get his attention.

Before he could do anything she strode across to the bed and made a grab for the remote control where it lay beside him, half covered by the *Standard* and an overflowing ashtray.

More than once it had occurred to her that Rory was brilliant at performing. Not for one second was he off guard. His hand came down on her wrist, pinning it to the bed and somehow in the same movement he jerked her forward so that she was half lying, half kneeling beside him.

'What was it you wanted?' he asked, twisting over,

pushing her onto her back to gaze down into her face. 'Or can I guess?'

She looked steadily back at him. 'Rory,' she said softly. 'Don't even think it. Not for a second.'

For a moment he gazed thoughtfully down at her and then flopped back on his pillow.

'Think what?' he asked, snapping the television back on, but this time the volume was down.

'Nothing,' Rosie answered, easing herself off the bed and moving towards the door. 'I thought we might have a talk about Tom. But I can see the challenge of real life is eluding you again.'

Her hand was already on the door. 'By the way,' he called after her. 'I've fixed a holiday.'

'A holiday?'

'Sure. Tom thinks it all sounds terrific.'

'Tom does?'

'That's right.'

'And when do we leave?' she asked icily. 'Not to mention where. It might not fit in with my plans.'

'I hadn't actually planned on you coming,' he said, blowing a cloud of smoke in her face. 'I'm flattered that you want to, delighted. You'll enjoy it. Monte Carlo.'

'Monte Carlo? No, I don't think so.'

'Well, that's where we're going, sweetheart, take it or leave it.'

The door slammed behind her. She heard him laugh as she ran down the hall and out of the house.

After sitting in a darkened cinema seeing a film she could not recall, she walked home trying to stem the rising tide of panic. Not yet ready to berate herself for believing this arrangement would work. She'd called Rory a dreamer. But what was she?

As she closed the door behind her she saw Rory coming downstairs with a pleasant-faced man carrying a black bag.

'Oh, there you are.' Rory looked harassed. 'God, I was so worried. Tom woke with a temperature and was practically delirious, I didn't know where you'd gone . . . you stormed out without saying where I could reach you . . . anyway, he's calmed down now. Dr Collins – John, isn't it? – came to my rescue.'

Rosie went to push past them. 'He was fine when I left,' she said ignoring Rory and addressing the doctor. 'What happened?'

Dr Collins looked at her with undisguised annoyance, snapping the lock on his case. 'There's no temperature and he doesn't feel sick any more. I expect it was a bad dream. He certainly is feeling quite upset about one or two things. Your husband had done a good job of calming him before I got here. He's nearly asleep.'

'I'll go up to him,' she said, taking the stairs two at a time. Tom was dozing, his face was cool. Briefly he stirred as she smoothed his hair back from his face, lightly stroking his smooth cheek.

Rosie was suffused with guilt that he might really have been ill and she had stomped off. She, so quick to accuse both her ex-husband and son of the same petulant behaviour. She took one of his hands and gently stroked it.

'Mum?' Tom murmured sleepily.

'Hi darling,' she said softly. 'Feeling better now? What was it?'

His voice was drowsy, only half answering her. 'I don't know. I don't remember, I just woke up and the doctor was there. Daddy was worried, Mum, I heard him tell the doctor.'

Rosie stiffened. 'Tell him what?'

'That you didn't want to live here any more, but that's not true is it, Mum? Dad made a mistake, didn't he?'

Rosie hesitated, not wanting to lie. 'I wouldn't go

anywhere without you,' she whispered. 'You know that.'

'Or Dad,' he insisted. 'I wouldn't want to leave Dad behind. He said you were having a breakdown, but you're not, are you?'

Shock made her sit back on her heels. 'Of course not,' she said trying to control the fury in her voice. 'If anyone's having a breakdown round here, it's not me.'

'Breakdown? What made you say that?'

'What made me? Just look at you. Storming out of the house because I arrange a holiday, blaming me for something you brought on yourself. You've got circles under your eyes, your work is all you care about . . .'

'That isn't true, Rory. Fixing a holiday without telling me or consulting me is not on. You must consult me where Tom is concerned. That's our deal.'

'Why? You never told me you would be out sightseeing with Harley . . .'

'Don't be absurd. Come to that, you never mentioned Ireland to me.'

Too late she realised he had moved her from the main point. They were now trading insults to justify their lifestyles, when they should have been discussing how to bring their relationship to an end. Admit failure, retreat to their separate bases. The problem for Rosie was that she didn't yet have a base to go to. And Tom didn't want to go even if she had.

Next day the doctor called her and suggested she might like to discuss her problems with a counsellor. 'As much for your sake as your son's?'

She tried to sound polite but her indignation got the better of her. 'I am not in need of counselling. Neither is my son. What kind of doctor are you to believe exactly what you are told?'

There was a short silence and then he said stiffly: 'I am

going to ignore that outburst and would simply urge you to rethink. Keeping problems bottled up is not going to help. Your son is suffering. You need help.'

# Chapter Thirty-One

In the interests of the holiday and Tom's feelings, Rosie decided that whatever the provocation she was going to rise above it all. It was a nice idea. It was of short duration.

The receptionist looked blank when Rosie announced herself and Tom at the hotel in Menton. 'There must be a mistake, Madame, there is no such reservation.' Even the manager when summoned insisted she must have the wrong hotel. Of course she could see the reservations book herself. Here. See? No Monteith Gores.

It took her another two hours to find Rory at the right hotel, by which time Tom was hot and fed up and Rosie was in a filthy temper and had seriously wondered why she was there at all.

With Rory was a worried-looking manager who sighed with relief when Tom fell out of the taxi shouting to attract his father's attention.

'Oh God, there you are,' Rory exclaimed striding from the hotel lobby towards them. 'I was worried sick. Where *have* you been?'

'Where have *I* been?' she cried. And so it started. Accusation and counter accusation until, worn out from travelling, hot, tired and now accused of incompetence, Rosie turned to the manager and demanded the key to her room. Telling Rory to cope with the luggage, she stalked off into the lift, leaving Tom to stare aghast after her.

As the doors closed the last thing she heard was Rory saying, 'Sorry, Michel. She's not well and you know what these career women are like, workaholics, you have to prise them away from their desks ...' He gave a small laugh. 'Tom and I will be fine. Thanks for your help.'

She struggled to press the 'door open' button to refute such a lie, but the mechanism, like life, seemed to be against her.

Rolling off the bed, Rosie pushed back the shutters that led onto a small marble-floored, glass-fronted terrace. It had been too late last night to see what now with a rush of warm air lay before her.

The sea was so wide, so blue, so near, at first she gasped. Away to her left the deserted ribbon of road, which yesterday had been packed with holiday makers, curved neatly around the bay and disappeared into a tangle of palm trees overhanging the usually bustling little boulevard until it disappeared towards the Italian border.

She stayed there mesmerised by the power of it all. The sea in the early morning sun an unmatchable mix of emerald green, navy blue and azure. Pinpricks of light were bouncing off the water in a dizzying display of flashes.

Irresistible. Ten minutes later with a cotton kanga pulled over her swimsuit, she scribbled a note for Tom and Rory in case they came looking for her.

Quietly she let herself into their room, crossed to the dressing table and moved a pile of Rory's clothes so that she could leave the note propped up. The smell of nicotine was unmistakeable. So too was the slender ribbon of a bow tie, trailing from one pocket of Rory's dinner jacket. He must have gone out again after she and Tom were asleep. Nothing changed.

For a while she gazed down at her son. Then she dropped the jacket where she had found it, propped up the note where Tom would see it if he woke early and as silently as she had entered she left the room.

\* \* \*

'How was the casino?' she asked casually a couple of hours later as the three of them sat down to breakfast on her terrace.

Rory, who was looking surprisingly alert on so little sleep, looked up from the morning paper with a wary flicker of surprise. 'No casino,' he replied, turning the pages of *Nice Matin*. 'James is staying at the Paris, left a message for me. You were asleep. You don't mind?'

'No, of course not,' she said, pouring more juice for Tom.

'We're going swimming in the sea, aren't we, Daddy,' Tom said, stuffing croissants coated in jam into his mouth. 'You can come too, Mum,' he offered generously. 'Only we're going to race, so you might not like it.'

Rosie was torn between the rare pleasure of just sitting with a book while Tom was entertained, knowing she could escape being around Rory baiting her, arousing her anger. But she also felt a bit left out. Common sense won.

'Quite right. Enjoy yourselves. I'll watch from the beach. Anyway, I've had enough swimming for one day.'

Tom's good humour was shortlived. At dinner that night, after a day that sounded more like preparation for the Olympics than a father and son enjoying themselves, Tom was a nightmare.

He was allowed to choose the restaurant just to keep him quiet and plumped for one in the bustling old town square next to a lively carousel and in full view of a rollerblade demonstration which fascinated him. It was not what Rosie or, to be fair, Rory, would have chosen. Conversation was limited, largely because Tom dominated the proceedings.

He swapped chairs with Rosie and changed his mind three times about his food. When it came he said he preferred her fettucini to the ravioli he had settled on.

Rosie gritted her teeth and exchanged meals, insisting she didn't mind what she had, and simply looked apprehensive when he insisted on sipping some of Rory's wine. His father muttered that he could drink the lot if it just kept him quiet.

They finished the meal in record time, no-one anxious to linger. Determined not to return to the hotel too soon, Rosie suggested they had coffee on the way back.

'We've still got to decide what to do tomorrow,' she said firmly and cheerfully as Tom started to moan about wanting to get back to watch reruns of Star Trek on cable TV.

'It's decided,' Rory said casually as they paused in front of a pavement café.

'What is?' Rosie asked.

'Tomorrow. Oh, didn't I mention it? Sorry, I meant to tell you. We're having lunch with Joel Harley.'

# Chapter Thirty-Two

'Where did you meet him?' she demanded, caught off guard and betraying more interest than she intended.

'Couple of days back. I was having lunch with a friend who knows him well and he was at the next table with his kids and his parents. I said you and Tom were joining me and Veronica Harley suggested we all came to lunch. They have a villa at Cap Ferrat but they thought it would be fun to have lunch on their yacht.'

Part of her was relieved. Rory's blatant networking. That's all it was. At first she refused to go, saying he could take Tom on his own. His anger left her unmoved. But Veronica Harley didn't. Failing to get his own way, Rory had phoned Joel's mother at the villa and whatever he said brought a call from her.

'Do come,' she said. 'I can assure you no-one is standing on ceremony. My grandchildren make sure of that. Besides, Joel and Nancy speak so highly of you that I would love to get to know you better. We hardly had time to say hello in Prague. And Joel says you're impossible to pin down while you're working.'

It wasn't vanity that swung it. It was not being able to refuse the genuine niceness of Veronica Harley. But at least both Joel and Nancy would know she was his mother's guest, not his.

And she was prepared. This time she would not confuse charm with interest. This time she was immune.

Joel was wearing an old and clearly favourite pair of faded cotton trousers rolled up at the ankles with white deck shoes, Ben was in cut-off Bermuda shorts and a ragged Counting Crows T-shirt.

You could not fault Rory's appearance but against Joel and Ben's casual disregard for fashion, his designer-labelled T-shirt, waist-pleated cotton trousers and navy loafers looked studied rather than comfortable.

Rosie's greeting to Joel was that of a friendly colleague. She'd been psyching up for the moment ever since she'd agreed to come. 'What a surprise,' she laughed, shaking hands. 'Your mother is hard to resist.'

'Well, I've always thought so.' He returned her clasp. 'Hope the rest of us can match up to her. Rory, good to see you and Tom.' He grinned down at Tom who was wearing an Arsenal logo on his T-shirt and had been rendered silent. 'I think Ian Wright's had a great season, don't you?'

'Just love "Sullivan Street",' Rosie smiled at Ben, mentioning a favourite track from Counting Crows' last album once the introductions were over and they were strolling across the marina to where the yacht was moored.

Joel raised an eyebrow. 'Good grief,' he murmured as he stood aside for her to follow Ben along the short gangway, 'I thought I was the only one earning brownie points around here.'

'You don't need to,' she pointed out. 'You're providing lunch.'

He laughed and said: 'You're sounding much better than I expected. Perhaps Rory was just being an overprotective husband.'

'I'm fine,' she protested, puzzled, forgetting to correct the mistake. 'Why? Did Rory say I wasn't?'

'I think he said you were feeling the workload a bit.'

'Nonsense.' Her voice was brisk. 'I can't get enough of it.'

'So I gathered,' he remarked. 'Ah, here's Lexie. Let me introduce you,' as the girl Rosie had last seen outside

Nancy's house swinging on Joel's arm appeared round the corner.

From everyone's point of view the lunch was a success. Geoffrey and Veronica Harley were hospitable and genial hosts, Veronica greeting Rosie warmly and endearing herself to her by saying she hadn't a clue where Nancy was. New York probably.

Joel's children were engaging if slightly bored teenagers, with flat mid-Atlantic accents. Ben, the mirror image of his father, was at fourteen a year older than olive-skinned Alexa, known to everyone as Lexie, who would, Rosie decided, eventually be as beautiful as her mother.

The Harleys had also invited two old friends who were charming but kept shooting anxious glances towards their daughter Claudie who had brought along her friend Tansi. Their appearance left Rosie in no doubt why Rory knew them. Claudie turned out to be the mutual friend who had introduced Rory to the Harleys.

They were both unreasonably beautiful, in silk shirts over bikinis, gold bracelets setting off the depth of the tans they had both acquired by liberal helpings of oil which they frequently smoothed on themselves and each other.

Rory greeted them both with double kisses, explaining that Tansi was in the film he was advising on and Claudie was an interpreter, which is how they'd all met. I bet, Rosie thought dryly, having instantly recognised why Veronica Harley made no real effort to speak to either of them.

At lunch Rosie was seated between Joel and Claudie's father and while her French was passable, even so she often had to stop to search for the right word. It was, however, its very fractured nature that was keeping the old man charmed.

'I was just telling Rory, you don't want this wreck, do you?' Geoffrey was calling across the table to his son.

Joel smiled. 'I love it, I just wouldn't use it and anyway

architects don't earn as much as industrialists or have the time to keep going on holiday . . .'

'So what's your idea of bliss if it isn't owning a boat like this?' Rosie asked him as everyone laughed.

'Oh, that's easy,' he said, stretching out and folding his arms behind his head, so that she had to turn slightly to look at him. He was looking straight ahead out to sea.

'Being a guest on someone else's yacht, my children near enough for me to know what they're doing, busy enough not to be a pain, all of which compensates for knowing I have my mother to thank for getting a difficult woman to have lunch with me.'

Rosie laughed. 'I knew it. There had to be a sting in the tail.'

'Oh, there is but that's not it.'

'What is it then?' she asked lightly, sipping her wine and wondering why she felt apprehensive. She couldn't see his eyes hidden behind dark glasses. But as she spoke, he pushed them back into his hair and said:

'I think she prefers houses to people.'

Before they had finished lunch, Rosie had made a couple of shrewd guesses about the Harleys' glamorous guests.

Back on deck after their swim Lexie, who'd been parted quite long enough from her Walkman, retired to a spot where she could veg out, Ben heroically took Tom off to play with some of his computer games, Joel disappeared to deal with some faxes that had come over, leaving Rosie leaning on the ship's rail in contented silence.

Rory, Tansi and Claudie were stretched full length on sun loungers, posing. No-one could possibly describe it as anything else.

Rosie turned away and gazed out over the sea. Her skin was now a golden bronze given even more depth by the black one-piece swimsuit she had changed into which also managed to make her already long slender legs even longer.

Her figure belied the fact that she had an eleven-year-old son.

'They look like they're auditioning for *Vogue*,' she grinned at Joel as he came towards her, indicating the perfectly positioned trio. He glanced along the deck and shrugged.

'Yes, but you look like you're in it,' he replied and she hoped he would mistake the blush for sunburn.

'Goodness,' she stammered. 'I must remember in future to have an ocean handy for when I want to look my best.'

He laughed, placing his hand on the small of her back. 'Come and sit up front where the kids can't find us and I won't have to watch my mother do her desperate best to ignore Claudie.'

'Claudie's stunning, isn't she?' Rosie remarked as they settled on adjacent cushions, their backs leaning against the side, only a distant view of another yacht gliding silently across the horizon to contemplate as theirs made its way back to the harbour. Bliss. She forced herself to remember her vow. Stay immune. It wasn't easy.

'Stunning,' he agreed. 'Shame about the brain. It's just that her parents have so spoilt her, that they either can't see or just ignore what's happening to her.'

'And that is?'

'Miss Colville.' He looked at her, feigning shock. 'Even my mother has that one sussed.'

Rosie blushed. As much for the sense of pleasure that he had not called her by Rory's name but her own, as the quality of the question. 'Sorry. Stupid of me,' she agreed.

A silence hung between them. 'Actually,' Rosie finally ventured, a wicked gleam in her eye but perfectly straight-faced. 'Would you mind not letting Rory know?'

'Rory?' Joel was startled. 'But he knows exactly what he's doing and what Claudie is about.'

'Mmm,' she agreed. 'But he does believe, poor man, that one night with him is all any woman needs to straighten them out. He honestly wouldn't recover if tomorrow morning he found out Claudie still prefers Tansi.'

'Good God, will it take him that long?' Joel asked solemnly, putting his hand playfully over her mouth as she struggled not to laugh out loud. 'Shh,' he chuckled under his breath. 'They'll all want to share the joke, if they hear you.'

Rosie knew she *liked* him. Liked the way his eyes crinkled when he laughed, the dry humour, the easy way they drifted into exchanging histories.

He told her about the days just after Yale when Harley Associates was just himself with occasional help from college friends working from an attic room in a disused furniture repository on New York's East Side.

He'd had a view there, over the river, from its huge iron skylights and at night he would sit in the twilight, mesmerised by the brilliant fiery glitter of the city, and he would shuffle its patterns of light and dark in his imagination.

'Very intense stuff, seems quite embarrassing now.'

Like most young architects he had begun by churning out designs for houses for friends and then for friends of friends, graduating as his contacts grew to bigger and grander houses and then onto schemes for small-town redevelopments and the offices of companies whose ambitions usually outstripped their budgets. Then the Alexander Museum had come along and changed everything.

'It was a competition. I knew I needed to win, to shift myself from that routine stuff to making sense of all the years spent at architecture school and Yale.'

Rosie understood. It was how she had felt when Nancy's commission had come along. She'd had to seize the chance, just as Joel had. Odd to think it was Nancy who had opened new horizons for them both. Just then Tom appeared, peering uncertainly round the corner. Joel saw him first.

'Hi, Tom, are we about to dock?'

Tom nodded shyly and disappeared. Joel rose to his feet, holding out his hand to pull Rosie to hers. For a brief second they looked at each other.

'Well.' She made the supreme effort. 'We'd better join the others,' and moved ahead of him.

'Rory,' she said as she neared them. 'It's been a wonderful afternoon, hasn't it?'

'Oh, sweetheart.' He looked up. 'I've got to meet James for a quick drink. Claudie's offered to drop me off. I'll be back later. Will you be all right to drive? I know you won't want to hang around – didn't you say you have all those phone calls to make to the workroom?'

He rolled his eyes to the assembled group, lazily watching the outcome of this minor domestic difference. 'If she could bring a phone with her she would,' he joked, getting to his feet. 'Joel, that was terrific. Veronica, what can I say? Darling, see you later.'

# Chapter Thirty-Three

'Don't be stupid, Rory,' Rosie said. 'You don't have to lie. If you want to screw Claudie Bergerard until what little remains of her brain drops out ... okay, Tansi then, it doesn't concern me. Just try not to let it be too public. I assume you know what you're doing and understand their er ... shall we say weaknesses?'

'What's that supposed to mean?' He wasn't whispering but she knew he didn't want to be overheard.

'Rory, sweetheart,' she mocked. 'If troilism and lipstick dykes with a coke problem are your scene, who am I to spoil your fun? Just do me a favour, Rory. Steer clear of the drugs. Okay?'

'I don't do drugs,' he told her coldly.

'No, of course you don't. Silly me. With your addiction to sex, I don't really see where you would find the time.'

It was not quite seven o'clock. She poured a glass of wine and pushed open the door to the terrace. By lunchtime next day, when Rory had failed to appear, she had recognised the pattern and had taken Tom up to spend the rest of the day in Ventimiglia, a little market town across the Italian border. Tom was now lying on his bed, watching TV.

Somewhere in the distance she could hear a quartet playing in one of the restaurants that lined the front and a band performing 'I Can See Clearly Now', the percussionist trying to keep time with the drummer and the singer oblivious to both.

The peace without Rory around was heaven. But Tom

kept asking when he would be back and she couldn't face a scene by saying he was back to his old tricks. Work, she explained. Dad was working hard.

The problem she had never really envisaged was that it would be Tom preventing her from leaving. Her house was months away from being complete but if Tom had been agreeable she would have rented a flat and got them both out. She had to fight down the panic.

A soft tap on the door made her turn. One of the desk clerks was standing there with a folded note. Rosie took it and glanced at the contents.

'Mr Harley rang but as there was no answer from your room, he left this message. He is taking the children to dinner at La Barque. If you get the note in time, would you and Tom like to join them?'

It was only later that she realised he hadn't included Rory. She rang the restaurant and left a message to say they would be there. Joel knew, as she did, that the people Rory was with in Monte Carlo would keep him fully occupied, blowing each other's minds. And much else besides, she decided.

They found La Barque without any difficulty. The old town square, a mere stroll from the hotel, was a fairyland of lights strung from trees, tables spilling out onto the narrow cobbled streets or cordoned off by colourful ribboned fences in the centre of the square, while waiters dashed between the crowds loaded down with trays of drinks and steaming plates of food.

A guitarist strolled between the tables of one establishment, a jazz pianist knocked out Fats Waller hits at another while the buzz of diners talking and bursts of laughter punctuated the warm summer night air.

Unusually for him, Tom accepted Rory's absence with less difficulty than she had dreaded when they discovered that Joel had been joined not just by Alexa and Ben but by his partner Daniel and Daniel's wife Stevie, and their two children, one of whom was Tom's age.

Tom was thrilled. It was moments like that when Rosie realised how much he had missed out being an only child.

It was an enchanting evening. A mini travelling circus had set up in the square, and this had the entire table in stitches not least because from where Joel and Rosie were sitting they could see behind the scenes where the two clowns were engaged in a furious feud about their act, only to switch to engaging hilarity once they ran through the tiny flap in the makeshift tent to perform like lovable old pals.

Helplessly laughing as much at Stevie who was practically sobbing with mirth as Daniel took pictures of the battle going on backstage, Rosie didn't even think as Joel, in no better state, simply handed her his napkin to mop her streaming eyes.

Rosie had rarely felt so relaxed. Or at home. Or had laughed with such genuine pleasure for a long, long time.

How odd it was that someone like Joel who, having achieved the sort of professional success that could buy him anything he desired, responded by wanting less and less.

His children treated him with an attractive but recognisable mixture of affection and teasing.

'Heard from Rory?' Joel asked, straight-faced.

Rosie shook her head solemnly. 'Not one to give up easily on that kind of challenge. I'll give him till Christmas, even Rory will be exhausted by then.'

Joel's laughter made the others look up in surprise and demand to know the joke.

'Too complicated,' Joel chuckled. 'Not with children present.'

'Oh, Dad,' protested Ben. 'What a killjoy. I bet it was X-rated as well.'

'That's right,' Joel agreed amiably. 'I meant, not in front of the girls.'

'Sexist,' Lexie and Charlotte screamed together.

'Now look what you've done,' Joel laughed at Rosie, ducking as the girls hurled their napkins at him. 'Another fine mess you've got me into.'

'Me?' she retorted, pulling her chair round to side with a grinning Lexie and Charlotte. 'I'd say you were the author of your own misfortune, don't you agree, girls? Pass me a napkin.'

'Architect, you mean,' Daniel pointed out as Lexie and Charlotte gleefully plied Rosie with weapons to hurl. Joel feigned indifference as they all laughed, reaching out to grab the napkin from Rosie's hand and to ease her chair back next to him, where he rested his arm lightly along the back.

After chocolate liégeois had been demolished all round and Charlotte had been asked to explain to her parents how she and Lexie knew so much about vodka sorbets, and the light had faded into night, Rosie leaned quietly back in her chair, content to observe.

Usually denied family life, she savoured it now. Robert and Tom were absorbed in watching Joel unravel a spaceship kit they had bought from one of the stalls, the others were making plans for the next day. For once she felt part of it. A gentle breeze lifted her hair, she pushed it away from her face and turned to find Joel watching her. He half smiled. 'Okay?' he mouthed. She nodded back, wondering if she was disguising as well as she thought a stomach that had lurched, and hoped her smile in return was not as drunk with bliss as it felt.

Much later they all walked Rosie and Tom back to their hotel where they left them, Stevie insisting they all get together in London, Daniel asking could he adopt Tom, Ben and Lexie teasing Rosie because she had claimed to be able to juggle and had been dismally found out and had been chased down onto the darkened beach to punish her.

They all kissed her, including Joel, who was due to take the children to New York to see Marianne before returning them to school.

'I'll ring,' he smiled. 'Maybe I can get you to break the habit of a lifetime and have a meal with me on home ground.'

She said that would be easily arranged. It must be for her own sake, she thought. Must be. She didn't add she would have dinner with him on Mars if that's what he wanted.

Rory had turned up from his stay in Monte Carlo the day before they were due to go home. Tom and Rosie were tanned and rested and something of their old relationship had returned without the fractiousness that seemed to descend on Tom when both she and Rory were around.

Rosie tried not to laugh when failure was written large on what he said when she asked about Tansi and Claudie.

'Oh, those two,' he said dismissively. 'Just a couple of yacht slags. Business came first as usual. Now what do you two want to do on our last night?'

They left the next morning, accompanied by the sideways glance of the manager at Rosie and his solicitous enquiry about her health.

# Chapter Thirty-Four

London was in the grip of an Indian summer and the haze of heat that clung to the streets of the crowded city made working a tedious affair.

Parks and commons were filled with office workers soaking up the unexpected heatwave and shops, packed since the beginning of August with cold-weather clothes, fretted at the lack of customers who could not bring themselves to think of winter while wearing sleeveless T-shirts.

Indigo skies and dusty sunbaked streets were at variance with the first hint of golden leaves on trees. A nervous feeling that was hard to fathom of waiting for something to happen had settled on Rosie.

In her bag was a letter she had received that morning from Joel, now back in New York, with copies of half a dozen photographs, some from the yacht and others from La Barque.

The one of her and Joel laughing right into each other's faces – a frozen moment in time, she thought – she slipped into her bag. Then she re-read, analysed in as many ways that it is possible to analyse one side of writing paper containing about what? – a dozen – lines. Finally she folded it and put it away out of sight.

She'd been down that road before. She would wait. It was now very important to her that she didn't get it wrong.

Rosie only wished she was enjoying similar success as a mother as she was a designer. So much easier, she reflected gloomily, when she used simply to announce to Tom how the day would run, the week would progress or what Tom was and wasn't allowed to do.

Now Rory had to be consulted. Or at least Tom had taken to consulting him when he didn't get the answer he preferred from Rosie. The harmony that had been revived in Menton had not lasted much beyond landing at Heathrow.

In the middle of September he returned to Old Farrells, all plans for sending him to a local school abandoned in the face of his opposition. En route to Oxford, where she left him with a sad sense of relief, they had dropped into see her mother whose catalogue of criticisms of her grandson's appearance ('That hair's much too long,'), table manners ('would he prefer a trough?') and failure to send her a postcard from France ('I assume he can write?') made Rosie vow to give her a wide berth until at least half term.

She gave Tom a more tearful hug than usual. Poor little fellow, she thought, blowing her nose hard as she headed for the motorway, and felt rotten all the way back to London.

Her mood was not helped by Jordan mentioning he had seen Rory looking divine the night before, even Nancy had said so.

'Nancy?' she asked, surprised.

'Mm. It was at Midge Etherington's party. And, Rosie, those curtains look beyond description. In fact Midge mentioned they had bought the de Lisle's old house, she may get a chance to save it for the nation after all.'

Rory and Nancy again, eh? Although Rosie had nothing to hide, she worried all the same. These days you just couldn't tell what either of them might say. Rory had disappeared almost immediately after Tom went back to school and Abbie chose the same time to take a holiday.

Since all normal communications with Rory had been suspended, she refrained from asking him what had happened to his course in estate management. She had never entirely believed he would do it, but she had thought his intentions were sound. Clearly his interest in the course had waned along with their relationship. She no longer cared.

It was a relief to have the place to herself and to catch up with her friends, see shows and exhibitions that in previous years she had been forced to pass on and even to get to the opera as Miriam de Lisle's guest.

Now that Rosie was on the A list of who to have at your party, Miriam found her an asset. It was the benighted Conrad de Lisle who was seated next to Rosie in his box at a charity performance of Wagner's deeply gloomy 'Parsifal'. Miriam's choice. How the committee ever let her get away with it was beyond him. And then he recalled his own relationship with her.

Still, there were compensations. Rosie Colville was one. Her head was ducked down, one hand pushed into the pocket of her satin trousers, the other idly sketching on the back of her programme the extraordinary lighting techniques that were used as the Knights of the Holy Grail gathered by the temple.

'Incredible,' she whispered back straight-faced as he asked what she was doing. 'I've got a client for whom this would work perfectly.'

Without saying a word he glanced around to where Sylvia Duxborough in a dress to rival anything on stage was looking suitably rapturous. 'Good God,' was all Conrad muttered back, to 'shsh' from nearby boxes. 'Is that where she gets her ideas?'

Conrad had to talk very severely to his weak side not to stare so obviously at the tanned cleavage Rosie was unconsciously revealing by the way she was sitting. He hoped she was as bored as he was with all that screaming and shouting going on over a stupid old bugger regretting his youth. Don't we all, he sighed to himself.

What Conrad found puzzling was that single attractive men also failed to rouse Rosie's interest. Now when that Harley fellow had met them in the lobby with Nancy Alexander, Miriam and Sylvia Duxborough had behaved like a couple of groupies. Rosie had simply continued her conversation with Oscar Duxborough.

That at least had livened things up a bit, or rather the way Sylvia had spoken to him. Lord, was he in for it when they got home. Conrad recognised the signs. With Oscar standing a bit too close to Rosie, clearly trying to get off with her, Sylvia looked ready to kill one or other of them. Not Rosie's fault. Attractive girl, on her own.

Since by this time his attention had wandered so far from the business in hand, by the time Act Three commenced, Conrad had entirely lost the plot. Amfortas mourning by his father's funeral bier was one sight too many and he could take no more. Scooping up the nearest programme, he made for the bar.

Relieved and happy he sat in the deserted bar, gulping down a gin and tonic and idly glancing at the programme. He chuckled. She had a nice sense of humour too.

Not bloody curtains at all. Her notes included a cartoon of the lead soprano playing the neurotic Kundry, clutching not balsam to tend the wounded king, but a huge pot of valium which she was shovelling down her throat like there was no tomorrow, wearing a dress identical to Sylvia Duxborough's.

He would have been amazed to discover that, far from dismissing Joel Harley with a friendly handshake, Rosie had initially been grateful for Oscar's company.

Running into Joel at the opera had been a shock. But she could hardly abandon Oscar Duxborough in mid-sentence, although the temptation was overwhelming. He really was a prat, leering like that under Sylvia's nose.

Irritated by his crassness, Rosie took matters into her own hands. Gently removing his arm, she leaned over and whispered: 'Quit while you're ahead, Oscar. We both stand to lose Sylvia. Not worth it.'

Red-faced, he straightened up. 'Can't think what you mean,' he huffed, but the exchange was not lost on Sylvia who had demanded to know what they were talking about.

'Our children,' Rosie lied.

'Really?' Sylvia's voice was loaded with suspicion. She flicked a look over Rosie and said sharply: 'Oscar? Miriam is waiting.'

It was not, however, Sylvia's hostility that had given her a sleepless night but the fact that Joel, who had given her every reason to believe he was warming to her, interested even, who had suggested lunch, had been back in the country for a week and had not contacted her. Rosie angrily punched her pillow into shape. She tried to sleep. At four she pushed the covers back and padded over to a small bureau in the corner. There she extracted a letter and a sheaf of photographs. Slowly she turned them over.

She was looking at them in another light. A light that said she had read too much into, wanted too much from, a soft summer night in a silly fantasy. Wanted too much from a man who was naturally hospitable, and especially so to someone working with a valued . . . what was Nancy to him? Friend? Lover? No, surely not? She couldn't believe that. Then why hadn't he phoned? Told her he was back? Been more ready to detain her when they had met in the foyer? But he hadn't. Polite. Nothing special. She could have wept. And would have done, if she hadn't felt quite so stupid. And angry.

At six she slipped out of the house and went around the corner to the workroom. There she knew where life was coming from. Joel Harley was going to be history where her feelings were concerned. She even practised her new resolution.

'I hear Joel's in town,' Carey told her when he phoned

to see if she could have dinner because Josh was away. 'Seeing much of him?'

'God, no,' she said dismissively. 'I need a difficult architect like I need toothache.'

There was a pause. Then Carey said mildly, 'Really? I thought you two had hit it off. I rather like him.'

Later that day, Abbie, emptying a waste bin, carefully pieced together a set of torn photographs and drew some interesting conclusions.

# Chapter Thirty-Five

Tom now disliked being hugged. Now he routinely demanded that his friends should be allowed to stay or he to stay with them rather than spend a weekend alone with his parents.

'You worry too much,' Rory said indifferently when after a particularly fractious weekend Rosie sought him out to discuss how withdrawn their son was becoming and to try and lessen the tension between them that was clearly causing it. 'He's just growing up. He knows he doesn't have to be responsible for you any more.'

'Responsible for me?' she asked, bewildered. 'How do you work that out?'

Rory lowered his paper. 'Because, my dear, you made him feel so guilty about wanting a life of his own, he felt he had to be with you each weekend.'

It could have been Piers all over again.

'Are you serious?' she exclaimed, not knowing which to laugh at first, what he'd said or the look on his face. 'For heaven's sake, Rory, he is only eleven years old. Of course he's dependent on me – on us.'

'Of course I'm serious,' he said coldly. 'That's always been a big problem with you, Rosie. You did it to me, and you were starting to do it to Tom.'

Suddenly she wasn't laughing any more.

'And that was what?' she asked, her hands clasped, her chin resting lightly on them.

'Oh really, sweetheart, you know I never denied my concern about Tom needing me in his life. No big deal. It's all in the past, but you really can be an emotional vampire

at times. I don't want him to have to go through all that
making you feel wanted routine. Bad enough I had to. You
know your trouble, Rosie, is you don't want me, but you
don't want anyone else to have me either. I faced up to
what you are a long time ago.'

'Which is what?' she asked, not even flinching at the
look of pure loathing on his face. Out of the corner of her
eye she saw Abbie hovering in the hallway. With her was
Syra. Immediately Rosie flashed a warning look to Rory,
but he ignored her.

'You're a manipulator, Rosie. You use people. You use
me. You wanted a rich husband, so you got pregnant. You
thought once you had the name you didn't need me. But
when it got too tough, you came running back to use me
all over again. You're a money-grabbing social climber,
Rosie, and that's a fact and I'm not the only one who's
sussed you out. Nancy knows it.

'Ask her, Rosie. She's got your measure. Don't ever think
you'll get Harley. He's unloaded one social climber, he
doesn't want another. Nancy will see to that. She made
you. She can ruin you.'

A move couldn't be achieved overnight, nor would Tom
take kindly to the idea, but move she was going to. Even
if her own house wasn't ready, she was now in a position
to rent something on a modest scale.

On her own she would have moved into a tent. But then
on her own, she would never have needed Rory back. Or
even have considered it.

The builders had already moved out of Nancy's house,
giving way to an army of electricians, carpenters and lighting experts. They swarmed over the building since Nancy's
pockets were deep and her patience short, and the decor-
ation began in earnest.

Conversations with Nancy were now so limited it was
only a matter of time, Jaye told her worriedly, before the

tabloids picked it up and would gleefully report the *froid-eur* that existed between the two women.

'They won't.' Rosie was blunt. 'Nancy would fire her entire staff and Livvie and Jordan wouldn't do that to me.'

'What about Rory? Or James?'

It was a possibility, she knew that, but for reasons she couldn't quite fathom Rosie knew they wouldn't. Such a vindictive act would have happened by now.

Jaye looked doubtful. 'Why don't you just go? Now. This weekend? I'll help.'

Rosie shook her head. 'Can't. Tom would go spare. And his feelings count more than mine. I'll do it gradually. But not without Tom.'

What she didn't add was that if it killed her she was going to make sure that Joel – oh God, so in Nancy's pocket – would be left in no doubt that her interest in him was being exaggerated. She was no more than a designer crossing his path and a path she fervently hoped she would never be asked to walk down again.

Avoiding Rory was easier than she'd hoped. But second guessing the movements of someone who had no sensible schedule was proving exhausting. She knew she was cracking up when she began to keep a record of how many times she had successfully dodged being in the same room as him.

Get a grip, Rosie admonished herself. She took to leaving the house an hour earlier in the morning to avoid both him and Abbie and eating out every night so that he would have left for one of his haunts before she returned.

She had begun to think it was working, that Rory had abandoned his spiteful remarks and unceasing attempts to drive her into a frenzy of anger until she heard that Tom would be staying with the Duxboroughs at their country home for the weekend.

Rosie tried to hide her disappointment. It should have been her weekend, but she gamely made it easy for Tom.

'Great, darling,' she said down the phone. 'I'll call Sylvia.'

'Oh, that's okay, Mum, Dad's already spoken to her. She phoned when you were out and they've arranged it. Felix told me. He said Daddy told his mother that you were so busy at work, he had better arrange it.'

Rosie choked back her annoyance. Rory listened to her protests that she could quite easily have spoken to Sylvia Duxborough.

'I was only around the corner,' she fumed.

'Sorry,' he said calmly. 'I just thought you didn't like being disturbed at work.'

'But that doesn't apply to Tom.'

'Well, no real harm done, is there, and a great deal avoided?'

'What does that mean?'

Rory looked at her carefully. 'The way I hear it, you were coming onto Oscar Duxborough right in front of Sylvia. *Tsk tsk*, Rosie and in full view of Nancy and lover boy. Getting a bit desperate for clients, are we, or ... something else?'

Rosie would have laughed if it hadn't been so insulting. Oscar Duxborough. Silly man. A drink too many and Sylvia making such a prat of herself in that dress and the way she cooed around Joel.

'Did Sylvia tell you that?'

'Sylvia? Good God, no. Heard it from someone who was there. Friend of mine.'

'Some friend,' she said dismissively, in no doubt it must have been Nancy. 'As I said, don't ever forget I'm Tom's mother.'

'I know you are. I was there, remember?'

'So you were, I'd forgotten.'

He stalked out of the room and seconds later she heard his Porsche, tyres screaming, career off down the road.

\* \* \*

They were sitting in Tom's favourite hamburger bar in the Kings Road when Rosie broached the subject of returning to live at Drake Street. With Tom she had learned first to say something he wanted to hear in order to get at what he was really thinking.

'Isn't it odd now going home to Marlborough Square instead of just walking back along the road,' she began. Silence.

'I mean,' she started again, 'that I sometimes miss our little house, don't you?'

'S'pose,' he answered thickly through a mouthful of hamburger.

'S'pose?' she encouraged. 'You miss it sometimes, do you?'

'I miss Kit,' he finally supplied.

Rosie leapt eagerly in. 'Oh, so do I. Sometimes.' She drew a pattern on the table cloth. 'Sometimes I wonder if it would be nice to live back there again, do you?'

Tom nodded vigorously. 'It's more fun. Nearer everything.'

She took a deep breath: 'There's nothing to stop us moving back, you know. In a few weeks when the house has been repaired.'

Tom looked up, searching her face. 'And Dad?' he said. 'Dad would come too?'

'Well, no. Daddy would stay where he is and come and visit . . .'

'No,' Tom said vehemently. 'No. Not without Dad. Only if Dad comes too.'

'We'll see. Buck up, we'll miss the start of the film.'

Rosie found time for her and Jordan to get to Decorex, held as usual in the grounds of Syon House. That morning she had got a commission abroad – a villa in Spain belonging to the third wife of a cabinet minister.

The strain of life with Rory was as usual effectively

disguised and by the end of the day it was generally being mooted that Rosie Colville was a success story.

It was true to the extent that for the first time ever, Rosie had hovered on the brink of telling Miriam de Lisle to take her decor problems to Jessica Milford.

For six weeks Rosie and Livvie had trawled through every colour combination to meet Miriam's exacting and exhausting requirements. That morning, with a sigh of relief, Livvie had ordered the material. Work could begin.

'Ros-ee,' Miriam said on the phone an hour later. 'I've been thinking. I don't like those colours.'

Rosie checked the gasp. 'But Miriam, you've been over and over this for six weeks and the fabric is ordered. Your mother moves in with you in less than a month.'

Miriam cut her off. 'So she moves in. So what? Yesterday I liked the colours. Today I don't. Tomorrow we choose some more.'

When Tom had a long weekend off from school shortly afterwards, Rory insisted that it was spent at Glencairn. Rosie was pretty certain by now from Tom's constant references to 'Helen' who mended his jeans, or 'Helen said we should have a picnic', that Rory was simply dumping Tom with his grandfather and the housekeeper and going off for a better time with his cronies.

Once or twice Rosie spoke to Helen, who was perfectly polite but discouraging, so she gave up and took to putting a note in with Tom's clothes if there was anything she thought they would need to know.

That too came to an end when Rory found out. 'Stop treating me as though I don't know how to look after my own son,' he stormed, brandishing the letter she had tucked into Tom's luggage.

'For God's sake, Rory,' she protested. 'It was only to say he's had a cold and not to let him go out in his trainers if it's raining.'

'Anyone would think you're the only person in the world capable of looking after an eleven-year-old. You know something? Half Tom's spoilt brat behaviour is due to you smothering him. Let go of him, Rosie, let him grow up, why don't you?'

# Chapter Thirty-Six

In spite of Rosie's obvious new-found professional security that had resulted in the dazzling success of the business, those who knew her well also began to realise she was paying a price. You only had to look at her to see that.

'Rory's such a self-satisfied schmuck,' growled Kit to Carey when they met for a drink. 'And Rosie's different now.'

'Like how?' asked Carey, signalling for the barman to refill their glasses.

'Well, she's kind of thrown a wall around herself. I don't know. I'm not sure the problem is entirely Rory any more.'

'I think you're right,' Carey agreed. 'She was on great form in Prague. Everyone adored her . . .' he stopped and frowned into his glass. 'I wonder.'

'Wonder what?' Kit leaned forward.

'Oh, nothing. Just thought she might be having trouble with Nancy's architect.'

'Well, she's certainly not one of his fans.' Kit took a draught of beer.

'No?' Carey shrugged. 'I expect you're right. Just a thought. Time for another?'

Just trying to keep a grip on the endless maze Rory wove was having an effect that alarmed her. Stress, Rosie told herself firmly. Just stress that was causing this lack of concentration. She wasn't going mad. But her memory seemed to be playing tricks.

Abbie had telephoned the workroom three times to ask if the house alarm had been turned off for any reason when

Rosie, who had been last to leave, could have sworn she had activated it.

But more worrying was that twice she had overlooked Rory's notes asking her to collect Tom when it was his turn. She'd protested there were no such notes, but was amazed when days later she found them stuffed in the basket where she threw her post each day.

Rosie looked blankly at the crumpled notes. Mr Farrell looked grimly at her the first time she had arrived dishevelled and weary after a dash down the motorway to collect her son three hours after all the other boys had left.

The second time he asked if anything was wrong.

'It's not good for the boys if they are made to feel anxious,' he admonished.

'Nothing serious,' she assured him, hugging a worried Tom. 'Just a mix-up in arrangements. Come on, Tom.'

'Don't leave notes,' she instructed Rory. 'Make sure you tell me.'

'Fuck that,' he replied, not even bothering to look up from his newspaper. 'I've got enough to do without organising your life as well.'

Tom was showing clear signs that this new pattern to his life was doing something to him. Bored with everything, annoyed that Rory was too busy to drive him back to school on Sunday or even to have Sunday lunch – for which Rosie was silently thankful – he had spent most of the weekend watching TV in his room.

By eight on Saturday night, Rosie had conceded defeat and dialled the burger home delivery. Piling a tray with hamburgers, french fries and milkshakes, she opened Tom's door with a flourish.

'Ta ra,' she announced. 'Special delivery by your personal chef,' and placed the tray on his bed.

She won a reluctant smile from him, but he continued to gaze at the television. After a few minutes of this and determined not to allow the wearing sulking to go on, she sat cross-legged on the bed beside him, affected a totally fake interest in the programme he was watching and began to eat her share of the meal.

Whether it was being made to feel better about himself or sheer hunger she couldn't tell, but two minutes later she saw him quietly reach out and pick up the hamburger.

All she dwelt on in the days that followed was the one immoveable fact that Tom would never forgive her if she now uprooted them and returned to how they'd lived before.

'Are you interested in that lamp, Madam?'

Rosie swung around, looking at the expectant face of the sales assistant.

'Lamp? What lamp?' Rosie gazed blankly back at the young woman and then down at her hands. 'Oh, you mean *this* lamp? No, I mean, thank you, yes. Just making sure it was the er . . . the er . . . right match. That's it. The right colour.'

'I thought that must be it,' smiled the girl pleasantly, leading the way to the cash desk and relieving Rosie of the small Tiffany lamp she had been absently clutching. 'You were standing there for so long . . .'

Rosie blinked. God knows how long she had been standing gazing into space in the middle of Christopher Wray's lighting emporium, but this had to stop.

David, Carey's producer, called her and because he was fun and she had to pull herself together, she accepted his invitation to dinner.

'Remember I told you, he's sometimes deaf,' Jaye warned her.

'Deaf?'

'He doesn't always hear it when you say no.'

Rosie laughed. 'I think he'll hear me.'

'How's Nancy?' asked Jaye. She was perched on a high

stool in Rosie's workroom, flicking through some sketches that were lying there.

'Okay, I suppose. I don't see much of her. I send messages through Tanya. She spends all her time with . . . Joel, when he's in town . . . and he's in town.'

Jaye looked up at the brief pause. Rosie busied herself with some papers on her desk. 'And what about Joel? Do you talk to him? Rosie . . . ? I said . . .'

'I know what you said. No. There's no longer any need.'

'And you're having dinner with David Mesinski?' Jaye ducked her head down and sideways to look up into Rosie's face. In spite of herself Rosie laughed.

'Rosie baby, anything you haven't told me?' Jaye asked innocently. 'Something tells me you're having dinner with the wrong man.'

'No, I'm not,' Rosie retorted. 'I'm having dinner with a man who is fun, uncomplicated and won't give me sleepless nights. Now I ask you, how can that be wrong?'

# Chapter Thirty-Seven

Ever since half term Tom's abiding conversation had been anything but school. In fact Arsenal seemed to occupy his every waking moment to the exclusion of all else, as his school report which arrived that morning testified.

It was dispiriting stuff. '*This term he has slipped back to an unacceptable level for a boy of his ability*,' read the stern comment from Mr Farrell. '*Tom is more concerned about his activities outside the classroom than maintaining his previous high standard and his behaviour occasionally leaves much to be desired.*'

Stuffing the report back into its envelope, Rosie went into the drawing room to leave it for Rory.

She shrugged. Rory had abandoned any pretence that he had reformed his slovenly lifestyle. Much of the time he was drunk or hungover and, since Abbie seemed incapable or disinclined to halt the steady march of confusion, Rosie was not surprised to find the room awash with untidy piles of letters, books and folders.

She looked around for somewhere to put Tom's report where Rory would easily find it and in doing so accidentally knocked a box file to the floor, spilling out the contents.

Some seemed to be personal photographs. Scooping them up, she stopped as a girl she knew stared sulkily back at her. Good grief. Rosie stared hard. It was Tansi. No mistaking those stunning, sensuous looks. A look she had last seen on Geoffrey Harley's yacht in the summer.

Rosie took a closer look, frowning. Tansie sitting on a stone wall as though she had just come in from riding, one booted leg slung across the other.

Slowly she shuffled the photographs and when Claudie appeared with Tansi standing behind her Rosie stiffened but not with surprise. It would have been more surprising if she hadn't been somewhere in the pack. The surprise was the background. She knew that room. It was Callum's. Dear God, they were in Scotland. But when?

She stared blankly at them trying to get a time, a date into her head when Rory had been there, furious that he could have invited them while Tom was there. Must have done.

Those ghastly girls. The only clue she gleaned was from the foliage in the background, the ivy clinging to the walls of Glencairn. It must have been after they came back from Menton. If she hadn't been so furious, she would have laughed.

'Rory won't give up until Christmas,' she recalled telling Joel. He was pathetic.

Stuffing the photographs back into the envelope, she tried to fathom the filing system of the card index, now lying in a clutter on the floor. It was a maze. The names appeared to be cross-referenced with other names. Frowning, she began to search for the name that linked them together. It didn't make much sense.

In fact this file was very odd indeed. Clearly unless you knew what Rory had intended, the code was impossible to follow. Rosie gave an exasperated groan.

Kneeling on the floor, she was so intent on what she was doing that she didn't even bother to look up when Abbie came in but she was startled by her sharp tone.

'Sorry, I knocked this off the table. It's okay . . . really, Abbie, I can do it.' Rosie straightened and stood aside as Abbie scooped them up and stuffed them back into a drawer finally turning to stare silently at Rosie.

'Tom's report,' Rosie explained. 'I was just trying to find somewhere to put it where Rory would see it. Tell you what,' she said as Abbie replaced the box file under the desk. 'I'll just tuck it here, under the lamp, he can't miss it then, can he?'

Surprisingly Rory was inclined to take a lighter view of it, not sharing her concern. Almost implying she was pushing Tom too hard.

'So what?' he said, running his eye down the pages. 'If you didn't make such an issue of it, he'd relax and get on with it. Anyway he won't be there next year.'

'Year after actually,' she replied, annoyed he couldn't keep track of Tom's progress. 'And as a matter of interest I don't push Tom. He's just had too much to cope with this last couple of terms.'

'Well, that's what I meant,' Rory said. 'And by the way – just to save you the trouble. If you want to read my letters, say so, you don't have to pry.'

'*Pry?*' Rosie looked at him in astonishment. 'Abbie didn't say that?'

'No, but you don't fool me for a second. What did you think you would find? Passionate letters from a mistress?'

It was not, she thought, even worth getting worked up about.

'Oh, no, Rory, I never thought you'd get a *letter* from a mistress. The candidates I've seen for that job don't look bright enough to write their name let alone sentences. All I ask is that you remember our agreement and keep Tom well away from anyone you're screwing. Is that clear?'

Jordan had convinced Rosie that being interviewed by the *Sunday Globe* lifestyle section would be the most brilliant advertisement for the company.

'You don't have to say a word,' he pointed out. 'Just look as wonderful as you do, and let the decor do the talking and have Rory looking wonderfully brooding in the background.'

It wasn't much of a surprise that Nancy too had been

persuaded into agreeing to have the finished house photographed. As long as no-one actually wrote about her personally, she was not at all averse to having her possessions and the Foundation mentioned every day of the week if it helped keep her profile as a philanthropist riding high.

The *Globe* wanted the pictures to be taken in Rory's house rather than the workroom. But Rosie refused. This surprised the picture editor since he had phoned Rory, apparently expecting to find Rosie there, and Rory had agreed.

'More publicity, Rosie dear?' Rory drawled when she saw him. 'Goodness, we *are* addicted to it.'

She turned on him. 'I didn't suggest this house,' she told him fiercely. 'They did. I didn't agree. You did. And I'm going to stop it right now.'

He glared at her, stubbing out his cigarette. 'Personally I don't give a fuck what you do,' he retorted. 'But try and think of Tom, will you? How do you think he'll feel knowing his mother didn't want to be photographed in his house? You tell him.'

'Rubbish. He doesn't even know it's an issue.'

'Yes, he does. I told him. I thought you'd be pleased.'

Rosie's instincts were to plough all her energy into her work and just let the clients roll in, but she was also a shrewd enough business woman to recognise that nearing the completion of Nancy's house was the right moment to establish just where she expected to draw her clients from in future. The *Globe* had enough clout to attract the right clientele. She welcomed but didn't need Jordan's enthusiastic encouragement. The right publicity worked every time.

It was still not quite light, but the way each day brought a fresh frantic wave of activity, she knew before she reached the glossy black door with its brass plaque announcing *Rosie Colville Interiors* in bold italics, that something would have to give if she was to get everything finished on time.

Finding a spare hour today was out of the question because the entire morning was to be taken up by the *Sunday Globe*.

Why was it that everyone wanted their homes ready for Christmas but didn't commission anyone far enough in advance to meet such a demand, she thought as she let herself into the silent Mews House.

She grabbed the post, flicking the central heating switch and the coffee machine into life before making her way up the narrow stairs, sifting through the packet of letters as she went. Livvie and Jordan were only minutes behind her.

Promptly at nine o'clock, Jane Grantham's scheme boards went off with Livvie. Jordan shot off to meet Joyce to supervise the hanging of the curtains in the flats in Little Venice, where the tracks had been fitted the day before. The photographer arrived from the *Globe* just as they both disappeared. Rosie checked all the immediate details were complete and suggested they go round to the big house.

With the memory of *The Herald* fresh in her head, Rosie resisted any pose that would suggest high-flying career girl and suggested instead that she sat on the leather club fender, one leg drawn up and her chin resting on her knee.

Much softer, more feminine. More approachable. Which is why she had bought a deep blue silk jacket, fitted with covered buttons, that flared gently out over her hips. Narrow black trousers and some lace-up boots took the panto-mime look down and the trash effect up. Jordan had clapped his hands in delight and asked if they did the jacket in his size. Rosie had assured him that they did.

The likelihood of Rory's house being recognised by his friends was now minimal, rendering him unable to score points. But there was enough to show Tom that it had been taken inside the house. Rosie thought Tom couldn't have cared less, but with Rory in his present mood she was taking no chances.

The first surprise of the day was that the *Sunday Globe* had sent a freelancer to conduct the actual interview instead of the style editor, a last-minute switch. She was already there in the workshop when Rosie arrived back from being photographed. An hour in the company of a professional who knew his job had relaxed Rosie to the point where she was beginning to chide herself for having been so uncertain about what she was doing.

Her good humour began to evaporate as she sat at her workdesk while the photographer took one last shot. Eyeing Bella Leigh, she could feel she was in trouble. Bella claimed the editor had decided that the lifestyle pages were wasted, readers wanted a more substantial text. Hence he'd sent one of his star writers. Rosie didn't believe a word of it. Not for an interior designer. Not in a hundred years.

Her instincts were faultless. Bella was out to be hostile. First she toured the workroom, carelessly picking up and dropping samples with a faint but detectable disdain that made Livvie, who'd just returned from Jane Grantham's, want to hit her.

The photographer ignored her. Rosie, talking to him in her usual friendly manner, was also keeping a watchful eye on Bella, at a loss to know what the ferocious behaviour was about.

Bella's opening remarks put paid to any lingering hope that she would be given a sympathetic treatment. It was like the beginning of a boxing match. She was hardly off the stool when Bella had punched her onto the ropes with a flurry of sharp, jabbing questions.

'How much did your feelings for your husband versus your need for personal success influence your decision to live with him again?'

Rosie looked stonily back at her. 'That's private,' she said politely.

'It's said that you have had a meteoric rise to the top in a short space of time – forgive me, I am no judge of these things.' Bella gestured to the workroom and Rosie's office. 'I take your word for it that all this is the trappings of success – could you have done it on your own?'

'I did do it on my own,' Rosie replied calmly, but her heart was thudding into overdrive. 'My son is our joint responsibility. My career is quite separate.'

Only one of them had gloves and a gumshield. All Rosie could do was duck and weave.

'But having a title to play with – I gather you are sometimes Mrs Monteith Gore and at others Rosie Colville – must weigh with the kind of clients you try to attract.'

Dear God, this had to stop. This girl's perception was based entirely on gossip, and distorted gossip at that.

There was just time. But only if Rosie worked fast. Excusing herself on the pretext of writing out some instructions for Livvie, she dropped a note in front of her.

'If you could just ring this client and find out those measurements and ring me at the house,' Rosie told her astonished assistant. 'I'm just going to walk over there with Bella.'

'Easier to talk there,' she smiled, standing back to let the journalist go first down the stairs. The scowling Bella, well into her stride, did not want an interruption but, as Rosie guessed, the idea of seeing her personal surroundings was too tempting. And it gave Rosie much-needed time to mount a rescue.

Fifteen minutes later, having spun out the walk to the house, leaving Abbie to make coffee for Bella and having insisted on showing her some innovative ways with curtain pleating, the call she was waiting for came.

'Yes, Livvie, you've got the details?'

'Okay,' came Jaye's rapid but calm voice. 'Bella is a dreadful writer, bright but a bitch. Most MPs she interviews have their passports ready in case they have to flee the country when she's finished with them. Do not under any circumstances lose your temper. I don't know why she's out to carve you up. Have you ever met her before, upset her?'

'No, not that I know of,' said Rosie, scribbling fictitious measurements onto a pad. 'That's great, Livvie. And what about the bedroom? Do we have any special instructions there?'

'Bedroom? Oh yes.' She could hear Jaye's laugh. 'All over town. She makes a tom cat look undersexed. Listen. Do you want me to get in a cab and come over? I can be there in twenty minutes.'

'No, that won't be necessary. It's all very straightforward now,' Rosie said calmly. 'Thanks, Livvie.'

An hour later, Rosie sank into a chair in her office and closed her eyes. An hour in which for ten minutes she had encouraged Bella to talk about herself, reducing the interview down to the point where the journalist would have little to go on.

She had swept Bella into the kitchen on the pretext of making more coffee, where they sat at the big pine scrubbed table. With a casualness that could have won Rosie an Oscar, the tape recorder that Bella had activated was rendered almost worthless as Rosie placed it next to the coffee percolator, still plugged in and emitting a low hum.

Every dangerous question fired was fielded without losing her temper or her charm. She played down her relationship with Rory, exaggerated her commitment to her work to soothe Bella, who was starting to look dangerous as time and questions were running out, and trod very carefully on the subject of Tom.

But Bella's reputation as a Rottweiler was not earned for nothing.

'Your relationship with your husband is platonic?'

'I never said that.'

'What did you say?'

'I didn't say anything at all.'

'But you live together.'

'Yes, with my son. We live together in this house.'

'What made you do that? You've been divorced for six years and were living separately. Is this a reconciliation or what?'

'A personal decision that was made jointly by myself and Rory. That's all, simply a decision.'

'It's said you don't speak.'

Rosie laughed. 'Goodness me, of course we speak.' She took a deep breath. 'We both love Tom. There's plenty to discuss.'

'So you'd consider remarriage, would you?'

'I would consider anything that was appropriate.' In years to come, maybe not even that long, Tom might see what was written. It must never hurt him.

Bella shrugged. 'Suit yourself. It's going to look odd.'

'I don't see why.'

'Well, after an acrimonious divorce . . .'

'Only according to the papers, unless you have another source?'

Bella chewed her lip. The pen she was holding wagged neurotically between her fingers: 'It's general gossip.'

'Is it?' Rosie said in a voice that betrayed nothing.

For a moment they held each other's gaze. Then Bella leaned forward and snapped off the tape which only Rosie knew was already useless to her.

'Is there anything else you need to know?' enquired Rosie politely, struggling between relief and amusement as Bella's eyes grew round with horror.

'Just a minute,' she screamed. 'How long has that percolator been plugged in?'

'I told him he should tell you,' Livvie was saying, giving Jordan a firm push in the small of his back. 'Go on, Jordan.'

Rosie stared blankly from one to the other. The morning's ordeal had left her well behind with her work and after a brief discussion with Jaye, she'd decided that all she could do was hope the silly girl with no notes or tapes to refer to would be limited in what she could write.

Now what? she thought as Jordan looked uncomfortably back at her.

'Don't tell me, you've left Jane's curtains in a taxi? No. Okay, you've told Sylvia Duxborough that Miriam de Lisle has more taste in her little finger than she has in her entire house. It can't be that bad.'

Shooting one last anxious glance at Livvie, Jordan said: 'The thing is it may not be anything at all . . . but Livvie – and Kit,' he turned for confirmation to Livvie, who nodded encouragingly back at him, 'thought I should mention it. Well, once or twice Bunty and I have gone to a club in Charing Cross Road – "Voltage" – and I couldn't help noticing once – a long time ago so it probably means absolutely nothing – but I saw Bella Leigh there, only I didn't know she was Bella Leigh until I saw her today.'

'This story hasn't got a happy ending, has it?' Rosie was studying Jordan carefully. 'What's wrong with that?'

'Well, the thing is, Liv was saying she was really giving you a hard time about Rory and I just thought you should know who I saw her with.'

# Chapter Thirty-Eight

'Abbie? Don't be ridiculous. You're quite mad.'

Rosie gazed furiously back at him. 'Mad? She's the one who's crazy. She's vicious and spiteful. I want her out. And I want her out *now*.'

At first Rory was nowhere to be found. James said he had gone to Paris for two days. Abbie had gone to stay with a friend.

'What are you talking about,' Rory asked coldly still with his overcoat on, his suitcases behind him in the hall. Syra was outside bringing in some parcels. Rosie checked the door to make sure they were not overheard.

'What journalist?' Rory repeated, sitting down on the fender.

'Bella Leigh. From the *Globe*.'

'Don't be absurd.'

'I'm not being absurd, Rory, I mean what I say. I want Abbie out.'

'Why, because that poofter you employ saw her in the same nightclub . . .'

'Not just in the same nightclub, *with* her. She was in this house with her, made her coffee, I was there the whole time and they talked like strangers. Why, Rory? Because I ticked her off about screening my phone calls, not letting her tidy my room? She's only the fucking housekeeper. How dare she make up those dreadful stories?'

'And what exactly was she making up?' He sounded interested. As though he were unclear of what was at the heart of her anger. 'That's obviously the way it looks to her.'

'What way does it look?' Rosie asked, struggling to stop herself from slapping him.

'That you're using me.'

'*Using you?* Not that again. You sound like a record that's stuck. And you're not using me, I suppose? Is that what you think?'

Rory shrugged. He looked coldly at her.

'You answer the question, Rosie. You're good at that. But before you do, ask yourself this. You're not here because of me, are you? Only what I can provide. A house big enough for all of us, a workroom that you've got at a rock-bottom rent – and you could have had it for nothing – security for your child and the space to make yourself the talk of the town. Which you have.'

'Rory, we'll discuss this later. I think Syra . . .'

'In my book that's called making use of someone. What do you call it? And you wonder why Abbie felt sickened by it? Now if you'll excuse me. Sorry, Syra, didn't see you there.'

But he had seen her. He was playing to the gallery, Rosie could tell. What she couldn't understand was, why?

Abbie removed her belongings while Rosie was at work. Mrs Milton had not minded at all taking on looking after Rosie's house as well as the workroom, at least until after Christmas. The extra, she said, would be handy. And it would give Rosie a chance to sort out the kind of permanent help she needed.

Unfortunately Mrs Milton had almost immediately fallen foul of Rory, who seemed content just to let things slide, by telling him calmly to wait a minute, Duckie, while she checked the laundry and *then* she would make him coffee.

For once Rosie had swept aside his complaints, telling him coldly that she would foot the bill for Mrs Milton, at the same time giving her instructions to ignore his bedroom and study, laundry and shopping.

Abbie's agency had found her another job. She had called Rory to ask if any post or calls could be redirected to an address in North London.

'Shouldn't think she'd need a job, selling stories the way she does,' Rosie couldn't help pointing out.

'She didn't get a penny,' Rory snapped. 'It's just your nasty mind. She didn't tell you she had met Bella because she was terrified of you. Always has been. You were very rough on her. Know what she said? She said she only stayed as long as she did because she wanted Tom to have some stability.'

'Some what?' Rosie sounded vague, deliberately leafing through a catalogue that had just arrived.

'Did you hear what I said?' he spluttered.

She turned a few more pages and began carefully to consult a list. 'I heard a lot of bullshit, if that's what you meant.'

Nancy's house as far as Rosie was concerned was finished, although she wasn't sure if you could ever put a final day of work on such a job. Last-minute snags cropped up that had her flying around London trying to find replacement accessories for some of the bathrooms, when the suppliers she had been using rang to say they couldn't complete the order. Two days before the curtains were to be hung, Joyce rang, begging for another day because the lining on one set was clearly not a match. Even then, Rosie and Jordan had spent days siting the furniture, which had left her wondering if a career with Pickfords might have been her true calling, and even more days arriving at dawn to over-see carpets laid, items being delivered, pictures being hung.

The *Globe* photographer had sent over some transparencies for Rosie to see, having said that he would arrange for a couple of spreads to be printed up for her to frame when the article appeared.

The drawing room, now restored to the original wood panelling, painted in a mist of blue and grey, gazed back at her. The four nondescript full-length windows had been treated as one, with puff-headed Italian strung curtains in aquamarine silk providing a visually stunning backdrop to a room that now boasted a newly installed nineteenth-century chimneypiece with a marble finish.

The antique furniture, with its Georgian footstool, was a triumph, as was the highly polished wood block floor enhanced by an Aubusson carpet in tones that reflected the colours of the room.

Rosie flicked through the transparencies, critically studying each, momentarily forgetting the exhaustingly long days with carpenters, painters, electricians, arguing her case, urging them along.

The neo-classic oak bookcases in the library looked as though they had been there for decades, blending so perfectly it had been worth waiting until the last minute to get the young designer Rosie wanted. Thank God Nancy had been talked out of white.

In spite of her own belief in Nancy's nature, which was selfish, hard and basically masculine, in the main bedroom Rosie had paid lipservice to Nancy's need to be seen as feminine and glamorous, leaving guest rooms to enjoy a softer look in pale buttermilk fabrics, striped wallpaper, colourful antique bedcovers and masses of white lace cushions.

A subtle blend of drama allied to softer patterns had satisfied the vain American's requirements. An antique gilt-wood corona was suspended above the king-size bed, from which heavy cotton curtains in a floral mix of pink, green and cream were draped either side, pinned to the wall by gilt ombras. Rosie had resisted the obvious idea of dramatic curtains for the three sets of windows overlooking the garden. French heading rather than something more ornate allowed the pattern to dominate rather than the design.

The furniture was kept to a simple minimum but the Philadelphia highboy had been included.

Mirrored glass doors concealed the faux stone walls of the bathroom, which suited Nancy's dislike of frills and femininity. That side of Nancy was for public consumption, privately Rosie knew that her client found it a bore. But in case she had gone too far in the other direction, Rosie had built a frame around the bath, draped with fake curtains looped on either side over brass ombras to soften the sharp effect.

Rosie gazed at the magnificent reception room with a sigh of satisfaction. She had heard from Jordan that Nancy was ecstatic with the spectacular effect of the rose-tinted curtains with their breathtaking swoop of swags and tails, looped into sweeping curves by tasselled cords.

The three chandeliers shipped over so carefully from New York were suspended like glittering and sparkling teardrops along the length of the room, the highly polished floor gleamed, the rococo chairs were grouped around the marble fireplace which dominated one wall.

But it was the staircase, the simple design with such a powerful effect, rising to a circular gallery housing some of Nancy's treasured paintings that made Rosie catch her breath. It had worked. All of it.

Without Joel she could not have achieved such drama. It was a sobering thought. But her inner self told her that it had been her own pushing for such a radical idea, arguing that she was competent, confident in her ability when on all sides she had been doubted, that had given him the opportunity to take the credit.

She wondered if he would. A small part of her said it was not in his nature. Her more cynical self said anything was possible.

Looking at the rooms from the photographer's point of view, Rosie was amazed at how it all hung together. And even more amazed that she had done it. Almost a year out of her life staring back from these two-and-a-quarter-inch transparencies.

Rosie ricocheted from elation to fear. Suppose it was snatched away? What if she couldn't repeat this success? Suppose . . . supposing this was it? And the next minute she was hugging herself ecstatically when each phone call brought another compliment, or another commission, and each one pushing the mess of her life with Rory into the background.

Alone in the workroom she sat back in her chair and closed her eyes. She had it all, didn't she? The job, the success, the name, the security. But God, what a price she was paying.

Curiously with Tom at the Duxboroughs for the weekend, she did have a small respite from deadlines. And from Rory. After such a hectic period, she needed a break, fresh air and exercise, and she planned to spend Sunday going for a long walk.

Her peace was partially shattered by the *Globe* publishing the four-page feature on Nancy's house and the interview with Rosie. Prominent, unkind, embarrassing.

A large full-page picture of Rosie sitting by the fireplace, one leg drawn up under her chin, with a smaller, more recognisable – to Rosie at least – drop-in shot of her in her workroom with Livvie and Jordan.

For a very brief second Rosie didn't recognise herself. For which she was thankful. The person gazing back at her was seriously confident and glamorous. A young woman who had no self-doubt, a confidence that assured her of success. Rosie knew she was looking at a stranger.

The text was every bit as bad as she had feared. It had done her no favours. Bella had drawn a picture of a woman obsessed with success, able to switch on charm to get what she wanted. Or as Bella had said:

'*Her charm is in the studied way she recalls your*

*Christian name, using it often and, some might say, unnecessarily. Her roots are middle-class but the men in her life have been plucked straight from Debrett's.*

*Marriage to Rory Monteith Gore, a failed relationship with society photographer Piers Imber and now back living with her ex-husband. She insists it is for the sake of her eleven-year-old son, who she sends to boarding school, a decision it is widely said not to be supported by her husband, but no-one would deny that her career has soared since she decided to once again make use of her marital aristocratic connections.*

*Among her clients, she told me, are millionairess philanthropist Nancy Alexander and Pedro Almarez who has just commissioned her to redesign a prestigious apartment block in Little Venice.'*

Rosie closed her eyes in despair. Not shared by Rory? Where on earth did Bella get that? And listing her clients. She had never mentioned one of them. What did it look like? God, had she got it in for her. Or rather Abbie had. But why? *Why?*

Bella also directed the force of her venom at the opulence of Nancy's house and, while the end of the feature was not designed to lift Rosie's spirits, it at least spared her from any further observations about her apparent ruthless scaling of the career ladder.

*'Nancy Alexander's house is the house of a woman for whom money clearly is no problem or object. Currently linked with architect Joel Harley who delivered this year's Alexander lecture in Prague, Nancy surrounds herself with women who are not afraid to use whatever connections they have to succeed.*

*Teamwork is where she excels, she says. And what a team she made with Rosie Colville, or should that be Monteith Gore?'*

Hurling the paper to one side, Rosie took herself off for a much-needed breath of fresh air. On her return she checked the machine hoping for a message from Tom, but there was nothing.

Her mother complaining about her daughter's absence, Ellie from New York – she and Judith were heading up to Connecticut for the weekend, Rosie almost wept with envy – Kit and Carey to see if she was free for dinner. But nothing from Tom.

Overcome with longing just to hear him, she rang Sylvia's country home. There she was told by the housekeeper that the family were in London.

'London?' Rosie echoed. 'Are you sure? I thought they were staying in the country?'

'No, Miss. Felix has a schoolfriend staying whose mother isn't very well, so Mrs Duxborough thought it would be easier to keep them both in town.'

Not well? *Not well?*

Rosie slammed the phone down and furiously stabbed at Sylvia's London number. Tom a mere mile away since yesterday. What was going on? At the Duxboroughs' home, she was told by the nanny that Mrs Duxborough had taken the children out to lunch before Mr Monteith Gore drove both boys back to school.

Rory? Driving them back to school? 'Where is Tom?' Rosie demanded. 'My son. Where is he?'

'No idea, Madam, I'm sorry.'

Why did they think she was ill? Why were Rory and Sylvia Duxborough having lunch without telling her? For the first time Rosie began to feel frightened at Rory's attempts to push her to the edge of Tom's life. And maybe even out of it completely.

She ordered the nanny to make absolutely certain that Sylvia called her the minute she returned. She also left a message at the school to ask that someone intercept Mrs Duxborough or Mr Monteith Gore and ask them to make contact immediately.

At five when Sylvia hadn't phoned, she rang the school

to hear the boys had arrived back at the normal time. Oscar answered at the Duxboroughs. He'd just got in from the golf course. No idea where Sylvia was. Yes, he would get her to call. No, Rory wasn't there. Why should he be?

She was waiting for him when he arrived home shortly before midnight. A faint aroma of whisky hung about him.

Rosie stood in the doorway. Her rage, having had several hours to abate, was well under control.

'Next time you lie to me, Rory, about Tom,' she said evenly as he crossed the hall and started to climb the stairs, 'I will take him and leave here and you can find whatever reason you like to tell Callum we failed.'

He paused at the sound of her voice and looked her over. She saw in his eyes that he was much drunker than she had first thought. Finally he repeated softly: 'Failed, eh?' He came back down the stairs and strolled over to her. For a brief moment she thought he was going to hit her and she stepped back. He laughed.

'Beating women is not my bag, sweetheart, but putting them in their place is.' The smell of alcohol, mingled with nicotine and the stale musk of perfume, made her wince. He began to recite, counting off on his fingers.

'My house, Rosie, my son, my future. If you weren't so aware that Tom wouldn't go with you, you wouldn't be here now. So don't ever try and threaten me like that. The world now knows what a user you are.' He tapped her lightly on the cheek with his hand. 'Got that?'

'I haven't *got* anything, Rory,' she replied, removing his hand, trying not to let her voice shake. Contempt almost overpowered her. 'I've told you what I *will* do. Not *might* or even *perhaps*. Crude threats from you do not move me. And by the way,' she said, turning away from him as he swayed unsteadily reaching out to hold the doorpost. 'If you're going to screw Sylvia, two things.'

She began to mimic him, counting on her fingers. 'My

son must never be allowed in the same company and two, do get her some decent perfume, will you? That one is as cheap as she is.'

# Chapter Thirty-Nine

It was nearly eight o'clock. Ginny had offered Rosie a lift after they had organised drinks and mince pies for all the crew who'd completed Nancy's house in record time. They'd stayed for one drink themselves but then tactfully withdrew, knowing the workforce wanted to relax, which they'd do more successfully without their employers around.

With one last attempt to persuade her to go with her to Stevie and Daniel's party, Ginny dropped Rosie at the corner of her road.

Standing on the pavement, Rosie waved her off and then turned towards her house. Slowly she made her way along the street, reluctant to go in, but with the Christmas festivities starting up all her friends were busy. She could have been too. But not at Stevie's. She was getting used to not seeing Joel. Why undo all that?

Very soon she would be able to bow out of that circle. They were his friends, Nancy's. Not hers.

She turned her coat collar up and gazed at the scudding clouds, the sharp wind gusting around her flattening her coat against her legs. She hurried the last few steps, anxious to be in out of the cold, anticipating beans on toast in front of something trashy on TV in a house that was clean and tidy. Perfect.

The switch flicked uselessly up and down in her hand as she stepped into the hall. That's all she needed. Fused.

Without the aid of a light, she propped the front door open with her bag, so that she could see to turn off the alarm. But there was silence. That was odd. It had its own backup if the electricity went down. In the drawer of the console table in the hall she felt around until she located a slim pencil torch.

The door to the drawing room ajar. Silently she registered what this meant. The alarm only worked if all the doors were closed. Maybe she hadn't put it on. But she had, she knew she had.

Standing in the hallway, she pushed the door open and swung the torch around. At first the room looked as she had left it. The beam travelled around the walls, then she stiffened and swung the beam back. The space above the mantelpiece where the Kneller hung was now empty.

Whirling round, the torch raked the shelf where the Bows figurines were displayed. Gone. So too were the Meissen snuff boxes. The doors of the chiffonnier swung open on their hinges. It was a bad night for Meissen. Some of the Swan was missing too.

She gasped out loud. Her hand flew to her mouth. Why hadn't Rory listened to her? She began to shake. Backing out of the room, she turned, too late to see a shadowy figure loom out of the dark. She felt a hard thump in her back that sent her flying to the foot of the stairs.

Her head swam. She heard, rather than saw, her assailant grab her handbag, throw the contents to the floor and then hurl the bag into the dark and leap out of the house. Seconds later she heard a powerful roar as a motor bike hurtled away.

Instinct made her crawl to the phone, her fingers trembling so much she had to punch the number in twice to get the police.

They found her huddled on the opposite side of the road, sitting hunched up against a neighbour's car in a state of shock. A policewoman slipped an arm around her waist and with a sergeant supporting her, they guided her to a police car, its blue light swirling around, the noise from their sirens having alerted some of the neighbours who were now standing out on the street. A second car joined them.

A blur of activity fell about her.

'Anyone else in the house, Miss? Sure? No visitors, children, au pairs or anything? Right.' She saw policemen going inside, their torches swinging eery laser beams across rooms that looked out onto the street until someone activated the fuse box and the ground floor of the house was flooded with light.

The police were practical more than unsympathetic, but pushed for time. Shivering now as much from cold as shock, Rosie was incapable of speech, tugging at the blanket that the policewoman had draped around her.

Someone asked if she could give them a phone number of a friend. Jaye. Jaye might be at home.

There was no possibility of going into the house until the police had completed their search, even up into the attic, the policewoman said. It wasn't unknown for a thief to hide up there until the hue and cry had died down and then make his getaway.

'But I saw him go,' she whispered.

'He might have had an accomplice. After all, you disturbed them.'

It was hard to distinguish cars arriving, cars leaving. Tugging at the policewoman's arm, Rosie tried to ask if she could get up, she thought if she stood she might feel better, but the policewoman's attention was being claimed by a new arrival. Rosie sank back against the seat.

And then she felt someone crouch down by the open door, take her by the shoulders and a voice curtly telling the policewoman he was a friend. She was being pulled gently out of the car and felt herself being hugged very tightly against someone, at the same time as a voice was saying: 'Oh, my poor girl, are you all right?' and she fell crying uncontrollably against Joel's shoulder.

# Chapter Forty

A dim light cast a shadow across the room. Her head throbbed and her limbs felt heavy and aching. At first she just lay there trying to remember what had happened. Then as the events of the evening flooded back, she started and tried to struggle up in the bed.

Almost immediately Joel was beside her, pushing her gently back, talking softly and soothingly.

'Take it easy and just listen to me,' he said, studying her face. He took her hand and held it. 'You're in your own bed. You're perfectly safe and you're not alone. I'm here and so too is Ginny. She'll be up in a minute.'

'Ginny? You . . . ?' Rosie was trying hard to keep his face in focus. She wanted to ask why he was there, was she dreaming and that whatever he might think, she had suddenly never felt so safe in her life.

Not since he had helped her into the house and stayed with her, a comforting arm around her shoulders while the police searched the garden and took a statement from her and said they would be back in the morning to fill in the gaps. Then Ginny and the doctor arrived and made her go to bed and she hadn't wanted to leave him. But he was still here.

'Why? I must think . . .'

She heard Joel hushing her as she attempted to talk. 'Don't try, the doctor gave you a hefty shot of valium. It's . . .' he glanced at the bedside clock. 'Nearly midnight. Try and go back to sleep. We'll talk when the valium's worn off. In the morning. Ginny's going to sleep in the dressing room. You're not going to be left alone. I promise. Now go back to sleep.'

Her face felt numb. It was hard to form words. Why had she been burgled, attacked, terrified? Why was he here, sitting by her bed at this hour? What was he doing outside her house when he should have been at Stevie's party? But the questions spun in a jumble in her head and, helpless against the tide of sleep that was engulfing her, she nodded and still holding his hand drifted into oblivion.

'Christ, not the Kneller? And the what? The Bows? Jee-zus.' Rory, woken in Glencairn at eight in the morning by Rosie feeling fragile and in need of sympathy, almost reduced her to tears when his questions had been aimed almost solely at what was missing and how they had got in, ignoring her injuries.

'Made it easy for them, didn't you?' he shouted furiously. 'Stupid of you, Rosie, I suppose you forgot the alarm again.'

'Rory, I didn't. I was here and I know what I did. I've had a rough time and I don't need this. I agree with the police, someone came in who knew the code. There's no sign of a forced entry anywhere.'

'Like who?' he retorted. Rosie hesitated.

There was someone. It had been troubling her. The motor bike that had roared past her was very distinctive. A Harley Davidson. James owned one. The only thing that made her hesitate was that for once the rider had not fallen off, as James tended to do. She took a deep breath.

'James?' he repeated. She heard him laugh. Impatient. Derisive. Disbelieving. 'Oh *please*. Is there no end to your vindictiveness about my friends?'

'Rory,' she protested weakly. 'Please not now. I just thought you should know. Okay?'

'Okay,' he said heavily. 'I'd better come back. I'll get the next shuttle.'

Rosie closed her eyes in despair. Slowly she eased her body to the side of the bed, swung her legs to the ground and waited until her head stopped swimming.

'Back into bed,' ordered Ginny, appearing at that moment with strong black coffee which she placed between them on the quilt. 'I blame myself for not making you come with me. Here, drink this, the doctor's coming at ten.'

'How did you know what happened?' Rosie asked, gingerly leaning back against the pillows.

'Didn't until Joel rang.' Ginny stirred her coffee. 'Stevie sent him when I told her you'd gone home. She insisted Joel went to get you. He rang me while the doctor was with you and said to come over. Caused quite a stir in that quarter,' she grinned mischievously.

'Where is he?'

'Gone. Left just after midnight. Said he'd call. Loads of messages,' Ginny told her. 'Nancy, Carey, Jaye – she'll be here in a minute. Stevie and Kit. He came round, said he'd be back later today. How do you feel?'

Rosie was very white, the shock of such a brutal attack was etched into her face. The base of her neck throbbed.

'I feel so . . .' she dashed a hand across her cheeks but the sheer fright of it all came back and her body was racked with sobs.

Ginny held her hand and let her cry it out, breaking off only to let the doctor in. Rosie groaned. Dr Collins, who had last advised her to seek counselling for her problems, trod across the room.

'Not much harm done,' he pronounced briskly, having examined the bump on the base of her neck. 'You'll ache for a couple of days.'

He then wrote a prescription for a strong sedative, told Rosie she might feel sleepy and weepy, but both were to be expected. Shock did that.

'Dr Collins . . .' she called after him as he turned to go. 'I won't need these.'

'You might,' he replied crisply. 'At least on this occasion please take my advice, if only for your family's sake.'

Rosie sank back on the pillows.

'Joel? I just wanted to say thank you for looking after me. Staying with me like that . . . and for so long.'

'Glad I was there.' He sounded cautious. 'And glad Stevie was so insistent about going to get you. I'm just sorry I wasn't there earlier. I might have saved you a headache. I'll call you when you're feeling better. Is Ginny still with you? And Rory? Good. Take care.'

She replaced the phone and burst into tears. Shock did that, the doctor said. Any kind.

# Chapter Forty-One

The police showed her the cellophane packet containing white powder which they found among her scattered possessions on the hall floor.

Rosie stared at the flat packet and then up at the detective's face. 'Rubbish,' she said flatly. 'I wouldn't use it or even know where to get it. Whoever burgled the house must have dropped it.'

They stared silently back at her. Rosie looked from one to the other of the two detectives sitting in front of her. They didn't believe her.

'It's true,' she insisted. 'I wouldn't touch the stuff.'

'Who else can get into this house, Mrs Monteith Gore?'

Rosie shook her head, trying to think. 'The only person who has the code apart from us is our former housekeeper, Abbie, Abeline Hart. She's a possibility because I asked Rory to fire her. Apart from that I've no idea.'

Four hours later – which seemed a ridiculously lengthy period to tell them she knew nothing and to complete her statement – a doctor arrived to take a blood sample.

She made no objection. They would find nothing. Maybe caffeine. But cocaine? Oh puleese.

Rory arrived just as the police were leaving. To her astonishment, he immediately crossed the room and gave her a swift hug and then with his arm protectively around her shoulders demanded to know what his wife was being accused of.

The detective rose to his feet. Rosie wriggled away.

'Nothing, sir. Merely helping us, as I hope you will.'

Rory threw an anxious glance at Rosie, not lost on the

occupants of the room, as he said: 'Of course. Sorry, officer. It's just that my wife – sorry, ex-wife – has been under considerable strain this last year. It's why she and my son are back living with me and I absolutely do not want to give her any further cause to feel under pressure.'

It was, as Rosie told Kit later, the most paralysing condemnation of her state of mind that she had ever heard without calling her deranged and the moment when she knew for sure Rory wanted to destroy her.

It was also the reason she immediately intervened. She got to her feet, managing to sound pleasant, far from how she was feeling, and leaned both hands on the back of her chair.

'Thank you, Rory,' she said firmly. She saw the tightening of the muscles around his mouth, but refused to be diverted. 'You forget it was at your insistence that I returned to help you improve your relationship with your father. To give you stability. Now, I'm much more concerned with being mugged and finding all this stuff in my handbag. Any ideas how it could have got there?'

'Coke? In your bag? Oh my God, Rosie . . . Officer, please, I can only repeat, my wife is under stress.'

'Don't be absurd, Rory,' she cut in. 'You know damn well I wouldn't touch the stuff. It must have been dropped by whoever burgled the house.'

'Honestly, love, don't go bringing James into this.' He turned, lifting his shoulders in an exaggerated display of frustration. Rosie wondered why he had never considered the stage. The police listened patiently but expertly to this exchange.

'Your husband mentioned someone . . . James? Is there any reason for that, Mrs Monteith-Gore?'

'I've told you, I heard a motor bike roaring away. James, Rory's partner, has one. If it was him he might know – have seen – whoever stole Rory's property. That's all.'

Rory shrugged helplessly at the detective. 'Darling, I told

you James was in Scotland with me. He couldn't have been in both places at the same time.'

In Scotland? Rory had never mentioned that. All eyes were on her.

'You didn't actually say that, Rory, but if you tell me he was in Scotland with you, I must have made a mistake.'

As she knew they would, the police questioned James who, with the help of several guests, confirmed that he had been with Rory at the Johnsons' in Scotland that night.

Rosie had reluctantly to accept that the noise of the attack had distorted her hearing. Her terror had obviously played a trick on her. The doubt that hung over her was obvious, but since the police could not see how she could have mugged herself, and because she was clearly distraught when they'd found her, they left the case open, particularly as they understood that Abbie was no longer in the country.

The blood test later showed not a single trace of any exotic substance but a brief and bitter exchange with Rory followed after the police had departed.

Rory was making no attempt to disguise his belief that she was implicated in the robbery through malice, stupidity or because she was cracking up.

He simply sneered when she asked icily if that was the case, how she could have attacked herself?

'Oh yes, I'd forgotten that bit,' he said admiringly. 'You'd do anything for attention, sweetheart, wouldn't you?'

'Meaning?'

Rory strolled out of the room, pausing at the door. 'Well, no longer able to attract mine, what a way to get Joel Harley's instead. Tsk tsk. All that hurling yourself into the street, first making sure someone would let him know that you'd be all alone.'

'Don't be ridiculous,' she snapped. 'Who told you he was here?'

He tapped the side of his nose, mocking her, outraging her, and closed the door softly behind him. Fury made her pull it open and stride after him. He was talking to Mrs Milton in the hall, the front door open.

'Tom is staying with the Duxboroughs next weekend,' she heard him say. 'If Mrs Duxborough calls, tell her I'll be in touch to arrange details.'

They both turned as Rosie spoke. 'And who arranged that, Rory?' she demanded furiously. 'Tom doesn't know that, does he? And you know I won't have him staying there.'

'I've arranged it. They're spending the weekend in Bridgewood. You need a rest, Rosie. Everyone knows that. It's nothing to be ashamed of, is it, Mrs Milton?'

Mrs Milton looked uncomfortably from one to the other.

'No, indeed not. You've been through an awful time, Rosie dear.'

Rosie wondered if any jury would indict her if she strangled Rory. He knew how to hurt her. How to frighten her. Winning Tom's confidence, his preference for his company, and now beguiling Mrs Milton into believing she was cracking up.

'That won't be necessary, Rory. As a matter of fact Tom and I have already made plans for this weekend . . .'

'Really? And they are what?'

'Well,' Rosie stumbled. There weren't any plans. She couldn't be specific.

'So.' He flicked some imaginary fluff from his sleeve and spoke like a man simply clarifying her intentions. 'No plans and no real reason to reorganise my arrangements?'

Rosie stared helplessly at him. 'I just want to spend time with Tom,' she said lamely. 'I've hardly seen him in the last couple of weeks and I am his mother.'

Rory took his briefcase from Mrs Milton and shrugged into his coat.

'So you are, Rosie,' he agreed calmly. 'So you are.'

When Dr Collins appeared the next day, summoned by Rory after Rosie had told him to stop nagging her about the theft and had finally shouted at him, she locked herself in her room, and refused to see him.

Outside on the landing she heard them conferring in low voices before retreating down the stairs. Sod them, she thought and turned over to try and get some much needed sleep.

Livvie and Jordan exchanged looks at the transformation in her mood. Clearly she was not operating with a full deck. They stared in amazement as she turned clients down, telling them she could not take on any more commissions until well into the New Year.

Wu Chang sent four faxes within an hour requesting her help to transform the headquarters of his company in London, where he was now moving full time, bringing with him several senior executives who all wanted their houses decorating.

She agreed to do the lot by March. 'But Mr Chang,' they heard her say. 'Have you got a pencil near you? Yes? Good. This is my telephone number. Do not give any of your executives the number of my fax. It exploded this morning.'

'It's that knock on the head,' Jordan whispered. 'Do you suppose she's got delayed shock?'

'Maybe,' Livvie replied. 'More like coming to her senses in my opinion.'

'Turning down chances like that?' he hissed. 'Are you as mad as Rosie?'

'No. Unlike you, I can see past a pretty face.'

Jordan was now utterly bewildered. 'Meaning?'

'Meaning that flaky ex of hers.'

'So beautiful and so . . . shallow,' Jordan ended mournfully, his fascination for Rory no longer what it was.

'And so vain,' Livvie finished. 'Hey, look at the time. I'll be late for the lecture.'

She began to hurl her work into an orderly pile on her desk. Slicking lipgloss over her mouth, ruffling her hair so that it shot up in sharp spikes, and exchanging the emerald green plastic baubles that hung from her ears for deep cherry triangles, she whirled out.

'What's the lecture?' Jordan called after her.

'"Letting Go Of Unrealistic Expectations",' her voice floated back up the stairs.

Jordan stopped what he was doing. Hastily he pulled his coat from the back of the chair. 'Hang on,' he shrieked. 'I'll come with you.'

Nancy was last to call. Rosie wasn't surprised. The great unveiling of her house was to take place next week. Whether she liked it or not, it would look odd if Rosie were not present. Equally, Rosie knew the dangers to her business of having her absence correctly construed, and so both women gritted their teeth.

Having her name linked with Joel in the *Globe* had done wonders for Nancy's spirits but very little for Rosie's.

'Sure you're up to it? I ran into Rory. He's so concerned about you. Doesn't want you to feel you're to blame.'

'I'm not,' Rosie told her icily. 'Next time you see Rory, tell him not to exaggerate.'

Nancy said, 'Glad you can make the unveiling.' Rosie knew she wasn't.

'Looking forward to it,' she lied. It was a toss-up which of them hit the cut-out button first.

A week later Rosie collected Tom from school at the start of Christmas break.

As they turned the corner and slowed to a halt, the sight of the front of the house brought shouts of pleasure from

Tom. He loved the wreath of holly and silver cones trimmed with red tartan ribbon that was on the front door and the miniature fir trees with nuts stuffed into the deep olive branches, placed either side of it.

'Dad,' Tom whooped. 'Dad!' he yelled, racing up the stone steps, his face lighting up as Rory appeared in the doorway. Rosie watched impassively.

A sight she had once yearned for being played out in front of her eyes was bringing her no pleasure at all.

'Dad!' Tom shouted hurling himself on his father. 'I'm home. Four whole weeks, Dad. Isn't that great?'

'Only four weeks?' Rory laughed, swopping mock punches. 'Well, we haven't got a moment to waste. Come on in here and let's me and you plan every second of it. Grandpa is longing to see you.'

With a hug and a ruffle of his hair, Rory ushered Tom ahead of him into the house, pausing only to glance briefly back down at Rosie, who was unloading her son's cases on the pavement.

A small half-sneering smile played around his mouth. For a moment in silence he just looked at her then he walked into the house and left her standing there, gazing thoughtfully after them.

It was not a scene she planned to have repeated. But Rory was not to know that. Not yet.

# Chapter Forty-Two

The party Nancy threw to celebrate Christmas and the completion of her house was a spectacular affair. There were too many plump wallets and generous spirits on the loose in London at that time of year for Nancy not to take advantage of them to help her beloved Foundation. She had filled the place with household names, diplomats and captains of industry.

By the time Rosie made her entrance, ushered in by Nancy's butler, the house she had come to know better than her own was overflowing. White-coated waiters moved amongst the guests, a glorious Christmas tree dominated the hall, and the magnificent staircase trailing swags of fircones and silver globes entwined in green leaves was every bit the show-stopper Rosie had known it would be.

To one side a string quartet dressed in Dickensian costume were playing a mixture of Mozart and Christmas music, flanked by branches of candles. The reception room was a blaze of light and colour.

Taking a glass of champagne from a proffered tray, Rosie made her way through the crowd to find Nancy. She knew at some point she would see Joel, but she was ready for it.

He'd phoned once but she was out for the day, and by the time she'd rung back he had left to collect his children from their respective schools and to spend a couple of days with them before they left for Christmas with Marianne at Martha's Vineyard. But he had rung. It was in turn something and then nothing, depending on how she thought of it. Which she did often. Too often. Earlier she had given herself a good lecture on the subject. Yes, she was ready.

She could see immediately that Nancy was on good form; her dry American wit coupled with the fact that she was a brilliant raconteur drew people to her. There was no need to question why Joel liked her, enjoyed her company.

Nancy, in her signature black with a scarlet-and-gold silk scarf, was in the midst of a group which included a prominent French banker and his mistress and the Minister for the Arts. He in turn was accompanied by a beautiful young man who Rosie recognised as the star of the latest BBC Jane Austen drama currently enjoying heart-throb status among the country's ecstatic female viewing public. And, Rosie noticed, Nancy's undivided attention.

For form's sake she simply smiled and raised her hand in greeting as Nancy caught her eye. At least Nancy, unlike some clients, acknowledged Rosie was the genius behind her acclaimed house.

She turned away, searching for Jaye. Her progress across the room was punctuated with other guests congratulating her on the design of the house. Like a first night, she reflected, knowing that by the time she reached the doorway to the dining room, she had secured at least three more commissions.

It was the boost she needed. For those who knew her well, the article in the *Globe* was a travesty. For those who didn't, she knew it would be a source of pleasurable whispered gossip. Joyce told Livvie that everyone had mentioned it.

After weeks of silence, Miriam de Lisle rang. Rosie knew her commiseration was as phoney as her voice suggested and made a superhuman effort to sound cheerfully unconcerned.

Ten minutes later, barely concealing her anger, Miriam replaced the phone convinced that Rosie had hidden depths. Most of which, according to Miriam, appeared to bottom out at barefaced brass. Not even a moment's gloom could she detect in her voice.

'Oh shut up,' she screamed at a peeved Conrad who she knew secretly admired Rosie and who chose that moment to ask why her face was flushed so badly and, mindful of the marriage counsellor's advice to be sensitive to his wife's moods and needs, enquired caringly if it might be a hot flush?

Miriam punched him before picking up the phone to ring Sylvia for a good bitch about Rosie.

It had not been Bella's intention, but she had made Rosie a name. Certainly this was as much her night as Nancy's.

'Quite right too. This looks brilliant,' Jaye said as they wandered into the other crowded rooms. 'How you put up with her ego is amazing. And so is that jacket by the way,' she added, looking enviously at the double-breasted pink satin jacket Rosie was wearing over a floor-length slim black crepe skirt.

'I should never have bought this,' Jaye wailed, indicating her black halter-neck dress, breathing sharply in to flatten her stomach. 'Let alone worn it. I need to lose at least a stone, oh God, and Christmas is in four days. This is definitely my last glass of champagne for two weeks.'

Rosie inspected her friend. She looked sensational. Sexy. Her mane of ash-blonde hair piled high with loose tendrils escaping around her ears.

'Dreadful,' she pronounced cheerfully, used to Jaye's inability to see herself as she was. 'And so disciplined. Fancy starting a diet in front of all that sensational food.'

Jaye peered over her shoulder, following Rosie's rapturous gaze. 'Hold on,' she commanded, seeing the table groaning with the most sinful food she'd ever encountered. She drained her glass and took another from a passing waiter. 'I think it would be awfully rude,' she said carefully, 'not to have just a little of each, don't you?'

The room where the buffet supper had been laid out,

like the rest of the house, was glittering. Lights reflecting off the silver Georgian candlesticks, the Garrards cutlery, Baccarat wine glasses, gold-decorated porcelain plates and balloon glass vases crammed with white Christmas roses all increased the fairytale atmosphere.

Already making inroads into the feast that Gerard had slaved over for two days with triumphant results, they spotted Livvie with Jordan, who was keeping Carey and Josh in fits with his predictions for their star signs. Kit was talking earnestly to Ginny, clearly not wanting an interruption. Jaye nudged Rosie and they both widened their eyes. Not like Kit to go for brains.

'*Ros-ee.*' She turned to see Stevie swooping down on her with Daniel in tow. 'You wicked girl.' Stevie hugged her. 'Are you feeling okay, over it? How's Tom?'

Rosie was then hugged by Daniel, who introduced her to Marc Corval, a guest staying with them from Paris, whose eye fell on her with delight. Her fringe had grown out, and she now wore her hair with a casual disregard for styling, which only made her look more French than English.

So delighted that, in the direct way the French have made their own, it took him just minutes to tuck Rosie's arm companionably through his and whisper straightfaced in front of Stevie that they were the most glamorous couple in the room and the evening had been saved by Rosie's arrival.

'Remind me to charge you for your stay,' Stevie teased him. 'Ignore him, Rosie, he knows perfectly well I am the love of his life.'

It happened so fast he was in front of her while Nancy was still greeting her. 'Rosie, hi,' drawled Nancy, exhaling a cloud of smoke.

'Nice to see you,' Joel smiled, turning to Marc. 'Are you planning to clutch Rosie all evening?'

'But no,' Marc said solemnly. 'This is just to get me

through until midnight. After that the air of mystery surrounding Rosie will be my duty to investigate.'

Rosie couldn't help laughing, extending a hand to Joel at the same time as she did so. 'How nice to see you,' she said. 'I think this,' she indicated Marc's arm, 'is called sexual harassment.'

Joel looked relaxed and amused. 'I thought that only applied at work?'

'Well, this is for me,' she smiled back, delighted that she could make it clear to both him and Nancy that she wouldn't be there otherwise.

'Then I insist you take some time off,' he ordered. 'This woman is going to be my stiffest competition,' he added to the others. 'Without her, it would never have occurred to me to resite that staircase.' His hand was under her elbow, guiding her away, ignoring Marc's protests that Joel was poaching. Nancy's face was a mask of fury.

'Nice of you to let Nancy take the credit for the table,' Joel said, smiling as her eyes widened. 'Don't worry, I won't mention it. I know Nancy well. Decor is not her subject. This is a remarkable job,' he continued, leading her up the wide staircase, sitting down halfway, the better to appreciate the scale of the gallery and the curve of the staircase.

Rosie sat awkwardly beside him, holding her drink, wishing she could look and feel more relaxed.

'Thank you for giving me the credit, but we all know it was your expertise.' She hadn't been mistaken. Silly to have thought he would be that vain.

He waved a hand dismissively. 'It looked very impressive in the *Globe*,' Joel was saying. 'What did you do to upset the dreadful writer?'

'Oh, who knows?' she shrugged. 'As long as they spell the name right, it's all good for the image.'

'You don't mean that,' he said pleasantly. He waited. Rosie stared into her drink.

'Am I that transparent?' she asked, carefully moving aside as other guests made their way down the staircase.

'Actually no,' he said 'As a matter of fact, you're not transparent enough. And that's the problem, Miss Colville . . . trying to second guess what's going on in your head.'

'Goodness, have you been taking lessons from Marc?' she asked. 'Making me sound mysterious when I'm really very straightforward?'

'Marc?' He glanced down to where the Frenchman was now talking to Nancy at the foot of the stairs, but making no secret of the fact that he was trying to catch Rosie's attention and quite often succeeding. 'No.' He gave a wry smile. 'But maybe I should.'

'No tie,' she said finally as he didn't seem too concerned that silence had fallen.

'No indeed.' He glanced down. 'I think my children are planning a particularly naff one for Christmas, which reminds me, I've been meaning to ask you something.'

'Ask away.' She tried to keep her voice from cracking. He was so damned near. 'You've obviously heard I'm on first-name terms with Father Christmas.'

'Not much escapes me, but as long as you don't use sleighbells or fur rugs, I wonder if you would be interested in redesigning my home?'

Rosie gaped at him.

'Is that a "no"?' he enquired after a few seconds when she didn't answer.

She shook her head. 'Sorry, it was just so unexpected. The commission, I mean. I've always thought architects preferred doing all that kind of thing themselves.'

'Well funnily, no,' he smiled at her. 'Not if someone can do it better. And I know you could.'

Rosie thought she would explode with fright and happiness. 'Well, yes, I'm flattered . . . love to . . . where shall we start?'

They were still smiling when Nancy called up to her:

330

'Rosie, your husband's just arrived, he's looking for you.'

Rosie's eyes flew open, she wheeled round, searching the throng gathered in the hall. 'Rory? Here?'

As she spoke she spotted him. Without having to be told, she knew he was already drunk.

'Excuse me.' She rose rapidly, wanting to put distance between them. Rory had other plans.

'Sweetheart,' he called out, seeing her sitting with Joel. 'There you are.'

He would never gatecrash. Not his style. But ingratiating himself with Nancy was. She must have invited him, but never mentioned it to her. Just how friendly were these two?

Beside Rory, James was grinning from ear to ear, incapable of making any attempt at disguising his own consumption of champagne.

Rory was mounting the stairs, eyes glittering. He looked, as always, impeccable. Slender, dark, brooding, the sexiest features any man was entitled to have, desirable. He left Rosie cold.

She felt rather than saw Joel glance up at her.

'I didn't know you were coming, Rory.' She tried to keep her voice from shaking as she started down the stairs to meet him. She could smell trouble. She knew the look.

'No, but then you rarely care where I am these days, do you?' His voice was soft but it carried. 'On the other hand, knowing Joel was here, I guessed immediately where to find you. Good evening, Joel.' He flashed a smile at him. 'Glad to see my wife knows – to quote the *Globe* – who to hitch her star to. I hear she's going to do your apartment. Well done, sweetheart, always get what you want, don't you?'

Joel was now standing beside Rosie, his eyes like flint, but Rory hadn't finished yet. 'Glad you let Nancy persuade you. After the theft at our house, Rosie needs good friends to restore her credibility.'

331

Rosie looked from one to the other, her face impassive, her insides doing cartwheels. Joel tried to speak, reaching out an arm as he did so. She shrugged him off.

'Thank you for reminding me.' She moved around Rory. 'I must be careful about the company I keep,' she remarked pleasantly. 'Now if you'll all excuse me.'

The grinning James was in her path. 'Perhaps if you hang around someone will ask you to decorate the Christmas cake,' he cackled weakly.

Eyes flashing, Rosie paused, casting a look of total contempt at him. 'As one who makes trash look Oscar material, I hardly think your opinion counts with anyone,' she said with icy politeness.

'You fucking bitch,' he screamed, clutching the banister. '*Trash?* How dare you?'

Ignoring him and the open-mouthed amazement of the onlookers, Rosie walked lightly and leisurely down the stairs, straight across the hall and out of the front door, Jaye and Carey racing after her, leaving behind the sight of James, incandescent with rage, too drunk to think.

Pushing Rory to one side he stumbled after her, missed his footing and rolled headlong down Nancy's magnificent staircase. The musicians in the middle of 'O Holy Night' scattered. James grabbed the nearest object to cling to.

With a collective gasp, the crowd now attracted by the screams watched horrified and helpless as the heavily decorated tree swayed and slowly sank against the far wall in a crashing shower of splintering glass.

James rolled to a halt at Nancy's feet, where he immediately rejected the two bottles of champagne he had consumed in the last hour. Nancy shrieked her disgust.

In the uproar that followed only Rory and Nancy, trapped between the door and the stairs, noticed that Joel too had slipped out of the party.

# Chapter Forty-Three

Carey caught up with her first. Jaye sprinted along on the opposite side of the road, her dress hitched above her knees, weaving wildly in and out of the traffic and, gasping, reached her as Carey swung her round.

Neither saw the black Range Rover slowing down and pulling to a halt in the centre of the road, just beyond where Rosie stood on a traffic island, her face chalk-white, trying to flag down a taxi. She was shaking violently. It was a bitterly cold night and her jacket was thin.

'Stay here while I go back and decapitate him,' Carey howled, hugging her as cars whizzed along on either side.

'Sue him,' shouted Jaye above the noise of the traffic, huddling against them. 'You'll get thousands. We'll all be witnesses. Oh Christ,' she moaned, seeing the Range Rover brake in front of them. 'Here comes Joel.'

All three gazed at him as he jumped out and strode back to where they were standing. He grabbed Rosie by the shoulders.

'Go away,' she ordered him, trying to push him away. 'I'm with my friends. Just leave me alone. Carey?' She turned to him, holding onto his arm. 'Carey?' she repeated urgently.

Jaye grabbed Rosie's other arm, glaring at Joel. 'Are you deaf? Let her go. Carey, what are you doing? No, I won't come with you, I'm not leaving Rosie.'

'That's right, Jaye,' Rosie commanded. 'Stay with me.'

Suddenly Carey, who had been glancing from Joel's face to Rosie's, surprisingly switched tack. 'You come with me,

Jaye. There's a great story going on at Nancy's. I think it's our duty to cover it.'

'Duty?' Jaye echoed, staring at him in astonishment. Carey looked steadily at her.

'Yes, duty,' he repeated emphatically.

'Oh yes, of course,' Jaye said, comprehension dawning. 'Absolutely our duty. In fact, I'd say we owe it to the nation. Race you. Rosie, I'll call you.'

'Jaye!' Rosie shouted desperately after them as they ran, clutching each other, to the other side of the street. 'Carey! You can't do this!'

'I think they just did,' Joel observed, his arm still around her. 'Come on, you're freezing. And attracting attention.'

A police car slowed alongside. 'That your car, sir?' enquired the driver, rolling down the window.

'Sorry, officer,' Joel called back, opening the passenger door and bundling Rosie in. 'I thought my companion was going to be sick. But she's fine now and we're just going, aren't we, Rosie?'

The policeman looked doubtfully at her. She certainly seemed white. Rosie nodded and allowed Joel to help her in.

They drove in silence, Rosie staring resolutely out of her window. Joel wasn't far wrong. Rory's outburst had horrified her. Humiliated her. She just had to get away.

She'd almost forgotten Joel, who didn't interrupt her silence at all. Finally as they reached the bottom of Kings Road and headed towards Chelsea Harbour she said tersely: 'Could you drop me here? I've got the keys to Kit's house. I can go there.'

'Certainly,' he replied, driving straight on.

'I said, could you drop me . . .'

'I heard what you said. But I'm not leaving you alone. Not in this state. When you're feeling better I'll drive you anywhere you want,' he finished, turning the vehicle into the cobbled street that led to his home.

He leaned out, activated a code and the garage door ahead of them slid noiselessly open, sliding down again once they were inside. Rosie remained silent. It was too undignified to start a scene. And in truth she didn't have the heart for it. She didn't have the heart for anything except to crave silence.

'Yes of course,' she said politely, following him into the lift where they travelled up four floors to the penthouse duplex.

Rosie stepped out into a warm corridor of highly polished woodblock flooring, the walls dominated with the hard-edged works of a clutch of modern American painters. Roy Lichtenstein, Warhol, she recognised immediately. Originals too.

Rosie followed Joel towards a pair of double doors at the far end. As he pushed them open, she had to stop herself from gasping with genuine pleasure.

Gazing out over the stretch of river it looked like fairyland. Downriver the lights on Albert Bridge and Chelsea Bridge cut perfect loops into the night sky. Lights from offices and apartments on the opposite bank reflected in the inky blackness of the water and downstream a mass of black shadows were all that could be seen of the warehouses that lined the river until it curved away towards Richmond and beyond.

'You don't need paintings.' She turned impulsively to him and back again, gazing out at the view, indicating the sweep of the bridges scattered upstream. 'This is all you need.'

The vast living area was a blend of minimalism combined with comfort. Other rooms linked effortlessly with each other, all managing to feel quietly luxurious with the minimum of fuss.

No clichéd Corbusier sofas or Philippe Starck chairs, but wide and white squashy sofas, sharp blue armchairs and a view that made Rosie feel the apartment was sitting in the middle of the river. It gave Joel's home a Mediterranean ambience. She thought of Menton. No wonder he didn't want the yacht.

Almost as quickly she told herself to forget Menton. This was London, and months later. At best this was business. In a minute she would go home.

The low purr of a phone distracted him. Rosie stood nervously gazing around until he was finished. The spacial flow of the entire apartment was so beautifully co-ordinated Rosie swallowed hard. Something was wrong.

The design of Nancy's house was where Rosie excelled. Bold, brave colours, intuitive mixing of the old with the new, pulled together with confidence and wit. Her professional instincts now took over. She was no more the designer for him than Jessica Milford.

Concealed radiators, sandblasted glass doors, no ostentatious technology but Rosie knew without being told that at the press of a switch, blinds would glide quietly into place. An expert – and for a minute her own natural curiosity took over and she longed to ask who – had produced lighting that didn't cast unnecessary shadows.

Joel interjected as though reading her thoughts. 'It's not used much in this country, but it works so well in my office that I asked for it here. It's white light, not that yellow effect you get from other lighting. No shadows. Shop fitters use it,' he added helpfully to her silent back. 'Mostly jewellers, makes diamonds sparkle.'

'Who did you get to do it?' she asked as casually as possible.

Encouraged by her sudden break from the cold formality he had so far encountered, Joel teased her.

'I'll let you know when you tell me your price. I cherish my secret army of suppliers too.'

Rosie turned slowly and faced him, not bothering to sit. 'No,' she answered him. 'There is no price. Assuming that you were serious about commissioning me to do all of this

– no, leave aside what Rory says – and if I were tempted, which I'm not, why would you want a designer like me?

'What could I do here? It's exactly how it should be. Why are you doing this?' Her eyes felt as though lead weights were on them, she knew she was beginning to shake.

'Doing what?'

He was leaning against the doorway, arms folded across his chest.

'Wasting my time.' In her head it sounded rational. Out loud it sounded neurotic. 'That's right,' she snapped. 'My time. Every bit as valuable as yours. Expecting me to be grateful for your commission. Well, I'm not bloody grateful . . .'

'*Grateful?*' Joel gazed at her in astonishment. 'Who asked you to be?'

'. . . not even noticing that my work is not like this. All this . . . this . . .' she tried to find the word, whirled round and threw her hands in the air. 'All this chrome and steel and futuristic drama. If you had *really* thought about me . . .'

'Thought about you? Are you crazy?' he cried in disbelief.

'. . . or even *noticed* what I did instead of your friend – or whatever Nancy is – telling you what to do, you would have seen I don't do this. It isn't me.'

'I know it isn't you. Nancy had nothing to do with it.'

'Then why ask me?' His eyes followed her as she stormed around the room. He appeared to have given up trying to argue.

'Is that it?' he asked.

She nodded, pride not allowing her to unleash the tears that were threatening to spill over. When you've behaved like such a fool, retreat is your only option, she told herself.

'No, you've said enough and – sit down – you're not

going anywhere. If you try and leave – come away from that door – I'll simply have to lock it – sorry, that way is a straight jump over the side – and that's the kitchen which as you will see has no windows.'

Rosie, struggling with what little dignity she had left, stood marooned in the middle of the room, her frantic pacing getting her nowhere.

'I'm afraid I must insist . . .' She got no further. Joel took her by the shoulders, removed her bag and pulled her down next to him on one of the sofas. She promptly wriggled away to the other end, sitting stiffly with her hands in her lap.

'Now, listen to me, just for once. I spend an entire summer trying to figure out what's going on in your life, sending you photographs with a note, hoping you'd pick up a phone. I ask you to dinner and then lunch and you refuse with some excuse.

'Not care? Not think about you? For fuck's sake.' He glared at her. 'And then it took that playboy you live with to get you so mad, I finally get you here, and you behave like an army general staking out an ambush. Is that how you treat all your clients?'

She looked back at him. Appalled. 'Thank you,' she said, taking deep breaths, making an heroic effort to speak calmly, pushing her hair behind her ears, straightening her shoulders. 'I'd like to go now.'

'Oh, for God's sake stop it,' he said. 'Just calm down and sit down. I don't really believe that speech was meant for me.' He shifted sideways so that he could see her. 'It's all because that evil little shit you live with is so desperately jealous he'd do anything to stop anyone else taking an interest in you. Do you want to know what I think?'

Getting no response he continued. 'I hadn't actually envisaged a relationship with you that involved being used as a punch bag, but if you want the truth, it's a relief. At least we're talking.'

Rosie turned and stared at him. 'What am I supposed to do? Mind read?'

He moved nearer to her, reaching out for the phone that purred that very second. He gave a muttered expletive as she instantly shrank further away. He disconnected the phone and grabbed her arm, pulling her back.

As he spoke his eyes never left Rosie's face. 'Tell me?' he invited. 'I'm a terrific listener. I might even be able to help. But I need to know one thing, well, two actually.'

There was a constriction in her throat. 'What's that?' she asked hoarsely, terrified he might doubt her innocence, that he might want to be reassured about all the things Rory said and knowing if he did, she had truly misjudged him.

'What makes you think even for half a second that an apartment designed like this, is the kind of place two teen-age kids would feel comfortable in? No, be quiet. What do you think I am? Some sort of style freak? I want a home for my kids to be able to sling their belongings down, make a mess if that's what they want, stick posters up, express themselves in whatever way they want.

'Sure I like the way this is done – I should do, I designed it. But it was never meant to be *home*. More an extension of how I work. I have clients here, so of course it had to be a continuation of what comes off those drawing boards downstairs. But nothing stays the same. My life is different now to when I made those decisions.

'I've bought a house – with a garden and a regular kitchen. It just needs so much doing to it. I was about to explain when Rory did his all-out attack on your reputation and you just shot off and arrived at all kinds of conclusions, none of which I'm glad to say are accurate.'

Devastated, she lifted her face to his. She knew she was now as flushed as she had previously been deathly white. Rosie eyed him nervously. Her hair was a tangled mop from running her hands so distractedly through it, there

339

was a crumpled and shredded tissue in her hand, her nose was shiny – oh yes, it was. Of that, if nothing else, she was entirely certain.

'Look.' She cleared her throat. 'I know what you must be thinking.'

'I doubt it,' he said easily. 'You might not stay for another two seconds if you did. Now,' he sat square on to her. 'Stop looking so trapped and tell me what's going on in your life. I'm sick of hearing it second hand.'

After a bit she blew her nose and tried to smile: 'God, you must think I'm neurotic and hysterical.'

'I wish you'd stop telling me what I think,' he complained.

'Okay,' she said. 'What was the second thing you wanted to know?'

He leaned forward, studying his hands and then looked sideways at her. 'Er . . . how good my chances are of getting you to have dinner with me?'

Someone in a voice that sounded nothing like her own said: 'Dinner? Yes. I mean, very good. I mean, your chances, not the dinner. If you see what I mean . . . I mean, yes, thank you.'

# Chapter Forty-Four

They didn't go out. Instead Joel produced a bottle of wine and, listening intently, moved her to a sofa near the windows, settling himself at one end, once replenishing her glass as she spoke.

Flashing strobes of light from cars crawling silently along the far side of the river and the chain of lights from the bridges suspended in the night sky cast a glow over the room.

'Financially, Rory stood to gain so much from it. More than me. Much more. Without us, Callum would have disinherited him. Otherwise he wouldn't have given a sod about me and Tom.

'And then when I . . .' she hesitated, she didn't want to tell him. Not yet. Too soon. 'When I rejected him, he couldn't handle it. Rory doesn't want me. He just wants power over me, over anyone who touches his plans.

'The only way he can make sure he inherits is if I co-operate and the only way in his terms that he can be sure of that is to have control over me. I'm going to get out, just as soon as I can persuade Tom that it's for the best.'

And it was so long since she had felt so at ease and just talked that when he said he would fix them supper she could not believe two hours had passed since she'd arrived.

'Oh please.' She jumped to her feet as he strolled off towards the kitchen. 'You mustn't go to any trouble.' He laughed and said he didn't intend to. Omelettes and salad were the height of his culinary powers, but she could sit and watch him whisk the eggs.

She teased him about the pristine state of a kitchen

obviously rarely used, and giggled helplessly when he had solemnly produced a bottle of ketchup and with a flourish gave it pride of place on the kitchen table.

As they ate, he told her that Stevie was fed up with him for not asking her out to dinner and that he didn't know what to do because he heard she was getting over Piers, she seemed so self-contained, never encouraged him to ask, always she seemed to be surrounded by friends, determined to put her son and her job first.

'You're hard to get near.' He flicked a look at her. 'You know it was never Rory that stopped me trying to get to you. It was . . . *is* . . . Tom.'

'He's been through so much.' She suddenly wanted him to understand. 'I don't want him to ever feel he wasn't the centre of my life. It's all I can give him. You and Marianne are so civilised about everything, Ben and Lexie have never not seen you for months on end, certainly not for a whole year, have they? But Tom has been without a father more than with one.'

Later she asked him about Marianne and the children and who his temporary distraction had been. He told her it was stupid beyond belief even to think of it now, but he had felt so trapped by so many things at the time.

'Marianne was not to blame. I have,' he said, swirling the wine around in his glass, 'enormous respect for her. She didn't deserve any of the stuff that happened, the divorce, the pain . . . she's a great mother.

'When I first started out all those years ago I wanted to do it on my own. Jack, my brother, had taken all the money my old man was willing to sling at him and he's ended up justifying his choices to him to this day. I didn't want that.

'Marianne thought it was a phase, but it wasn't. I knew if I was to be anything I had to grit my teeth and get down to it on my own. Hurt my father, of course. My mother understood. Jack thought I was off my rocker.'

He might, he said leaning back, closing his eyes, just

remembering, have remained an architect of small vanities if it had not been for the first competition he won.

'I married Marianne in the same year I was about to crack it. Worst mistake I ever made.'

'Which?' asked Rosie. 'The marriage or the competition?'

'Trying to do both at the same time. Cocky sod I was then. But all the trappings of making money got in the way of what I was doing and most of all got in the way of my marriage. I had a limousine I didn't use, a penthouse in London, an apartment in the Village. Just business toys, you know how it is, and then Daniel was around and said we needed a helicopter so I bought one.'

'Helicopter?' she repeated. 'Where is it?'

'It was ridiculous,' he said. 'A game we were all playing. The year Marianne left me I sold it to the guy who piloted it for me, but if I need to go somewhere in a hurry, I only have to call him. Much saner.'

'What happened between all that and London?' she asked, accepting a brandy. She rarely drank the stuff, but then she rarely did any of the things she had done this last year.

'Too much I expect,' he said. 'But what happened actually was Nancy.'

Rosie felt a small lurch in her stomach which she hoped wasn't reflected in her face.

'Or at least her father. He asked me to design the Alexander Museum in Detroit. It was waiting to happen. The Alexanders had – still have – money to build on the scale of the pyramids. Red tape disappeared, the best engineers materialised, technicians queued up to work on the project. I was . . . *gone*, but so too was my marriage, although I didn't know it then.'

It was a familiar story, too many hours spent with Nancy Alexander overseeing the project. One night too many sleeping at his office because he didn't know when to cast

off for the day. His children seeing less and less of him –
'So I do understand, you know' – and then Dale Klonack
came along.

'I didn't notice. And by the time I did, it was too late.
She was in love with him and the rest is history.'

Well, not quite.

'And what about Nancy?' Rosie asked, desperately trying to inject a friendly interest into her voice.

'Nancy?' He sighed. 'Marianne was so wrong, whatever
the papers say. She's a good friend. She saw off the Houston
deb. Said she wouldn't have looked at me, if it wasn't for
the family money. Yes, I know.' He gave a dry laugh as
she stiffened, misinterpreting her stare. 'Very flattering.'

He reached out and took her hand, and just looked at
her. Then he said: 'I never thought the first time I got you
to myself it would be like this ... especially as I've got
some bad news for you.'

Her eyes flew to his. Bad news? But his eyes were
laughing.

'How bad?' she asked.

'Well.' He removed her glass. 'I can't drive you home
because I've drunk too much and I am surprised – not to
say a little shocked – that you appear to have matched me
glass for glass and so you can't drive either.'

So she had, although she knew it wasn't the drink that
was making her brain feel odd and not even thinking about
resisting as he pulled her gently towards him.

'So, er ... what do you suggest?' Rosie asked, adrift in
something that was so delicious, she wanted to stay floating
there for ever.

Silently he pushed her against the back of the sofa, kissing her softly on her cheek, her chin, her neck. 'What I
suggest,' he said, moving briefly away to douse the lights,
'is that we concentrate on you compensating me for the
past six months and then drive home in the morning.'

Rosie privately thought she would be incapable of

driving anywhere for a year. She tried to tell him this as he took her hand and led her down the stairs to his bedroom.

'I've got great ideas for this room,' she managed to say, hearing him laugh as she took in the vast white bed, the only furniture in the room.

He didn't bother with lamps, since none were needed. The lights from the river, and a moon appearing rhythmically from behind scudding clouds, were in Rosie's now arrested ability to think straight, quite enough.

'I bet you have,' he murmured and then, without taking his eyes away from her face, he slowly ran his hand down her neck, her breasts and then unbuttoned her jacket, slipping his hands underneath it, sliding it in one movement from her shoulders.

He was kissing her mouth and drawing her down with him onto the bed. She shivered, wrapping bare legs around his, her arms reaching up to pull his head down, gasping as she felt his body against her own, and then passion and longing and need took over and Rosie gave up caring about anything, knowing only that she finally, at last, felt complete.

# Chapter Forty-Five

Christmas Day was every bit the nightmare Rosie had dreaded. After a small show of not being able to say if she could come, Caroline announced she was putting her family first and would grace them with her presence after all. With no-one but themselves to make the day work, forced together by circumstances and family ties they fell back on their various props: Rory to drink, her mother to criticising.

By lunchtime, Rory was drunk - it was not even particularly well disguised either. Her mother kept up an unceasing and exhausting monologue about the imagined and real slights she had had to endure from her family and friends, and therefore didn't notice her ex-son-in-law's increasingly glazed expression.

Caring only for Tom, a note from Joel in her pocket, Rosie was still dazed from the speed with which she had become his next thought.

Part of her was glad he was not in town; she needed the space to think. The other half counted days, divided into hours and minutes until she might see him again.

The absence of Abbie meant the weight of the day fell to Rosie. While this did not trouble her in any way, she did miss the lively, laughing company of Carey and Jaye and Kit who were all spending Christmas in Carey's house. And she missed Joel.

Several times her eyes strayed to the phone, wondering if it would be worth risking a call to New York where he had flown with his children for Christmas and New Year with their mother.

There was no reason in the world to keep what was now between them a secret. But neither wanted to share it, Rosie for Tom's sake and Joel because of Lexie and Ben. Neither wanted anything or anyone to damage what they might have together.

Rosie also knew Rory would be even less manageable if he knew and just hoped that he would reach his bedroom before drink-induced sleep overcame him.

Nancy's party lay unspoken between them. Rosie realised that Rory was furious at having to be associated with James' drunken performance. The fact that Rory's business partner now was in hospital recovering from multiple injuries sustained in her home did nothing for Nancy, who was freely described in the tabloids next day as 'eccentric hostess' or 'madcap American heiress'.

Nancy had still to get used to British newspapers' ability to reinvent personalities according to the latest events and with a wonderful disregard for the truth.

There was no mention of Rosie, who privately and unjustly a bitter Nancy blamed. She was even denied the pleasure of reading her name coupled with Joel's, which was not mentioned either. Kit, who had witnessed the aftermath, told Rosie that for an awful moment such was her fury and hysteria that they all thought she would be stretchered off with James.

If it were not for Tom, Rosie would have happily spent the day sitting staring into space with a silly smile on her face. It was the need to make it enjoyable for her son that sustained her through a Christmas Day that she recalled in later years as the Christmas from Hell.

Her brother Patrick had sent cards and presents for them all and had incensed his mother by forwarding a photograph of himself with the third Mrs Colville, having not let anyone know she existed. Lucky Patrick, Rosie thought, handing the offending picture back to her mother. Out of it all.

Tom, fêted with presents and up since dawn, seemed not to notice – or if he did, not to care – that his parents made little attempt to talk and had his first tantrum of the day when his grandmother had made it her business to count his presents.

'Disgraceful,' she pronounced stiffly, having completed her task. 'And still the tree to come.'

Rosie surveyed the mountain of wrapping paper, string and labels that engulfed the room with misgiving. On his birthday and Christmas she behaved like someone who had gone through a skilful extraction of her sense of judgement. But this year Rory's contribution to demolishing their son's sense of values made her regard Tom's pile of presents with dismay and alarm.

For appearances' sake she had bought Rory some cuff links and Polo aftershave, as well as some stocking fillers that she had wrapped up the night before along with a stocking each for her mother and Tom. Automatically she piled in some tights and soap for herself so that Tom wouldn't think she had been left out.

To her horror, Rory presented her with a cashmere sweater, Safari perfume and a John Galliano sliver of a belt with a silver buckle.

'How very generous of you, Rory,' her mother exclaimed, peering at the pale grey sweater in Rosie's lap as her daughter struggled to smile. She felt powerless to stop Caroline who, feeling more than satisfied with the amber-and-gold necklace and matching earrings Rory had presented to her, thought Rosie was indefensibly brief in her thanks.

Fuelling Rosie's wrath was Tom's anguished whisper that maybe they hadn't bought Daddy enough. It was written all over her mother's face that for once her grandson had got it right.

It was written all over Rory's that he had scored the point he was looking for.

The day ended near to midnight with Tom over-excited and angry because the grown-ups all refused to play one more game of Ultimate Soccer Manager, and who had become almost tearful when Rosie insisted that he should go to bed.

Caroline, horrified at her grandson's tantrums, opened another bottle of wine. For the first time all day Rory showed some interest in his former mother-in-law and in silence they finished the bottle together.

Of the two, Rosie preferred her mother. When finally the house was silent, Tom asleep and Rory out cold in his room, she slipped under the covers of her own bed and drew out the note Joel had written and which she had carried with her all day. It was a quote from Jean Genet:

'*My heart's in my hand and my hand is pierced, and my hand's in the bag and the bag is shut and my heart is caught.*'

For the first time in a long time, she slept.

# Chapter Forty-Six

In a week she would have to tell Rory about her decision. But first she had to get Tom on her side.

In the month since the night she had first slept with Joel, she had spent every possible moment she could spare from Tom with him.

It wasn't a lot. Lunch, the odd dinner and miraculously two whole nights together just before Tom returned from New Year in Scotland with Rory, and while Ben and Lexie had stayed with Joel's parents in Wiltshire prior to returning to school.

Rory was preparing to leave for a winter holiday in Barbados with James and quite probably the dreadful Betsey and Syra, but Rosie was now beyond even the mildest interest.

Her concern was Tom. As she drove to collect him she battled with several arguments to persuade him that life in Drake Street would be wonderful, even if it wasn't completely renovated. What with Nancy's house and other work piling up, her own home had been relegated to last on the list. In a matter of a week or two it would at least be livable in. Rosie was anxious to restore the house to how it had been before, warm and welcoming, with the same colours and as far as possible the same fabrics. All to make it easier for Tom to feel the adjustment was not too strange. In her bag were the prospectuses of two schools that would mean he could live at home.

Rosie was now completely convinced that Tom's feelings about his school had not undergone, as Rory kept insisting, a dramatic change since they had moved back to live together, but that he was nursing some private anxiety.

Joel had mentioned it. He said it had occurred to him when they were in Menton. 'If he doesn't think the answers matter, he's a great kid. Ben said so. But sometimes he sounded as though he was giving the answer Rory wanted, rather than what he really wanted to say.'

The weekend before had been full of Rory's attempts to undermine her. Arriving back too late from staying with some of his cronies in the country to spare much time for Tom, he had infuriated her by insisting that they all went to Planet Hollywood for lunch.

Since Rory was back on a bender of indulging Tom beyond reason, she tried to dissuade him. But it failed when Tom ranged himself on his father's side. In the end, she suggested they go without her, pleading work. She didn't want Tom's return to school marred by witnessing the ill-disguised hostility that lay between his parents. Far better to let them go alone.

Joel, occupied with his own children, had managed to make a brief call to her and they made hurried plans to see each other the following week.

Whether it was because she was so crazy about Joel or because she had grown so used to Rory baiting her, this last month had taken on an air of comparative peace.

Rosie saw it as a new beginning. A chance to work on a future with Joel, one where they might even decide it was strong enough to start incorporating each other's children into their lives. It gave her the energy to approach the intervening weeks with an optimism she had only recently thought impossible.

That morning, Nick Newall had been informed that she would be leaving Rory's but she had yet to give him a firm date. As she drove towards Tom's school, Rosie knew that all that was left between honourably keeping her side of the bargain with Rory – one year, that was all – was Tom.

What in the end was a month or two short of the deadline when they could all be spared?

The drive at Old Farrells was already filling up with cars as parents arrived to take their sons home for the weekend. She pulled in behind a Volvo and made her way towards the wide reception hall where the assembled boys were waiting.

She saw Tom standing on his own and waved with both arms in the air to attract his attention. Her subconscious told her something was wrong. He didn't race to meet her. Just got slowly to his feet. He looked pale, as though he had been crying. Out of the corner of her eye she saw Sylvia Duxborough who was hustling Felix towards her car.

Rosie ignored her, intent on pushing her way through the throng of little boys to reach Tom.

'Darling, what is it?' she asked in alarm. 'You've been crying.' She tried to pull him into her arms, but he pushed her away backing against the nearest wall, and fresh tears began to roll down his face.

'Mrs Monteith Gore,' a voice said at her elbow. It was the school matron. 'Perhaps you'd like to come into my room?'

Rosie looked blankly at her. 'Tom?' This time she caught hold of him, refusing to let him out of her grasp. 'Tom,' she said, trying to soothe him. 'What is it? What's happened?'

'Mrs Monteith Gore. It would be much better . . .' Matron's voice butted in again. Several pairs of eyes were on them as she clasped Tom's thin little shoulders.

'Go away,' he sobbed. 'I want Daddy.'

It was like being slapped hard across the face. 'Tom,' she said desperately and, oblivious to the stares, pulled him into the side room where Matron was waiting but not before Tom had sobbed loudly enough and clearly enough for several bystanders to be a witness to his next words:

'I hate you. Why didn't you tell me?' He scrubbed tears

away from his face that was now streaked with dirt.

'Tell you what?' she cried, frantically trying to hold onto him.

'Tell me that you're going to leave me and Daddy.'

The shock of what he had said made her blink. It didn't make sense.

'Tom, that's nonsense. Where did you hear that? Who told you such a thing? It's not true. I'll never leave you.'

'It's true, though, isn't it? Don't lie. You're leaving me so that you can marry Joel and I *hate* him.'

Treading carefully was no longer an option. On the drive back, Tom had eventually fallen into an exhausted heap, refusing to be comforted. Felix Duxborough. That was his informant.

Rosie's first instinct in her blind rage was to drive straight to Sylvia's house and damage her in a way that Tom had been damaged. How in God's name did she know about her and Joel? And if she knew, then Rory must.

The viciousness of the story, the dreadful lie to pour into the ears of a child, left her breathless.

So too had Matron who, having watched silently while Rosie reduced and soothed Tom's tears to a manageable level, had asked to speak to Rosie on her own with the headmaster.

'Mrs Duxborough will certainly be distressed to hear Felix passed on such information, but it would have been much kinder to Tom to have heard from you that your relationship with his father had broken down and you were contemplating marriage with someone he barely knows and clearly dislikes.'

Rosie allowed her to finish, glancing every now and then to Mr Farrell whose place on the moral high ground was as usual firmly established. At least until Rosie was allowed to speak.

'And if this school,' she said in a voice that miraculously

retained its control, 'had one ounce of consideration for the boys' welfare instead of seeing them merely as the fuel to stoke its bank account, then a child like Felix and his mother would be standing here now and not me, the innocent victim of a particularly nasty slur.

'And the reason for that, as you well know, is that until recently I have had to be very frugal in my own lifestyle to be able to afford your outrageous fees, whereas the Duxboroughs have enough spare cash to line the walls of the gym.

'No, I can quite see that the choice between an inconvenient investigation into the facts might have stemmed the unceasing flood of Duxborough money into the coffers. I can only say – and please don't interrupt, Matron, your face is so red I strongly suspect you have been drinking – and for your sake I hope you have, because it can be the only possible explanation for your outrageous handling of this affair.

'Mr Farrell, you had better get your calculator out because by the time I have finished suing Matron personally for slander and you for causing mental distress to one of the pupils, you will need all the money you can get to bail you out. And indeed to live on until you can both get new jobs.

'I can only suggest that you keep grovelling at the altar of Oscar Duxborough and remember to call the new swimming pool they have donated, the Dux Pond. I'm amazed you haven't thought of it yourselves.

'Meanwhile I await your written apology. Tom will not be returning here after the summer term.'

Sylvia Duxborough refused to take her call. So too did Oscar. His office claimed he was out of the country.

There was no sign of Rory that day or the next. When Joel rang from Frankfurt, Tom was in the room, so she kept the conversation brief and rather than blurt out the

354

truth, told him she was frantic with work and would call later. Joel would have to wait. Tom came first. Always. Always.

Rosie realised the moment she saw Rory that Sylvia Duxborough must have alerted him to the scene at the school. It was almost as though he was expecting it. The swagger in his walk, the smirk, showed a man who cared nothing for the distress it had caused his son, only satisfaction that his son's mother was angry beyond belief.

'But it's true, sweetheart, isn't it?' he sneered, slumping down into an armchair, swinging one leg casually over the side and surveying her over the rim of the tumbler of whisky he was clutching.

'Which bit?' she sighed, trying to let Rory make the running.

'You and Harley. I'm sorry Sylvia told that stupid child of hers. Quite spoilt my fun, my dear.'

Rosie gazed at him in disbelief. '*Your fun?*' She could hardly breathe. 'Fun about what? Tormenting Tom. You're crazy.'

'Not mad,' he yawned, glancing at his watch. 'Just keeping an eye on my investments. We had an agreement, Rosie, you've broken it. We said no relationships in this house . . .'

'Joel has never been in this house,' she pointed out, still refusing to acknowledge that she was involved with him, wanting to protect such a decent part of her life.

'No? That's not my information. Now run along, there's a good girl. Lover boy will be back in a day or two and you can tell him all about it then. Meanwhile do try and remember our agreement. You seem to break it at every turn.'

She knew he was mad, or drunk, or both. 'You told Sylvia all this, didn't you? With no proof, in a vicious attempt to get your revenge because I wouldn't sleep with you, because you felt rejected. God, you are unpleasant.'

They stared at each other with such a dreadful loathing that Rosie felt physically sick. This had to stop. For Tom's sake.

'Rory,' she appealed to him. 'Tom is too distressed to put up with this any more and so am I. It hasn't worked. You know it hasn't. We said we would review it all in a year and that's nearly up. We're leaving. Now. Me and Tom. I can have my house back . . .'

'I know you can. Your builder has finished.'

'How do you know that?'

He gave a snigger. 'I make a note of these things. You're not the only one anxious to end all this.'

'Then, let's try and part on some kind of reasonable and amicable terms for Tom's sake,' she suggested eagerly. 'Visit him all you want. I'm going to enrol him at a new school so we can both see much more of him. So much better for Tom. For all of us. Take him to see your father in Scotland all you want. But we can't stay here any longer.'

She was surprised he hadn't interrupted. Just let her finish.

'Whatever you want, sweetheart. Go now if you like. There's the door.'

'Don't be silly, Rory,' she said wearily. 'It will take a few days . . .'

'Not for you, sweetheart,' he told her without altering his bored tone. 'I said, *you* can go. Tom stays.'

'*Tom stays?*' Her voice cracked. 'Stays where?'

'God, you can be thick,' he sighed. 'Let me see if I can explain it any more clearly to you. You go. Because you want to and I agree, you are a mess and I'd rather you went. But my son, Tom, my heir, my father's grandson, stays in the school he's at, until he is ready to go to my old school in Scotland. Meanwhile he remains in his family home. Which is here. Got that?'

He was bluffing. She laughed. 'You're mad. What old school? You were thrown out and there is no way Tom is

356

going to be so far away from me and he won't stay here without me. You know that. No court would allow it. I've done nothing that could make them decide anything else.'

'No?'

'No. Now stop this. In a week, Tom and I . . .'

'What a bore you are,' he said mildly. 'Here.' He strolled across to his briefcase and took out a slim envelope. 'Like me to read it to you?'

Rosie snatched it from him. It was marked from the Family Divorce Division of the High Court. A letter from a firm of solicitors in Scotland accompanied it. In a blur Rosie scanned the contents.

They had noted his instructions. His wife's solicitors would be informed and steps were being taken to revert residency for Tom Monteith Gore to his father with reasonable access granted to his mother, Mrs Rosie Monteith Gore, née Colville, on the grounds of her inability to conduct herself in a manner conducive to their son's wellbeing and welfare.

She read it twice and then folded the letter and let it drop to the floor. 'You know what you are, Rory,' she said, hating every inch of his body. Loathing the very thought she could ever have touched him. Shared a child with him.

'Go on,' he jeered. 'A shit?'

'God, no, nothing so interesting. "Twisted" is the word I was looking for.'

357

# Chapter Forty-Seven

'For a start he can't have a hearing in Edinburgh, he's just trying that on. Psychological advantage, trying to rattle you, distracting from the real issue. Take no notice, I'll have that slung out in seconds.'

'Sure?' Rosie asked, turning away from the window. Nick Newall briefly nodded, already into the second page of the letter. He looked up, scanning her anxious face.

'Don't worry. Any variation on the order about Tom has to be heard in the court where you were granted a divorce and that was the High Court here in London. Unless there are exceptional reasons for not doing so.'

'Like what?'

'Like you were both now living in Scotland or abroad. Not that it matters. The outcome is likely to be the same whether it's heard here in London or in the Court of Sessions in Edinburgh. It's the welfare of Tom they are both concerned about.'

'No difference at all?' she asked anxiously.

He shook his head. 'Scotland's a bit more formal, that's all. Wigs and gowns and it's held in an open court, but even then Tom's identity would be protected by reporting restrictions. In England it's heard in chambers. Still formal, but less intimidating.

'I suspect what Rory wants is to get as many of his cronies as he can to listen to the lot and let Callum know what a saint he is. He'll be denied that if it's heard down here.'

'Rory's insane,' she said flatly. 'Anyone can see that.'

'You didn't,' Nick pointed out. 'Not until he said he was going to challenge you for Tom.'

'But he can't take him away, I've done nothing wrong,' she protested, the sickening shakes that had engulfed her since she heard of Rory's plans taking over. She lapsed into silence, halted by Nick's raised eyebrow.

'Listen to me. Rory will have to prove you've done something pretty dire for any court to alter the order they've made. Sometimes it can be renegotiated because circumstances change.

'A boy like Tom, for instance, as he gets older might benefit more from being with his father, in which case the behaviour of either parent unless it was outrageous isn't an issue. But that isn't the case here, is it? Has Tom said he wants to stay with Rory? If he has, he'll be listened to. He was twelve last week.'

Rosie looked silently back at him and then returned her gaze to the square outside his window.

Nick Newall shuffled the papers in front of him, peering at them over the top of his glasses. The silence in his room was broken only by a ticking clock and not, as she thought, by her jangling nerves, as he went through the pile of witness statements in front of him.

'Vindictive little sod,' Nick ventured at last, removing his glasses and rubbing his eyes. 'And you had no idea?'

'None. And none of it is true . . .'

Nick motioned her to stop. 'I know that, you know that. We have to make sure the judge knows that. All these people,' he tapped the sheaf of papers in front of him, 'are prepared to say you neglected Tom by putting your work first, that you're emotionally unstable, and that you falsely accused them of everything from theft to adultery. It also says that you are possibly dabbling in drugs. All are reasons that would give the courts pause for thought if they can be made to stand up.'

Rosie looked down the list of statements Rory's solicitors

359

had compiled. James, Syra, Betsey, Sylvia Duxborough . . . *Sylvia*? Abbie, Mr Farrell, Matron. The list was unending of those Rory had rallied to support his vicious claim on Tom.

Rosie briefly closed her eyes. 'When did he start gathering all this shit about me? What evidence have they got? None. Just ghastly little minds that have been poisoned by Rory.'

All reciting the incidents they had witnessed of Rosie making Rory's life a hell, her erratic behaviour, her hysteria. James said she had lost him a half-million-pound deal because she was so rude to his American clients and that he had personally heard her tell Rory she had no time for Tom. Sylvia recited the number of times she was asked to care for him, adding a strenuous denial that she had slept with Rory. Matron and Mr Farrell stated that she had been both abusive and threatening.

The list was horrifyingly long. Even the manager of the hotel in Menton had been prevailed upon to say that Mrs Monteith Gore was overwrought when she arrived on holiday and Bob, the former tenant of the Mews House, no doubt under orders from the Girlfriend from Hell, claimed she had insisted that Rory evict him.

The most damning statement came from Abbie, reciting a catalogue of incidents that painted a picture of a selfish, ambitious hysterical woman who leeched off her ex-husband and who accused her of collaborating with the press.

'She's not a defenceless sixteen-year-old. She's got to be thirty-five if she's a day. Why didn't she just leave?'

Even that reaction had been catered for. Such apparently was Abbie's fear and distrust of Mrs Monteith Gore that she stayed only because she felt so sorry for Tom and indeed Rory, who was trying his best to deal with his neurotic wife. She was now, she added, living quietly in London with a very nice family.

Rosie's eyes rounded. 'Here? The police said she wasn't in the country when they were looking for her when I was mugged.'

Nick sighed; 'She probably wasn't then. Must have come back. Want to read Rory's?' he asked, indicating the fattest report on his desk. Rosie hesitated, nodded and held out her hand.

It was still a shock. Ten minutes later she replaced the document on Nick's desk and dusted her fingers.

'What do I do?' she asked quietly. 'Apart from justifying everything he says by feeding him rat poison?'

Nick cleared his throat and beckoned her to come and sit in one of the armchairs either side of the fire which was licking comfortably into the chimney.

'At the moment you are doing fine. There's no evidence at all that you take drugs, for which you were tested at the police station. No previous convictions, of course. No syringes falling out of your bag. It would be hard for him to make that one stand up. But the police will say quite truthfully they found cocaine in your belongings and they know you accused James of the theft.'

Rosie dropped her head into her hands.

'And you must be honest with me, Rosie. He mentions you resumed an intimate relationship with him . . .'

'It's a lie,' she flashed back. 'Once. That's all. And I never wanted that . . .'

'You mean he raped you?'

Rosie gazed back at him. 'I don't know. I just thought it was easier to get it over with.'

'That is still rape. You didn't consent but you didn't resist either for . . . what? Your own protection? Your safety?'

'Nick, I was once married to him. It didn't seem like rape. I'd been with him all evening. I just don't know . . .'

'Did you ask him to stop?'

'Yes.'

'And he refused?'

'Yes.'

'Why did he?'

Rosie bit her lip. Her knuckles were white. What do you say about something that was so brief, urgent, nothing. A familiar routine. When did rape stop, curiosity take over and consent begin? She still hadn't found the answer.

'I didn't say anything. It happened. I let it happen.'

Nick looked sharply at her. 'Did you want it to happen?'

'Nick, it's no good asking me. It's over. I'm just angry with myself for letting it happen. But I made it perfectly plain that it was never to happen again. It never did. To say we had a relationship is madness. And neither do I want Tom to hear me accuse his father of rape. I just want the subject dropped.'

Nick wrote something on the file. 'Give it some thought, my dear. Rory was very specific. And I doubt he will be so sensitive.'

Rosie shook her head. She could see Rory's face. The frightened flicker in his eyes. Bluffing it out, not wanting to face up to knowing that physically she found him distasteful.

'I'm not so sure.'

Nick glanced at her in surprise. Rosie looked thoughtfully down at the statement. Bitterness, revenge might be written all over it, but pride was too. 'I know him better than anyone,' she went on. 'He wouldn't risk anyone knowing he'd been rejected. It's the only power he has. And I'll fight him all the way. Watch me.'

'Hmm,' Nick grunted doubtfully. 'Our best course of action is simply to rebut everything he says and present a stronger case.'

'The truth, you mean?'

He hesitated. 'Yes, that too. Meanwhile, try and keep Tom from being too stressed. Allow Rory to see him whenever he wants within reason. I do not want anything to jeopardise your position.

'Now here's some advice you won't need. But I'll tell you anyway. Until this case is over, do not start to over-react. No making sure everyone sees you at the school, no courting good opinions. Never works. And it's too late for all that. Lastly, perhaps more difficult, Joel Harley. Are you going to marry him?'

Rosie shook her head. 'I don't know. He hasn't asked me. We're only just getting to know each other.'

Nick gave her a long look. 'Okay. If Tom knew him, liked him, it wouldn't matter. But I must be blunt. Until then this relationship is not significant in the eyes of the court. Not . . . stable. You understand. don't you?'

Rosie looked steadily back at him. 'I know. I won't lose sight of that. Tom,' she finished bleakly, 'must come first. I'll tell Joel.'

She got up and walked back to the window. After watching her for a few minutes, Nick sighed and resumed his reading. She had yet to see the statement from Callum Monteith Gore.

Meanwhile Rosie stared down into the square outside Nick's office, resting her head against the pane. How could she have been so blind? What she had assumed was an attempt to make her life difficult because she had rejected him had been a carefully orchestrated campaign to have her declared unfit to be in charge of Tom.

Time after time she had fallen unwittingly into the trap. Railed at her ex-husband, stood her ground, goaded into retaliating in public.

Now she looked back on it, all Rory's accusations had been in front of witnesses, delivering the final coup at the moment when someone was conveniently around to remember it all, to use it.

And Joel. Rory's most malevolent barbs were plunged in where he knew he could do the most damage. Rosie's public pursuit of the man, flaunting her relationship with him, and finally in devastating detail a log of the time she had spent with Joel, including the nights she had stayed with him.

He must have had someone watching her. She shivered. To know she had been so closely observed by such a desperate man.

Buffeted between the flawed arguments of shared parenting, her mother's insistence that she must make it work for Tom's sake, resisting when her friends advised caution, she had been forced to dance to the tune of a weak and feckless man. What was worse, she beat her fist tightly but gently against the pane, was that she had been the one leading the way.

# Chapter Forty-Eight

He was waiting for her as she let herself into his penthouse. He didn't move, but watched her carefully as she came over to where he was lounging against the windows, a mug of coffee in his hand.

His hair as usual looked as though he had just scraped it back from his face. Brown cord trousers, a serviceable denim shirt and boots. No fuss, just, Rosie thought, a great smile.

'I can't stay long,' she told him, as he reached out to hold her. Surprise flickered in his eyes.

'Let me say hello, first,' he said but she moved away. 'What's the matter?' he asked frowning as he scanned her face. She knew she was looking pale, blusher only made it worse.

'I've just come from Nick's,' she began, not daring to touch him, withdrawing her hand as Joel leaned his back against the window.

Thus far she had resisted telling Joel the whole truth about that night with Rory. There was not a shred of doubt in her mind that she loved this man, wanted to share everything with him, but a stray remark had made her hesitate.

*I don't know how he could keep his hands off you,' he murmured as they lay in his bed, watching the dawn come up over the river, a white blanket of frost gripping the roofs, the water still grey and silent, protected from the world wrapped in each other's arms.*

*Rosie stayed silent. 'Did you ever feel you wanted to*

sleep with Marianne again?' she finally asked, keeping her voice drowsy, allaying suspicion.

'Sure. There was nothing wrong with the sex. Just something wrong with us. But I never did anything about it. If you have sex with your ex, it's unfinished business, isn't it? It would have meant there was still something there. And we both knew there wasn't.'

He said simply: 'Five days without you. I was beginning to think we were destined to be those ships you mentioned once before.'

'Ships?' she repeated blankly.

'Yes, when we were in Prague. You said . . .'

She nodded. 'I remember. Joel . . .' She took a deep breath. She couldn't look at him. 'Joel, I think we might be.'

When he didn't reply she gave him a quick nervous glance. He was watching her steadily. 'Go on. Tell me why.'

It came out in a bitter, angry rush: 'Because life is unfair, and nowhere is it written that we are entitled to be happy and because Rory is a shit and I have fucked everything up and I don't want to screw it up any further and I have to think of Tom . . . and you.'

There was a brief silence. 'You want to be on your own, is that it?' His voice was calm but his eyes were those of a man who has been hit by a tank he hasn't seen coming.

She turned, impulsively reaching out with her hand. 'No. Never that. But until I've got this case over and done with, Nick says . . . Nick says the court would view a relationship with you as casual and that won't look good.'

'Is that how you see it?' he asked, replacing his mug on a table beside him, folding his arms and looking back at her.

'Of course not. But we don't know where it's going, do we? You know as well as I do . . . Oh God, Joel, we're not

366

teenagers, we've both got children, responsibilities . . .'

'Which we take seriously. For Christ's sake, Rosie, just because that fucking little creep starts to throw all this shit around, doesn't mean anyone will believe him. What can he say that any judge would listen to for a half a minute?'

'He's got a twelve-year-old boy who may well say he prefers his father because he doesn't trust his mother any more. Who has a lover he dislikes. And because . . .' She stopped.

'Go on . . .'

'Because he's also going to say that our relationship was a sexual one and that I was a willing partner to a reconciliation and that my behaviour deteriorated when he realised it wasn't going to work and he stopped it.'

Joel laughed, disbelief written on his face. 'Is that it? That's his evidence? Oh my darling girl, you just tell the truth . . . you wouldn't have let him touch you with . . .' He hesitated. 'I mean, that *is* the truth. Isn't it?'

Rosie got up and pressed her face against the window. She knew he was watching her profile. The river was choppy, a black swell thrusting it angrily against the sides of the embankment. It was growing late, lights were already on. In a minute dusk would plunge the skyline into night, obliterating it all. A beautiful view. A beautiful life.

She turned her face and looked at him. Saw the uncertainty lurking there. Get it over with. There didn't seem to be any other way.

'Not quite,' she said. 'Not quite.'

Moving back into Drake Street was so unlike the dream she had kept in her head all those months with Rory that she got drunk. She also got drunk for another reason, but she didn't want to think about that.

Her suitcases were piled in the hallway, the house was cold, the walls bare and the fridge empty. It wasn't how she'd planned it, but she was grateful to be there and so relieved she cried and slept and woke and cried some more until finally she succumbed to exhaustion and slept in her clothes, waking in bright sunlight since the windows had no curtains, with a head that felt like it was being squeezed through a steel door and a raging thirst.

But she was home. It might not yet have the decor she wanted, but in a way that was strangely comforting. She was back where she started. A chance to begin again more wisely, as her accountant had said. She just hoped her wisdom hadn't come too late. Only the knowledge that Tom would be joining her at the weekend moved her to organise his room to make it as near as possible how he remembered it.

Tom was a different matter. By the end of the first evening he spent there, Rosie, who had prayed he wouldn't make a fuss, was praying he would. Anything would be better than the polite agreement with everything she suggested. 'I don't mind,' or 'If you want,' were offered with monotonous regularity to everything she said.

'Give him time,' she told herself. 'Time. That's what we all need.'


Nick decided that of all the names Rosie could give him to counteract Rory's claims, Carey and Kit were important. As Tom's godfather, Carey would testify to Rosie's concern for his welfare, and Kit as a neighbour and friend who had closely observed them both while they lived next door would verify that she entered into all Tom's interests and was both mother and father to him for long periods at a time. And Jaye would verify that Rosie had twice turned down a job at the *Clarion* because it came between her and Tom.

Roland Whittington, her former editor, wrote a letter saying Rosie had resigned as Style Editor of *Focus* magazine because the demands it made on her time were not conducive to Tom's wellbeing.

Livvie and Jordan wrote to Nick Newall saying rather recklessly that they were willing to sign anything to help Rosie, thereby promptly wiping out their use as credible witnesses.

Judith phoned from New York with an offer to get the first plane back when they gave her the word. A joint letter from Jed Bayley – carefully describing himself as a respected social observer rather than gossip columnist – and Ellie, offering whatever character references she needed, followed hard on its heels.

All good stuff, said Nick, but all these people loathed Rory and loved Rosie. Not as credible as, say, a client.

Rosie shook her head. 'It's out of the question. They don't want to be dragged into all this.'

Nick thought Nancy would be a good name. Rosie said she would rather die. Nancy. Territorial, snobbish, ruthless. And meddlesome. It was as kind a description as Rosie could allot her. She knew who was behind the letter which had arrived that morning from Marianne. Rory had not wasted a moment. Marianne could only have known the details of the case from one source, and that was Nancy. And Nancy was in Rory's pocket.

Jane Grantham, however, was a breakthrough. Summoned – which she afterwards insisted was the only way to describe it – by Jordan to check some colour charts which she could have sworn she had already done, she eventually was forced to ask him if he was all right when he had sighed heavily for the fifth time.

'So awful,' he said mournfully, having pressed her into staying for a coffee. 'That dreadful Sylvia Duxborough – oh dear,' he clapped his hand across his mouth in a show of dismay which did not fool Jane.

'Forget I said that. I'm sure Rosie will get used to not having Tom around – although it will probably kill her.'

Jane's cup clattered into the saucer. 'What will kill her?' she asked sharply. 'Jordan, where *is* Rosie?'

Jordan crossed his legs, clutching his arms around his body, dropping his voice to a whisper. 'No-one will speak up for her and that *dre-a-dful* ex of hers is going to cart Tom off to Scotland. But please, Jane, not a word. She'd murder me. Livvie and I have offered to speak up for her, but it's no use. We're not grand enough.'

Jane eyed him thoughtfully. 'I see,' is all she said. 'Now, I think the darker blue would work best. Very sensible of you, Jordan, to ask me in. No need to tell Rosie I dropped by, is there?'

Jordan saw her out and then whisked himself upstairs, colliding with Livvie, who'd been straining to hear what was going on.

'Well?' she demanded.

'Easy peasy. Probably ringing Nick from her car right now,' he grinned smugly. 'Shsh. Rosie's coming.'

Nick was delighted with Jane's call, which resulted in a letter paying tribute to Rosie as a devoted mother and competent businesswoman. Jane's impeccable credentials would go down well with the judge.

Surprising support came from Conrad de Lisle who quietly and privately wrote to Nick Newall, saying he had always regarded Rosie as one of his wife's saner contacts and had always thought Tom a grand little fellow when he used to come round to play with Garth. That had been long before Rory came back into his life.

The rage Miriam flew into when she heard this was cosmic. But torn between lending her support to Sylvia Duxborough, who looked the likely winner of this domestic fracas and therefore not worth alienating since they moved in the same circles, and Conrad's refusal to withdraw the letter, she went on holiday until the fuss died down.

From Caroline there had at first been a silence. This did not surprise Rosie in any way. Her mother could write a government white paper on why women should disregard infidelity, but Valerie Cottisham had chosen that moment to recall that Rory had once made a pass at her daughter while married to Rosie and Caroline's allegiance to Rosie was assured. For Rory to seduce women who were strangers was one thing, but to prefer Valerie Cottisham's ghastly daughter to her own was indefensible. A week after Rosie had parted from Joel and moved back to her old home, Caroline boarded a train for Paddington.

Shortly after six o'clock Rosie opened the door to find Caroline plus a suitcase standing on the doorstep, a taxi with meter ticking over outside.

'Pay that man,' Caroline commanded, breezing past her surprised daughter. 'Oh my God,' she wailed, staring at the drying plaster. 'Is this what you're reduced to?'

Rosie passed a hand wearily across her eyes. On a list of ten things she needed most at the end of another anxious day, her mother didn't even figure.

'Actually, Mother dear, you're looking at evidence that I'm doing rather well,' Rosie pointed out. 'I couldn't have Tom living in a hotel and, anyway, he knows this place better than anywhere else. But I can now afford to have the whole place redone. My team have promised to work overtime and get it all finished in under a month.'

'I see,' Caroline said doubtfully, flicking a chair with her handkerchief before she sat down, her face registering quite clearly her regret that she hadn't waited the extra month to make this generous gesture.

It could not be said that Caroline's visit was a success, eventually it subsided into a long harangue about the ills she suffered at the hands of an unthinking Bridge committee not to mention the various tradesmen with whom she was forced to deal.

But Rosie was touched by her show of solidarity and when she waved her off at Paddington at lunchtime a few days later, she promised to come and stay for a weekend, just to get away from it all.

'And as for Callum,' Caroline snorted, her head poking through the small window of the carriage, 'saying you think only of your career and accusing Rory of trying to cheat him, that's fine talk from a man who openly supports devolution.'

'And slanders his former daughter-in-law?' Rosie asked, straight-faced.

'Yes, of course, that too. Bye, darling,' she called as the train began to move. 'And do something about your hair,' she shrieked above the noise of the train. 'Appearances really do count. Take it from me.'

Rosie groaned and walked back up the platform and out to where she'd parked her car.

In her bag were two letters. The first was from Nick, saying the court hearing was a month away and to let her know that Rory's team had subpoenaed Dr Collins to give evidence about her emotional stability. Rosie gritted her teeth. No comfort there.

The second was from Marianne Klonack. She understood that Joel was involved with Rosie and wanted her assurance that on no account would his name be dragged into the proceedings.

I have two children to think of [she warned]. I will not tolerate anything or anyone who disturbs their lives. They have been through a traumatic time with the breakup of my marriage to their father and we all deserve a little less attention from the media, particularly when the trouble is not of our making.

Joel is a private man. I am certain he wants none of this either. Please don't make it difficult for him. You can only end up hurting him and his children. I do not expect you to concern yourself with my feelings. But I urge you to think of my children.

Rosie couldn't hate her for the letter, or blame her. Wasn't it exactly what she was doing with Tom? Protecting him, preventing any public fight with his father over custody?

It wasn't difficult to trace how Marianne had been made aware of the state of things. Rory had recognised in Nancy a natural ally and fuelled her resentment about Rosie by casting her in the light of an opportunist out to further her ambitions on the coattail of a titled or rich man.

Failing to prise Joel away from Rosie, Nancy's final weapon was to alert Marianne Klonack to do the work for her.

In response to a worried phone call from Ginny, Daniel had come over and using his emergency key let himself into Joel's apartment. He found him unshaven, sprawled in a chair and still sober after consuming a bottle of Scotch unaided.

'Hey, man,' Daniel said. 'Don't frighten me. What happened here?'

'Happened?' Joel rose unsteadily to his feet, his voice little more than a croak. 'The bag is shut, that's what's the matter. Sorry, Dan. Give me five. I'll be with you.'

'The bag's shut? What's that supposed to mean? Are you ill? What *is* it? Hang on, you've dropped something,' Daniel called after him, picking up a crumpled photograph. He smoothed it out.

For a minute he couldn't see who it was, the creases were so ingrained, and then he recognised it was Rosie Colville and Joel and they were laughing and it was summertime in Menton.

He raised his eyes to Joel. Comprehension dawned. 'What . . . ? I mean. For fuck's sake, Jo. Does Stevie know? Why didn't you say?'

Joel shrugged. 'Nothing to say. I got caught, that's all. I didn't understand what it all meant. I'll live.'

\* \* \*

Rosie paused at the top of the ramp leading from the train platform. In her pocket, rather worn around the edges, was the card with the quote from Jean Genet in Joel's handwriting. Rosie halted and pulled it out and reread it, as she did every day and every time she wanted some proof that it had happened.

'*And my heart is caught,*' she recited softly to herself, oblivious to the masses of people surging past her, the sharp burst of wind that pushed her hair back from her face and tugged at her coat.

Folding the sheet she thrust it back into her pocket. 'And I threw it away,' she said it softly, to no-one in particular. A couple of young girls looked at her curiously. Several commuters skirted around her as she looked unseeingly into the sky.

Then she took a deep breath, lifted her chin and walked briskly in the direction of her parked car, and was swallowed up in the crowd.

# Chapter Forty-Nine

Across the courtroom Rory was sitting staring straight ahead. His suit was expensive, his hair cut shorter. He carried a black briefcase and when spoken to listened carefully, nodding agreement, looking thoughtful.

Occasionally he allowed a small, fleeting smile in response to a friendly hand clapped on his shoulder by his legal team. Rosie knew that smile. So practised. So effective. Behind him talking in a low voice to Basil Claythorne, Rory's expensive solicitor, was the even more expensive barrister he had retained to fight his case, Donald Crowe.

None of it came as a surprise to Rosie as she took her place next to Nick, since she had been well warned what tactics Rory was employing to get control of Tom.

On Nick's advice she had opted for him handling the case, ably assisted by two members of his staff, since the expense of a QC would make savage inroads into her resources. She did not qualify for legal aid, her earning capacity having exceeded such a consideration, but equally she knew she would be ruined if she lost.

'But if . . . I mean, *when* I win, I won't have to pay any costs, Rory will. So why shouldn't I have a QC too? Nick? Nick, I *am* going to win, aren't I?'

'Of course you are,' he assured her. 'Provided everything you've told me is the truth.'

Nick, on the other hand, was nevertheless uneasy and at a loss to know why Rory's legal team were permitting him to pursue the case.

'I know why,' Rosie told him bitterly. 'Rory has insisted. He isn't listening to anyone. He never has. And you have to remember this is the end result of a strategy he's been weaving for months.'

The warring couple had entered the side courtroom of the High Court within minutes of each other but steadily ignored the other's presence, partly on counsel's advice and mostly because the idea of speaking was anathema to them both.

Tom had spent the previous day with Rory, who had insisted on sticking rigidly to his access rights. Such was his confidence that he would win this case, he had made no attempt to stop Rosie removing Tom from the house and installing him back in Drake Street.

'Make the most of it,' he had sneered softly from the doorway, as she packed. 'In a few weeks, Tom will be living in Scotland. From now on, you'll dance to my tune. You all will.' That day all the locks were changed. Notice to quit the Mews House served on her.

It was clear from Tom's mood when she spoke to him on the phone the previous night once Rory had delivered him back to school, that Rory had not wasted the day.

Every last detail of the case had been fed to the boy. Rosie told him Daddy had exaggerated, that he wouldn't listen to the truth. But Tom wasn't listening either.

Not once did he mention Joel, and nor did she. She had given him her word, she was not going to go back on it. And besides, she no longer had that option. It wasn't hard to fulfil her promise. Just hard to live with it. So very, very hard.

She glanced up as Nick spoke to her in a low voice: 'Most of the statements will be read out, except for that of the doctor, who will be cross-examined. Try not to look too anxious. All right? Stand up. Here we go.'

Rosie thought Donald Crowe was preposterous. The hearing, as in all child custody cases, was a private one, but he could not resist playing to the gallery even though apart from court officials it was empty.

At least Rory looked impressed, satisfied his money was being well spent. The statements that were read out on Rory's behalf were a description of someone she didn't recognise. Baleful, manipulative and uncaring. She was relieved that the shock of what they contained had passed many weeks ago, but it still sounded unreal.

Rory's expression was schooled into one of pain and suffering. Occasionally he passed a hand wearily across his eyes. Rosie thought she would throw up.

Rory was concerned that his ex-wife was suffering some kind of breakdown, a result of a broken relationship which she had been confident would result in marriage. After that came a fire, some disastrous business decisions, all of which had led to the serious emotional neglect of their son.

Donald Crowe droned on. When Miss Colville had persisted in her desire for a reconciliation, having unrestricted access to his son at a significant point in the boy's development swayed his client. He was, however, stunned by having a legal agreement drawn up expressly to protect her interests and to promote her career. The document was before the court. Sexual relations were restored, instigated by Miss Colville.

Nick rose and began to argue the point as being inadmissible. Rory glanced at Rosie; a mocking smile hovered briefly on his lips. Their eyes locked. An imperceptible shake of her head warned him she was prepared to fight. He tried to brazen it out. Her gaze didn't falter.

She saw him tug at his solicitor's sleeve and whisper something. Donald Crowe asked for a short break. The three conferred.

'My Lord, at my client's request, that last statement will be withdrawn.'

A raised eyebrow from Nick, who glanced suspiciously at Rosie, now the picture of innocence, and the case proceeded.

The last straw was an affair with a man who Tom

disliked and the dreadful discovery from a schoolfriend that his mother was going to remarry without mentioning it to him.

Nick objected. 'There is no truth at all concerning my client's remarriage. She has no plans now or in the foreseeable future for such an event with the person mentioned.'

For the first time, surprise made Rory forget himself. He shot her a startled look.

James was harder to refute since on her own admission Rosie had implicated him in the theft from Marlborough Square and had told Rory she would never allow Tom to live under the same roof as him. Three months later she had.

Abbie was not required to appear, but Nick found it more difficult to demolish what she had to say since she was a daily witness to life in Marlborough Square.

Taken wildly out of context, as Nick had emphasised over and over it would be, it still sounded dreadful that so many people could have misinterpreted her behaviour. Rory in his evil genius had made certain they did.

Early the following morning, Dr Collins was called.

It was like listening to a rather bad movie plot. His notes reminded him that she had shown no emotion when she had arrived back very late from a night out, when he had been called by Mr Monteith Gore to attend their son.

He described Tom as anxious and, in his view, stressed. He was in tears and had expressed his anxiety about his mother's health. He said he feared his mother was having some kind of breakdown.

Donald Crowe looked grave. Rosie studied the ceiling. The judge was listening attentively. 'Was it your impression that Mrs Monteith Gore's behaviour was as the result of alcohol or other substance use?' asked Donald Crowe.

'I have no idea. There was no occasion to examine her. She merely appeared unmoved by what had taken place. I suggested to Mr Monteith Gore that if he and his son both believed Mrs Monteith Gore to be in emotional turmoil, that he should try to get his wife to see a counsellor. I was concerned only that an eleven-year-old boy should be suffering such anxiety.'

'What opinion did you form about Mr Monteith Gore at that time?'

'That he was naturally anxious and at rather a loss to know how to cope. My own experience of his wife showed that she had a forceful personality. Because of this he told me he was reluctant to insist, because Tom might be further damaged.'

'Did you in fact take any action?'

'Yes. I telephoned Mrs Monteith Gore the following day, but she refused to listen although I urged her to seek some kind of counselling.'

'You were then summoned to see her after a robbery at Mr Monteith Gore's house, is that correct?'

'Yes. Mrs Monteith Gore said she had disturbed a burglar and had received a blow to her neck. She was distraught and tearful. I gave her a shot of valium.'

Nick intervened. 'Police evidence shows she did disturb an intruder; that is not in question. It isn't an unsubstantiated claim.'

Donald Crowe smiled thinly and went on: 'You did not, I understand, think it prudent that she be left on her own as Mr Monteith Gore was in Scotland. What was the arrangement for her care?'

'She had a friend with her. A Mr Harley. He said he would stay.'

Rosie frantically tugged Nick's arm. He quietly removed her hand, giving it a squeeze as he did so.

'And did he?'

'When I left at around eleven in the evening, he certainly had that intention.'

'Who else was in the house?'

'As far as I know, no-one.'

'Did you see Mrs Monteith Gore again professionally?'

'Yes. Next day at the request of your client. She was hysterical and he called me.'

'What did you do?'

'There was nothing I could do. Mrs Monteith Gore had locked herself in her room and refused to come out.'

# Chapter Fifty

At the end of the day, she arrived home uncertain, afraid and not quite sure where all this was going. 'Into the lawyers' pockets,' Jaye said cheerfully, allowing Kit to refill her glass while she cooked lasagna in Rosie's kitchen.

'And I'm staying the night,' she added firmly.

Rosie looked at them both. Loyal, supportive and working overtime to keep her spirits up. Not a word of reproach. Not one 'I told you so'. She didn't deserve them.

Over supper Kit mentioned he had seen Piers. A few weeks ago Rosie would have shown more interest in her ex-lover, but now she simply nodded and gave a small smile, glad to know he was happy.

By the time the court broke for lunch the following day, Nick had done an excellent job, but Piers' letter was the unlooked-for bonus.

He wanted the court to know that far from being a careless or indifferent mother, Rosie Colville had on all occasions during their professional and, more importantly, personal, relationship put her son first, even losing commissions if he needed her. Their intended marriage had foundered for those reasons.

There was a personal note to Rosie, The first communication in nearly two years. *'Let's meet. I'm happy, but I'd be happier still if you were too. I've missed you.'*

They adjourned for lunch, Nick confident that Rory would now back down. But Rosie wasn't so sure. Not even a flicker of surprise had crossed his face as the letter was read out.

No wonder. After they reassembled, Donald Crowe rose to his feet and produced a letter from Tom.

Rosie gazed white-faced at Nick. Donald Crowe was droning on: 'This would demonstrate the bond of affection between father and son and the twelve-year-old boy's own desire to be with him.'

This court, he concluded, had the power to take into account the changing circumstances of a child's life and with or without the evidence before the court, the child himself was now at an age when residence with his father would be more beneficial and the court had not been presented with any evidence that should preclude that possibility.

Nick asked for and got an adjournment to study the letter alleged to have been written by Tom to Rory. It included:

I don't want you and Mum to be bad friends, but I don't want you to be together any more. I don't want to live with Mum and someone I don't like. If I live with you can we still go and see Grandpa? I like it at Glencairn.

Rosie refused to allow Tom to be questioned but Nick insisted. He was given time by the court in which to satisfy himself that Tom meant what he said. Rory was behaving with the supreme confidence that comes from a man who knows his name is already on the winning ticket.

A frustrating day trying to build a case followed but without Tom's input Nick had very little to help him.

The letter sounded to Rosie unreal. Carey thought the boy had been pressurised into it. Jaye agreed and Kit was all for having Rory decapitated. Rosie would not even phone Tom at school. She was adamant. He was not going to be forced into taking sides. She was determined that Rory's track record as a father should be the influencing factor. The only factor.

Livvie and Jordan had been keeping *Rosie Colville Interiors* ticking over as well as trying to find new premises, but the last few weeks without Rosie's constant presence and input had started to take their toll on the business and on them. A tentative phone call from Livvie asking if there was any chance of her dropping by gave Rosie something to hang onto while Nick was working on the letter from Tom.

There was nothing she could do but try to keep her mind off it. Within minutes her already overstretched nerves nearly snapped.

'So much for post-New Age interface with workers' equality,' Jordan shrilled, two bright spots of colour on his usually pale cheeks. Livvie was steaming, pointing to the faulty dye matching in the lengths of fabric she was clutching. 'And to think you almost ordered this ... we would have lost a client and ...'

'*We? We* would have lost?' Jordan gave a mock laugh. 'Who was it said it was time to break out, experiment?'

'Oh for God's sake put a sock in it,' Livvie retorted. 'And if we're talking about mistakes, what about that Soho loft you thought would be right for us ...'

'I did not,' he stormed back, his nose inches from hers. 'All I said was ...'

'All right, all right,' Rosie intervened, holding up her hands. 'That's enough. Livvie, get me the order book. Jordan? Where's the revised schemes for Pedro? Right, now let's move it. I have to be out of here in one hour.'

Throwing each other one last fulminating look, they got back to work. Rosie's head was pounding. Twenty minutes later, Jordan appeared with some strong black coffee while Livvie had gone downstairs to see a rep from a blinds company.

'Sorry,' he mumbled, putting a cup in front of her. 'You didn't need all that.'

She looked up and gave him a wan smile. 'No, but then

you and Liv don't need the weight of all this either. Hey, why don't you give Livvie a cup? It's not like you two to fight.'

'No,' he agreed with a sigh. 'Only sometimes, it's awfully difficult living up to Livvie's standards. She's terribly idealistic. She says Bunty and I are codependent, not compatible, and that I should assert my rights in this relationship, but you know it doesn't feel *comfortable*.

'The theory is fine, it's the reality of it all that gets me. I *love* Bunty. Liv's so disciplined.'

Rosie stared at him. She gave a hollow laugh. Jordan asked her what was wrong. 'Nothing,' she assured him, holding out her cup for more coffee. 'Just me living a theoretical life instead of a real one.'

At seven she went looking for a cab back to Drake Street, having organised life for the next couple of weeks so that the business could now continue relatively smoothly while they found somewhere else to operate from.

She had just emerged from the mews and crossed the street when a Jag with headlights full on swished around the corner and pulled up outside Rory's house. Instinctively, she shrank back behind one of the pillars at the entrance of the house opposite, fearful it might be Rory, that he would see her, suspect her of spying.

As she watched, out stepped the familiar figures of James and the ever-faithful Syra, followed by a woman whose back was to her as she climbed out of the rear seat.

Rosie stiffened. She knew that back. Knew it well. It was Abbie. Definitely Abbie. She pulled herself as far into the porch as she could, not wanting to be detected, just praying the owners would not choose that moment to leave or arrive home.

James' indifference to the two women was obvious as he quickly mounted the steps. Rory answered the door, leaving it ajar for Syra and Abbie to follow. Rosie shrank further back into the shadows, waiting until the two women disappeared into the house after him.

But they didn't. Syra in her trademark micro skirt, long legs and high heels, was immediately ahead of Abbie as they walked around to the pavement and started up the steps. Suddenly Abbie shot out an arm and pulled Syra backwards and behind her. Rosie was too far away to hear clearly what they were saying. Next second she jumped with fright as Syra screamed, stumbled and almost fell, flailing out at Abbie as she tried to steady herself.

Ignoring her, Abbie began to climb the steps but was stopped by Syra. A furious lunge brought Abbie spinning round. Across the street, Rosie gaped in amazement as Abbie's hand came up, followed by a stinging crack as she slapped Syra across the face.

'You fuckin' bitch,' screamed Syra, holding her face. 'I'll fuckin' sue you.'

Abbie glared back at her as the noise brought Rory and James back to the door. 'Sue me?' Abbie shrieked. 'For what? I'm not for rent . . .'

'*Rent?*' Syra gasped, ignoring James ordering them both inside as curtains in a neighbouring house flicked back. 'At least I've got a price,' she howled. 'I haven't got to give it away.'

It was too much for Abbie. Rosie watched in fascinated horror as Abbie grabbed Syra's slicked-back hair and shoved her hard against the railings. James leapt down the stone steps followed by Rory, who pulled the screaming women apart.

One arm around her middle, the other controlling her flailing fists, Rory bundled Abbie inside the house. Syra was prevented by James from following. There was a heated exchange, ending when Rory reappeared. James left him to deal with the sobbing girl.

Digging his hand in his pocket, he peeled off some notes from a roll of money and, thrusting it into the sobbing Syra's hand, he turned on his heel and tried to re-enter the house. She tugged at his arm, trying to hold onto him, the bundle of notes fluttering around her, but he pushed her away.

'What for?' Rosie could hear she was sobbing. 'Haven't I done enough for you? For fuck's sake, Rory . . . *Rory?*'

As she screamed at his back he turned, one foot on the bottom step, followed by a swift glance in each direction. Then he walked back to where she was standing. It was over in seconds. Rosie could hear the sickening crunch as he punched Syra in the stomach, the dull thump as she fell crumpled to the floor. Rosie's hand flew to her mouth.

The door closed, leaving Syra slumped against the railings. From her vantage point Rosie watched while the distraught girl rolled over, groaning, weakly and ineffectually clawing at the money that had fallen around her feet, wiping the back of her hand across her nose. With a hurried check either way, Rosie raced across the street.

'C'mon,' she whispered urgently to the dazed and bleeding girl. 'Hold onto me. I've got to get you away from here.'

She pulled Syra's arm around her neck, and hauled her to her feet. She was heavy and stunned. The workroom. Rosie needed to get her round the corner to the workroom. There she could sort this out.

Frantically she glanced back over her shoulder. She knew she should confront Rory. But she knew also that the scene she had just witnessed had frightened her. Not just for its violence but the fact that she had been very blind indeed.

'He didn't have to do it,' Syra whispered in a weary voice as Rosie wrung out a cloth and wiped the wretched girl's face and hands. 'He said he would get rid of Abbie, that he was just using her, and that we would be together. But he didn't mean it, did he?'

Rosie removed the glass of water from Syra's hand and pushed her back against the cushions, slowly shaking her head. 'No, Syra. And whatever he's promised Abbie, he doesn't mean that either. He only wants Tom. And that because it's the only way he can inherit all his father's money.'

Syra was rocking herself backwards and forwards. 'He shouldn't have done that to me,' she muttered. 'Not after all I've done. Not for that fucking bitch.'

Silent tears racked her thin shoulders. Rosie dropped to her knees beside her. Her voice was calm but urgent: 'No, Syra, he shouldn't. Listen to me. Please let me call a doctor . . .'

'No, please don't.' Syra tried to struggle up, sounding frantic. 'I've had worse, this will go in a minute. Please.'

Rosie grabbed a chair and pulled it up to where Syra was half lying, half sitting on the sofa in the reception of the workroom. The door was locked and the blinds pulled well down. Terrified Rory would come round, she left the lights off. The room was lit only by the light cast through the blinds from a lamp outside.

She spoke rapidly. 'Syra, Rory mustn't be allowed to get away with all this. He's crazy. Even before he hit you, I knew he was. I can't let my son live there, be taken away from me. But he's so plausible. He relies on all of us not wanting a fuss to get his own way.'

Syra shook her head, struggling to get up as Rosie leaned forward and pushed her back against the cushions once more. 'No police, no doctors,' she panted. 'Just give me a minute.'

Rosie waited. Syra was silently taking deep breaths. Rosie glanced at the clock; it was nearly eight. Tomorrow morning she had to go into court and hear the judge sign away her life. If they knew how brutally he had assaulted this girl, he wouldn't have a chance. No matter what Tom wanted. At the very least she could delay the court's decision.

All the time she listened for the sound of Rory's car which he parked outside. Syra couldn't stay here. Nor could she. She tried again, but Syra stopped her. 'Why do you need my help?' she whispered, her face beginning to recover some of its colour, curiosity replacing shock. 'He's scared shitless of you. Why are you looking at me like that? You must know that.'

'No I don't,' Rosie replied, knowing Syra had misunderstood. 'Rory is scared shitless only of what I might find out. You could tell me that, couldn't you, Syra? Either you help me or I go to the police. I have nothing to lose, except my son.'

She started to get up. 'You can stay here until you feel better . . .'

She didn't get any further. Syra could see she was serious. She held out a long bony hand, nails like talons, and gripped Rosie's wrist. Fear flickered in her eyes.

'No. You mustn't. I'll tell you. What do you need to know?'

# Chapter Fifty-One

'Call girls?' Rosie echoed. 'From his house? My God, and I didn't even suspect.'

'No, not from the house.' Syra shifted impatiently. 'Just his telephone. Rory's too smart to run a sweet-shop operation. I used to do tricks for James' clients. I was part of the package. Don't look like that. It's a great deal more honourable than poncing off a man you married and rationing him in return for the mortgage.

'Easy stuff, you know, commuters looking for a little relief before Haslemere or Sevenoaks. Clients if they were in town on their own. Then Rory came back from the States bringing Abbie with him, and it all changed.'

'*Abbie was in the States with him?* What changed?'

'We went international. Became more specific with requests . . .'

'Specific? You mean sexually specific . . .'

Syra nodded. 'Betsey was recruited. House parties arranged. Abbie was in charge of the girls. It was what she was doing in New York. Rory met her there. She recruited in clubs, always handpicked. Never from cards in telephone boxes or ads in papers.'

'How many girls on the books?' Rosie asked, not even surprised she felt no shock. It was after all what Rory was good at.

'About thirty. All professionals . . .'

'You mean actresses, models, that kind of stuff?'

'No.' Syra looked surprised. 'Maybe one or two models, but they need professionals. Lawyers, a couple of headhunters. There's a couple of medical students and a journalist.'

'Bella Leigh?'

Syra nodded as Rosie gave a rueful grimace.

'Oh c'mon. Anyone can pull a brain the size of a grape. Think about it. What's the big male fantasy?'

'Screwing a woman with a brain guaranteed not to tell him to fuck off?'

They both laughed.

'Abbie only takes the ones who speak another language or won't look out of place at a conference. Some are with other agencies, but Rory and James get location work. Abbie keeps everyone's diary full, but not mine. I decide. Not her.'

Rosie let Syra ramble, unloading her points scored, small battles won against the scheming housekeeper. But how could she have been so blind? Abbie who had rounded on Rory when she found Syra's knickers. Abbie who appeared on the stairs when a drunken Rory tried to seduce her. Abbie recruiting Bella Leigh in the club. Abbie wanting to get her off the scene. Jealous, vindictive Abbie.

The way she dressed. Her obsession with Rory's background. It all made sense. Rosie would have laughed if she hadn't felt so foolish.

'Sure. She's nuts about Rory. He's been stringing her along for a long time. She hated you, but she had to put up with it. Best time I ever had knowing she had to pretend to be the cleaner.'

Syra laughed for the first time. 'But she knew it was me he loved.' She glared defiantly at Rosie. 'And she couldn't stand it. And he really did love me . . . once.' She broke off, her voice a sob. 'I know he did. But he needed Abbie. She's so tough. All the girls are in fear of her. Not me though,' she added proudly. And then her face crumpled and she began to cry.

'Syra, you must calm down,' Rosie insisted, now having no difficulty at all in seeing Abbie in the role of a madam.

Knowing, as the pathetic girl in front of her would soon realise, that Rory loved no-one.

Sex was the weapon he used to control everyone. She shivered. She knew now why he had tried to seduce her. Why he hated her. Once his sexual power over her was gone, she was dangerous.

'I have to get some proof,' she muttered, rising swiftly to her feet, pressing her hands against her temples. 'There must be something . . . I must *think*.'

*Proof?* She stood very still. Of course she had proof. She didn't need Syra to tell her where that could be found. The photographs on Rory's desk. Tansi, Claudie. The airline tickets.

Syra shook her head. 'No use. It isn't illegal even if you do find them. He always said to me, no-one could touch him. If anyone asked, he would just say, they were friends. All just friends. Nothing criminal in that. He must be making a fortune, but he's obsessed with his inheritance. Can you understand that? A lousy crumbling pile stuck on a hillside at the backside of beyond, it's all he seems to want. Why can't he just have it? Why does he need your kid to get it?'

Rosie shook her head. 'It doesn't matter. But it matters to Rory. Without the title, he's nothing. Just another punter earning a living. He's such a nobody without it. Such a waste of space. But a title tells him he's something. He lives in a fantasy world. I know him, you see.'

She began to pace up and down, watched uneasily by Syra who was beginning to recover and to realise exactly who had come to her rescue.

'Look,' Syra began, painfully rising to her feet. 'I'm, you know, grateful and all that for you giving me some space. But I'd better go. Rory will kill me if he thinks I'm here . . .'

Rosie glanced around as if remembering the girl's presence. 'Then don't tell him,' she said calmly. 'I won't. Not if you help me.'

Syra licked her lips. Her legs were beginning to show bruises where she had fallen against the railings. Her eyes were swollen from crying. She was pathetic. But she stood between Rosie and Tom.

'Help you? How?' She eyed Rosie warily.

'I'm going to search Rory's office. Now. But I need someone to come with me. I don't have any keys to get in.'

Syra stifled a scream. 'He'll beat shit out of me. And you. You're crazy.'

'In which case it will have to be the police.' Rosie reached for the phone.

A small strangled sound erupted from Syra. 'Please, no. Okay, okay. What do you want me to do?'

Inside Rosie was weak with relief. She punched in Kit's number. 'Not a lot. Kit? It's me. I want to stay with you tonight. I'm bringing a guest.' She paused and gave a small grateful smile. 'You're the best of friends. About an hour?'

She replaced the phone and raced upstairs to the workroom and rummaged through her workdesk until she found a heavy bronze pair of scissors. Then she rejoined Syra. 'Okay,' she said briskly. 'This is the plot.'

When she'd finished, Syra gazed at her in a mixture of awe and amazement. 'And you think he wasn't scared of you? Fucking hell.'

Fifteen minutes later, every car alarm that could be activated in Marlborough Square burst into life. Doors opened, lights came on, owners spilled out onto the pavement.

Rory, Abbie and James joined them, racing for keys and switches to control the noise. For reasons they could not immediately fathom, James' car was now parked fifty yards up the street. All three raced towards it, rushing past residents clambering to get to their blaring vehicles.

Pandemonium reigned as car doors were opened, voices yelled at each other ordering everyone to shut the noise off. Vehicles with owners who were absent continued to blare out their high-pitched wailing, lights flashed on and off. James' car was left to wail itself out.

Syra still had the keys to it. Angry and frustrated, James clenched his fist and hit the roof of the pulsating Jag, which started wailing all over again.

Later the seven-year-old girl who lived opposite, who had been peering from her bedroom window, told her mother that she had seen two ladies push every car along the street and then run away when the alarms went off.

Rosie stood motionless behind the door of the study. As the occupants of Rory's house had streaked out onto the street, she had slipped in through the open door.

She had thirty minutes. Then Syra would act. Abbie's voice came floating in, arguing with James. 'Why didn't you take the keys away from her? She must have had second thoughts about stealing it and just dumped it. Do I have to think of everything round here? Angel, I'm *not* talking about you . . .'

Rosie winced. *Angel?* Merciful heaven. Rory an angel?

She held her breath as she heard the drawing-room door close. James could be heard calling a garage. If Syra had followed her instructions, he was wasting his time. Carefully she pressed the handle of the door down needing the light from the hall to guide her. The passage was empty. She stiffened and stepped back, as Rory emerged from the drawing room and made for the study.

Her heart hammering, she slithered behind one of the velvet wing chairs and just prayed his visit would be a short one. The lights snapped on. Rory didn't linger. She could smell the faint aroma of his aftershave. From the drawer at the top of the desk he pulled a folder and then left.

Weak with relief, it was a minute before Rosie could steady her hands enough to begin. She crossed to the window behind the desk and carefully opened it. Just in case. Waited. Silence.

Nothing. Then, crouching down, she examined the lock on the desk, gently easing it up and down. Possible. Very possible. Made as a decorative piece of Georgian furniture and not for security purposes, Rosie's expert eye knew it would yield to pressure. It would wreck the wood, spoil the value, but there was a greater prize at stake than the anguish of an expert from Sotheby's lamenting the destruction of a fine piece that would have easily fetched a four-figure sum.

From the back pocket of her jeans she slid the bronze scissors and eased one blade into the crack between the top of the drawer and the desktop.

Sliding it along, she felt it hit the steel bolt. Her hands were clammy, pausing every few seconds to listen for Rory or Abbie. With teeth gritted, her grip on the steel handle making her knuckles show white, she levered the makeshift weapon up and down as hard as she could go. Over and over, grunting with the effort.

Once James had emerged to use the loo, and Abbie went to the kitchen. But no-one disturbed her as she crouched in the dark breaking into Rory's desk.

She remembered it was a rolex file, kept in his bottom drawer. Twice she thought her heart would stop when the phone rang right in her ear, sending her diving for cover.

And then, sweat making her hands slippery, her hair sticking to her forehead, she heard the welcome crunch of splintering wood as the lock was prised clear of the frame. At the same time the scissors slid off the edge straight into her thumb. With a cry of pain the scissors fell to the floor, blood spurting from the wound.

For a few seconds she sucked at the wound as a red trickle ran across her palms. She searched each way for something to staunch the flow. Finding nothing, she seized the scissors and carefully, painfully, cut a slice out of the tail of her white shirt. Using her teeth she pulled a make-shift tourniquet between her thumb and wrist, a red stain immediately seeping through the thin linen.

She'd see to it later. Carefully, hands trembling, she pulled the drawer out. It was of double depth. She saw the rolex file immediately, slung carelessly on top of a series of buff folders. Carefully she lifted it out and placed it on the floor beside her. Then she turned her attention to the buff folders.

Rosie gazed despairingly at them. Which one mattered? With no time to sift through them, she pulled the lot from the drawer and took them with her.

Through the crack she could see the hall was empty. The grandfather clock on the opposite wall showed it was another three minutes before Syra would be waiting outside.

It felt like days. Then it came; the phone rang twice and then stopped. Fifteen seconds later it rang twice. This time, heart pounding, she heard Rory behind the closed door of the drawing room repeating: 'Hello . . . hello?'

It was her signal. Syra was outside. Holding her breath until her ribs ached, the blood from her thumb seeping down her hand, she walked silently across the hall, waited. To open the door she had to put her precious cargo down.

The door catch slid back, Rosie bent and scooped up the files and the rolex file, easing the door open with her hip. Once outside, she held the door so that it didn't click shut until she could see the headlights of James' car.

Lights flashed and dipped, letting her know that Syra had seen her, then the car slid silently forward. Only as it drew level did Rosie let go of the door, hurled herself down the stone steps and was in the car and roaring out of the square before the bang of the front door alerted the occupants that something was amiss.

# Chapter Fifty-Two

Kit was waiting as they fell out of a taxi in Drake Street, Syra having dumped James' car where it would be clamped.

They made a sorry sight as they recovered in his kitchen. It occurred to Rosie that it was odd for Ginny to be there, but for the moment she was having trouble explaining Syra, blood streaming from her hand, a ripped shirt, blood-soaked scissors, a pile of by now equally stained files and why she wanted them both to stay the night instead of in their own homes.

'Don't you see?' she explained impatiently, trying to staunch the flow of blood from her thumb and to shrug Kit off. 'Ouch, careful – it needs stitching. It's too late to lodge this lot in the bank tonight, I'll have to wait until morning, so Rory mustn't know where I am until he's agreed to withdraw his claim on Tom. I'm going to phone him – your number is stored, isn't it – he can't check it?'

Kit shook his head, sealing the fresh bandage with tape. Ginny was rounding up coffee and drinks. 'No – but Rosie,' he urged in a whisper, glancing around to where Syra was crashed out in an armchair. 'Don't you think you should tell Nick? You're way in right over your head. I mean, just look at this stuff.' He picked up the rolex file and flicked through it.

'Naomi: Lawyer. HR, H, TS,' he recited out loud. 'Hand relief, head and troilism, I suppose. And this. Listen. Sami,' he began and then paused. 'Good grief, what's that?' He pointed to the girl's speciality. Rosie twisted her head to read the card. 'No idea, ask Syra.'

'And this? Christ, I thought I knew the lot . . .'

Rosie took the file from him and shoved it into a plastic bag. 'Stop it, Kit. It's grubby enough as it is.' She felt sickened by what she knew. The squalid, twilight world that Rory inhabited frightened her.

She had suspected drugs, she knew he drank, ripping off Arabs and Tokyo businessmen was routine, but not this. She felt revolted by it. Ashamed. She gave herself a shake.

Histrionics could come later. There were more urgent matters to deal with. Tom for a start. Tom. Oh God, how could she? She turned her eyes to Kit.

'Here,' he said gently, handing her a drink. 'None of us knew, no-one suspected. He could go down for a couple of years for this. Best place for him.'

Rosie gulped down the drink and shook her head. 'No. No he won't. Not via me. Listen. No, listen, please. How do you think Tom would ever survive if he knew his father was in jail and for this? I can't do it. I can put him out of business though, and I won't have to fight him for Tom. That's all I ask.'

Kit looked at her dumbfounded. 'You mean after all he's done, he's going to walk away scot free, to start up again? You can't. He beat Syra, he's damn well nearly destroyed you.'

Rosie glared stubbornly back at him. 'You don't understand. I've removed the evidence, there's not a single thing on any one of these sheets that links them to Rory. He won't start again, he couldn't. Even if I can't prove it, he won't risk forcing my hand. What have I got to lose if I don't have Tom? The publicity would kill him. No-one would touch him.

'In return for my silence, he's got to agree to drop all claim to Tom and get out of London. I don't care where he goes. Let's see what bloody James comes up with now, shall we? He's in this too – up to his thick, bloated neck.'

As she spoke she flicked through the buff-coloured files

dragged from Rory's desk. She recognised the one that had caused Abbie such concern and now she knew why.

Its contents made her eyes grow round. 'Look at this,' she breathed, flicking through the lists of names and addresses. Businessmen, politicians, actors, a judge and several football managers. There was even a newscaster and an investigative journalist. A couple of earls and the governor of a major international bank.

'He'll kill you,' Kit beamed. 'And probably me as well. Now what?' He stopped, noticing she was paying no attention. The details in the file were absorbing her, her hand held up to quieten Kit.

He leaned over her. 'He's not turning Glencairn into a museum, but a bloody brothel,' Rosie said slowly. 'Look. Private country club, planning permission for a pool and saunas . . . oh, of course it *isn't* a country club. After all this stuff?' Angrily, she tossed the files to one side.

'Don't worry, Kit,' she said dryly. 'Callum will kill him long before he can get to me. Where's the phone. What? Oh, fiddle to that. What's a drop of blood on the floor . . . well, a few drops. All right, call a doctor. I'm calling Rory.'

He laughed. 'Well, well, well,' he drawled. 'Housebreaker now. And a letter as well, eh? So let me see. You now have evidence that I am running a sweet shop – but you're prepared to remain quiet provided I drop my claim to Tom? If anything happens to you, your lawyer has permission to open the letter which will incriminate me.'

Rosie gripped the phone: 'That's about it.'

There was a pause. 'Of course that makes you an accessory,' he pointed out. 'But if I'm prepared to go along with this – and there's no saying at the moment that I will – how long will you stay quiet for?'

'You have no reason not to trust me. I would never hurt Tom.'

She could hear someone distracting him in the

background. She guessed it was Abbie. 'Let me call you back,' he suggested. 'Give me a moment to think this over.'

'Nothing to think over, Rory. Take it or leave it.' Call her back? He must think she was stupid. Briefly she closed her eyes. Must think? He didn't think it, he knew it. So stupid. Blind. Naive. Shattered. How long had it been going on? Since Tom was a baby? Since she left? And what did it matter now?

'Okay.' Rory spoke lightly, indifferently almost. 'You win. I'll call Donald . . . but Rosie.'

'Yes?'

'You haven't won, my precious.'

Rosie stiffened. 'Won? Neither of us has won. What do you mean?'

Rory yawned down the phone. 'Tom will never accept anyone in my place, and I mean anyone. Still. Win some, you lose some. That's life.'

Rosie replaced the phone, conscious only of sickening relief. She took a deep breath. Later she would try to come to terms with the kind of man she had married. Even later she would come to terms with the one she couldn't.

Next morning Kit accompanied Rosie to court just in case James or Rory decided to exact revenge in a manner that was perfectly within the experience of them both. Her thumb was now expertly stitched by Kit's doctor but, apart from being sore, she was relieved she'd sustained nothing worse.

As the court went into session, there was no sign of Rory as Donald Crowe explained to the judge that his client, in the interest of his son's welfare, had phoned him earlier that morning with instructions to withdraw his case.

My Lord looked over his glasses and said, he was only sorry Mr Monteith Gore could not be fined for wasting the court's time. Residence and care and control remained with Mrs Monteith Gore and from the look on his face as he dismissed the case, Rosie could see he was glad to be rid of the lot of them.

Nevertheless as she caught his eye she smiled and mouthed thank you. He grunted and disappeared, clearly believing a good old smash and grab would be easier than these outwardly civilised people who played mental games with each other.

Rory had been warned to stay away from her but as Rosie let herself into her silent house in Drake Street she shot a nervous glance up and down the road before she went in. She had arranged to pick Tom up at five. No point in going to the workroom.

Looking Nick in the eye had been difficult. He'd stared piercingly at her when she told him that she had persuaded Rory to back down but beyond a grunt, he said nothing.

Livvie and Jordan, now reconciled – the result, Livvie said when Rosie rang, of attending a new age affirmation workshop that had polarised their previous spiritual ineptness which by an amazing coincidence occurred just as Jupiter was travelling through that sector of both their signs that governed love and harmony – had already heard the good news but they were still in celebratory mood.

Rosie thought better of pointing out that the newly restored harmony between them probably had more to do with their generous consumption of Jack Daniels after the meeting and the fact that Livvie had that morning seen some premises that might well suit them, than the position of Jupiter.

'Great, Liv, I'll take a look on Monday morning. Don't stay late, will you. And Liv? Thanks. You – and Jordan too – you've been absolute bricks. Normal service resumes Monday. Me? Well, just me and Tom. I thought we'd have a quiet weekend. Lots of love.'

She yawned, sifting through the letters on the doormat. Carrying them and a mug of tea into the newly restored drawing room. She looked around, liking what she saw.

Tom would like it eventually. He had once before. At some point she would have to see Rory. The idea of him ducking out of Tom's life was from her point of view wonderful, but she knew Tom would be distraught if it was to be permanent.

She needed to regain his trust. Ease him into accepting only spasmodic visits from Rory. Come to some arrangement with Callum.

It wasn't over. Not yet. Rory had to close down his business or at least the part of it that could send him down. She sank down onto the chaise longue and swung her legs along its length.

The post did not interest her because she knew it contained nothing from Joel. He had kept his word. Sometimes she felt so weak, she wanted to reach out and call him. Tell herself that Tom would just have to accept him.

She didn't want a future without him, but he had let her walk away and she knew he had been right. It had all been a dream. Too perfect. Life wasn't like that, never had been, never would be.

Before she closed her eyes, she rang the operator and asked to be rung in one hour and then, with the afternoon sun warming the room, she pulled a cushion under her head and thought about what might have been. And then she slept, the tears still wet on her cheeks, and dreamt what in her waking moments she wouldn't dare.

The school drive still had evidence of the tail end of parents' cars as she pulled in. She had rung them at the beginning of the week to explain that the court would not rise until four o'clock so it might be six before she came to collect Tom.

It was a warm sunny afternoon, as March began to fade and April took its place. Rosie had not seen Mr Farrell or Matron since that awful afternoon in January and she didn't particularly want to see them now. But she guessed it might be inevitable.

The hall was deserted. She walked across and tapped on the secretary's door.

No answer. Tom was probably still in his dormitory. She mounted the oak stairs and made her way through the corridor to Tom's room. It was empty. She checked his locker. That was cleared. He must be downstairs.

She shook her head. Stop it. Nothing's wrong. But she found herself running across the courtyard to the block that housed Matron and Mr Farrell. The school was unnaturally quiet. All the boys had gone home for the weekend. Her feet crunched into the gravel as she ran, skirting across the lawn. Tom would be waiting for her.

Only Matron was there. Her face stiffened when she saw who was banging on her door.

'Dear me,' she said acidly. 'I didn't expect to see you here ... Tom? Well he's gone home. With his father, of course. Mrs Monteith Gore, what is it? How dare you push past me like that?'

Rosie couldn't stop shaking. Nick tried to calm her. Matron stood ashen faced behind her as the door opened to admit Mr Farrell.

'I have no idea,' Rosie almost screamed into the phone to Nick. 'Matron said he came here this morning. It's now five o'clock. They could be anywhere. No, I have no idea why they let him go.' As she spoke she turned and looked into the horrified faces of the head and Matron.

'Ports alert? Yes. Just in case. The house, check the house first, Nick.' But even as she said it she knew Marlborough Square would be empty.

Jordan confirmed it, racing there and back while Rosie waited hanging onto the phone. 'Jordan, ask Livvie to book a flight for me to Edinburgh. I think there's one at around eight thirty. I'll go straight from here. I'll collect my ticket at the check-in desk. Jordan ... Tell Kit. No, don't come. I'll be quicker on my own.'

She slammed the phone down. Mr Farrell stepped forward, trying to bluff it out.

'Why should we have stopped him? He's the boy's father. This really isn't our responsibility ...'

He got no further. Rosie pushed him with both hands against his shoulders, shoving him as she spoke.

'When you knew there was a custody hearing.' Shove. 'You decided that he was the right person to have my son.' Shove. 'And you, you revolting little man, let an innocent child go.' Shove. 'Against the wishes of the court.'

Mr Farrell was up against the wall, his breath coming in quick bursts. Matron was paralysed with fear. 'But the custody ... surely Mr Monteith Gore was awarded ...'

'Why? Why should he be? I was. No court in the world would have allowed my ex-husband to have custody of a flea. And you have now aided an unscrupulous man, about to be the subject of criminal proceedings, to take my son because he oiled your greasy little fist, smirked at you and charmed you, and you believed all those wicked stories spread by him and that vicious Duxborough woman.'

Mr Farrell cringed, a dreadful vision of his future swimming before his eyes, a vision which included explaining his hasty actions to a board of trustees. Rosie had reached the door and was beyond reason.

'You preferred to think Tom would be given to him, because you had more to gain.' She almost spat the words out. 'Oh, get out of my way, you ghastly little shit. Oh, was that your foot, Matron? I'm sorry it wasn't your smug face.'

# Chapter Fifty-Three

Livvie had booked Rosie's ticket. A car would be waiting for her to pick up at Edinburgh and a room booked at the nearest hotel to Glencairn, should she need it.

From the concourse she called Nick. He said there was still no reply from Callum's house. The police had sent a patrol out there and reported back that the house was deserted. Meanwhile, he was speeding through an injunction to stop Rory leaving the country with Tom.

Customs had not reported anyone taking a schoolboy on a long-haul flight or to Europe under that name. Ferries had not reported any sightings or had the channel tunnel rail links.

But that was no proof he hadn't slipped through. Not all passports were checked and he could have used false names. The possibilities were endless but the probability to Rosie was that it had to be Scotland. Nor did the police seem inclined to intervene.

Rory was not – yet – a wanted man. But they had decided taking Tom away without his mother's consent was strong enough reason to mobilise a Ports Alert.

'But *why* won't they do something?' she almost sobbed down the phone. Nick tried to calm her down. No recriminations for deceiving him. That might come later.

'I'm sorry, Nick,' she choked. 'I didn't want to lie to you, but I had to think of Tom.'

'Not now, Rosie,' he hushed. 'Let's just get Tom back. I've had to tell the police about the files. There was no other way. But for the moment they don't have any reason to arrest him other than for abducting Tom. It's a domestic matter, Rosie. I promise you it's better at this stage to let me do what I can. Please don't go to Edinburgh on your own. It could be a wasted journey.'

But Rosie was no longer listening. Mr Farrell said they were in a hired car, not Rory's. Rory was definitely not going back to London. It might be days before the car was located if Rory had just dumped it at the airport or near the coast.

All of this she told Nick. 'London is the last place you'll find him,' she said wearily. 'And if he hasn't left the country, Scotland is the most likely place. Callum must know something. I'll call when I get there.'

All Rosie had with her was a shoulder bag with her wallet and the clothes she stood up in: faded jeans, canvas baseball boots, a sweatshirt under a bomber jacket. When she left the house, she had after all been planning nothing more adventurous than a trip to school to collect her son, not a frantic dash to Scotland.

Be practical, she told herself sternly. Even if she found Tom tonight, there was no way she could get him back to London until tomorrow.

Clutching her ticket and boarding pass, she made for the concourse shops. In twenty minutes she had bought a holdall, and enough supplies to keep her going for the next day or two, all the while mentally berating herself for her stupidity in taking her eye off the ball.

She should have known what Rory would do. Known he wouldn't just leave it at that. But to snatch Tom? Oh God. Tom. She could hardly breathe. People milled around her with dizzying speed, the panic had risen to her mouth. For a few seconds she was paralysed with fear.

Minutes before she boarded the flight she called Nick once more. There had been no news on Rory but the police reported that James appeared to have fled from his office. Desks were empty. All the signs of a hurried departure were evident. Betsey too had disappeared.

Of Abbie there was no sign. Rosie rang Kit. Syra, who was still cowering in Ginny's flat, had no idea where they could have gone. She was now terrified Rory would be coming for her. Or at the very least James.

'Can Ginny keep her for a day or two? Oh Kit, thank her for me. That's such a relief. There's my flight. I'll call you when I get there.'

Tom. On the loose with a man who was dangerous and mentally unstable. And what had she done to prevent it? Moved in with him, let Tom get close to him and then fallen asleep wallowing in self pity about her own future while Rory was spiriting their child to God knows where.

Guilt engulfed her brain. While her son was being abducted she had been weaving schemes that would at once restore her relationship with Joel while making Tom see it would work.

Rosie's more rational self was in deep denial. By the time her flight was called she resented the hold Joel had over her. Could see how Tom felt threatened. By the time she boarded the plane, she had made every pact known with God that if he restored Tom to her safely, she would never ask to see Joel Harley again.

Rosie had not driven out to Glencairn for nearly eight years. Not much had changed but the darkness distorted the shape of the road, sending shadows to obscure bends, hiding signposts.

As the road swung out of the town and plunged deeper into the countryside she was too absorbed in following the only guide she had, a snake of cat's eyes down the centre of the road, picked out in the beam from her headlamps, to be concerned about her nerves. In truth the darkened countryside held no fear for her. Her terror was what was waiting for her at journey's end.

It was nearing midnight when she arrived at the house, further away than she remembered, larger than she recalled. But the familiar granite lodge looming up out of the dark on one side of a pair of black wrought-iron gates was unmistakeable. Two carriage lamps lit the entrance as she swung the car into the long drive up to the house.

There were lights burning on the ground floor. In the drive a Mercedes estate was parked and behind it a black BMW. From inside the house Rosie heard a jangle as she tugged the bell pull. The sound of a door opening, a light illuminated the porch as a woman's voice called through the door asking what she wanted.

'It's Rosie. Rosie Monteith Gore. Please open the door. I'm looking for Rory and Tom.'

There was a silence and then the heavy bolts were pulled back and the door opened. A woman wrapped in a service-able dressing gown peered out into the dark, her streaked grey hair pulled back into a clip.

She stared at Rosie in amazement and suspicion. 'Rory? Here? Of course not. At this time of night? Why would he be here?'

'Because he's snatched Tom and I can't think where else he would be and I must see Callum. I know he's unwell, but this is so urgent. Are you Helen?'

The woman looked blank. 'Helen? Good heavens, no. I'm Annie McClellan, Callum's housekeeper. I'm sorry, did you say Callum was unwell?'

Rosie thought she must have misunderstood. 'Well, a bit frail, I think Rory said. But I must see him. I don't want to upset him, truly, but this is desperate and he might be able to help.'

'Is he expecting you?' the woman asked, preventing Rosie from going in. It was after all past midnight.

Rosie shook her head. 'I tried to phone. There was no answer. So I just came. The police have been here, didn't you know?'

The housekeeper looked shocked. 'The police? No. It's my day off. I only got back at eight o'clock. Sir Callum and Mrs Sinclair were over dining with the Montroses and got back an hour ago.' She hesitated. 'You'd best come in. I'll get Sir Callum.'

Rosie followed her through to the sitting room at the back of the house. The housekeeper bade her wait. Eight years before Rosie had said a bitter farewell to Callum. She had never wanted to see him again. The feeling had been entirely mutual.

Nothing had changed in this house which Rory had always loathed. To Rosie, however, the sense of timeless continuity in the furnishings and the paintings was reassuring. However much she disliked the inhabitants, she had never disliked the house with its panelled walls, inky black portraits, deep comfortable sofas alongside chintz-covered chairs.

The silver-framed pictures of Rory as a schoolboy. One of Tom taken on the first visit he had made with Rory last spring. One or two of Rory's mother, holding Rory in her lap, and others more recent that Rosie did not recognise.

'Come with me,' said the housekeeper from the doorway. Rosie replaced the picture she was holding and followed her across the hallway and into the drawing room. Taking a deep breath she entered.

For a moment they simply stared at each other. Callum was greyer than she remembered. The once-raven hair and thick dark brows were now streaked with white. But the black piercing eyes that Rory had inherited and in turn, Tom, looked thunderously back at her. He looked strong and fit and unwelcoming.

Rosie glanced at his companion. Probably in her early fifties but she looked younger, perfectly groomed, in a soft grey sweater and pearls, attractive with cropped blonde hair, holding a tumbler of whisky.

'Hello, Callum,' Rosie said evenly, moving further into the room. 'I need your help. This is difficult for me.'

'And not for me I suppose?' he cut in, making no attempt

to introduce his companion. Rosie watched her as she immediately rose and placed a restraining arm on Callum's.

He responded to her touch and stopped. The woman turned to Rosie:

'I'm Helen Sinclair. We've spoken briefly on the phone.'

Helen? This sophisticated woman was the housekeeper? Rosie's amazement showed. Tom had only said she was nice. Rory dismissed her as a relic. Of the two, Tom was more accurate.

'We know about Rory. There was a phone call from your solicitor – and Rory's. Darling . . . please let me . . .'

Callum had opened his mouth to intervene, but at that he turned and gazed into the fire, his arm leaning along the fireplace, one foot pushing at a log smouldering in the grate, sending sparks shooting up into the chimney.

Helen beckoned Rosie to a chair but Rosie shook her head. 'I'm sorry, my dear,' Helen began. 'But your journey is a waste of time. Rory isn't here. The police were here as we left for dinner and we can only tell you what we told them. Rory was last here at New Year, very briefly to drop Tom off with us. He spends most of his time with the Johnsons. Gordon Johnson. Have you asked him?'

Rosie shook her head. 'I hardly know them. It's been years.' She was also having to cope with a scene unfolding before her that contradicted everything she had assumed about Glencairn.

Helen was no more a housekeeper than Abbie. But there all similarity ended. No wonder Rory had stopped her writing those notes. But why didn't he tell her the truth? And Callum. He looked as if he could toss the caber with one hand at the Highland games. Rory had said he was sick and frail.

She knew why. A fit and well Callum could easily be disturbed by Rosie, who had been prevented from accompanying Tom by the threat that Callum might keel over at the shock of seeing her, knowing how much he disliked her.

The presence of a glamorous companion was quite likely to arouse her suspicion. Helen had to be a dumpling of a woman wearing a pinny in keeping with a frail old gentleman. Not an attractive intelligent woman who was clearly more than a companion.

Poor Tom could not be blamed for the confusion. He thought Jaye was elderly. What would he have made of this middle-aged woman?

The phrase 'dropped Tom off' meant what? That Rory then took off? To where? Rosie turned to her former father-in-law and tried to appeal to him:

'Callum, if you know what's happened, then please help me. Where could Rory have taken Tom?'

'Away from you, obviously,' he snapped. 'Look what you've driven him to. Aren't you satisfied with keeping my family from me all these years without all this? What kind of woman are you? You nearly drove him to a breakdown the first time and now this. And you dare to come here with your lies and accusations. Jealous because I've had my son and grandson restored to me. No, Helen, I won't be quiet. This woman has destroyed my son. I hope to God he destroys her. I wouldn't lift a finger to help you. Now get out.'

Rosie listened white-faced. Trembling with anger.

'With pleasure.' Her voice was shaking. 'And when your rage has subsided and those blinkers that you have worn to view the world for God knows how many years finally wear out – because I doubt you'd be brave enough to remove them yourself – you might live to regret that you never got to know your son.'

'Get out,' he roared, his face now pink. Helen stood rooted at this explosion.

Rosie turned to leave, pausing in the doorway. 'And that's a pity,' she said, continuing as though he had not spoken. 'Because you could have done so much more for him, saved him a great deal of the punishment he will now have to face. I could save you and Rory from scandal. That's right. Scandal that has nothing to do with me, but now you leave me no choice.

'Have you ever wondered what Rory was doing in London? Did you ever bother to come and see? Did you ever contact Tom in all those years and suggest taking him out, away on holiday? Did you? No. You chose to go on sulking and being resentful that I wasn't good enough for your son. Preferring Rory's version of our marriage so that you wouldn't have to sully yourself with acknowledging me.

'Well, I'm sorry I wasn't born to the House of Windsor, with a pedigree as long as your arm, but I have something so much better than that. I have dignity, Callum. You have none. All you have is pride and, believe me, that is not the same thing at all. What a shame you never taught your son that. Please, don't say anything else. I'm leaving.'

It was after one in the morning when Rosie reached the small lochside hotel, grateful that the owner did nothing more than give her a mild reproof at the lateness of the hour as she let her in.

But she couldn't sleep. All she could think was that Tom must be okay. Rory wouldn't hurt him. But he would be bewildered about being taken so swiftly from school. She was certain Rory would not tell him the truth.

The Johnsons were now her only hope of unravelling where Rory could possibly be if he had come to Scotland. Nick was right. He wasn't here. But the answer might be. Her head was thumping, she felt so tired she couldn't even cry and eventually she slipped in and out of a troubled sleep, until at seven she was roused by a soft knocking on her door.

Bleary-eyed, Rosie fell out of bed and pulled the door open.

'You have a visitor, my dear,' said the owner. 'A lady. She's waiting downstairs. She didn't give her name. Said it was private.'

In less than ten minutes Rosie peered round the door of the small lounge. Standing by the window, her back to Rosie, was Helen Sinclair. She turned as Rosie came in and gave a faint smile.

'You won't of course tell Callum, will you?' she said. 'But I think I can help you.'

# Chapter Fifty-Four

'Please.' Rosie darted forward. 'Anything. Please help. Callum doesn't understand. Rory is evil . . .' She stopped. She no longer knew who to trust.

Helen glanced at her watch. 'I can't be away for long. I've left a note saying I've gone for a ride. And you must respect my confidence. Strange as it may seem to you, I am devoted to Callum, but where Rory is concerned we are on either side of an almost unbridgeable chasm.

'I'll be frank with you. I would be happy if Callum never saw Rory again. But most stories don't have happy endings. I'm not sure this one will have one for me. But I just took one look at you last night and thought Callum's loyalty to Rory must stop.'

Rosie stared at her. 'What do you mean?'

'I mean,' sighed Helen, 'that he has spent his life trying to compensate his son for being motherless, wanting the best for him, indulging him, blaming everyone else for leading him astray. If I've heard Callum once I've heard him a thousand times saying: "*But he's my only son*".'

'I see,' Rosie said. Helen wrapped her arms around herself, chafing her arms to keep them warm. Rosie felt cold too. The fire was not yet strong enough to have warmed the room.

'A child is a child, but not to the exclusion of everything and everyone,' Helen was saying. 'Rory's spirit has never been allowed to grow because he has always known he could wind his father round his little finger, well, not just his father. And now look at the mess he has become.'

Rosie waited while the owner deposited a tray of coffee

on the table, promising to arrange breakfast when they were ready.

'For better or worse Rory is all Callum has left to him. And Tom. He's a proud man. It might be meaningless to you, but the Monteiths and the Gores have been at Glencairn since Bannockburn. He's still in shock, not able to take in what's happened. You see, he believed Rory. Oh all right, wanted to believe him. When he turned up here after such a long absence it was only because he had heard through Callum's lawyers that he'd be disinherited if he didn't.

'In which case, all Rory would get is the house, which is only in great shape because of Callum's own personal fortune being ploughed into it, but Callum said he wasn't going to leave his son the money. However, Rory knows the buttons to press with Callum.'

It could have been Kit talking. '*I suppose this is knowing which buttons to press?*' Rosie gave herself a shake.

'My dear, he told Callum that you wanted a reconciliation – we know now that isn't true. That he really wanted to settle down. Callum said if you were still together after a year, then he would rethink everything. But for once he wanted to see Rory stick at something.

'In fact he nearly didn't give him a chance. It was at least another four months before you moved in with him after your house was damaged in the fire. I thought you were using Rory. I never knew how fortuitous that fire was for him. It came only days after Callum said he had run out of patience.

'Then Rory would arrive here with Tom, bringing with him all these stories about how you were neglecting the boy, concerned only with your career. It was so difficult for us because we never saw you. All we saw was Rory trying really hard and getting no support from you. I know, I know, he was playing us all off against each other.

'Callum didn't want to believe Rory would have

snatched Tom for no reason, no matter what Rory's solicitor said, or the police. And then there was this man you got involved with . . .'

Rosie stopped her. 'That is my business,' she said shortly. 'And besides, my relationship with the person concerned was of short duration. It is now over. There was never any question of marriage. It was Rory who made sure Tom was told such a wicked story. Don't insult me any further.'

Helen looked troubled, uneasy, clearly beginning to regret this visit. 'Please understand. If Rory was duping you, he was also duping his own father. By now Callum will be mortified at the scene last night. He's got to blame someone. He'll come round. The trouble is,' she paused looking at Rosie's rigid face, 'I fear you won't. I came to see if you could meet him halfway. But I think it's too early for that, isn't it?'

'I'm not going to waste your time putting all of that in context,' Rosie said politely. 'Just tell me one thing. Why was it necessary for Callum to have my co-operation? Why not just let Rory bring Tom to Glencairn? I wouldn't have stopped it.'

Helen laughed. 'Oh my dear, don't you know? You were the condition. Callum had many years to reflect that the only time Rory was on the straight and narrow was while he was with you. It's been many months now since I began to doubt Rory. It was that note you sent when Tom had a cold – if you were so careless, you would never have done that.'

'Rory was livid,' Rosie told her. 'He said I was undermining him in front of his father. He said so many things. I got a shock when I saw you, he said you were the housekeeper. He told me Callum was frail and ill and any shock from me turning up might kill him.'

Helen sighed. 'The only reason I was tolerated is because I'm clearly not going to have a family. Callum's second wife gave up after a couple of years. Rory drove her out.

Rory might look like Callum, but he is temperamentally his mother's son.'

'I never met her,' Rosie said. 'I don't know what that means.'

'I did,' Helen's voice was brief. 'Years ago when she was first married to Callum. She was a . . . frankly, Rosie, she was a slut. An alcoholic slut. Ignored Rory right from birth, screwed anything that wasn't actually pinned to the floor and died from liver poisoning. Callum only married her because she was pregnant.'

Rosie gaped. 'I had no idea.'

'Callum saw history repeating itself when Rory got you pregnant. He lived in terror that Rory would one day get into real trouble, so he insisted he married you or he would cut him off without a penny. Rory did a great job of convincing Callum that making him marry you – sorry, my dear but the situation is too serious to be polite – was a grievous error. You were painted as a whining, clinging woman interested only in the title. When you left Rory, Callum's view was Rory's. He couldn't see that anyone would willingly walk away from a Monteith of Glencairn. You'd secured a sinecure for life. Your son was the next heir. I know, I know. Silly title. But he was prepared to hand it all over to Rory to run as a museum.'

'Brothel, actually,' Rosie said calmly.

Helen choked on her coffee. 'Brothel? Are you mad? Callum said you claimed it was a club of some sort. But not a *brothel*.'

Shock was written all over Helen's face. Rosie could see that her hand was shaking as she put the cup down.

'Just call Nick Newall, better still, Donald Crowe. They have copies of the evidence. None of it matters, Helen.' Rosie looked bleakly at the older woman. 'How can you help? Where has he taken Tom?'

'What? Oh, yes. I'm sorry, I had no idea . . . no matter,' Helen said, giving herself a shake. 'Taken Tom? That I don't know. But I am certain that dreadful oaf Gordon Johnson will have a hand in it. That's where they all stayed when they were up here. Not with Callum.

'I think Rory must have got Tom out of the country. And I think he used Gordon's private plane to do it. They used it for everything. We never saw Rory at all. He was always with him, always flying off somewhere.'

'Where?' Rosie asked hoarsely. But she already suspected.

Kit phoned her back two hours later. 'Don't ask. Just listen. Gordon Johnson's plane is registered in a small company name and regularly flies out from a private airstrip near Edinburgh to the Côte d'Azur.

'Ginny had it checked and it landed there late yesterday afternoon but it is now back in Scotland. What does Gordon Johnson say?'

'Fuck off, basically,' Rosie replied. 'Says Rory is a friend, hasn't seen him for a few weeks. Prove it is the bottom line where he's concerned. But I think he's frightened. I don't think he knew about Tom being abducted. Okay, Kit, I'll call Nick ... oh, you have ... I'm going straight to Monte Carlo.'

She found Claudie's number through her parents. The apartment block where Claudie lived was in the centre of Monte Carlo. Rosie arrived late in the afternoon, booked into a small hotel on the outskirts of the town and called Claudie's number but the phone switched to a machine.

It was April and warm. Under any other circumstances a stroll in this affluent place would have been a pleasure to be savoured. Rosie would have revelled in the gentle evening heat of the sun, the streets not yet overcrowded with tourists. But she hardly noticed as she walked the few blocks to Claudie's address.

There was no reply. The porter was unhelpful. Rosie

could guess why. Girls like Claudie relied on a blind eye and a discreet tongue and were prepared to pay for it. This dishevelled English woman was not enough to endanger such *largesse* from the flaky one on the top floor.

Having checked that there was only one entrance to the block, including the underground car park, Rosie crossed the street and sat at a pavement café where she could keep an eye on who arrived and left.

Once the heat of the sun combined with her own travel weariness nearly sent her to sleep, and once she started up thinking she had seen the beautiful French girl and was halfway across the street only to realise her mistake and slump down again.

As dusk faded into night she was rewarded. A black convertible pulled up and out stepped Claudie, leaning across to kiss the driver full on the mouth. No mistake. The tan already even, the hips even slimmer than Rosie recalled.

She could faintly hear an exchange in French and then with a laugh Claudie turned and disappeared into the apartment block. Rosie paid her bill – good grief, five coffees – and crossed over the road.

The porter rang Claudie's apartment. 'She is not home Mademoiselle,' he intoned, having given Rosie's name to the voice on the other end of the phone.

'No?' Rosie asked politely in French. 'Please tell Miss Bergerard that she is mistaken. She is most definitely at home to me. I have her photographs. Otherwise I might have no option but to leave them with the police.'

The word 'police' acted like magic. Mademoiselle Flaky was on her own. He handed the phone to Rosie. 'What do you want?' Claudie demanded. A less guilty woman would have been more accommodating.

'My son,' Rosie told her in English, hoping that the porter would not be fluent enough to understand. 'All the evidence I need is locked in a safe in London. If you co-operate your name is taken from the file. If not – and Claudie, listen carefully – and if anything happens to me or Tom, the police in London have instructions to arrest every name on the list. Yours included.'

'What list?' Claudie was dismissive. 'You have no proof of anything, *n'est ce pas?*'

Rosie turned her back on the porter who was clearly more fluent than she had hoped judging from the way he was sitting so still, not turning one page of his newspaper.

'Proof, Claudie,' she whispered softly into the phone. 'How distasteful. But if you insist.' It was not hard to recall Claudie's card in the rolex file. Or Tansi's. Both were versatile and indeed pioneering in sexual pleasures.

Kit had said it made de Sade look restrained, explaining one or two practices that Rosie had never heard of and frankly thought were hysterical.

All of this she relayed to the silent girl on the other end of the phone.

'Now I'm going to cross the street and wait for you in that café. If you have any sense you will help. You will not call Rory and you will simply hand me an address or phone number where I can find my son and your name will never be mentioned.'

Claudie came running across the street. 'I did not know about the child.' She was breathless and agitated. 'My parents . . . You will tell them about this?'

'If Rory says you warned him, then yes. Otherwise you have nothing to fear from me. Don't you trust him? No? Good decision, Claudie. Now make a few more.'

Claudie slumped down in front of her. 'I want to stay out of this,' she whispered, nervously lighting a cigarette. 'I may be getting a part in a movie. It's my chance. This could ruin it. I have no idea where Rory is. But he uses this house.' She scribbled the name down and handed it to Rosie, who glanced at it and stuffed it into her pocket.

'Will I find Rory there?' she asked.

Claudie raised her hands in a negative gesture. 'Maybe, maybe not. Arrives without warning, goes in seconds.'

'By private plane? Gordon Johnson's?'

Claudie's eyes flickered warily. She nodded. 'I don't ask questions. It is not good. I do what I am told. Tansi asked questions . . . she wanted to get out.'

To Rosie's surprise, Claudie's eyes filled with tears. 'Tansi?' she prompted. 'What about Tansi?'

Claudie shook her head, dashing a hand across her eyes. 'Nothing. She'll be fine.'

Rosie handed her a napkin to wipe her face. A mental flash of Syra being punched by Rory came back. 'Somebody beat her up, is that it?'

Silence. 'It doesn't matter,' Rosie said, a resigned note in her voice. 'I know she was. Is she badly hurt?'

The other girl just nodded, dragging heavily on a cigarette. 'Is Joel with you?' she asked suddenly.

Rosie's eyes flew to her face. 'No. Why should he be?'

Claudie shrugged. 'No reason. Maman said he looked happy with you.' Rosie felt a rush of longing, quickly quelled. She was getting used to it now. 'I thought he might have come with you.'

'No. I don't see Joel,' Rosie explained carefully. 'He doesn't even know I'm here. There's no reason for him to.'

'I don't want him to know,' Claudie confessed. 'Or Veronica. She is so disapproving. They all are. My mother listens to Veronica. It is so difficult to live your own life, to get away from them. You don't understand. No-one does. About me.'

Her voice was full of self-pity. Rosie wasn't sure what it was the world didn't understand about Claudie. But she was rich, beautiful, spoilt and now too dangerous for Rory to let her walk away.

'Of course Joel knows what you do,' Rosie said, not unkindly but refusing to collude in the fantasy that Claudie was weaving. 'So does Veronica. I don't know her well, but it seemed to me that she wouldn't hurt your mother in that way.

'Get a life, Claudie,' Rosie advised more gently, dropping a flurry of notes on the table to pay for the coffee as the sultry girl stared up at her.

'But what can I do?' she beseeched. 'My parents. Rory ... he'll get me the same as Tansi.'

Rosie stopped her. 'There are other ways of earning a living apart from doling out remorse and punishment to ageing movie moguls – get out of here now while I'm distracting him.'

'But where would I go?' Claudie sounded appalled.

'Anywhere. Anything has got to be better than living in fear in luxury.'

Claudie blew a cloud of smoke and tapped her lighter on the table. 'You don't understand ...'

'Probably not,' Rosie cut in impatiently.

'But you don't understand.' Claudie reached out and grabbed her wrist. Rosie paused.

'Understand what?'

'He'll kill you.'

'Nonsense.'

'But it isn't.' Claudie licked her lips. Her voice was barely audible. 'He's already tried.'

# Chapter Fifty-Five

In a saner moment, Rosie would not have driven off into the night through the French countryside not knowing what awaited her at her destination. But an entire day of agonising inactivity had been the spur.

Tom had now been missing for three days. Every minute that passed was eating away at her sanity. To sit doing nothing was beyond her, the thought of sleep did not enter her plans.

Her hand was hurting where the stitches had been inserted. There were navy-blue circles under her eyes, even the addition of hurriedly purchased cotton trousers, sneakers and T-shirt could not disguise the neglect in her appearance.

Rory's violence was dished out in direct proportion to how much opposition he encountered, she had seen that for herself. The miracle was that she was not dead in an alley with her throat slit.

Claudie's revelation that Rory had tried to have her killed had shocked her, but only because she had been so unaware of the danger she was in.

'You must believe me,' Claudie had urged her. 'We knew nothing until Abbie came here, one weekend. She was jealous because Rory had taken Tansi for the night.' She stopped and flicked a glance at Rosie. 'She had no choice. It was nothing. Rory was careless.

'She hated anyone who came near him. But Rory just laughed at her and then she became very drunk and told Tansi that he would kill her if she stopped interesting him – and that he had already tried to kill you.'

Claudie took a drag on her cigarette. Rosie sat very still. Claudie was serious.

'A fire? Was it a fire? He thought you might be killed and then he would get your son. But you escaped. Why did you live with him? To me, this is madness, yes?'

Rosie's hands felt sticky. She was surprised at how calmly she was listening to Claudie. She had moved in with a killer. She didn't have to be told about the robbery. Was that another attempt?

'Did he put the idea into Veronica's head to ask us to lunch?'

'He told me to arrange it. He and James need respectable people, to be seen with them. Credibility is so vital to them. But Joel had already heard you were here and he suggested it.'

There were some compensations in this bleak tale.

'We didn't ask questions, you must understand, it is dangerous. But, *pardon*, Rosie, Rory did not speak kindly about you, I was surprised when we met. You were not as I imagined and we began to feel Rory was not, how do you say? All there? And then one night Tansi was having a row with Rory because she wanted to get out and she said, if he didn't let go she would tell the police he tried to kill his wife.'

Claudie's voice broke. 'They took her away and a couple of hours later she was found half-dead on the beach. She was so badly beaten she couldn't walk or talk. I did not know her in the hospital, I thought it was an old woman. Terrible.'

'Did Rory . . . did Rory arrange it?' Rosie's voice was hoarse. Claudie nodded.

'With our boss' approval – you know the head of Create, the model agency? Well,' Claudie drew deeply on her cigarette, 'he hires the girls. Oh, not for *Vogue*, believe me.' She gave a bitter laugh. 'He puts girls like me and Tansi on planes around the world to sick old men who couldn't get it any other way.'

She stubbed out the cigarette and immediately lit another. 'Some get out, because they're too old to be useful. Some still oblige, even if they are now married and respectable. Some try like,' her voice broke, 'like Tansi to just go. But she was so beaten, so terribly beaten.'

'Where is she now?'

Claudie's eyes were filled with tears. She brushed them away with the palm of her hand. 'At the boss' house.' She nodded her head in the direction of the hills, exhaling a cloud of smoke. 'Above Paul de Vence. They've told everyone it was a car crash.'

'What part does Rory play in all this?' Rosie's hands were clammy. How would anyone believe she didn't know?

'Rory pulls in clients and girls. New girls, young girls, maybe no more than fourteen or fifteen. Those disgusting old bastards like them young. English aristocracy.' Claudie spat on the pavement. 'That's what I think of them. But Rory pushes the girls to take risks.'

'Like what?'

Claudie laughed and reeled off a list of household names who had been serviced by the girls, and even one or two highly paid models who had started their careers doing tricks for Iranian noblemen.

'Next time you see a president or a prime minister making a speech, there may be one of our girls giving him head under the table. Rory is a pimp. I'm sorry, Rosie, but I'm very frightened. If he ever finds out what I've told you, I'm dead because he is so powerful and is murderous if he is crossed. You must promise me, *swear*, you won't tell him. And now, please, you will get my name off that list, yes?'

Rosie thought this was all happening to someone else. She scarcely heard Claudie's next question. She knew too much, Rory would kill her rather than give Tom back.

Claudie was watching her carefully. 'Why does he want to kill you, Rosie? It doesn't make sense to me. Why?'

Rosie looked blankly at her. Then gave herself a shake. 'Sorry, Claudie. I was miles away. Why does he want to kill me? Oh, because he's tried every other way to get my son away from me. It's all that's left to him. I promise, if I get my son back, I will do everything I can to keep you out of it.'

She gave a faint smile. 'I must be very stupid. Until now I never dreamed he wanted to kill me. I must be either very vain or very thick not to have realised how much he hated me.'

Nick had said the French police were being alerted. But the police inspector simply shook his head. The paperwork was not through. His hands were tied. In the morning, Madame. Yes, he knew where she was staying. He would stay in touch and yes, the address was helpful.

'If your husband is here with your son, we have powers to detain him and return them both to England. Be thankful he hasn't taken him to a country outside those covered by the European or Hague convention. You are both English citizens, it would be different if your husband was French. As it is, we have no interest in the matter beyond co-operating with our English colleagues. Now I have a note here that the Lord Chancellor's department in London have made the necessary request, but I must wait for the documents to come through. Please, take my advice, go to your hotel and rest.'

Rosie almost screamed with frustration and disbelief. He adopted a kindlier tone.

'Believe me, we take a poor view of such behaviour. If you stay calm until we can see him ourselves, then there is no need for you to feel any alarm. Call us if he tries to contact you or molest you. Remember, it is unlikely he knows you are here.

'Madame,' he said severely when she began to argue in restricted French that surely it was not beyond their mandate to come with her now. 'You must trust me? Are you in danger?'

Rosie hesitated. 'I believe so,' she finally said. 'I have witnessed my husband use violence.'

The villa was approached up a narrow dirt track that led off the road inland towards Peille. Rosie prayed she wouldn't meet another car coming down. At the end of the dirt track the road divided. Guessing, she took a right and ten minutes later found herself back on the main road.

Swearing under her breath, she swung the car round the sharp bend to the right back up the narrow road and started down the dirt track again. The instructions from the man at the petrol station were clear, if accompanied by a strange look.

Rosie was confident that her French was fluent enough not to have misunderstood his directions. The thought that Tom could be just minutes away from her kept her going.

A phone call from Nick when she arrived back at the hotel was the final straw. 'There was a hitch in the papers. It may be Monday before they are processed.'

'*Tomorrow*? Nick, I can't wait that long. Tom will be worried sick.'

'He may not be, Rosie. No, listen. He is used to going away with Rory. Heaven knows what he's told him, but there is a very good chance that Tom will not be too worried.'

He was wrong. Tom always called her. He must wonder what the silence was about. Nick was however right about one thing. God knows what Rory had told him.

She left a message on Kit's machine, telling him what she planned to do. Of necessity it was a short message, but sufficient to let him know that she wasn't prepared to wait any longer.

This time she turned left, bumping over ruts in the road. Claudie said the house was secluded, surrounded by out-houses and a barn that was converted into a pool house.

Parties, she'd said. Private parties were held there. Movie people mostly. She shuddered. Pigs. All of them.

About halfway along the track, crouching forward over the wheel, searching for a road sign, it was some minutes before Rosie realised there was another set of lights in the rear mirror. A much larger vehicle was following her.

Panic gripped her. Finding a reason for trawling along this dirt track after dark would be difficult if Claudie was to be believed. The house was isolated. Ahead of her she saw a gap in the wall and without warning swung the car through and waited.

Relief swept over her as the heavy vehicle lumbered past, the driver giving no sign that he had seen her. She gave it a few minutes and then did a careful U-turn and continued on up the lane.

A wide farm gate was the first indication that the house was not far ahead. Rosie doused the lights on the car and crawled nearer.

The house itself was tucked into a cobbled courtyard, surrounded on three sides by a high rough stone wall. At this point it seemed prudent to proceed on foot. She pulled onto the grass verge under some trees, closed the door of the car and then ran swiftly to the wall.

On either side there were clumps of trees. Now what? Rosie hovered, uncertain about what to do. Knocking on the door would get her nowhere. She could see that the courtyard was empty. No sign of cars. They must be parked at the back of the house because at least one had passed her with nowhere else to go but here.

There was no light to guide her except for the glow from the house and occasionally the moon when it appeared from behind scudding clouds.

Nothing for it. She took a deep breath and ran forward.

She didn't hear or see anyone until a firm hand was clamped across her mouth, an arm around her waist started to drag her backwards kicking and struggling into the thicket. A second shadowy figure grabbed her legs and between them she was overpowered.

Terror more than bravery triggered the fight she put up as she tried to escape, clawing ineffectually at any limb within her grasp, and finally with nothing else left, she sunk her teeth as hard as she could into the hand that was across her mouth.

She heard him swear softly under his breath, but she was no match for two assailants. Not a word passed between them as she was silently pinned to the ground before the hand was removed.

'Thanks,' a very familiar voice whispered as she was finally released, her face covered in mud.

Rosie twisted round, spitting out grass, straining to see in the dark. '*Kit,*' she gasped, wiping her face, recognising one of her captors. 'Oh, my God,' she breathed, her eyes swivelling to the other. 'What are you doing here?'

# Chapter Fifty-Six

'Trying to stop you getting killed,' Joel whispered. 'Kit, I'm going to see what else is behind that wall. Stay put. I'll be a couple of minutes.'

Kit nodded. Recovering her wits, Rosie grabbed at Joel's arm. 'What are you doing here? For God's sake be careful, he's already tried to kill me . . .'

'I know,' Joel said briefly. 'Claudie told me,' and disappeared into the dark.

'Kit, what are you doing here?' she whispered into his grinning face, dragging her gaze from the gloom swallowing Joel. 'What's going on?'

'Exactly what Joel said. When you weren't at the hotel we guessed what you'd done and came here. We followed you up the track, only you started playing clever and turned into a field, so we just waited until you followed us.'

'But why is Joel here?'

'Nancy.' Kit kept his voice down, peering through the shadows, straining for a glimpse of Joel's tall figure. 'When she heard Rory had done a runner she got a bit queasy about having greased up to him like that, and told Joel all the stuff he's fed her about you just going after rich blokes.'

'*Rory?* You're kidding me? Not Nancy and Rory?'

Kit nodded. 'He might be a bit older than the rest, but it seems she er . . . liked his mind.'

Rosie was grateful she was already sitting. No private detectives telling Rory about her and Joel. Just a jealous and threatened Nancy.

'At the same time Ginny rang Joel and asked if the guy

who pilots him around could find out about Gordon Johnson's plane. Then early this morning, Joel came over just as Ginny and I . . . I mean . . . oh, you know what I mean. By that time you'd already taken off so we couldn't contact you. We told Joel everything that had happened and he said he was getting the next flight down here because in your state you were likely to get killed and I said I was coming too . . . hang on, he's coming back.'

They both shuffled to make room as Joel slipped in beside them.

'It's pretty quiet. Claudie says . . .'

'You've seen her?' Rosie cut in.

'Didn't need to. I guessed she'd be your link. This ex of yours does a great line in terror, doesn't he? I told her to get the next plane to London. She'll use my apartment until she feels safe about returning. Anyway, she says, there are French windows all along the back facing onto a terrace . . .'

Rosie started to move past him, but he pulled her back. 'If you want Tom safe, listen to me,' he told her grimly.

In silence, she waited.

'Tom is old enough to know something is wrong, but there's no need for him to witness any ugly scenes. And Rory's not alone. I can hear raised voices. Any better ideas?'

They both shook their heads.

'Okay, here's what we do. No histrionics. This isn't NYPD. We're civilised people . . .'

'Which is why we're huddled in the middle of the country planning a raid,' Kit observed sarcastically.

'Shut up, Kit,' Rosie hissed. 'Joel's right. We're civilised. I wonder if a jury would indict me, if I got someone to rearrange his features?'

'Atta girl,' Kit chuckled.

'Grow up,' Joel ordered.

At first she refused to wait in the car, but Joel insisted that the sight of her might spark a scene that would, in Tom's interests, best be avoided.

'Kit, there appears to be a side path around to the back to the left of the house. If Claudie is right that's where they'll be. I'm going to knock and get Rory to the front of the house, but if he tries to leave with Tom through the back you can stop him long enough for me to get to you. Okay? Let's go.'

Clutching her stomach, Rosie watched as they sprinted away. When this was over she would think about Joel. Not now. Now she could only think about the danger they were all in.

She was too far away to hear but in a few minutes the door to the house was opened. Rosie peered through the gloom. Abbie. Of course. She would be here. She had to grip the steering wheel to stop herself racing across the courtyard to tear her hair out.

She saw Abbie take a step back and then Joel simply pushed past her into the house. Of Kit there was no sign.

Then there was silence. Nearly ten agonising minutes passed before the door opened and Joel came back. She opened the car door and ran to meet him.

'Tom's with him. He's fine.' He caught her as she slumped forward, jerking her roughly to her feet. 'Rory wants to talk to you alone,' Joel continued without preamble. 'He says five minutes of your time in return for Tom and your word that you'll destroy the files in the bank. Kit's waiting in the courtyard. You don't have to do it, Rosie. I can get Tom out of there. Rory doesn't look safe.'

Rosie stared towards the stone house. 'No,' she said quietly. 'I doubt he is, but I want Tom out of there without a fuss. Rory's his father after all. Just five minutes?'

For a moment he gazed down at her, and then with a

muttered oath directed at the sky, he propelled her forward, rapidly giving her instructions in the few seconds before they arrived at the lighted entrance.

Kit was now waiting by the open door. 'Go in with her,' instructed Joel. 'Say you decided on the spur of the moment to take a holiday with her. Then you leave with Tom and drive straight to the hotel. I'll now drive to the end of the track so Rory will think I've gone too, but I'll come back on foot and be outside.'

Rory was standing leaning against the wall in the sitting room, a tumbler of whisky in his hand, an odd smile on his face, as Rosie entered.

Next to him Abbie was holding the back of a chair. Rosie's eyes swept the room. Tom was sitting in an alcove and leapt up as she came in, followed by Kit.

It took every ounce of willpower for Rosie to greet him normally, fighting back the tears. But she couldn't let go of him, stroking his hair, kissing him.

'Mum.' He finally began to struggle. 'Everything's all right now, isn't it? Dad says you're friends.'

'Are you all right?' she gulped, smoothing his T-shirt, taking in the grubby jeans. Anything to hold him, keep him next to her. She could feel him wriggling away.

'Course I am. *M-um*,' he muttered in her ear as she hugged him again. 'You're making me look a prat. *Kit!*' he whooped, catching sight of him behind Rosie. 'Hey, this is great.'

'Hi, Tom,' Kit said easily, ruffling his hair. 'How's it going? I'm playing truant. Couldn't resist a holiday. Made your Mum bring me along. Rory, would you mind if Tom went on ahead with me? It's late and I still have to check in at the hotel.'

Rosie couldn't let go of Tom. It was Kit who came to his rescue, easing the boy from out of her grip.

'My mother used to do the same to me in front of

complete strangers, she really is a wally sometimes, isn't she?' he joked.

'She's all right,' Tom said, grinning up at her. 'Just soppy and forgetful. Can you believe they *both* forgot Dad has to go to New York tomorrow?'

Rosie's eyes flew to Rory's face. In that moment she was grateful to him. Tom had never been afraid. He'd been expecting to see her. The swift lie that they had both forgotten he had to go away had worked.

'Rory?' Kit's soft insistence made Rory shift his gaze from Rosie to Tom.

'Oh, sure. See you, kid. Sorry about the business trip. Just one of those things. Go easy on your mother.'

Tom looked back at him. He made no move towards him. He completely ignored Abbie. 'Sure, Dad. See you around.'

Left alone, the only comfort Rosie derived from her situation was knowing that Tom was safe and that just outside the door Joel was waiting.

'Sweetheart,' Rory drawled. 'Lover boy tells me you're ready to do a deal.' He pushed himself off the wall where he had been lounging and came towards her. He reeked of whisky. She flinched as he stopped within touching distance of her. He didn't miss the revulsion on her face, nor could she mistake the flicker of anger in his.

'Sure, Rory,' she said. 'You have my word. I've got Tom. All the evidence will be destroyed. I'd like to go now.'

'Rory, don't listen to her,' Abbie broke in. 'We have no guarantees at all. Do what I tell you. Take her with us, until we can get the files back. We can go anywhere, start again. She's a bitch, Rory. You've always said it. She's lying.'

Rosie eyed the door nervously. 'Rory knows me,' she said evenly to Abbie. 'He's always trusted me.' She held Rory's gaze. 'You know what I'm going to say, don't you, Rory?'

433

He nodded, taking a slug of whisky. 'I don't want Tom to be involved in a scandal,' Rosie explained for Abbie's benefit. 'Things are bad enough. I care about his feelings, not wanting to see his father splashed across the newspapers. I care about his future. Rory knows that's his guarantee, always will be, that I'll keep my word.'

'Are you kidding?' Abbie jeered. 'God, you make me sick, all this mother love, Tom this, Tom that. Tom fucking everything . . .'

'Fuck off, Abbie,' Rory drawled, not even looking at her. 'Rosie and I understand each other. Me and Rosie. We're special, aren't we, sweetheart? Always were.'

Abbie stood where she was. 'Stop that, Rory.' Her voice was sharp. Rosie detected a hint of fear in it. 'I'm not going,' Abbie said flatly. 'I have every right to be here.'

'Go, Abbie.' Rory ordered, his gaze never leaving Rosie's face. Abbie looked from one to the other.

'Why? You hate her. You've told me so. No, I won't be quiet.'

'Abbie.' Rory sounded bored. 'How can you understand something like me and Rosie, eh, sweetheart? What did you call it, Rosie? Unfinished business? I like that. Abbie, are you still here? Disappear, my pet, I want to talk to my wife.'

Rosie knew he was rambling. Why couldn't Abbie see that? Why didn't she just humour him? Get this over with?

Abbie was trembling. 'Your wife?' she breathed, her chest rising and falling alarmingly. '*Your wife?*

'Have you forgotten something?' she screamed, tears beginning to course down her cheeks. She was trembling so violently, Rosie instinctively took a step forward to help her but before she could reach her, Rory's head swivelled towards the window.

'Shut up, both of you,' he ordered. Rosie froze. Listening. Oh God, had he heard Joel? But it wasn't Joel. The distinct sound of cars crunching to a halt in the courtyard outside made Rory hastily pull the blind aside. Lights from police cars blazed into the room.

Abbie began to scream. 'I told you, you wouldn't listen. Fucking bitch. It's the police.'

'Rory,' Rosie began, appalled. 'It wasn't me . . .' She got no further. Rory was opening a drawer in a small bureau behind him. Rosie held her breath as she saw the small automatic pistol flash in his hand.

'No . . . Rory, don't.' She darted forward, pulling the gun from him but the stitches in her thumb made her cry out in pain and she felt her arm being twisted up her back, knew the stitches had split. There was a roaring in her ears as the pain seared through her, mingled with Abbie screaming.

'We're leaving,' Rory panted, pushing her towards the door. 'Me and you, Rosie,' he gritted, scooping up his passport with his free hand from the same drawer, shoving it into his pocket followed by a roll of banknotes. There was an anguished moan from Abbie. She tugged at his arm.

'Rory, don't go. What about me? *Rory* . . . '

He shoved her away with such force, she overbalanced and fell against the armchair.

Rosie blinked, turning her face away from the arc of lights in the courtyard as she stumbled ahead of him. A voice ordered Rory to stop. Pushing Rosie ahead of him, he screamed at them.

'Back, get back.' A rapid order was given in French. Rory was pulling her backwards, frantically looking from side to side, across the gravel to one side of the yard. Rosie tripped and fell, feeling her legs burn through her cotton trousers as the stones ripped at her legs. Rory dragged her to her feet as they reached a motor bike parked against the wall.

Pain and fear kept her immobilised other than to do as he said. Rory ordered her to pull the machine round to the entrance. Her hand was now pouring blood from the split stitches, but she dragged the bike to where he wanted it, trying to stifle cries of pain.

'Rory,' she sobbed in fright, begging him as he began to mount. 'Don't do this. I didn't call them. I gave you my word . . .'

'Doesn't matter. You're coming with me. Me and you, Rosie. The dream team on a clean machine.' He gave a crack of laughter. An ugly, hysterical sound.

He kicked the bike into life as the police inspector shouted at him to be sensible. Rosie was dimly aware of movement, but the lights were too strong to let her see what was happening.

Above the roar of the machine he was ordering her to get on, to drive it. 'Just do as I say,' he screamed, fanning the gun around as the police tried to move forward. Rosie swung a leg over the bike, Rory got on behind her, reaching round her to release the brake, his legs steadying the machine as he prepared to go.

Rosie made one last desperate plea. 'Rory, let me sit behind,' she screamed. 'We'll both be killed. You won't get away unless I'm with you. I'm your only chance. If I get killed they won't care about shooting you.'

A fraction of a second. He held the gun at her. She slipped off as he pulled himself forward. In that instant she was grabbed and pulled clear of the bike, hitting the ground as Rory swivelled round, wildly firing the gun. Then the bike rose on its back wheel and Rory spurred it forward across the courtyard, scattering panic-stricken police in his wake.

'Lie still,' Joel ordered, covering her body as the young policeman who had helped him yank her from the saddle lay panting beside them, helpless to stop Rory from making his escape.

It was over in seconds. Rosie pushed herself up and twisted round. Watching in horror as Rory blindly weaved and dived between parked cars but failed in the dark to see the police car parked just beyond but immediately across the gates.

A sickening roar, the black machine soared into the air, the shattering sound of splintering glass and metal as it plunged back to earth on top of the police car and then silence. Just the swish as the wheels of the bike spun uselessly round, yards from where Rory's twisted and broken body lay lifeless.

Abbie got to him first, bending over him, cradling his head in her lap, sobbing, calling his name. Rosie raced to crouch beside her. The police inspector summoned a doctor over the radio, but it was too late.

'Madame,' the policeman said gently to Rosie as she knelt beside Rory, tears rolling down her face. 'We did our best. Mademoiselle Bergerard came to us. She said your husband might kill you . . .'

He stopped as Abbie began to scream at him, beating him with her fists. Sobbing wildly: 'Her husband? Don't any of you know who I am? I'm his wife. Me. Not you. I'm Mrs Monteith Gore.'

# Chapter Fifty-Seven

Rosie watched as the oak-lined coffin was slowly hoisted onto the shoulders of the pall bearers outside the crematorium in the tiny graveyard on the hillside above Glencairn.

The day was sunny but a wind whipping up from the loch shook the hedgerows, the silence unbroken except for curlews swooping in graceful arcs out across the shimmering water, carpets of deep mauve heather covering the peaceful hills that swept around the church in a majestic protective shield.

Wild flowers moving in the small gusts that tugged at their heads heralded the highland summer that Rory would never see again.

She glanced down at Tom tightly clutching her hand, holding in his other Rory's family bible, and read the bewilderment in his young face.

Then as the chaplain indicated that they should follow the coffin into the chapel, she gently squeezed Tom's hand, leaned down and kissed his head. With a small reassuring smile she led him through the small knot of mourners, who parted silently and respectfully to allow Rory's young son to lead them, flanked by his former wife and his father.

Sun streamed through the stained glass as they filed into their places. Rosie glanced across at Callum, whose devastation at the loss of his only son was etched in the glazed look and the muffled sobs he gave way to, as the disparate group rose to sing 'The Lord Is My Shepherd'.

Abbie's statement had been the stuff of melodrama. In return for the truth, having secured Callum's agreement to settle all Rory's debts, she followed the advice of her newly acquired psychiatrist that a frank confession would sound so extraordinary no-one would challenge her mental instability.

Even more attractive to Abbie, was the promise that such a move vastly improved her chances of avoiding Holloway. An open prison was beginning to appear attractive.

Rory took all the blame. Poor Rory, Rosie reflected as the chaplain gave a brief sermon confining it to the grief of his family, his father and his brave young son and how they should try to remember only the good things about Rory.

Rosie chose to remember his smile. She saw it now, gently mocking her, even white teeth laughing at her, a cigarette clamped between them his face tilted to the sun, his black hair tousled and dark as a raven's wing. That's how she would think of him.

Let everyone else blame him. She couldn't. They had given life to the child next to her. Part of Rory was in him. To remember him in any other way was beyond her, even now. And without him she would have gone under. Rory's interest in her future was zero, always had been. But unwittingly he had given her a chance. Rosie chose to be grateful.

And where, she wondered bitterly, were all those hangers-on, who couldn't even make the journey to Scotland for his small dignified funeral? The ones who had conveniently dumped their guilt along with his death? No longer of use, a liability. Distance is what they craved. Contempt is what they achieved.

Rosie had ordered flowers to fill the chapel and cover Rory's coffin, to create a scene of serenity and tranquillity to compensate for the violence of his death. When she realised so few would attend, she'd instructed Helen to tell the local paper it was a private funeral. What Rory would have wanted.

Once again on the advice of her psychiatrist who had

recommended a long stay in a private clinic in one of the leafier suburbs of London, the widow did not travel to Scotland. Nor did she send flowers. Abbie's statement to the police sickened Rosie.

I married Rory Monteith Gore in New York two years ago. I know now it was not because he loved me, but because he needed money and my business acumen.

I believed him when he told me that Rosie Colville, his first wife, had deliberately set out to alienate him from his father and to secure Sir Callum's wealth for her own son, out of which she would benefit handsomely. I now know this is untrue. I was deceived and agreed to help him recover what I believed was rightfully his.

He suggested I posed as his housekeeper in order to lure her back to living with him, which would satisfy his father's stringent demands, and to get custody of his son who he said was being emotionally neglected by Miss Colville.

He did not believe it was wise to tell his father of our marriage until he had convinced him he was a proper parent to his and Miss Colville's son. A fact which weighed heavily with Sir Callum.

His plan was to remove his son from her neglectful custody and to arrange for the boy to live in Scotland with his grandfather, thereby restoring his and his son's rightful place in Sir Callum's life.

And his will, Rosie thought savagely. Rory's death had shocked her. But more shocking was that while she was his target for disposal, she had in the end been the one to bury him.

A handful of distant relatives had filled the pews out of respect for Callum, the sun streaming down onto Rory's oak coffin as it slid silently out of sight, his ashes to be interred in the family plot alongside those of his mother.

At the back of the chapel, listening to the simple service, were the lawyers. Behind the immediate family, Kit, Jaye and Carey with Josh, stood together, heads bowed, Rosie knowing they were there out of respect for her and Tom.

Tom, holding her hand very tightly and bravely singing 'Jerusalem' in a wavery voice, made Rosie's heart swell with pride and when he had then led the mourners as they filed out of the chapel into the chill spring air, she knew he was proud of himself that he had been there for his father.

A sad crocodile of people who were unsure how to react since one half never saw Rory and the other had been the recipients of his venom, trooped back across the silent graveyard, up the hill to Glencairn, where Helen did her best to make them feel welcome.

Callum closed the door of his study and stayed there until the last mourner had gone, leaving his former daughter-in-law to do his duty for him.

It was Basil, Rory's lawyer, who gave her Abbie's statement to read. 'I did what I was obliged to do for my client,' he said stiffly as he joined her by the window staring down over the loch.

Rosie gave him a brief smile. What did it matter now? 'I know,' she said. 'I don't blame you. None of us could handle him. Why should you? I'll read this later if you don't mind.'

I did not know until much later that he had deliberately set fire to Miss Colville's home to force her to live at Marlborough Square, relying on her financial difficulties to ensure this.

He threatened me with violence if I went to the police when I discovered this. Later he stage-managed a theft from his own home, planning to implicate Miss

Colville by taking certain valuables from the house. These are now in a safe-deposit box at a bank in Edinburgh. Rory assured the police that he was in Scotland at the time.

Rory said he had to make it look realistic and used violence to stop her discovering his presence when she returned home earlier than he expected. I believe he had heard she would be at a drinks party but she changed her mind. He then used a private plane owned by Mr Gordon Johnson to fly to Scotland to join me and James Cooper and other clients of Mr Cooper's at a house party.

Mr Johnson confirmed to the police that both Mr Cooper and Rory had been with him since late afternoon. But that was not true.

The statement went on in much the same vein, covering all the ploys and stratagems Rory had used to get access to Tom and his father's fortune.

Throughout Abbie cast herself in the role of the duped wife, so in love, so trusting. Her specific talent for selling vice was not mentioned. Her occupation was given as personal assistant. The police were actively looking for James. Betsey had fled to New York. Syra had gone home to her mother.

Before she left Glencairn, Rosie took a walk back to the hillside where Rory was now at rest. She sat down on the grass by the bank of wreaths that surrounded the family plot, hugged her knees, looked out over the loch and talked to him. Remembering the good things. Forgiving the bad.

What did it matter, she asked herself, with a last look at the grave. She bent down and touched the soil, smoothing it with her fingers, letting it trickle through them. What did any of it matter now? Slowly she got to her feet, turned her face to the last warm rays of the sun.

She could hear his voice, calling after her, a soft whisper. 'Only you, Rosie. Only ever you.' She turned and walked away without looking back.

# Chapter Fifty-Eight

'I'll be there in five,' she mouthed to Kit as she plucked the milk from her doorstep, holding up her hand. He threw the window up.

'Well, don't be longer. Otherwise you don't get a lift to the airport.'

'And you don't get your blinds for free.' She poked her tongue out at him and disappeared into her own house.

September was still hot and the city was stifling. It was a treat to be able to walk home from the new workroom near Sloane Street, a relief to know the move was over and all links with Marlborough Square were at an end.

Especially good to know that with an enlarged staff and Livvie and Jordan hopelessly addicted to their new premises, she could have a holiday without phoning back home every five minutes.

Lisa, the glamorous new live-in help she had hired to keep an eye on Tom now that he was enrolled at Johnny Grantham's school in London, had left a note to say the boy had phoned from Cap Martin where he was on holiday with the Granthams and could she ring?

Rory's death had stunned Tom. He had sat white-faced, bewildered, wanting only Rosie to be with him in the days that followed. Before they boarded the plane bringing Rory's body home, Joel had asked her what she was now going to do.

'It's going to take time,' she whispered, wishing they weren't in such a public place. 'I'll think more clearly after the funeral. He's so young, so damaged and it's as much my fault as Rory's. I'll work something out. Just me and Tom for a bit.'

Joel hadn't attempted to kiss her, merely nodded and walked back to his car. He was not leaving on the same flight. Five months ago. Five months and four days to be precise. Rosie resolutely began piling clothes into a suitcase.

Her mother had phoned too to say goodbye before she left for Chicago to visit Patrick, and to wish Rosie and Tom a good holiday, and did Rosie think Patrick's third wife was going to be any better than the other two?

'Possibly. This one's pregnant,' Rosie pointed out. What a fractured family they were.

Even with the help of Amy the new trainee, Mrs Milton and Sam, the dazzlingly efficient secretary Rosie had taken on last month, it had been non-stop activity all week and a brief break with the Granthams was an attractive prospect. Kit promised to drive her to the airport en route to a weekend in the country with Ginny.

Tom, Jane reported in her last phone call, was having a great time and they were all longing to see her.

There was a letter from Callum for Tom which Rosie knew contained some holiday money. She tucked it into her bag to take with her.

Poor Callum. Rosie was just pleased he had Helen and now that the shock, if not the grief, of Rory's death was receding, not to mention the revelation that he had an unknown daughter-in-law, it was likely they would marry.

Tom's future was settled by Callum. Arrangements were in place for Glencairn eventually to be turned into the museum Callum had always longed for, with a special memorial plaque to Rory to be placed above the door.

Rosie had refused all his offers of financial help. 'Treat Tom, Callum,' she suggested when he had arrived in London to take her to dinner. He wanted to put the past right. But for Rosie it was over. 'Take him on holiday with you and Helen. Come and stay down here – you're always welcome. Keep in touch. Tom doesn't need money. He needs family. His family. And he needs a man in his life. You're perfect for the task. It's what Rory would have wanted.'

And Callum had tried, was still trying. Odd man. Helen was right, nothing of Rory could be traced in him. But plenty of Tom. She smiled, closing her suitcase. It was just nine. The flight was at eleven. She called Tom in Cap Martin and got Jane.

'He's on the beach. Stevie and Daniel are here with their kids, so bring ear-plugs. I'll pick you up at the airport, we'll dump your stuff here and get over to Stevie's early afternoon. How does that sound?'

Five months since Rory had died. Five since she had last seen Joel. The Arlingtons would be painful reminders, but like walking through Mayfair, or going up to Glencairn as she and Tom had done last month, it could be borne. Everything else and everyone else seemed to have moved on. And so could she.

Kit and Ginny were an item. Miriam de Lisle had made the necessary overtures to establish herself back in Rosie's clientele. Oscar was suing Sylvia for divorce and Rosie heard from Jordan, who got it from Jessica Milford, that Sylvia was fighting a horrendous legal battle to hang onto at least the small flat in Victoria for herself.

Salina Bhandari was as troublesome as ever, but as it never seemed to occur to her to take her decor problems elsewhere, they resigned themselves to her as a fixture.

On the other hand, they had become fond of Wu Chang who, apart from having a seemingly inexhaustible string of relatives and friends all descending on London before Hong Kong was returned to China, had surprised them by inviting the whole company to a champagne dinner at his Wimbledon home, where he personally cooked them an authentic Chinese meal.

They thanked him next day by fax.

Mr Farrell had been suspended from the school by the trustees and the outcome was still pending of the investigation into charges of negligence.

Nancy had sent flowers to Rosie and a note saying she hoped when everything had settled down they could meet and she would be given a chance to explain. Rosie made no move to take up her invitation.

Jaye was on holiday and Carey and Josh had taken themselves off to motor from London to Madrid for an arts festival. August was indeed a quiet month.

'If you need me you know where I am,' Joel had said as they parted. He sounded weary. He had witnessed her shocking grief when Rory had died. But it was grief for Tom, and a wasted life.

He had made no attempt to contact her and she had not expected him to. The horrors they had shared needed time to fade. The burden was easing. Not so hard to carry on after all. Life went on.

*Rosie Colville Interiors* was a success. TVN wanted to talk to her about a slot on their morning magazine programme and Jed had phoned from New York to say his Long Island home was awaiting her touch, as was the magazine he had agreed to give exclusive pictures to once it was finished.

Tom was once again the Tom she knew, albeit a little older; life had touched him early, in a particularly painful way. She knew he would survive. She could even listen to him telling her bit by bit, a week or a month at a time, the way in which Rory had fed him ideas, made him anxious to make the right decisions, warned him not to upset Rosie by wanting to come home.

'He said you were so busy it would be difficult for you, but that's not true, is it? I mean, if it was, you wouldn't have let me go to school with Johnny, would you?'

She never prompted him. Just waited for him to talk.

447

Hugged him. So little, so impressionable. Wanting to do the best by everyone.

'I do miss Dad. But he wasn't always truthful, though, was he, Mum?' he'd said a week before he went off to join the Granthams in the South of France. 'And Abbie was awful. She used to tell me that Dad had given up so much for me. But I couldn't see how that was, because I hardly knew him. Not really. Not like Johnny knows his Dad. And she said that it was only you Grandpa didn't like. But Grandpa said he did. He said . . .' Tom thought for a moment. Rosie waited. 'He said you hadn't always understood each other, that was all.'

'That's all. Silly, eh? It doesn't matter now,' she agreed, sliding omelettes onto plates and carrying them out into their small walled garden, followed by Tom carrying a bowl of salad.

'Mum?' he said, pulling the tab off a tin of Coke and pouring it into a glass.

'Mmm?'

'That was an awful thing Felix told me. It wasn't at all true, was it?'

Rosie paused. 'No. Don't worry about it any more. Joel was always, is, a friend. Nothing more.'

'You don't see him though, do you? Felix said you were going to go and live in America with him.'

'Without you? Not see Arsenal? Good heavens, there are limits,' she joked.

Tom laughed. 'I did used to try, Mum. You know, be like Dad. But I wasn't good at it. I'm sorry about that.'

Rosie leaned over and hugged him. 'We all tried to be what Daddy wanted us to be. But I think even he would say, we're okay as we are.'

He was coping. So could she. She was not a teenager.

At the last minute she bought some ear-plugs and on the plane, hunting for her passport, a small, rather battered slip of paper fell out. She tucked it back. She didn't need to know what it said. The bag was indeed shut.

Better get it over with. She blinked in the strong sunlight, slipping her glasses on as she came down the steps with Stevie. She guessed he would be there.

For a while the occupants of the pool were so engrossed in their game her presence went undetected. She spotted Tom at once, his skinny brown body hurling itself on top of the ball, and then she saw him swim frantically towards Joel, throwing the ball to him, shouting with delight as Joel got it past Ben standing in goal.

'Ye-ay, Joel,' she heard him yell. 'Gimme five.' Joel pushed his hair out of his eyes and with a grin held his own and Tom's hand aloft in a victory salute.

'Mum!' Tom spotted her and swam to the side, hauling himself out and tearing across the grass to where she was standing, laughing delightedly with Stevie, squealing as he shook water all over her, hugging her.

'C'mon in. Me and Joel and Robert are licking them hollow,' he reported. 'Aren't we, Joel? Rob, wait, I'm coming,' and he was off diving into the pool, surfacing at the far side as Dan called half time.

In the round of greetings that followed, Joel was last. Rosie found it difficult to look at him.

'So, hi, you,' she finally said. 'Nice to see you.'

'And you,' he said and for form's sake kissed her lightly on the cheek.

It was Joel who suggested he drove her back to Jane's, claiming she had just mentioned she was tired. Rosie blinked.

'I'll come back for Lex and Ben. Or better still,' he said to a straight-faced Stevie, 'why don't you bring them all to La Barque this evening? We'll join you there. Rosie can wait for me while I change at my place.'

'Oh, poor Rosie.' Jane was immediately contrite. 'There I was forgetting you've been working all week. Joel, I can run Rosie back ... Ouch, Stevie, you're kicking my shin.'

Tom, when informed of this arrangement, simply said, 'Cool, Mum,' and turned upside down, disappearing into the pool. 'Mum,' he called, surfacing. 'I forgot. Joel's changed his mind. He likes Arsenal now.'

They both needed to get this conversation out of the way. They drove in silence for the first few minutes and then Joel pulled the jeep over to the side of the road where it overlooked a sweep in the bay and slid back in his seat, looking straight ahead: 'So, what's the decision?'

She knew what he meant. 'That I'm getting there,' she said. 'That I can live with myself. That was the important bit.'

'What about Rory? Is he out of your system?'

Rosie leaned back against the head rest. 'Poor Rory,' she said softly. 'He fantasised. We never knew each other. I didn't have to bury anything with Rory. I was never in love with him. It was an obsession. A young girl's fantasy. It was never given the chance to wear itself out.'

She looked at his profile, staring resolutely ahead. 'Real life isn't like that. I had Tom. I'm so grateful for him. I can't ever regret that. But no-one in all that time came along to show me what love could be like. Should be like.

'And what about you?' she asked carefully. 'I mean, it's been five months?'

He gave a reluctant smile. 'Er ... I did work that out for myself. And there was never anything for me to decide. The bag was shut, remember? Marianne should never have written you that letter ... yes, I know about it. But she didn't understand. Nancy was just being ridiculously protective.'

Rosie stared silently ahead. Let it go. Nancy was history. 'I just couldn't cope with someone putting me third on the list,' he said. 'It wouldn't work. I've been there. Got the T-shirt. And the scars.'

'No-one has to be first or second in my life,' she said. 'Just there. That was Rory's problem. Poor Rory. He was right about one thing. I put Tom before him. But,' she turned and searched his face, 'if I had loved Rory, that wouldn't have been a contest for either of us. How can I blame him for everything that happened? I was as much to blame . . . oh, not the second time, he was so unstable, it was frightening.

'I needed to sort out the tangle everything had got into. Don't you see, everything I did failed. I thought I'd failed my mother – never the daughter she wanted. Then I met Rory and I couldn't get him to love me, not being able to cope with being a single mother.

'No, don't say there are thousands of single mothers all feeling the same. I only cared that I felt such a failure. So Tom was going to be my success. Had to be. I was going to be the perfect mother. Not let him suffer.

'It's so easy to say it was absurd. I know that. I just wanted him to have everything I didn't. He wanted a father so much. I wanted him to have one so much. We both cast Rory in a role he could never fulfil. And there I was to blame. I let Tom believe he was a good father. I got him into it. I had to get him out of it. By myself. It had to be my success.'

He hadn't interrupted, letting her talk. Not trying to touch her. Very still.

'Without anyone else in your life?'

She shook her head impatiently. 'No. Don't you see? It was *because* there was someone else. You were so special, so important. It wouldn't have worked unless I'd worked through the guilt of it all on my own. Got it out of the way.'

'And now? Now what do you want to do?'

Rosie turned and looked at him. He was leaning forward

on the steering wheel, his glasses pushed up onto his head. So patient. So understanding. Not rushing her. Giving her space.

The heat was beating down. She estimated it must be in the nineties. The occasional gust of wind, so slight as to make no difference. It was very silent. Across the bay a small white boat drifted slowly across the horizon.

'Only to find something to do between now and going to La Barque,' she said softly, reaching out gently to touch his cheek. Slowly he turned his face and looked at her, searching her eyes and then he pressed his mouth into the palm of her hand.

'I mean,' she said, as he pulled her towards him. 'It's awfully hot to be out in the sun. We could, of course, admire the view. Or I could tell you about all the latest designs I've completed.'

'Or maybe,' he suggested as he let her go and started the engine, holding her hand under his on his knee, turning the car towards his house lying empty and waiting a mile up the road. 'We could just see where we go from here.'

She smiled. 'Just one other thing.' He glanced sideways at her as she gazed straight ahead. 'It's important we get it straight now.'

He stared at her in surprise, beginning to brake. 'What's that?'

'I take it,' she said sternly, 'that you're serious about Arsenal?'